BOOKS BY VINCENT LOCOCO

Tempesta's Dream:

A Story of Love, Friendship and Opera

BELLAFORTUNA SERIES

A Song for Bellafortuna - Book 1

Saving the Music - Book 2

Sicilian Melody - Book 3

SICILIAN MELODY

A NOVEL

VINCENT B. "CHIP" LOCOCO

Cefalutana Press

Musical Selections used in the novel

Sicilian Folksong: *Lu me sciccareddu*
O mio babbino caro from Gianni Schicchi by Giacomo Puccini
Sicilian Folksong: *Sicilia bedda*
Va Pensiero from Nabucco by Giuseppe Verdi
Easter Hymn (Inneggiamo) from Cavelleria Rusticana by Pietro Mascagni

FOR THE WOMAN WHO TAUGHT ME TO LOVE STORIES

MY MOTHER
LYNDA GOODIER LOCOCO

CONTENTS

In Sicily, women are more dangerous than shotguns.

— THE GODFATHER

SICILIAN MELODY

PART I

THE DON

AN ATTACK AT DAWN

*J*ust as the sun had risen on that early Monday morning, Adriano Umbretto stood over the crumpled body lying at his feet, sweat running down his face. His heart raced as he fought to catch his breath. In his right hand, he held a bloody knife.

The cool March breeze carried the scent of oleander and rosemary through the open second-floor bedroom window of Adriano's spacious villa. Outside in the morning mist were the rolling, gentle hills of Castelvetrano, a region of Sicily known for its fertile soil. The hills were perfectly lined with olive trees covering the majestic terrain. The serenity of the countryside stood in stark contrast to the scene of violence inside the bedroom. The scents wafting through the window, and the coppery smell of the dead man's blood splattered across the floor gave the room a strong, pungent odor.

Adriano lowered the knife and wiped the blade against

his pajama pants. His pants quickly became stained red as his steely eyes remained intently locked on the dead man lying before him. Blood oozed from the man's chest, precisely where Adriano had plunged the knife deep into the intruder's heart.

Adriano had killed before, a few times to be exact, but that was ages ago when he was still a young man and finding his place in the violent world of the Sicilian Mafia. Now, at sixty-five and as head of one of the most powerful *coscas* in all of post-war Sicily, others handled that dirty part of the business for Don Adriano Umbretto.

Just then, Adriano heard footsteps running up the stairwell near his bedroom. He turned toward the door and raised the knife, gripping it tightly, as his body became tense. A man burst breathlessly into the bedroom, carrying in front of him a *lupara*, the sawed-off shotgun that was the most favored weapon used in Sicily for protection or to exact a vendetta, depending on one's situation. Adriano quickly relaxed and lowered the knife when he realized it was Luca Speranza, his forty-two-year-old confidant and *Capobastone*, the underboss and second in command within the Umbretto *cosca*.

Luca stared at the scene before him and noticed his boss's bloodied pants. He lowered his *lupara* and hurriedly asked, "Don Umbretto, are you hurt?"

"No, Luca. The blood is his, not mine."

Luca sighed in relief as he quickly made the sign of the cross.

"Is Francesca safe?" Adriano asked.

"She is. Some of the men are with her."

Adriano dropped the knife on the floor and then pointed

to the dead man. "How in God's name did this scumbag get into my villa?"

Luca gulped hard. He had worked for Don Umbretto for a long time. He loved him like a father, yet he feared him just the same. "We are still trying to find out, Don Umbretto."

Suddenly numerous footsteps could be heard running up the stairs. Mario Zucello, with his *lupara* slung over his shoulder, was the first to come into the room, followed closely by three other men holding their *luparas* at the ready.

Luca turned to Adriano's soldiers as they entered the room. "Relax, gentlemen," he exclaimed. "Don Umbretto is fine. He killed the intruder."

Mario asked Don Umbretto, "What happened? How did you kill him?"

"I awoke early this morning and was writing some letters over at my desk by the window. I went to get some papers from the other side of the room. This *bastardo* must not have seen me behind the door. When he entered the room, I came up from behind, wrestled his knife away, and then stuck it in his chest."

"How lucky," replied Mario. "He must have just stumbled upon your bedroom, and thankfully you were able to surprise him."

Adriano chuckled. "Luck. If that's what you want to call it, Mario."

Mario added, "We have secured this part of the villa. Some of the men are sweeping the rest of the villa. But, we believe he was alone, Don Umbretto."

Adriano asked, "Does anyone know this man? Does anyone know who he works for?"

All of the men in the room looked down at the dead man's

ashen face, his open eyes locked in a death stare, and then shook their heads negatively.

Adriano continued, "I want a meeting in my study in one hour. Those in attendance better come to the meeting with answers." He looked down again at the body by his feet, and then he turned and looked into the eyes of each of the men in the room before saying, "I do believe someone just declared war on us."

At that moment, a young woman in a flowing pink nightgown came running into the room, followed closely by two gentlemen holding their *luparas*. Entering the room, the girl stopped short upon seeing the dead body. Her hand came up to her mouth as tears began to flow down her cheeks. Adriano stepped over the body and made his way over to her. He grabbed her tightly.

"Papa, are you hurt?"

"No, *fanciulla*. I am fine."

"Did you kill him?"

"I protected myself." He then said to everyone in the room. "Leave my daughter and me, and take this piece of trash with you."

Three of the men picked up the body and carried it out of the bedroom, leaving a trail of blood behind as the Don held onto his daughter. When the men carrying the dead man had left the room, Adriano motioned to Marco Moretti, one of the men who had entered the bedroom with his daughter and, at nineteen years of age, the youngest member of Adriano's *cosca*.

Adriano told Marco, "Wait outside my bedroom door, and when my daughter leaves, walk her back to her room and stand guard until we figure all this out."

Marco turned and smiled at Francesca before looking at Adriano, replying, "Yes, sir. I will protect her." He left the room and stood in the hallway.

Adriano turned toward Luca and said sternly, "Luca, one hour."

"Yes, sir. One hour."

Luca departed the room and closed the door.

WITH THE ROOM CLEARED, Adriano stroked his eighteen-year-old daughter's golden blonde hair as she laid her head on his shoulder. He then pulled away and stared into her deep, blue eyes. "You look so much like your mother," he said. "Beautiful, just like her. I still remember the day I first gazed upon those eyes of hers in your grandfather's olive grove."

She fixed her gaze on her father's eyes. "Papa, how did that man get inside our home?"

"I don't know, but I will find out."

"You killed him?" she repeated the question she had asked earlier.

"*È così!*" (It is what it is.) Adriano answered her with his favorite phrase, an Italian expression used when one is resigned to the outcome of a situation, accepting it for what it is. He said, "Now, I need you to do something for me, Francesca."

"Of course. Anything for you, Papa."

"You need to stay inside today and over the next few days. You cannot leave. Do you understand?"

"Papa, I was going to my voice lessons later today."

"You cannot go, *mia cara figlia.*"

"Why can't I go? It's just in town. What's going on?"

"I'm not sure yet. But I'll know more soon. So, until then, you cannot leave the villa."

"Papa, please. Why not?"

"Because I said so. I will post Marco outside your bedroom door at all times. Because he is Salvatore's nephew, I trust him completely. You will be safe. Make sure your window is locked. Now go. Marco is waiting for you in the hall to walk you back."

She frowned, showing her displeasure. But there was one thing she had quickly learned in living with her father. One could never change his mind.

He kissed both her cheeks, wet from her tears, and she left the room, avoiding the blood trail across the floor.

AFTER SHE HAD DEPARTED, Adriano turned and looked over at two portraits on the wall above his dresser. They were of his wife and son. He had lost both of them to the business many years ago. He stared intently at the portrait of his wife.

Her long blonde hair hung down just below her breasts. Her blue eyes were ever-piercing from the portrait. He walked over to the portrait and spoke lovingly to her. "On my honor, I will protect her. I will do so with my life if I have to. That is my promise and what I owe to you. It's all that I have left now."

He kissed his fingers, brought them up to the portrait, and placed them on his wife's lips, saying, "*T'amo, Santa. T'amo.*"

He glanced at the portrait of his son but turned quickly away from it. It was too painful to even think about him.

A photo of his fraternal grandparents sitting atop the dresser caught his attention. Adriano sighed heavily and then walked to the bathroom to clean off and change his clothes before the meeting.

2

A DYING WISH

As Adriano stood in front of the bathroom mirror, he tried to gather his thoughts, but the chaotic events of earlier left his mind unsettled. Adriano knew those feelings were part and parcel of choosing a career in the business.

The business. That was how the *Mafioso* members described it. Every person who chose this life had his own reasons. For some, it was financial, while for others, it was a means to pursue power. Others joined simply in grateful reciprocation for the actions of their Don in handling a situation for them or their family. For Adriano, deep down, he always believed life had offered him no other alternative than to join the business. It was a decision he had both come to love and despise.

He looked at himself in the mirror. His feelings that morning roused in him for the first time a sense of vulnerability. Death had come to his very door. But death was not a stranger to Adriano. Tragedy had touched him at an early age, and it remained a constant walking companion with him his entire life.

His thoughts drifted to his grandparent's picture while memories of his youth came to the forefront of his mind. The tune of the Sicilian folksong, *Lu me sciccareddu*, sprang into Adriano's head, a song that both his grandfather and father had always sung to him as a child.

Music had always been a part of Adriano's life, and it was the one thing he could always rely on, even during the worst of times, to soothe him and give him peace. Music always provided him a respite from all the tribulations life would throw at him.

While still wearing his blood-stained pants and staring into his bathroom mirror, his thoughts wandered back some 53 years, to his early life when he grew up in the nearby city of Monreale, and to the time he came to live with his grandparents.

ADRIANO WAS the second child born of Giacomo and Elena Umbretto of Monreale, Sicily, where Adriano grew up. When Adriano was only six years old, his parents and older brother died in a supposed tragic wagon accident when a spooked horse caused the wagon to plummet off a high cliff. But Adriano's grandfather, Calcedonio Umbretto, never believed it was an accident. As head of one of the most influential *coscas* in all of Sicily, he knew that his son's death was meant to send a message to him. After all, many wished to wrestle control of Monreale away from him.

Calcedonio worked quickly after his son's death to

uncover who was involved in the plot. Days later, Calcedonio and his associates confronted those men in a dark alley in the nearby city of Palermo. The plotters admitted their guilt, foolishly begged for their lives, and ultimately paid dearly for their crime against the Umbretto family - with their own lives. Calcedonio personally slit the throat of the supposed ring leader of the little group.

After the death of his parents, Adriano went to live with his grandparents, Calcedonio and Carina Umbretto, who raised him in their palatial villa on the outskirts of Monreale. For Adriano, residing in the Umbretto home meant that he would grow up front and center in the world of loyalty, power, corruption, vendettas, and protection. In other words, he was now living under the roof of one of the most powerful Dons of the Sicilian Mafia.

Although Adriano's father had been part of the business, Adriano was never fully aware of his father's deep involvement nor what the business was all about. However, living with his grandfather quickly made Adriano aware of that life and all it entailed.

It was a life lived according to traditions, the unwritten rules passed down from generation to generation. It was a life of loyalty, obedience, honor, respect, and, ironically, a deep religious faith. The most notable tradition was *omertá*, the all-important code of absolute silence, reflecting the ancient Sicilian belief that a person should never go to government authorities to seek justice for a crime and never cooperate with authorities investigating any wrongdoing. Silence was expected and obeyed.

His grandparents soon became like parents to Adriano, as

their relationship grew in closeness and love. As Adriano learned more and more of his grandfather's "business" dealings, he quickly grew in awe of his grandfather and noticed the deep respect and regard people had for him. He also became acutely aware of the command and authority that his grandfather possessed over the entire region under his control.

Adriano's brief weekly strolls with his grandfather across the main square of Monreale would always confirm for him the immense power Calcedonio enjoyed. While walking across the piazza, his grandfather would stop and speak with one citizen, then another, and then another. He conversed with each person briefly and without excitement, usually in a hushed undertone. By the time they reached the opposite end of the square, it was obvious that these brief conversations were not chit-chat but were, in reality, commands. Within a few minutes, his grandfather had issued orders to each person he spoke to that would affect all of Monreale and its countryside.

As he got older, Adriano knew he was lucky to live in comfort with his grandparents, while much of Sicily suffered harshly. For you see, life in Sicily at the turn of the century was much as it had always been, a life of hardship, poverty, and immense suffering for most of the island's inhabitants.

The Mafia had established its foothold in Sicily well before Adriano was even born. Sicily was essentially a feudal system, with peasant laborers working for wealthy landowners. Around the time of the unification of Italy in 1860, the government that was supposed to ensure civic order across Sicily was corrupt. Poverty was an ever-present acquaintance. Some of the poorer inhabitants of Sicily turned to crime to survive. In turn, the wealthy landowners began paying groups of men to protect their property. This was the birth of the Mafia, a word derived from the Sicilian adjective *mafiuso*, which means swagger, boldness, or bravado. These groups soon became their own clans and began to exert great power as Sicilians started to rely more and more on them for protection. Each of these *coscas* came to be ruled by a single boss, known as the Don. In return for the *pizzo* payments made to the local Don, the landowners were offered protection and security. The Don soon came to be regarded as the sole source of order in a very harsh land.

For the past thirty years, one man had controlled the Mafia in and around Monreale with an iron will, a strong fist, but with a sense of justice and compassion for those under his protection. That man was Don Calcedonio Umbretto.

The Don embodied the paternalistic "man of honor" and lived his life steeped in the old traditions. As a result, he was blessed with loyalty by both those who worked for him and those to whom he offered his protection. Calcedonio never forgot his humble beginnings as a peasant, even after ascending to his position of absolute power. As a result, he was always willing to help those in need. If you came to Don Calcedonio Umbretto in need and showed him respect, your needs were met and then some, even if what was being asked was contrary to law.

Don Umbretto's word was his bond. In the mind of the Sicilians, he was the trusted enforcer of law and order in that part of Sicily, instead of the corrupt government officials, police and judges. If a husband under his protection lost his life, Don Umbretto was known to assist the widow with monthly payments to help raise her family. If a person under his protection was wronged in any way, his response was swift and strong and, in his mind, utterly correct and deserved. In that regard, Don Umbretto singularly played the role of police, judge, and appeals court. And if you ever hurt someone in his clan, it meant certain death.

The men inside his *cosca* were fiercely loyal, and most had been with him since the beginning of his rise to power. He protected them and treated them with respect. However, it was his grandson, Adriano, on whom he showered all of his love.

Don Calcedonio Umbretto was a towering force to deal with across Sicily for those thirty years in power. He had to be since his region of control in Monreale was so close to Palermo, the bastion of the Mafia. But when he reached the age of eighty-five years, his heart began to fail him. Carina began to work closely with some of his *cosca* members to relieve her ailing husband of some of his burdens. The Don's men soon referred to her as *"donna d'acciaio,"* which meant "woman of steel." Even Adriano took note of his grandmother's expanding role, and he became aware of the high esteem and respect that was shown to her by the citizens of Monreale under the Umbrettos' protection. In a world and time dominated by men in business, politics, and almost all aspects of society, his grandmother's position showed young Adriano that women could be just as powerful and accomplished as men.

As her husband began to slow down more and more, the aura of power and untouchability that surrounded him as a younger man disappeared. In the world of the Mafia, a sign of weakness was not just a bad trait but a trumpet blast announcing to others that a door was open, and one could attempt to walk in and take control.

It was on an afternoon in November 1900, while Don Calcedonio was on his way back from a meeting in Palermo, when his perceived weakness was pounced upon. A single gunshot blast from a *lupara* as his car passed a busy Palermo intersection left the Don mortally wounded and barely clinging to life in the back seat of the vehicle. His men brought him back home to the villa and to the arms of his distraught wife, who made him comfortable as the death vigil began. Adriano visited with him every day as the Don lay in his bed, in severe pain from his wound and drifting in and out of consciousness. Carina rarely left his side.

Finally, by the end of the week, it was obvious to all that the end was near, as the Don slipped into a coma. The next day, Carina had two chairs set up next to his bed as she prepared for a meeting with her husband's former *capo*.

Carina was seated close to her husband's head. She glanced to the door, anxiously waiting for her visitor, who was late to arrive. A simple gold crucifix hung on the wall above the bed. Carina had sent word that morning for the man to come see her about an urgent need. Carina looked at the empty chair. She was not concerned. There was no doubt in her mind that the man was coming. The man owed it to her husband.

Just then, she heard footsteps outside the bedroom, and in walked Don Gerlando Spatuzza. Don Spatuzza was, at fifty years of age, thirty-five years younger than Don Umbretto. For years, he had worked under Don Umbretto until he left his employment at the behest of his boss to become the head of a *cosca* in Castelvetrano, a small Sicilian town blessed with surrounding fertile soil that produced some of the best olives in all of Sicily. Thanks to that move, Don Spatuzza had become extravagantly wealthy and powerful in his position of power. Carina knew her husband's young protégée owed him one last favor.

Don Spatuzza said not a word when he walked inside the bedroom but stared intently at Don Umbretto lying peacefully on the bed. He knelt next to the bed and then bent over, kissing Don Umbretto on his right hand, a gesture of gratitude for the Don's many years of generosity to him.

He turned toward Carina. "I'm so sorry, *Signora Umbretto*."

"They finally got him, Gerlando. He is dying."

"Who did this, *Signora Umbretto*? Who?"

"Onofrio Fausto. That's my belief, as well as the belief of your Don, before he slipped into this coma."

"Onofrio Fausto? The young Don from Villalba?"

"*Si*. Not confirmed. Just a belief." She was quiet for a moment before saying, "But I know my husband is right."

Don Spatuzza stood up and took a seat on the other chair. "*Mi scusi, Signora Umbretto*." he said. "Why did you call me here? To make war against Onofrio on behalf of your husband? What is it that I can do for you?"

Carina took a deep breath. "All these years, my husband has controlled Monreale. You know how tough it has been, with the constant threat from *coscas* in and around Palermo, who would love to control this area. He fought them off all these years. But now it's over. He will be gone in a very short time."

"His *cosca* will defend what he has strived to protect all these years. Someone from among his men will rise up and take control and defeat them."

"If our son survived him, then perhaps that is true. But now, I do not doubt that upon his death, his *cosca* will be obliterated."

"*Signora Umbretto*, are you asking me to help defend your husband's *cosca*? Is that why you asked me here?"

"*Nulla*. I don't want anything from you. Instead, I want you to take something away."

"I don't understand."

"My grandson, Adriano, is now twelve. He is a good-looking boy. He looks more like me than the Umbretto side of the family."

Don Spatuzza chuckled. "I have not seen Adriano since he was a little boy."

"He has not been involved in the business. He's smart. He has the heart of a lion, and I can see in him the willingness to defend what he believes to be the truth, the right. My husband always thought that he would make a great Don one day. I need him taken to a place of safety right after my husband's death, before Don Onofrio Fausto, or, if not him, some other Don and his *cosca* sweep in and kill everyone in a fight for control."

"Why me, *Signora Umbretto*?"

"My husband has killed and had killed many men, Don Spatuzza. Many men. Yet, he lived a life of honor. You, like him, have lived the same way. A sort of rustic chivalry in a very harsh land. Not like this new crop of young thugs who rule for themselves and for themselves alone. There is no honor. No loyalty. No tradition. One of the last things my husband discussed with me was the safety of Adriano. He told me that when he died, he wanted you to take Adriano back with you to Castelvetrano and raise him in the tradition of a man of honor, like himself and you. He owed that to Adriano's father. So, when Adriano comes of age and begins his life in the business, he will be like the honorable men of old. I feel it in my heart. I ask you to do me this favor, both for me and for my husband, whom you loved."

Don Spatuzza stood up from the chair. He glared at the crucifix on the wall. Then, he looked down at Don Umbretto. He turned toward Carina and said in a loud voice, "*Signora Umbretto*, I owe Don Umbretto my life for all that he has done for me. I will raise Adriano myself as if he was my own."

"*Grazie*. My husband shall die in peace."

"I know over these last few months you have taken over much of the duties of your husband. Even in Castelvetrano, we have heard rumors of the *donna d'acciaio* ruling over Monreale. You have served him well."

Carina was surprised when Don Spatuzza knelt in front of her. He grabbed her right hand and brought it towards his mouth and then kissed her hand.

Later that night, Don Calcedonio Umbretto died. All of the *cosca* chiefs in Sicily came to the majestic Cathedral in Monreale for the funeral two days later, outwardly to pay their respects while inwardly planning for the impending war to take control of the Don's holdings. One of those was twenty-five-year-old Onofrio Fausto from the small Sicilian town of Villalba, who had quickly become a powerful Don in his own right. Evil, vindictive, sadistic, ruthless, yet brilliant, he was on the rise in the world of the Mafia. He was fully aware that control of Monreale would bring him the immense power that the small town of Villalba could never afford him. Don Calcedonio had always been a perfect judge of character.

His belief as to who fired the shot that finally took him down was correct.

Don Calcedonio Umbretto's funeral was also attended by the landowners to whom he had offered protection over all these years. They wore black as a sign of how distraught they were, not only for the passing of the Don but for the inevitable war that would come.

After the service, the funeral procession passed through the streets of Monreale to the cemetery. So many citizens attended that the procession stretched almost the whole block of the *Via Appolonia*, which led to the grave. The Don's associates carried his coffin on their shoulders, as Adriano, with tears in his eyes, walked closely behind his grandfather's casket, with Carina and Don Spatuzza walking beside him.

After the burial, all of the *cosca* chiefs came up to pay their respects to the family. They first offered their condolences to Carina. When they came to Adriano, they kissed the young boy's cheeks under the ever-watchful eye of Don Spatuzza. The last was Onofrio Fausto, who, as he kissed Adriano's cheeks, knew that in just a few days, after he had destroyed Don Umbretto's *cosca* and killed his wife, he would personally plunge his knife into the heart of Don Umbretto's sole heir, young Adriano Umbretto.

Before dawn the next day, Adriano kissed his grandmother and then climbed aboard a horse-drawn cart driven by Don Spatuzza. A small suitcase with all of Adriano's belongings was placed in the cart.

Carina, along with two of her husband's longest *cosca* members, came to tell the boy goodbye. "Be a good boy,

Adriano, "she advised. "Listen to Don Spatuzza. He will teach you how to be a man."

Don Spatuzza jumped down from the cart and walked over to where Carina was standing. "*Signora Umbretto*, please. Come. Come with us."

She sighed. "Don Spatuzza, my place is here."

He leaned in close to her and, in a whisper, called her by the name her husband always used for her. "Cara, you will die here. Do you understand?"

She smiled at him and then pointed to the men standing nearby. "My place is with them. With all of them. In my husband's mind, there was no greater trait in a person than loyalty. He lived his life immensely loyal to those around him, and he expected and received loyalty from those who worked with him over all these years. He was loyal not only to them but to me our entire married life. He would never abandon his *cosca* members, many of whom have been with him from the beginning. I thank you for the offer, but my place is here. Loyalty demands it."

She then reached out and grabbed Don Spatuzza's right hand and kissed it. The gesture caught the younger man off guard. A tear slowly ran down his face. He knew she was passing her husband's torch to him. The student now would become the teacher.

Don Spatuzza made his way back to the cart as Carina turned and walked over to where the men were standing. That was the last time Adriano would see any of them alive.

As the cart departed the villa in the darkness of that morning, Adriano sang, under his breath, his grandfather's favorite Sicilian folksong, *Lu me sciccareddu*.

Avia nu sciccareddu, davveru sapuritu,
ora mi l'ammazzaru, poviru sceccu miu.
Chi bedda vuci avia paria nu gran tinuri,
sciccareddu di lu me cori, comu ju t'hai a scurdari?
E quannu cantava facia:
iha, iha, iha…
sciccareddu di lu me cori, comu ju t'hai a scurdari?
Quannu 'ncuntrava 'ncumpagnu subitu lu ciarava
e dopu lu raspava ccu granni carità.

I had a little donkey, really special,
and now it's been killed, my poor little donkey.
What a beautiful voice he had, he seemed like a great tenor,
donkey of my heart, how can I ever forget you?
And when he sang he went:
hee-haw, hee-haw, hee-haw
donkey of my heart, how can I ever forget you?
When he met another friend, he would get along with him
and he would caress him with great tenderness.

Don Spatuzza held the reins tight but tapped his foot to the lyrical song sung by Adriano. The cart slowly proceeded westward out of the town and down into the beautiful Sicilian valley surrounded by the hills in the distance. Just as the sky began to brighten in the early morning mist, Adriano finished the song. He then turned in the cart and looked up toward Monreale for one last glimpse. The cart continued westward.

And that is how Adriano Umbretto, at the age of twelve, avoided death at the hands of Onofrio Fausto, left his hometown of Monreale, and began living under the safety and tutelage of Don Gerlando Spatuzza in the small town of Castelvetrano.

***

ADRIANO LOOKED DOWN from the bathroom mirror and stared at the blood on his hands from the dead man in his bedroom that morning. He placed his hands under the faucet and washed them. The water basin turned red as the blood from his hands curled down toward the drain. He pictured the faces of Calcedonio and Carina.

For Adriano, death was as constant in his life as a summer rain. He splashed water on his face in an attempt to shake his mind to the present. He thought of the events of earlier and who may have been behind the attempt on his life.

Adriano concluded that there were three men he would put at the top of the list of those who might have orchestrated the attempted hit on him: Don Carlo Butera from Siracusa; Don Gianni Costa from Palermo; and lastly, Don Sergio Genovese from Campobello di Mazara, a man whose family Adriano had been in battles with before, and whom of the three Dons, Adriano would place at the very top of the list.

Adriano would make certain that the man responsible would pay for his crime, unlike what had occurred with Onofrio Fausto, the killer of his grandfather and his grandmother. It was a few years after those events that Don Spatuzza had finally told Adriano that Don Fausto was the man responsible for the killing of his grandparents. But by the time Adriano had finally come to power, Onofrio was too strong a Don and too entrenched in Monreale for Adriano to exact his revenge.

Years later, when Adriano was finally in a position to make his move against him, Onofrio and his family had already left the shores of Sicily for the New World. Onofrio Fausto had evaded retribution. Adriano swore he would never allow an opportunity for revenge to escape him again.

Whoever had sent the man to kill him this morning would pay with their life.

3

A BETRAYAL

*W*ithin one hour after the intruder's death, Adriano sat at the head of a long table in his first-floor study of his villa on the outskirts of Castelvetrano. The room was dark, as the windows were closed and shuttered. Around the table sat six of his most trusted men. Adriano sat quietly as he waited for the meeting to start. Luca was seated next to him.

At the opposite end of the table sat Giancarlo Fanucci. As the *Caporegime (or Capo for short)* of Don Umbretto's *cosca*, he was not only responsible for the dealings with all of the Don's soldiers, but he also took on the role of head of security for the villa.

As Giancarlo waited for the meeting to start, he nervously tapped his right foot on the floor. With the intruder having come inside the villa earlier that morning, he knew this would be a very tense meeting. Nerves rising, he got up and walked over to the small bar in the corner of the room. He grabbed a bottle of *Vino di Bellafortuna*, the Don's favorite wine that was produced locally in the small village of Bellafortuna, a hill-top village situated close to Monreale. Giancarlo filled a wine glass and quickly drained it as he tried to calm his nerves.

Meanwhile, Don Umbretto sat upright in his chair in complete silence, waiting. The door to the study opened, and in strode Don Umbretto's *consigliere*, Salvatore Battaglia. A huge muscular man with a bushy mustache, he said not a word upon entering, only nodding his head to the Don. Salvatore took a seat not at the table but in a chair situated in the corner.

Salvatore Battaglia was a shadowy figure inside the Umbretto *cosca*. He was not only Don Umbretto's advisor, but was his enforcer. He was responsible for handling anyone who did not comply with the organization's policies, rules, or deals, both outside the *cosca* and sometimes inside it. Because of his specific job for Adriano, Salvatore did not reside at the villa, as Adriano did not want him to become too close to any of his associates, as he was fully aware that there would be times when Salvatore would have to take actions against members of Don Umbretto's own *cosca* members.

Once Salvatore was seated, Adriano said quietly, "*Inizieremo*." (We shall begin.)

Giancarlo returned to his seat. Don Adriano eyed each of the men around the table. Besides Giancarlo and Luca, the other associates at the table were Ferruccio Fonsato, Alfredo Maestri, Flavio Fontana, and Mario Zucello. They listened intently as the Don began to speak.

"This villa is my sanctuary. This villa is where my daughter lives. This villa is supposedly protected by men that

I pay very handsomely. Yet, somehow, this morning, a man entered my sanctuary."

Giancarlo spoke up. "Don Umbretto…"

Adriano shot a glance toward him, silencing him. "I am not finished." Giancarlo nodded as the Don continued, again speaking quietly.

"As you know, our position at this time is precarious. The fascists were not our friends. Before the war, so many involved in this life were thrown in jail by Mussolini, or left for America, while others fled into the hills to avoid jail or death. But now with the war over and the fascists gone, we suddenly find ourselves back in power. The Allies, in charge of Sicily after the War, turned to the Dons of old and installed many of us as Mayors of towns all across our island. The Allies have looked to us as the people they could trust to put in positions of power among our Sicilian friends, as they know we hated the fascists and were never loyal to them. The Allies knew we would have no allegiance to the now defeated fascists. So, the Mafia came out of hiding. I, along with others, rose back to power. I gathered my associates and re-formed my *cosca*. With me being installed as the Mayor of Castelvetrano and my dear friend, Don Calogero Biscotti, appointed as Mayor of Monreale, our power is slowly being regained. However, with our rise to power comes a fight for control among the clans. Areas are being divided up, and families are controlling certain locales. Castelvetrano and its surrounding areas are once again mine. There are many who would love to control this area. Just as there are many who would love to take down Don Biscotti in Monreale. That's where the six of you come in. My most trusted men. I need to rely on you to solidify my control. The landholders in and around Castelvetrano are once again paying us for protection. Now let me ask you this. Why would they trust me with protection if I can't even protect my own home? This very morning, my sanctuary has been disturbed. I want to know how, and I want assurance it will never happen again."

The tone of his voice then changed as he growled loudly. "In other words, how the hell does an intruder come into my villa? And not only does he come into my villa, but comes to my bedroom. What if instead of my bedroom, he went to my daughter's? Who then is dead on the floor? *Che*? *Che*? Who?"

Giancarlo gulped hard before responding. "We do not yet know who the man worked for or where he was from. He had no identification on him. We will begin immediately speaking discreetly to some of our friends in the community and see what they are hearing. If someone knows something, we will find out."

"I'm not asking who he worked for," Adriano said. "I am asking you how he came into my villa? A villa that is supposedly protected and secure."

Giancarlo looked directly at Adriano. "He climbed the fence in a perfect spot, unguarded, and by the time we saw him, he was already entering the villa." He looked around the table before saying, "I don't think he found your bedroom by accident, though."

Mario Zucello suddenly spoke up. "Sir, I think he just happened upon your bedroom once he found his way into the villa."

Giancarlo shot a quick glance at Mario and was about to answer him, but he was quickly cut off by Don Umbretto. "I don't care what you think. I want to know how he came into my sanctuary? First, tell me if the villa is currently secured?"

"It is," replied Giancarlo.

"Will it happen again?"

"An intrusion? No," replied Giancarlo.

All of the men around the table followed Giancarlo's response and said, "No, Don Umbretto."

Adriano reached below the table and pulled out the knife he had used to kill the man just an hour earlier. He said, "I don't care who this man is. What I want to ensure is that it will never happen again. And there is only one way for that to happen. Giancarlo, come here."

Giancarlo got up and walked over to where Don Umbretto was seated.

Adriano stood up. "You are the head of security. Place your right hand on the table."

"My hand?"

"Yes, your hand."

Giancarlo did so. Adriano said, "With your other hand, take the knife." He extended the knife to Giancarlo, who took it.

Adriano reached down and grabbed Giancarlo's wrist of the hand lying on the table and held his hand in place. "You failed me. You failed my daughter. You allowed someone into my villa."

"Don Umbretto, I swear, it will not happen again."

The other men in the room shifted uneasily in their seats.

Adriano continued, "You are damn right; it will not happen again. You will always have something to remember your failure by. I want you to take the knife and cut off your pinky."

"What? Don Umbretto? Please," pleaded Giancarlo.

Some of the men at the table glanced at each other

uneasily as they took in the scene before them. Off in the corner, Salvatore stroked his mustache with one hand as his mouth twitched with an arrogant smirk.

Adriano yelled, "They could have killed her. Now, cut it off."

Giancarlo breathed deeply as he brought the knife down to his pinky finger. He pressed the knife against his finger, drawing a slight touch of blood from the sharp knife.

Suddenly, Adriano released his grip from Giancarlo's wrist. "*Basta,*" Adriano thundered. "Enough. You have proven your loyalty to me. I trust you, Giancarlo. I trust you."

Giancarlo sighed heavily as he lifted his hand off the table and handed the knife back to the Don.

Adriano sat back in his chair. "Everyone leave the room except for Giancarlo, Luca and Salvatore."

The men quickly stood up from the table and bowed to the Don as they filed out of the room, relieved the meeting had ended.

AFTER THE OTHERS had left the Don's study, Giancarlo rubbed the touch of blood off his pinky with his thumb and sat next to the Don. Across from him sat Luca. Salvatore remained seated in the corner.

Adriano said, "Gentlemen, we have a traitor among us."

"Who?" asked Luca.

"The one man who came into my bedroom this morning with his *lupara* hanging off his shoulder. I knew right then and there I had been sold out. My betrayer knew he did not need to protect himself from an intruder, whom he had assisted in his endeavor. However, imagine this traitor's surprise when he came into my room, and found me alive, standing over that dead man. Giancarlo, you said earlier that you believed the intruder did not find my bedroom by accident. I do agree with you. That traitor disagreed with you and made sure he voiced that opinion. And that's the second time today he has done so."

"Mario?" asked Giancarlo

"Correct. He knows the answer as to whom this man worked for. He provided information to whoever it is that moved against me. The intruder knew what area of the fence was unguarded. He knew right where my bedroom was inside the villa. Thankfully for me, I got up earlier than normal. Something my betrayer did not expect. A knife in the heart while I slept was what he thought was going to occur. At the meeting, I used the knife to put the blame on you and to show my anger against you. To give the appearance that I was not interested in who the intruder was and who he worked for, but more interested in protecting my villa. Yet, I knew the moment the killer came into my bedroom, he had assistance from a traitor among us. So now my path is set before me. I need to not only find out who is trying to take control from me, but I need to confirm who is the traitor among my men."

Luca asked, "What do you want us to do?"

"I want the both of you to track every move Mario makes. I think this evening, he will leave at some point to make his report to the person or persons he sold me out to. Watch where he goes. See who he speaks to. In doing so, I think we will find out who is at war with us. Don't be surprised if his trail leads to the Genovese family. My guess is Don Sergio

Genovese is finally avenging the death of his father, Vincente, who, as you know, made war against my family many years ago. Vincente paid the ultimate price for those actions against me, with his life. I believe Mario betrayed me to Vincente's son, Sergio. I am convinced. Follow Mario when he leaves."

"We will follow him," replied Giancarlo.

Adriano then said, "All of this must remain quiet. We cannot have the citizens of Castelvetrano become aware that their Mayor was almost killed inside his own villa. Do you all understand?"

"Yes," they both replied.

"*Bene.*" (Good). Adriano then added, "Giancarlo, report back to me the moment you know where Mario goes."

"I will."

"Now, the two of you leave me. Salvatore, you stay and let me speak with you."

Giancarlo and Luca stood up to leave. Giancarlo hung his head down before he said, "I'm sorry for letting you down, Don Umbretto."

"Just find out who is behind it. I want to know."

The men left the room as the Don sat at the head of the table alone. He rubbed his temples, tired from the events of the day. Salvatore got up from his chair and joined him at the table.

"Once I have confirmed that Mario has betrayed me, you know what must happen?"

"Of course," replied Salvatore. "It will be done swiftly. Just tell me when."

Adriano closed his eyes and became silent as he thought about Mario. For Adriano, loyalty was the most important quality in a person. Adriano was fiercely loyal to those who accepted him. Mario's lack thereof is what stung him the most. He opened his eyes. "Betrayed, Salvatore. Since the death of the intruder this morning, something has unsettled my nerves. Now I know what has been bothering me. I guessed it within moments after the event. I have finally been betrayed. And by one of my men who has been with me the longest."

"Times are changing, Don Adriano. It's a new world. The Mafia in Sicily is changing to meet that new world. The days of the rural Mafia and the Don being a social intermediary for those under his protection are of the past. Now, real power and real money in post-war Sicily is what the new Dons are after. You have to change to stay in power and control."

Adriano sighed. "Perhaps you are correct. But, with all my power, I will strive to keep the old way alive. The way my grandfather and Don Spatuzza taught me. Now leave me."

Salvatore stood and nodded to the Don and left the study.

Adriano hung his head low. Life in the business provided Adriano with great wealth and power, yet there was a major price to pay. There was always someone out there ready to take your place, remove you, and grab what you controlled for themselves. Loyalty from those around you was required, not only to stay profitable, but to survive. But today, he had been betrayed by someone within his own *cosca*. He had never been betrayed in all of his years in the business.

Mario would pay the price for his betrayal. The rest of Adriano's *cosca* had to know the price for such infidelity.

4

FATHER GIULIO GIANUZZI

The next morning, far removed from the world of vendettas, betrayal, and *omertá*, in the secluded hill-top village of Bellafortuna in central Sicily, Giuseppe Sanguinetti sat in the front pew inside *Chiesa della Madonna*, the small, Baroque-style church located in the main piazza. Giuseppe was always the first to arrive for the weekday morning Mass. Here, in the sacred silence of his little village church, Giuseppe would be alone, deep in prayer. Not all of his prayers were directed to God. He spent a few moments every morning praying to his son, Biaggio Sanguinetti. It was more like a spiritual conversation than a prayer, a way to stay close to a child whom he loved deeply.

This church, which sat on the southern side of the *Piazza Santa Croce*, had a long connection to Giuseppe and the Sanguinetti family. It was here in this church that Giuseppe had been baptized, just as his father and grandfather had been before him. It was also where Giuseppe had served as an acolyte as a young boy and where he later pledged his marital vows to both God and his wife, Maria. The village church was also where his son, Biaggio, had been baptized and where, as a newly ordained priest, his son had celebrated his first Mass with all of the residents of Bellafortuna in attendance. It was also from this same church that, within just a few years of becoming a priest and working at the Vatican under Pope Pius XII, Giuseppe's beloved son was laid to rest.

It was a deep, dark time for Giuseppe and Maria during those first few months after Biaggio's death as they navigated the devastation that grief brings to a person. The little prayerful moments Giuseppe spent with his son every morning sustained him in those early days. Now four years past Biaggio's death, the utter shock and then despair at his death had subsided somewhat for Giuseppe and Maria, yet they still struggled daily to overcome the pain and emptiness in their hearts.

Slowly the church began to fill with its typical number of occupants for a Tuesday morning Mass, which meant about half of the number that would be in attendance for a Sunday service. Giuseppe finished his prayers to his son with his usual, *"Addio, mio figlio. T'amo. Domani."* He stood as Monsignor Mancini entered the sanctuary. A very young priest accompanied the monsignor, and the Mass began.

Monsignor Pietro Mancini, the long-time pastor of the village, led the service. After the opening prayers, he read the readings of the day, and after the Gospel, he gave a short sermon and then introduced the new young priest. He had just arrived in Bellafortuna the day before to study under the monsignor for a few months.

After the introduction, the young priest stood up and

made his way to the pulpit. He strode up the steps of the pulpit and placed both hands on the lectern. He smiled at all of the villagers sitting in the church. The women out in the crowd quickly took notice of the young man's striking appearance, his athletic build, his close-cropped, dark hair, and his very expressive blue eyes.

"Buon Giorno, Signor e Signori. Mi chiamo Padre Giulio Gianuzzi. First, I want to thank Monsignor Mancini for welcoming me here to your beautiful village and for his kind words in introducing me. As he said, I come from Cefalù. I've been a priest for only a month. I was sent here to learn under the much respected and, I know, much loved Monsignor Mancini. I look forward to meeting all of you over the next few weeks. Although none of you know me, I know all about your village. You see, I came here as a child to see an opera at your outdoor theater down in the valley with my father. It was Verdi's *La Traviata.* I still remember how moved I was by the opera and the beauty of this place. I hope while here this summer that I will have the opportunity to see an opera. So once again, thanks for having me, and I look forward to meeting each one of you as the weeks go by."

The villagers clapped their hands. Father Gianuzzi smiled and welcomed their warm wishes. The Mass then continued with Monsignor Mancini being assisted by the young priest.

When Mass ended, Giuseppe Sanguinetti walked out of the church, where he warmly took the extended hand of his good friend, Monsignor Pietro Mancini.

"Impressive young man, Pietro."

Monsignor Mancini smiled. "That's because he showed love to your opera and the summer festival."

"That's true," Giuseppe said. "Let me go introduce myself."

"Giuseppe, *aspetta.* Did you speak with Santo Vasaio last night by chance?"

"No, I did not see him."

"He wanted to meet with you. Yesterday evening, he saw a car with three men inside in dark suits parked near the Boccale Winery down in the valley. He attempted to go speak with the men, but they quickly drove away when Santo approached."

Giuseppe took a deep breath. "Did he mention the type of car?"

"He said it was an Alfa Romeo?"

"An Alfa Romeo. Did he say the color?"

"Gold."

Giuseppe raised his hand to his mouth and stroked his chin. "*Freccia d'oro.*"

"Golden arrow?"

"Yes. It's a new vehicle the company is producing now. Only the very wealthy and powerful would be in such a car."

"Who do you think these men are?" Monsignor Mancini asked. "What do they want?"

"I don't know for sure, but I do fear we may soon find out. If I had to guess, these are the men of our nightmares, Pietro. The men we have successfully kept out of Bellafortuna all these years."

Monsignor Mancini leaned forward and asked in an almost whisper, "Mafia?"

Giuseppe sighed loudly. "Well, let's just say farmers don't drive a *Freccia d'oro.*"

"Do you think they work with Don Biscotti?"

"No. I think these men are working for someone else, someone who, I'm afraid, will not leave us alone like Don

Biscotti does. I'll speak with Santo later today at the winery before I leave on my wine trip. Thanks for letting me know."

Giuseppe turned and walked a few feet to where Father Gianuzzi was standing. He was busy meeting the other villagers departing the church before heading to their workday in the vineyards and olive groves down in the valley. Giuseppe stood waiting his turn, speaking to each of the villagers as they finished talking to the young priest. "He reminds me of your son," a few villagers told him as they walked away. Giuseppe smiled awkwardly in return while he felt the instant pain in his heart as if an arrow had pierced it.

Anna Baldini, the wife of Lorenzo, the only *farmacista* (pharmacist) in the village, said to Giuseppe, "You should consider using our new priest to stand in as Jesus at our Holy Thursday celebration."

Giovanni nodded his head in agreement. The Easter celebrations in Bellafortuna were rich in traditions and had been celebrated in the village for centuries. One of the events most looked forward to by the villagers was the recreation of the Last Supper out in the piazza on Holy Thursday evening before Mass. However, the Good Friday procession was the highlight of Holy Week.

"*Signora Baldini,* that's a wonderful idea," Giuseppe replied. "I will speak with the *Società* at our meeting later this week as we prepare for the upcoming Holy Week celebrations, which are now less than two weeks away."

"I think the villagers would like that."

"Tell Lorenzo I will pick up his medical supplies and medicines he wanted me to get for him while on my trip."

"He is so thankful for all that you do, Giuseppe."

"Well, with Dr. Incaprera being our closest doctor miles

away in Palermo, your husband fills the role of much more than just a *farmicista* for us."

Anna wished him a good day while Giuseppe waited until the last villager finished speaking with the young priest. Giuseppe walked up and extended his hand. "It's so nice to meet you, Father Gianuzzi, and I hope you enjoy your stay in our little village."

The priest grabbed Giuseppe's hand. "*Grazie*. Please call me Father Giulio. I do look forward to my stay. It's so beautiful here."

"I am Giuseppe Sanguinetti. I run the wine store across the piazza from here, *Il Paradiso*, and I am also in charge of the opera festival in the summer. Thanks for your endorsement from the pulpit."

Giulio cocked his head. "Sanguinetti? Your son was Father Biaggio?"

"*Si.*"

"A priest of the Vatican. I heard everything about him from Monsignor Mancini. You must be a very proud parent. I'm very sorry for your loss."

"He was a wonderful son." Changing the subject, Giuseppe said, "Our *Società della Bellafortuna* is a group of leaders of the village. I am a member. We are meeting later this week to discuss the final plans for Holy Week. I would like you to come, sit in, and meet all of us."

"I would love that."

"*Molto bene, Padre Giulio. Benvenuto in Bellafortuna.*" Giuseppe paused, before adding, "*É un luogo magico.*" (It's a magical place.)

"That's what I have heard. Let me know about that meeting."

"I will. Take care. And please, come stop by the wine store and pick up a bottle of *Vino di Bellafortuna* produced at the Boccale Winery down in the valley. It's some of the best wine found here on Persephone's island."

"I shall. *Ciao, Signor Sanguinetti.*"

Giuseppe turned from the church and walked across the Piazza Santa Croce. In the middle of the piazza sat the statue of Enzo Boccale, the founder of the village and the winery. He was also the man responsible ages ago for moving the village from its earthquake-rattled original location down in the valley to its current location on the top of the hill. The left hand of the Boccale statue extended east toward the fertile valley of Bellafortuna.

During the war years, the base of the statue was home to the fascist mandated poster of that movement's leader, Benito Mussolini. It had been removed by the villagers with *Il Duce's* downfall. Giuseppe was always filled with regret whenever he looked at the space where the fascist leader's image had once stood. He had envisioned that with the fall of fascism and with Italy declaring Sicily an autonomous region in 1946, life in his village would improve. However, life here was still difficult.

The fact was that life in all of post-war Sicily was grim. For most residents of Sicily living in the bigger cities, food, particularly fruits, vegetables, cereals, and meats, was very difficult to obtain, and the black market became the main source of acquiring these foods. For those living in the countryside or smaller villagers, like Bellafortuna, life was hard but not as bleak. The farmers in and around Bellafortuna provided foodstuffs to the other villagers, with the food being exchanged among the villagers rather than being bought. But with that blessing came a curse.

From his wine travels around Sicily, Giuseppe knew firsthand that the Mafia was rising in power once again and in a fight to control the black market. The Boccale Winery and vineyards of Bellafortuna would be quite a prize for a Mafia Don.

Either by luck or divine intervention or perhaps a combination of both, the Mafia had never established a foothold in the tiny secluded hill-top village. One thing was certain. The history and fortune of Bellafortuna were always intrinsically linked to the city of Monreale, for whoever controlled Monreale had always played a role in keeping the Mafia out of the village.

Long before Don Biscotti came to power, the man who had controlled Monreale the longest was Don Calcedonio Umbretto, who left Bellafortuna untouched by the Mafia. After his death, then came the blood bath for control, with Onofrio Fausto coming out as the victor. Every citizen hated him. As for nearby Bellafortuna, there was one blessing in having Onofrio Fausto as the man in charge of the area in and around Monreale at the turn of the century. He had distant relatives, the Vasaio family, who had long lived in and controlled the village of Bellafortuna. With the assistance of Onofrio, and his close friend, the Archbishop of Palermo, the Vasaios, who were Santo's family, were allowed to solidify their control of the economic life of the village free of the Mafia. Eventually, Bellafortuna was able to free itself from the Vasaio family with the strange union of Giuseppe Sanguinetti and Santo Vasaio, but that is another story in the long and fascinating history of the village of Bellafortuna.

As for Onofrio Fausto, during Mussolini's war against the Mafia, he chose to flee to America with his son, Castranzio Fausto, where they settled in New Orleans, joined the American Mafia there, and became very wealthy during Prohibition.

It was after the Fausto family had fled to America that Calogero Biscotti rose to power and became the man in charge of Monreale, and unlike his predecessor, was loved by the inhabitants of the city. Don Biscotti allowed Bellafortuna to continue unfettered by Mafia influence. The villagers were well pleased when word had reached them that the Allies had reinstalled Don Biscotti as the Mayor of Monreale after the war.

Giuseppe thought back to his conversation with Monsignor Mancini. Who were those men in the car by the Boccale Winery? If they were *Mafioso*, who did they work for? And what were they doing by the winery? One thing was certain, if one were to make a move for control of the winery in Bellafortuna, it would have to be a very powerful family willing to take on Don Biscotti. It would be a risk many families would be willing to take to gain control of Monreale, and the fertile farmlands of Bellafortuna.

Giuseppe knew he had to do something. But, he was a changed man after the death of his son. He no longer had the desire to be the leader and protector for his little village and the inhabitants whom he loved. Yet, deep down, he knew he would never allow the fertile farmlands of his beloved Bellafortuna to one day become the battleground for control by the Mafia, at least not without a fight. He made his mind up. He would go see Don Biscotti and alert him to the men who were seen scouting the area of the winery. Don Biscotti knew the Sanguinetti family well. But where Don Biscotti had had a strong relationship with Antonio Sanguinetti, that relationship flourished with Antonio's son, Giuseppe.

Giuseppe reached his wine store on the opposite side of the piazza from the church. His sole employee, Kurt Hofmann, was already inside sweeping the floor.

Kurt, a Jewish musician from Vienna, had fled the Nazi death grip during the war. With the highly secret aid of the Vatican and the assistance of Father Biaggio Sanguinetti, Kurt, along with a group of other Jewish musicians from across Europe, were sent to hide in Bellafortuna, where the villagers protected them. That, too, is another story in the history of the small village of Bellafortuna. While living in Bellafortuna, Kurt fell in love with a local girl, Elizabetta Adorno, married her, and was the only one of the Jews to remain in the village after the war.

"*Buon giorno*, Kurt," Giuseppe said when he entered.

"*Buon giorno, Signor Sanguinetti.*"

Giuseppe excitedly asked, "Guess who I received a letter from yesterday?"

"Who?"

"The Adlers," replied Giuseppe.

"Really. *Meraviglioso.* (Wonderful.) How are they?"

"They are all settled in California, and Ludwig has already secured a movie contract to provide the musical score for a movie with Errol Flynn. Anikka is doing well. The children are all in school, including little Josef."

"That's wonderful. May I read their letter?"

Giuseppe walked behind the counter and pulled out a small gold box. He opened it and removed the folded letter, sitting atop other folded pages of paper. He walked over to

Kurt and handed him the letter. "It was so good to hear from him and that he and his family are doing well."

"We are all doing well, Giuseppe. Heinrich is all settled in New York. And Alfred just informed the both of us a few weeks ago about his life in Vienna. It seems as though all of our friends who came to live here during the war are settled into their new lives. I certainly know I am happy in my life with Elizabetta and working for you here at the wine store. Although we lived through hell, we at least are all scratching out a life for ourselves."

"I'm so glad to hear it. I pray for all of you every day and for all the European Jews who suffered so much. I'm so glad Bellafortuna was a place that offered all of you care and protection. Maria was so happy to hear the good news about the Adlers."

"I know she loved them so much. Both Ludwig and Heinrich are making music once again. And we all have your son and this village to thank."

"Indeed. Now, help me get ready for my trip this week."

"Where are you going this time?"

"Just to Monreale and Palermo. I have a large delivery for some wine stores at each spot. While I get the cases ready, can you please go to the Pandolfini stables and ready my cart and horse? And then, we can load the cart with the cases of wine. I'll be back on Thursday."

"I will. I'll pull it around to the front of the store." Kurt began to walk toward the door but stopped and turned back to Giuseppe. "*Signor Sanguinetti,* you do know if you ever bought a truck, you could certainly get where you are going faster?"

Giuseppe did not answer as he walked to the front door of

Il Paradiso and opened the door. As he led Kurt out, Giuseppe said simply, "I'll see you in a bit . . . with my horse and cart."

Kurt laughed as he left the wine store.

Giuseppe closed the door behind him, and before walking to the door in the back that led to the upstairs living quarters, he turned to his left and saw on the wall, above an old gramophone, three frames, one of which held a Jewish star with writing and signatures on it. A smile came to his lips. "They are all doing well, Biaggio. You saved the music."

He walked through the store toward the stairwell leading to the living quarters so he could speak with his wife and prepare for his trip, with his first stop being Monreale and a visit to Don Calogero Biscotti.

5

DON BISCOTTI'S COMMITMENT

*L*ater that day in Monreale, before Giuseppe would visit the largest wine seller in the city, he made his way to the *Piazza Vittorio Emanuele*. He parked his wagon at a close acquaintance's house who had a stable just a block from the piazza.

Giuseppe walked up the *Via Roma* and came into the beautiful piazza. A large fountain sat in the middle of the square, surrounded by three churches, including the majestic and famous Duomo with its spectacular mosaics. Palm trees dotted the landscape and made the entire area very attractive. Interspersed between the churches were small cafés, each with a few people having light lunches or espressos at the outside tables.

He passed one café that used to be the home to his in-laws' candle shop, which building had been sold soon after they had passed away. As a young man, and having married his wife, Maria, who was from Monreale, he had spent many an hour walking around this piazza and taking in all that it had to offer.

He approached a large palace on the piazza, which had been built by the Norman princes centuries ago when they had invaded the city and which now was the town hall and seat of the city's government. During World War II, it had served as the headquarters of the Allied army during the invasion of Sicily.

Since the installation of Calogero Biscotti as the mayor of Monreale by the Allies, the town hall was no longer open to the public. One would either have to make an appointment or be let in by his security men, who were all members of Biscotti's *cosca* and always present when the mayor was in his office.

Giuseppe knocked on the door, and a tall, muscular man opened the door.

"May I help you."

"I'm Giuseppe Sanguinetti from Bellafortuna. I would like to see Mayor Biscotti."

"Do you have an appointment?"

"I do not. But I was hoping he would see me. If he knows I am here and that I have a pressing issue, I'm sure he will want to see me."

"Stay here, *Signor Sanguinetti*."

The door was closed. Giuseppe turned and looked out toward the piazza and waited. He chuckled to himself, knowing that because of his position and years of working in the wine business throughout all of Sicily, he could just show up at the office of a mighty Don, and he would most likely be seen. He thought how ironic it was to be so close to many of the powerful Sicilian Dons yet, at that same time, hate everything that they stood for. But for a businessman in Sicily, you better know how to play the game. And no one played it any better than Giuseppe Sanguinetti.

The man returned to the front door and escorted Giuseppe to Don Calogero Biscotti's office, the mayor of Monreale. While walking down the hallway, the man said, "I am Dondo Gufinisti. I'm one of Don Biscotti's associates."

"Nice to meet you."

"Come, Don Biscotti's office is right here."

Giuseppe entered the office and was immediately met by Don Biscotti, seated at his desk in his large office. "What brings the opera man from Bellafortuna to me this afternoon?" asked Don Biscotti.

Giuseppe walked in and took a seat on the opposite side of the desk. As he did so, he replied, "To speak to you about an issue."

"Well, before you do, please tell me how is Maria?"

"She is doing well, as well as can be expected."

"I miss her parents so much. I hope her grief from the loss of her son is abating."

"It's a daily struggle, Don Biscotti."

"I see her brother from time to time. I know he retired from his opera career and is now teaching here in Monreale and Palermo."

"Indeed. We see him from time to time."

"So, tell me. What is your issue that you bring before me?"

"It concerns our winery. A *Freccia d'oro* with three men in dark suits was seen scouting the winery the other day. When Santo Vasaio attempted to approach them, they drove off."

Don Biscotti stroked his chin. "In 1944, I came to this very building where I was installed by the Allies as the Mayor of Monreale. At the same time, my good friend, Don Adriano Umbretto, was named Mayor of Castelvetrano, a man whom you know well from your wine business. Since that day, as Sicily has arisen from the ashes, I have been fully aware of forces moving against me and against Don Umbretto so as to remove us from power and take control. Many families lay dormant for so many years, in hiding and in exile. But now, they breathe again. But with that rebirth, comes a fight for control. The black market is extremely lucrative. This is what the most powerful families want to control. Areas, such as your village of Bellafortuna, that were untouched prior to the exile, are now on the radar of the new breed. So, you are most likely correct that these men scoping out the winery were there for nefarious purposes."

"I thought it important to come see you and tell you."

"I'm grateful for it. I can tell by the tone of your voice, this occurrence does cause you great alarm."

"It does."

"Have no fear, Giuseppe. As it was prior to my exile under Mussolini, and now, since my return, Bellafortuna has my unequivocal commitment to protect not only its industry but its people. I will put some of my best men on discovering who came to your winery. I know they will find out who it was. The word will go out to stay away from Bellafortuna. Everyone will know that your village remains under my protection and you will have the support of not only me, but of my entire *cosca*."

"I knew your support would be unwavering, as it always has been. We are blessed to have you back in power, Don Biscotti."

Don Biscotti stood up from behind his desk and walked to the empty chair next to Giuseppe. He sat down and said in a serious tone, "Sicily has entered uncharted territory. With one hand, Italy has freed us from their control, granting us our autonomy, while with the other hand, money from Rome and Milan is flowing in to rebuild our devastated cities. So although we are supposedly now free, in reality, the mainland still controls us through their purse strings. And when I say money, I mean lots of money. Groups are vying for control of that money, as well as power and control of many parts of Sicily. I'm sure I don't need to point out to you that your winery would be one such place."

"Indeed, as that is my fear."

"Long before the war, when I first took over control of Monreale after Onofrio Fausto left for America, your father came to me and opened his heart to me. Antonio's words to me way back then still rest in my soul. His words made me commit to the same arrangement that Don Calcedonio Umbretto had with your village when he ruled Monreale all those years."

"My father loved Bellafortuna, and would do anything to protect it."

"Your father was a great man, Giuseppe. A great man." He then bore his stare into Giuseppe's eyes. "*Tale padre, tale figlio.* (Like father, like son.) I've always respected you, Giuseppe. Always. My commitment to Bellafortuna remains the same as before."

"Don Biscotti, knowing we have your support will help me rest more easily."

"Thank you for advising me of this, Giuseppe. I will begin

trying to find out who was visiting your winery. In the meantime, please give Maria a kiss for me."

"I will, and thanks for seeing me."

"You're welcome. Before you go, tell me what are the operas this summer at the festival in Bellafortuna?"

"We are doing Puccini's *Madama Butterfly*, Giordano's *Andrea Chenier* and Verdi's *I Vespri Siciliani*."

"Sounds like a wonderful season. I've never seen Verdi's opera concerning the overthrow of the French by the Sicilians. I will definitely have to come see it."

"It should be great. We were lucky to secure some really great young singers. I'm most excited about the soprano. Her name is Renata Tebaldi."

"I'm looking forward to hearing her."

"Our tenor was to be Alfredo del Monte, but he was injured during the bombing of La Scala during the war and is most likely done singing now that he is blind."

Don Biscotti shook his head. "A tragedy. He was such a good, promising singer. A Sicilian. I heard him sing in Palermo."

"Indeed. Mario Filippeschi is replacing him."

"I hope you realize the joy you bring to our island with your festival. You provide to all of its citizens the majesty and beauty of opera in a spectacular location. It truly makes for a stunning evening of music, and allows one to get completely absorbed into the music. I'm so happy the festival has returned after being shuttered during the war years. I look forward with great anticipation to the upcoming season. If there is nothing more, I must get back to work."

As Giuseppe went to stand up, Don Biscotti extended his hand ever so slightly with his palm down, expecting it to be kissed. Now, Giuseppe Sanguinetti did play the game, but his father had taught him from an early age to never bow to anyone and never show inequality, as then you are the slave to the master.

Giuseppe always hated this part as it was always so awkward. But he had watched his father do it for so many years with his dealings with these men of power. Giuseppe gracefully stood up from the chair while paying no attention to Don Biscotti's outstretched hand. Once standing, he said, "*Grazie*," and quickly walked toward the door. When he opened it, Dondo was standing in the hallway.

As Giuseppe began to step out of the office, Don Biscotti stood up from the chair. He yelled out, "*Signor Sanguinetti*."

Giuseppe took a deep breath and then quickly turned back toward Don Biscotti.

"Bellafortuna will be protected," Don Biscotti said. "You have my word."

Giuseppe smiled, nodded his head, and then departed from the office.

6

AN INITIATION

It was late in the afternoon on that Tuesday when Adriano waited patiently in the study of his villa for the arrival of Luca and Giancarlo. He stood behind his desk, looking out the window that overlooked a small courtyard. Mario Zucello's believed betrayal had kept Adriano awake most of the night before and made him sick to his stomach all of the next day.

There was a knock at the door. Giancarlo Fanucci and Luca Speranza walked into the study and stood opposite Adriano's desk.

With his back turned to both men, Adriano asked, "Was I correct about Mario?"

Giancarlo took a deep breath. "As you said would happen, Mario left the villa late last night. We followed him. Mario met with a man in Corso Borgatti."

Without taking his gaze away from the window, Adriano

asked with surprise, "Corso Borgatti? Who did Mario meet with?"

"That's just it," Luca replied. "We are not sure. We can confirm that the person he met with was not a resident of Corso Borgatti. We think it was just a meeting spot to make his report."

Giancarlo interjected, "By the time we discovered that the man Mario met with was not from the town, he had already slithered away."

Adriano turned around. "So you lost him?"

"We did," responded Giancarlo. "The man left the city and we don't know where he went. Who Mario met with remains a mystery."

Luca added, "But this does confirm your suspicion that Mario was behind the attack on your life."

Agitated, Adriano said, "And yet, we have no idea who he betrayed me to. I was hoping that you would not only confirm Mario's betrayal, but my belief that Don Sergio Genovese is the man responsible."

Giancarlo said, "We will continue to investigate and hope to have an answer soon."

"I know you will. Is Mario back at the villa?

"He is," Giancarlo responded.

"Don Umbretto, what are we to do with him?" Luca asked.

Adriano folded his hands in front of him. "We cannot allow a traitor to continue to live among us. This is a job for Salvatore."

Both Giancarlo and Luca took a deep breath at the mention of Salvatore's name. Adriano considered Salvatore to be one of the most loyal members of the men under his control, and when he was presented with a task, it was executed with precision. As for the members of Adriano's *cosca*, Salvatore always made them feel uneasy.

"Giancarlo, tell Salvatore to take Mario up to the mountains today, to the area above Seliniunte," Adriano continued. "While there, tell Salvatore to encourage Mario to advise us as to who he sold me out to."

"I will."

Adriano was quiet for a moment before he said, "Please relate to Salvatore that whether Mario relinquishes the information or not, the traitor shall not see the sun pass below the hills this evening."

"It will be done," assured Giancarlo.

"And Giancarlo, make sure Salvatore allows Mario to make his peace. Now, leave me."

After his two most trusted members of his *cosca* left the study, Adriano slumped into his chair. A traitor within his own *cosca*. Salvatore would make sure that the rest of Adriano's associates would see him take Mario away. They would all know what that meant.

Mario deserved to die. Adriano was convinced he had sold him out to Don Genovese. Sergio Genovese had to be the man behind it all. After all, there was a long history between the families.

Sitting at his desk, Adriano thought back to his beginning years in the business. His thoughts drifted back to the very early difficult years as he made his place in the business and to his run-in with the Genovese family.

ADRIANO'S INITIATION into the business occurred while he was living with Don Gerlando Spatuzza in Castelvetrano. When Adriano first came to live with Don Spatuzza after the death of his grandfather and grandmother, he slowly began to be given chores within the business. As the years passed, he grew closer and closer to Don Spatuzza, and the members of his *cosca*. Don Spatuzza began to entrust Adriano with more and more tasks. But there was one day that changed Adriano's life and set him on a path that would make him a full-fledged member of the business.

It was a late afternoon in March 1906 when then 18-year-old Adriano, holding an envelope containing a letter from Don Spatuzza, walked up the winding dirt road that led to Salvatore Buccino's hill-top farm, just a few miles southwest of the town of Castelvetrano. *Signor Buccino's* farm was the farthest out of Don Spatuzza's properties for which he exerted his protection. Adriano had heard the Don's associates talking about a group of men from the nearby town of Campobello di Mazara who had been harassing *Signor Buccino* over the past few weeks and stealing his cattle. Don Spatuzza believed these men worked for the young but powerful Don Vincente Genovese from Campobello di Mazara. The letter that Adriano carried contained the name of the men that Don Spatuzza had secretly discovered were the perpetrators. The letter confirmed Don Spatuzza's commitment to end the harassment and his steep price to rid *Signor Buccino* of his problem.

As he continued walking up the road on that late afternoon, Adriano wiped the sweat from his brow. Although he was exhausted from a hard day's work, Adriano took in the spectacular views the road offered of the valley below.

Since his early days of coming to live with Don Spatuzza, Adriano loved hiking all across the rolling hills and mountains of Western Sicily, and he often pretended he was like the bandits of legend and lore hiding in and exploring the deep, dark caves.

Delivering the letter for Don Spatuzza that day was his last chore. Adriano didn't mind the trip, as it offered him the chance perhaps to see *Signor Buccino's* beautiful daughter, Vittoria. At seventeen, she was only a year younger than Adriano. He had befriended her at a very young age, and they often stole a few secret moments to speak together. And just a few weeks ago, behind her father's oil press, they had kissed. They promised each other and God that they would wed each other one day, but for now, they kept that a secret.

When he reached the summit, he realized something was wrong. As the Buccino farmhouse came into view, it was the loud voices that first caught his attention. He stepped off the dirt road and hid behind a grove of bushes as he took in the scene unfolding before him.

Three men stood outside the door of the farmhouse. Salvatore Buccino and his wife, Caterina, were kneeling on the ground. The three men were talking very loudly to Salvatore, who seemed to be disagreeing with what was being said to him.

Adriano scanned the area around the farmhouse but did not see Vittoria. Just then, from behind the farmhouse, a single gunshot could be heard. As the three men turned and looked at each other, Salvatore stood up as his wife began to cry uncontrollably.

Salvatore began yelling, "Vittoria. Vittoria."

The older man of the group took the butt of his gun and

plunged it into Salvatore's stomach, making him crumble to the ground. Caterina reached over and held her husband close.

Adriano stayed hidden behind the bushes. He was outnumbered and had no weapon, and knew there was nothing he could do. Adriano noticed a younger man walk from around the side of the home, holding a pistol in one hand. The man took the pistol and stuck it into the waistband of his pants before reaching down, zipping up his pants. A long, deep scar ran across the man's face.

The older man who had been questioning Salvatore angrily walked over to the young man, yelling at him. "Why? Why did you do that? I said to have fun with her." He proceeded to slap the young boy's face.

Caterina was crying uncontrollably while Salvatore raised himself to his knees. "I curse all of you. I curse all of you to hell."

The older man ripped the pistol from the younger man's waistband and proceeded to execute Salvatore and his wife. Adriano watched in horror from his hiding spot, as his body jumped with each gunshot.

The men quickly left the property.

When they had gone, Adriano leaped from his hiding spot and ran to the back of the farmhouse. He found Vittoria lying near the olive press. The top of her dress was ripped open with her breasts exposed. The bottom of her dress was raised above her stomach, and her undergarments were hanging on her right ankle with her legs spread open wide. Tears flowed down Adriano's cheeks as his eyes stared at the single bullet wound in her forehead. As he kneeled by her body, his hands began to shake with anger. He picked up her hand into his, and, in the same spot where he had pledged to marry her, he swore to both her and to God that he would get revenge.

He leaned over and kissed her lips, bright red from the blood running down her face from the wound. He pulled the top of her dress over her breasts and then reached down and grabbed her legs, closing them. He lowered her dress over her exposed womanhood. With tears streaming down his face, he kissed her one last time. From his pocket, he pulled the letter he was carrying from Don Spatuzza. He ripped it open and read the names of the men Don Spatuzza believed were harassing the family. "They will die for this, Vittoria. *Giuro*. I swear it. I swear it on my life."

He stood up and began running away from the farmhouse toward Don Spatuzza's villa.

DON SPATUZZA SAT in his chair in his study, listening intently to the story being told by Adriano, who often cried during its telling. Adriano ended his story by saying, "I want to kill them."

Don Spatuzza leaned forward in his chair. "Slow down, Adriano. Slow down. One thing required in this business is to act prudently. A plan must be established and followed with precision."

"They need to die, Don Spatuzza."

Don Spatuzza smiled at Adriano. "*Amico*, you have already learned that if justice is what you seek here in Sicily, you must seek it out for yourself. Without doing so, there is no justice in this land. But one must also be cognizant that every action you take creates a reaction. These men work for

Don Vincente Genovese. A young, powerful man. You desire to kill four of his members. You must always know what the consequences of your actions will be."

"They killed her in cold blood. One of them took advantage of her before they did so."

"So we consider the consequences. But we must do so without emotion. This girl. You loved her, no?"

Adriano did not respond as Don Spatuzza continued, "And now she has been ravaged by another. However, none of that matters when you consider revenge. You must look at the results of any and all actions. Don Genovese is strong, but he will not want to take me on. Not yet. So, revenge against members of his *cosca* can be pursued."

Don Spatuzza got up and walked to the door. He opened it, and Ernesto Cesaretti, the Don's chief bodyguard, was standing outside the door. "Call the men, Ernesto, at once." Don Spatuzza then turned and glanced toward Adriano before turning back to Ernesto. "Tell the men we will have an initiation." He then walked back into the room and said, "Adriano, go get dressed in a suit. Then come down to the foyer and wait. *Capice?*"

"Where am I going?"

"Tonight, you are becoming a man of honor."

AN HOUR LATER, Adriano, dressed in a blue suit with a red tie, walked down the hall with Ernesto, where he was led into the small billiard room. Upon entering, he was met by twelve of the Don's soldiers and associates, all of whom were dressed smartly in suits and ties. On top of the billiard table were a lit candle, a gun, a knife, and a prayer card with St. John the Baptist, the patron saint of Castelvetrano. The only light inside the room was from the single candle. Chairs were arranged around the billiard table.

Directly opposite the door from where Adriano entered sat Don Spatuzza. "Come, Adriano, sit next to me."

Adriano made his way around the table as the men took their seats. Those who did not have a place stood around the room.

When Adriano took his seat, all the men repeated at once, "Don Spatuzza, we owe you everything, even our lives."

"*Grazie* to each and every one of you," Don Spatuzza replied. "Now, what is your purpose tonight."

Ernesto walked over to where Adriano was seated and, placing his hands on his shoulders, said, "Tonight, Don Spatuzza, this boy becomes a man, a man of honor."

"Rise, rise, Adriano Umbretto," Don Spatuzza said.

Adriano gulped hard and then rose out of his chair. Ernesto moved closer to him.

From across the table, Gennaro Giduciano pointed to the gun and said, "Adriano, pick up the gun."

Adriano followed the command.

"Place your finger on the trigger," ordered Gennaro.

Adriano did so.

"Now, with your other hand, place the gun back on the table, but leave your trigger finger pointed out," instructed Ernesto.

Adriano again followed the request.

At that point, Don Spatuzza stood up and grabbed the knife. He took Adriano's trigger finger in his hand and pricked it with the end of the knife. Ernesto picked up the prayer card and held it under Adriano's finger as drops of blood fell onto the saint.

Ernesto then took the prayer card and held it over the candle flame. The prayer card burst into flames.

"Adriano, hold out your hands," Don Spatuzza said.

Ernesto placed the burning card inside the cupped hands of Adriano.

Don Spatuzza nodded. "Now, move the paper back and forth, from hand to hand, and repeat after me."

Adriano began passing the burning card back and forth between his hands as the flames licked the palms of his hands. He moved the card faster and faster to avoid burns from the prolonged contact.

"If I ever betray any member of the family, my soul will burn like this saint."

Adriano repeated the words, and when he finished, the card had been consumed by the flames. Adriano rubbed his hands together.

"Your father, your mother, your brother, and all of your grandparents are dead," Don Spatuzza said. "We are your only family. Tonight, you are now officially one of us. You will learn everything there is to know from Ernesto, who will be your mentor. Welcome to the family, *amico nostro*."

All of the men in the room repeated, "*amico nostro*."

Adriano kneeled and kissed the extended right hand of Don Spatuzza.

Just then, two men came into the room carrying glasses of Chianti wine. They were handed out, and then they were all raised toward Adriano.

"You are now an '*omu d'onuri.' Salute*, Adriano Umbretto," exclaimed Don Spatuzza.

"*Salute*," the men repeated.

The wine glasses were drained, and then each member came up and kissed Adriano on both cheeks.

When the ceremony was over, Adriano walked with Ernesto and Don Spatuzza back to the study. Three men in dark suits were waiting by the door of the study. The three men had not been at the ceremony. Don Spatuzza acknowledged the men, and they all entered the study. The door was closed, and Don Spatuzza sat behind the desk.

"I thank all of you for coming at this late hour," he said. "Tonight, we plan. Tomorrow, you execute."

The men nodded their heads, signifying their understanding, as Don Spatuzza continued, "Tomorrow you will proceed to Campobello di Mazara where you will find the killers of the Buccino family. You will make them pay – pay with their own lives. No one hurts people under my protection and gets away with it." He turned to Adriano. "And our new member will join you."

Adriano smiled as he thought of Vittoria.

BY 3PM THE NEXT DAY, three of the killers lay dead in the streets of Campobello di Mazara with single gunshots at the hands of Ernesto. Only the young killer of Vittoria remained at large.

He was found working in a vineyard. Adriano saw the man and stared at the scar on his face, confirming his identity. The young man was on his knees assisting other workers cutting weeds away from some of the vines. He sensed

Adriano walking toward him, and when he looked that way, his eyes caught the glare of Adriano. He stood.

"*Come, va?*" asked the man. "*Che fu?*"

Adriano pulled a knife from his belt, and the man began to run. "*Aiuto. Aiuto,*" the young man screamed, but no help was coming from the other workers who watched the pursuit in silence. As the man crossed a ditch, he tripped and fell. Adriano reached him and stood over him with his knife drawn.

"*Come ti chiami?*"

"Franco Calobrenese. I did not do anything."

By this time, Ernesto and the other men arrived, along with some of the vineyard workers who stood off to the side. Adriano stood over the man. "You took her from me. You dishonored her."

"*Perdoni me, Signor.* Please, I have a wife and family."

"I don't care."

"My uncle is Don Vincente Genovese."

"He cannot help you here," replied Adriano.

The man got to his knees and pleaded. "Please don't hurt me. I did not mean to kill her. She bit me. I lost my temper."

"And now you lose your life." Adriano then raised the knife and said loudly, "*Ecco il suo ultimo boccone, pezzo di merda.*" (Here is her final bite, you piece of shit.) Adriano grabbed the young man by the hair and slowly slit his throat as blood poured from his neck. The man crumbled to the ground.

Adriano, standing over the dead body, looked around and said to the workers standing nearby. "Let Don Vincente Genovese, as well as all of the residents of Campobello di Mazara, know that Adriano Umbretto has avenged the death of the Buccino family who were under the protection of Don Spatuzza. Let this be a lesson to all of you, or I will personally come find you and kill you."

Ernesto looked at the men with him and chuckled. The other men laughed.

The vineyard workers quickly began walking away as Ernesto walked over to Adriano. He whispered to Adriano, "You have become a man today, Adriano. But never kill without allowing the person to make peace with God. Remember this always. You owe that to the man whose life you take. You are one of us now."

The Don's other men extended their hands, and Adriano shook them all.

"Let's go home, gentlemen," Ernesto said.

"*Aspetta*," said Adriano. He then ran towards a vineyard worker, who froze with fear when he saw Adriano hastening toward him. Adriano reached into his pocket and pulled out a wad of cash. He extended it to the man and said, "Can you purchase some flowers and send them to *Signora Calobrenese*? Give the rest of the money to her."

"*Si, Signor*," replied the man before quickly scurrying away.

Adriano made his way back to Ernesto and the others. As they turned to leave, Adriano turned and looked back at the dead man lying in the dirt. Adriano's anger and feelings of revenge had subsided with the man's death and were now replaced with emptiness. Adriano had taken a life. The man had it coming. The man deserved to die, but the feeling of emptiness only settled in deeper and deeper. Yet, justice was done. Justice was what Sicily lacked, and justice is what Adriano knew Don Spatuzza brought to the island. And

Adriano was fully aware that Don Spatuzza had learned his sense of justice from Adriano's grandfather, one of the most respected Dons in all of Sicily. That is how Adriano would dedicate his life. He was in the business now, and for the money he would make from it, he would provide justice for those who paid for it. He had killed a man. He knew he would most likely have to kill again. He vowed he would never murder anyone. Killing and murder were different in his mind. He killed Franco Calobrenese; he did not murder him.

Just then, Ernesto put his arm around Adriano. "Yesterday was the ceremony. Today, was the action that truly makes you a man of honor. You restored that young girl's honor. You are now part of the business."

Adriano took a deep breath. The image of the man's frightened eyes right before Adriano slit his throat was seared into his mind. That was all he thought about as the group continued back to Castelvetrano to make their report to Don Spatuzza.

Meanwhile, within the hour, Don Vincente Genovese was told about the death of three of his men and of his nephew, Franco Calobrenese. Don Genovese was also given a name, the name of the killer of his nephew, the name of one Adriano Umbretto. Don Genovese was a smart man, wise enough to know that his family was powerful but not yet powerful enough to take on Don Spatuzza. Revenge would come one day, and when it did, Adriano Umbretto would pay the price for the killing of his nephew.

As for now, Adriano Umbretto returned to Don Spatuzza's villa. With his initiation into Don Spatuzza's *cosca* and with the killing of Franco Calobrenese, Adriano Umbretto became a simple soldier for Don Spatuzza.

ADRIANO'S REMEMBRANCES were disturbed by a knock on his door.

"Who is it?" he yelled to the closed door.

"It is Luca, Don Umbretto."

Adriano rubbed his temples as the thought of Mario Zucello's betrayal came back to him.

"Enter," he said as he rose from behind his desk.

Luca walked into the study and announced, "Salvatore is here. Giancarlo has already spoken with him. He will be taking Mario away shortly."

Adriano took a deep breath. "Thank you, Luca. I'm not to be disturbed the rest of the day."

Luca nodded his head, and departed the room.

Adriano slumped back into his chair. Why would Mario betray him? Why? No one had ever done so before, even after all these years in the business. Adriano sighed. Mario would be dealt with by the end of the day.

Revenge was a strange bedfellow. Immediate gratification was almost always complimented with later remorse. Adriano learned from an early age that killing, no matter the reason, took its toll on you. He was not looking forward to the feelings he would experience when he received word later about the fate of Mario Zucello.

7

THE BOCCALE WINERY

Santo Vasaio slowly walked down the dirt path that led from the Boccale Winery over to the wine cellar that centuries ago had been hewn into the base of a hill in the Bellafortuna valley. It was late Tuesday night.

As Santo approached the wine cellar, he yawned. He was tired, as his day had begun early, as it did every day, out in the nearby vineyards, meeting with his workers in the predawn hours, walking his vineyards as he checked his crops, deciding which to trim, tie-up, cutback, or prune. That was all done before he would head over to meet with the men who worked on the barrels that stored the wine the Boccale Winery produced.

Before any wine from the Boccale Winery was placed in an oak barrel, the barrel was fire-roasted for a short time. That would give the barrel a distinct vanilla and cinnamon aroma, which would ultimately mix and become part of the wine stored inside. That was one of the key ingredients of *Vino di Bellafortuna.*

It was not an easy process, for if the workers roasted the barrel for too long, the barrel would give off a smokey smell, which was how most of Santo's competitors treated their barrels. But perfecting the barrel roasting process was not something that one could just try to imitate and expect to obtain the same result. The process used by Santo had been passed down from winemaker to winemaker. It had originated with Enzo Boccale himself ages ago, and was taught to Santo by Antonio Sanguinetti.

Once Santo finished meeting with the barrel makers, he would proceed to the winery, where he would check on the production of *Vino di Bellafortuna.* That's where he would spend the rest of his day, working in the winery on production, barreling, and bottling, and writing letters to his contacts at all of the different wine suppliers throughout Sicily and Italy. His days were long, but he loved every moment of it and still relished seeing a bottle ready to be shipped.

A few times a week, as he did this night, he would end his day in the wine cellar, tasting wines from the barrels and checking on the process of wine aging. He came to the double doors of the cellar, each emblazoned with the letter "B" on either door for Boccale. He entered and took the small stairwell down into the bowels of the cellar.

He entered a cavernous area filled with stack upon stack of oak barrels. It was here in the stillness of the cave that the miracle of wine creation through time came to fruition. The scent of vanilla and cinnamon permeated the entire room.

Santo walked over to an upright empty barrel on which

sat wine glasses and a long glass tube. He picked up a wine glass and the long glass tube, which he referred to as "the wine thief." He then walked over to one of the barrels and uncorked the top. He placed his wine thief inside, which quickly filled with wine. He removed the glass tube from the barrel and then filled his wine glass from the tube. The wine from this barrel had been aging for 13 months now. Most of the wines were bottled between 13 to 14 months after barreling. They would only be bottled when Santo, and only Santo, approved that the barrel was ready. He raised the glass to his nose and breathed in deeply. The wine was appealing on the nose, big and powerful, packed with spicy aromas, with hints of vanilla, cinnamon, truffles, tobacco, and pepper.

He walked toward a small table and sat down. He placed his wine glass down and waited as he let the wine inside breathe. As he did so, he heard footsteps on the stairwell that led down to the cellar. He turned and smiled when he saw his wife, Mirella. In her hands, she carried a small pail.

"You must be starving. I brought you a little something to eat," she said.

He stood and met her halfway toward the table. He kissed her. "*Grazie*. Come sit."

As she did so, he walked over to the empty wine barrel and grabbed another wine glass from the top. He then returned to the other barrel and used his wine thief once again. He then poured his wife a glass of his creation. He brought her glass back to the table and sat down. "Let it breathe for a few moments."

He opened the pail that she had placed on the table in front of him and pulled out a mortadella sandwich with a small container of olives. He asked his wife, "Did you eat?"

"I did. Matteo and I ate earlier. He said you would be late tonight."

"He was right."

"Soon, you need to teach your son this part of the business, so that you can end your days earlier."

Santo picked up his glass and raised it to his nose once again, breathing in deeply. He swirled the wine around the glass, checking closely as the contents ran down the sides. "I will show him everything. One day." He smelled the wine once again. "This is the most important part of all that we do. The most important step. It must be just right. It's all about the timing. One misstep here, and all the months of the process are a waste."

"You need to teach your son, like Antonio and Giuseppe Sanguinetti taught you."

"I've taught Matteo everything about the production, and I have slowly begun to teach him this part. It will take time, but he will get to understand this process in the years to come."

Santo picked up the glass and smelled it one more time before he raised his glass to his wife. "*Salute.*"

She picked up her glass. "*Salute, mio amore.*"

They both took a drink at the same time. "Well?" he asked.

"It's perfect," she replied. "But I'm sure you will disagree."

Santo chuckled. "Another week, then perfection."

Santo picked up his sandwich and took a bite. As he ate, he said to Mirella, "I spoke to Giuseppe this morning before he left on his wine trip. I mentioned to him about the car I saw near the winery. He was as concerned by the news as me.

He assured me that when he returned from his travels, the appearance of the men would be brought up to the *Società della Bellafortuna*. Without a doubt, he is very concerned about Bellafortuna due to the rise of the Mafia."

She looked around the wine cave. "If Bellafortuna ever lost this place, it would mean the end of our village."

"It is a special place. Once the economic conditions improve across Sicily, I would love to open our winery to the visitors who come to the opera festival every summer. They could spend a few hours touring the wine facility and then we could take them down here where they could taste the wines. I think they would gladly pay something to do so."

"I think people would love that."

"I will mention that idea to Matteo. It might be something he can be in charge of, and in a few years, we can try it."

As Mirella finished her wine, she said, "You can wait a week if you want, but your wine does taste perfect."

Santo laughed as he passed his empty dinner pail over to his wife.

She reached out and gently grabbed his hand. "Come to bed soon, Santo." She gave him a wink.

"I will. I promise."

A short while later, after she had gone back to their home, as Santo was about to place his wine thief inside another barrel, he paused and looked around the wine cave. He owed all of this to Antonio and Giuseppe Sanguinetti. After the removal of his own father, Vittelio Vasaio, from the economic stranglehold that he had once held over the villagers, the Sanguinettis turned to Santo to take over the winery, and they taught him everything there was about the business and the production of wine. He came to love this place and knew the importance that the Boccale Winery held for Bellafortuna.

He dipped the wine thief into another wine barrel and drew some of the product from the barrel. He smelled the wine inside the glass. Just by the smell alone, he knew. He immediately raised the glass to his lips and tasted it. Perfection, as he had guessed.

A feeling of pride rose inside him as he relished in his creation. His thoughts turned to his conversation with Giuseppe about the Mafia. His mind was emblazoned with one thought and one thought alone; he would fight and defend the Boccale Winery with his own life if called upon to do so. He owed that to his father, his wife, his son, the villagers of Bellafortuna, and to his friend, Giuseppe Sanguinetti.

8

FRANCESCA UMBRETTO

 driano was seated in the villa gardens that Wednesday morning, drinking a strong espresso. Here, among the hedges and the flowery garden beds, he would try to forget all of his troubles, and just get lost in the majestic beauty of his well-kept grounds. His momentary respite was ended when Salvatore Battaglia entered the gardens and came over to where he was seated.

"It is done," said his trusted enforcer.

Adriano gulped hard, as Salvatore went on to report that Mario Zucello did not admit that he was a traitor, nor did he provide the name of the person with whom he had made contact in Corso Borgatti when he betrayed his boss.

"I did what I could, but Mario was afraid for his family," Santo said. "I think Mario got in over his head, whoever he got in bed with. I believe he came to the conclusion that he would rather face your wrath alone than have his family face our unknown enemy. For that reason, he died without coming clean. He knew you would leave his family alone."

Adriano sighed. "You are probably right. In the end, he found honor by saving his family. I will send his wife some money to help with the funeral."

"I'll make sure she will get it."

"As for Francesca, I will speak with Giancarlo and advise him that the increased security will remain in place."

Salvatore agreed.

"Your nephew, Marco, is with her most of the time."

"*Va bene*. He is a good, trustworthy boy."

Adriano looked directly at Salvatore. "Other than you, Luca, and Giancarlo, Marco is one of the few members I trust, and that's because of his relationship to you." Adriano sighed again. "At this point, I need to surround myself with the people I can trust."

"I understand, Don Umbretto. Mario paid the price, and all of your associates know what that price was."

"Thanks for your duty, Salvatore."

Salvatore stood up. "*Prego*, Don Adriano." He then turned and walked out of the garden, leaving Adriano seated alone.

***

LATER THAT DAY, Marco Moretti was leaning against the wall outside of Francesca's bedroom. Since the day the intruder had come into the villa, Marco had stood guard outside Francesca's bedroom door under Don Umbretto's orders. Giorgio Silveri would relieve him for a couple of hours at night so he could sleep, but mostly Marco had just stood his post hour upon hour. It made sense to him. The intruder who had come into the villa could have killed not only Adriano, but his daughter as well. He knew how much Adriano loved his daughter. That was obvious. No matter what was going on, the moment she walked into a room, Adriano would stop everything and speak with her. Theirs was a father-daughter relationship. But Marco had recognized when he first came to work for Adriano how captivating her beauty was, and, how all eyes always turned on her whenever she entered a room.

On both Monday and Tuesday night, while standing guard, Marco could hear Francesca crying intermittently as he stood outside her bedroom door. He felt sorry for her, as he often was her driver to her singing lessons in the town and knew how much she loved going to them. Her life was a musical life, a craft that she worked hard at trying to perfect.

Marco quickly grew in awe of her dedication to music. The villa would often be filled with the sound of her playing the piano in her room, while she practiced her art and sang the majestic and beautiful opera arias written by the greatest composers the world had ever known. One could say it was her singing voice that first made Marco's very own soul fall in love with the daughter of his boss when he first had come to work for Don Umbretto. Of course, she did not know it. And he was certain Adriano would never approve, nor would she pursue anything with one of her father's associates. His love would have to remain a secret locked within him forever.

Since the coming of the intruder into the villa, the music had stopped for Francesca. Not one note was played on the piano inside her bedroom, nor did one song come from her mouth during that time.

On that Wednesday afternoon, the quietness in the

hallway outside her bedroom was broken suddenly by the sound of the piano. A smile came to Marco's face as that sound was soon joined by the lilting singing voice of Francesca. The piano punctuated the melodic line that her voice was producing. Marco laid his ear against her door and listened intently to her intoxicating voice.

O mio babbino caro
Mi piace è bello, bello
Vo'andare in Porta Rossa
A comperar l'anello!
Sì, sì, ci voglio andare!
E se l'amassi indarno
Andrei sul Ponte Vecchio
Ma per buttarmi in Arno!
Mi struggo e mi tormento!
O Dio, vorrei morir!
Babbo, pietà, pietà!
Babbo, pietà, pietà!

Oh my dear papa
I like him, he is so handsome.
I want to go to Porta Rossa
To buy the ring!
Yes, yes, I want to go there!
And if my love were in vain,
I would go to the Ponte Vecchio
And throw myself in the Arno!
I am pining, I am tormented!
Oh God, I would want to die!
Father, have pity, have pity!

Father, have pity, have pity!

If Marco had known anything about opera, he would have known Francesca was singing an aria from Giacomo Puccini's *Gianni Schicchi*. But he did not, so all he could do was relish in the words of the aria about a young woman's plea to her father to allow her to marry the man who had touched her heart. The gorgeous music was matched perfectly with Francesca's stunningly beautiful voice.

He listened to her singing aria after aria all afternoon.

LATER, when she finished, she opened the door, and found Marco standing across the hallway, staring out the window. He turned toward her when the door opened, and he smiled.

Francesca stared at his dimples, as usual. Marco always smiled whenever she spoke to him. And her eyes would always rest around his mouth as she waited for his dimples to appear. Of all her father's associates, he was the most handsome. He had rusty brown, close cropped hair and sparkling green eyes. In some other life, she would have liked to have gotten to know him better.

"*Signorina Francesca*, what can I do for you?"

"I want to go see my father. I'm sure you are going to tell me you have to escort me."

"Yes, I do. I think he is in his study."

"Any word on how much longer you will have to be my babysitter?"

"Babysitter? I'm no babysitter. I'm merely protecting you after the event from a few days ago."

"Well, I'm done with it. Please take me to my father."

As they walked toward the study downstairs, Marco said, "I heard you singing earlier. I just wanted to tell you how beautiful you sounded."

"Well, if I can't get back to my teacher, then what is the point?"

They reached the study. Adriano was seated behind his desk. He stood up when Francesca walked in. He motioned to Marco to shut the door, which he did, leaving father and daughter alone.

After Francesca spoke her piece, Adriano responded, "Listen, I know you feel like you are in prison. But we are still working things out after what occurred here just a few days ago. Until then, let's just keep the status quo."

"I've lived my entire life according to all of your rules. I have followed them all. Singing is the one thing I have. The one thing that is mine. I was making such strides with *Signora Lucia*."

"And you will again, soon."

"Soon? But Papa."

"Look, I don't want to scare you, but these are dangerous times. And we are not even sure who we need to worry about. So, my answer is no."

"Then if I can't go to her, will you allow her to come here?"

Adriano nodded his head. "You are relentless, just like

your mother. I will make the arrangements. Beginning next week, I will send someone to pick her up and bring her here to meet with you. I'm sure she won't mind, as I will make it very attractive for her to come."

"*Grazie, Papa. Grazie.*"

She ran behind the desk and kissed her father, before almost skipping across the room to the door. When she opened the door and walked out into the hallway, she was met by Marco who smiled at her. She smiled back, before she turned toward her father again and said, "*Grazie, Papa. Mille Grazie.*" She then walked down the hallway with Marco, as she excitedly told him what her father had agreed to.

Adriano watched his daughter walk down the hallway. He thought to himself how his daughter had so much of her mother's spirit. A spirit to stand up for what she wanted. His daughter was becoming a woman. He had raised her well and fulfilled the promise he had made to Santa when she died.

He remembered back to when he fell in love with Santa Antonini. Reflecting back on that time made him well up with emotion. Adriano closed his eyes, and the image of his wife's face, her scent, and her touch permeated his entire being, as he thought of laying eyes on her for the first time.

As THE YEARS passed following Adriano's initiation into Don Spatuzza's *cosca*, he quickly moved up the ranks, taking a very active role in the business. Under the tutelage of Don Spatuzza, and under the constant direction of Ernesto,

Adriano was being groomed to one day become the next Don of Castelvetrano.

Adriano went about his job and worked tirelessly for Don Spatuzza. When he got older, Don Spatuzza would always tell him that he needed to find a wife, as life as a Don was hard and lonely, and one needed a family to make the sacrifice worth it all. As for Adriano Umbretto, he never thought marriage was in the cards for him after Vittoria Buccino's death. However, at the age of 28, that all changed. One day, he was walking along a grove of olive trees with a farmer, Matteo Antonini, who was under the protection of Don Spatuzza. The farmer's workers were hard at work, picking olives from the trees. It was exhausting, physically demanding work.

As Adriano passed one of the olive trees, he heard from above him the voice of a girl singing an old Sicilian folksong.

Sicilia bedda, nun ti pozzu cchiù scurdari,
Granni è 'st'amuri quantu granni e profunnu lu mari.
Ma quantu sù beddi Nu-Yorki, Berlinu e Milanu
Ma quantu cchiù duci è la vuci di 'nu paisanu.
'Sta terra ca chiama li figghi ca sunu luntanu,
'Sta matri ca è matri dui voti e mai ni scurdamu.

Beautiful Sicily, I can't forget you,
This love is great, like the sea that is great and deep.
But how are beautiful New York, Berlin and Milan,
But the voice of motherland is sweetest.
This land calls their sons who are far away,
This mother is the best of all and we'll never forget it.

Adriano noticed a ladder leaning up against the olive tree. He glanced upward and saw the young woman at the very top of the ladder. She had a wicker basket slung over her shoulder in which she was placing her just picked olives.

Adriano stopped walking and stared at the girl. She wore a simple blue dress, that ended near her ankles, just above her white socks and black shoes. Her golden hair shone brightly under the afternoon sun. She went about her tedious work, all the while singing her folksong, without paying any attention to the young man staring up at her.

The farmer had continued on, unaware that Adriano had stopped. The girl finished her song, and became aware of the young man at the base of the ladder. Her deep blue eyes locked on his eyes, and she gently smiled, before she turned back to her work. With that smile, Adriano felt weak in his knees.

The farmer meanwhile turned to speak to Adriano, and quickly realized that he had stopped walking some yards back. The farmer moved toward him. Adriano was standing still, staring at the beautiful girl on the ladder, while her dress blew in the gentle wind of the afternoon.

The farmer asked, "You like what you see?"

"She has a lovely voice."

The farmer chuckled. "My son, you are not staring at her voice."

Adriano turned toward the farmer before he laughed in return. He responded, "You are right."

The farmer looked up at the girl as he said to Adriano, "My son, women inspire the melody of our soul. They are the true melody of Sicily. So, I ask you again. Do you like what you see?"

"I do, very much."

"Good, because that is my eighteen-year-old daughter, Santa."

Without looking at her father, and all the while staring at the young girl, Adriano said, "*Signor Antonini,* your daughter will never have to pick another olive ever again."

AND THAT IS how Adriano Umbretto met Santa Antonini from Castelvetrano. Their engagement was a whirlwind, but in a very traditional, Sicilian way. The couple was never left alone during their entire engagement. Their walks together were always followed closely behind by female members of the Antonini family, lingering just far enough behind to provide the couple a few moments to speak freely so that they could get to know each other, yet watched closely by the entourage. If Adriano got too close to her, he would catch the *malocchio* stare from the ladies. It was during these walks that Adriano confided in her as to what he did for a living. He went on to explain to her his whole life story. Santa was not a naïve girl. She was the daughter of a farmer in the rough, grim life in Sicily. She knew what way of life Adriano could provide to her, and she was acutely aware that her father approved of the match. During their engagement, the only time Adriano and Santa touched each other was at the family dinner, when Adriano would secretly rub his foot up her leg under the table. She would get excited at his touch, and looked forward to the family dinners because of it. She was falling in love. And the best part was that, unlike most Sicilians whose marriages were arranged by the parents, their relationship was based on desire from their first sight of each other, which eventually turned to love and affection.

After a few weeks, their marriage occurred in a beautiful nighttime ceremony in the Church of the Holy Trinity in Castelvetrano. For Adriano, as it is for most Sicilians, his wedding day was the most important day in his life. Santa arrived at the church on horseback surrounded by women carrying torches that lit the road. She was adorned in a simple, white wedding dress.

The sacred religious ceremony was filled with music and was packed with Sicilian traditions passed down from generation to generation. Don Gerlando Spatuzza served as best man for Adriano. After the ceremony, the couple climbed aboard an ornately decorated *carrettu sicilianu,* a two wheeled carriage pulled by a donkey. The cart was decorated with vivid colors of reds, yellows and oranges. The wedding party and guests walked with the cart, holding torches, as they travelled to the Antonini farm. Once at the farm, the women of the Antonini family brought forth plate after plate of food from the main house, and placed the food on tables all around the yard. Antipasto came first, of course, consisting of arancini, prosciutto and figs, salami, stuffed mushrooms, calamari, and Castelvetrano olives.

Next came the fruits, salads, *Pasta alla Norma,* bread, meat, cheeses, and of course, wedding soup, followed by three different types of veal dishes to choose from. That's not even to mention the desserts like cannoli, cassata, torta di ricotta, and the wedding cake.

And of course, during the entire evening, the guests could choose from wine, champagne and limoncello. Music and dancing filled the night. The couple's first dance was the traditional *Tarantella.* All throughout the evening, one could hear yells from the guests of *"Evviva gli sposi!"* (Long live the newlyweds) and *"Per cent'anni!"* (For one hundred years!) At one point in the evening, the couple handed out the *confetti,* fancily wrapped sugar almonds, to all the guests in attendance. Interspersed among the guests were a few members of Don Spatuzza's *cosca,* standing guard with their *luparas.*

As the night finally began to wind down, the younger men in attendance suddenly appeared carrying torches, while some had musical instruments. They came and encircled the couple. Santa's mother and father came into the circle and hugged their daughter. As *Signor Antonini* shook Adriano's hand, Santa's mother whispered into her daughter's ear, "Don't be afraid, tonight. Make him happy, Santa."

The men with the torches then led the couple down the road away from the farmhouse, while the men with the instruments played love songs. The couple, now free to show affection toward each other, walked hand in hand as husband and wife, as the torchbearers surrounded them on either side. As the newlyweds continued toward Don Spatuzza's villa, the love songs soon turned to raunchy songs that the men sang the entire way, like *C'e la luna mezzo mare* and *We', Marie, We', Marie.*

When they reached the villa, the couple waved to the men before going inside. Santa said not a word, as they moved toward the bedroom.

Once inside, Santa stood perfectly still, with her hands at her side, facing him. Adriano grasped her shoulder and slowly turned her around. He grabbed her hips from behind and pulled her into him. He whispered into her ear, *"T'amo Santa.* You are the melody of Sicily."

She sighed, as she gently bent her back forward and pushed her backside into him. He slowly began to unbutton the buttons on the back of her white wedding dress. As he slipped her dress past her hips, her slip became visible. It had lace at the bottom, and lace around the breasts. This was her mother's and grandmother's slip, which they all wore on their wedding night.

Santa stepped out of the dress. She reached up to her right shoulder, and pulled down the strap of her slip, and then the left strap, which allowed it to fall to the ground. She stood in front of her husband in her white bra and underwear.

Adriano began to remove his clothes, as she undid her bra. His eyes glanced at her chest as her breasts were exposed, and she could see his excitement in his pants. She pulled off her underwear, as he pulled down his pants. She trembled with nerves as she brought her knees in, crossed her feet, and placed her hands in front of her intimate area. He pulled off his underwear. Her eyes drifted down, and they widened as she looked at him.

He reached for her hands, which exposed her to him. He said softly, *"Vieni, Santa. Vieni.* Come. You are so beautiful. Come. I will be gentle."

He led her to the bed, and they climbed under the sheets. They kissed, haltingly at first. But once his fingers entered her, her kissing became more intense. Her hips began to move with the thrust of his hand, until she finally pulled his shoulder toward her letting him know her intention. She laid flat on her back and he climbed on top. She reached and grabbed his manhood, and slid it into her wetness. It hurt as he entered her, but felt good at the same time.

He began to thrust inside her, and her pain intensified with each push. Soon though, she began to match his rhythm as her wetness allowed her to grind her hips deeper and deeper into him. Their pace quickened as their breathing intensified and they both made sounds of enjoyment. As she contracted, his tension released. She laid naked on top of him for a bit, before she got up to go clean up in the bathroom.

As she did so, he got out of the bed and looked at the bedsheet that was stained with her blood. He took the sheet off the bed, opened the window, and tied the sheet to a chair by the window and hung it out the window. As Sicilian tradition demanded, he made sure that the blood stain on the sheet hung out the window proving to all who could see that his wife was a virgin. He took out another sheet and laid it on the bed. She returned to the bed in a nightgown, made the bed with the new sheet, and then slipped under the covers. They kissed deeply.

"T'amo, Adriano."

He smiled and told her again he loved her. She rolled on her side, and he wrapped his arms across her breasts. She stared out the open window as the sheet with her blood flapped in the night breeze. Adriano and Santa began their life together as husband and wife.

9

MIRELLA VASAIO

Early that Thursday morning, Father Giulio Gianuzzi sat inside the Boccale Winery. Mirella Vasaio had just completed giving the young priest a tour of the entire complex.

"And now Father, here comes the best part."

"How can you top the tour?" he asked.

She stood up from the table and walked over to where two wine glasses were stationed and a bottle of *Vino di Bellafortuna Riserva*. Walking back to the table, she said, "This is how I can top it."

She poured both of them a glass. Raising his glass to her, he said, "*Salute, Signora Vasaio.*"

"*Salute,*" she responded, as they both took a sip.

Father Gianuzzi smiled after taking that first sip. "This must be what the wine tasted like at the wedding feast in Cana. I love your winery and I love your wine."

"Thank you, Father. The *Riserva* is my husband's pride and joy."

"Well, I can tell why. How did he get started in this business?"

Mirella went on to tell him how the Boccale Winery had been the mainstay of the village for many years, but had been shut down when Santo's family had come to the village and took over control of most of the economic life of the village.

"It was because of my husband and Giuseppe that eventually my father-in-law relinquished control. Giuseppe and his father reopened the Boccale Winery. Over time, Antonio Sanguinetti turned this place over to my husband, and taught him everything about this business, which tells you the type of people the Sanguinettis truly are, and how they held no grudge against my husband for his family's action."

After taking another sip of wine, Father Gianuzzi said, "Monsignor Mancini speaks so highly of Giuseppe and Maria, as well as your husband and you."

"That's very kind of him, but the Sanguinettis are the real leaders of this village. Unassuming people that they are, yet leaders just the same. I grew up here, and remember life under the rule of the Vasaios, as well as when they finally stepped down. It's an amazing story." She went on to describe those events in detail.

Father Gianuzzi smiled. "God has indeed touched this place. Not only in its beauty, but in its history."

"My parents loved this place and passed that love down to me and my two sisters. After my parents' death, my sisters left for Palermo with their husbands. I remained. My life is here. My life is here with Santo and our son. Now, I hope and pray that God will protect our village with the return and rise of the Mafia."

"The scourge of Sicily, *Signora Vasaio*. I had hoped that they would remain in exile as what occurred during the time of Mussolini. At least most of them. Mussolini failed to eradicate all of them. Some stayed hidden, while others continued their business but in a much smaller and less public way. Of course, we were all thrilled to see Mussolini defeated. But with his defeat, the evil has returned. The snakes have slithered out of the hills, and are now fighting for control."

"It's a scary time."

"Indeed it is. The Mafia is ruled by one thing and only one thing, violence. Violence is what gives them power. Violence is what gives them control."

"I fear our beloved winery will draw their interest."

"My hope is that Bellafortuna remains unmolested by them. But I will be honest with you. All you have is prayers. If they single out your village and its winery, Bellafortuna will not be able to stand up to them."

Just then, Mirella's husband and son passed outside the window coming in from the vineyards. "Oh, good. Come outside with me, Father. I want to introduce you to my family."

He took his last sip of wine, and stood up from the table. "You have been a most gracious host, *Signora Vasaio*."

"Please, come anytime you wish."

They departed the winery and went out to meet Santo and Matteo.

10

EXILE

*L*uca Sperenza sat in the study inside Adriano's villa. His boss was seated not behind his desk, but in the chair next to him.

"Betrayed, Luca. Betrayed. And I never saw it coming."

"How could you? Mario has been with us a long time. Neither I nor Giancarlo saw it coming either, and that's our job. For that I'm truly sorry."

"Luca, you have been with me the longest. You have been with me from my rise in power, to exile, and to my return. You witnessed first hand the loss of my wife and son to this business. And the entire time you have shown me nothing but loyalty."

"Don Adriano, when my father died many years ago, it was you who comforted my mother and offered me a job in your *cosca*. For that I am eternally grateful. For that, I pledge to you my never ending loyalty."

Adriano paused momentarily, turned his head and gazed

out the window, before finally saying in return, "It gives me great pleasure to know it, as loyalty is what I need most of all right now. In this hard, difficult life, loyalty is the only way to survive. Loyalty is what brought me to where I am today. Loyalty is what made you my *capobastone*."

"I promise, Don Umbretto, I will do everything in my power to assure you will never be betrayed again."

"Betrayed. I must get word soon to Don Biscotti of the attempted attack on me. Of course, it must be done privately. Perhaps over the weekend, I will send you to Monreale to meet with him and personally relate what has occurred. To let him know of the attack as well as of the betrayal within my own *cosca*."

"I will do whatever you ask of me, Don Umbretto."

They spoke a little longer about other issues before Luca departed. Adriano shut the door and returned to his desk.

Luca was like a son to him. After all, he had been with him for such a long time. He had witnessed first hand the ups and downs of the business. And throughout it all, Luca had remained steadfast in his loyalty to his Don. This was a tough life. But Adriano had persevered. He had come out on top and remained there. He would do whatever was necessary to protect everything that he had worked so long and hard for all these years.

Sitting down in his chair, Adriano thought back to his early difficult years in the business. It was a period of lows and highs, of happiness and grief, and of power and exile. Adriano closed his eyes and remembered.

As the months passed after their marriage night, Santa fell more and more in love with Adriano. She became fully aware of his life in the business. She knew Don Spatuzza protected her father, and truly believed that the benefits offered by him and his *cosca* for the people of Sicily far outweighed its darker side. In her mind, both Don Spatuzza and her husband were somewhat of a modern-day Robin Hood, protecting families whom she had known her entire life.

Two years after their marriage, Don Spatuzza died, and Adriano became the Don of Castelvetrano. All of Don Spatuzza's *cosca* members stayed and worked for Don Umbretto. Ernesto became his first *consigliere*.

Don Adriano Umbretto was very well respected by the citizens of Castelvetrano, as many knew him from his years of service under Don Spatuzza. Adriano was known for his integrity and for his unwavering loyalty to those under his control.

Over the years, Castelvetrano's olive production almost tripled, as the hills in and around the town became filled with olive trees. Adriano protected, for a hefty price, almost every farmer in and around Castelvetrano. His wealth, power, and prestige grew quickly.

In 1920, a young fifteen-year-old boy from Taormina after the death of his father joined Adriano's growing *cosca*. That young boy was Luca Speranza.

That same year, through God's providence, ten years after Adriano's marriage, Santa gave birth to a son, Giacomo Umbretto. From an early age, Adriano began to slowly train his son in the code of being a man of honor, just as Don Spatuzza had done for him.

Adriano believed his life would continue much as it had

for his grandfather and Don Spatuzza. However, in May, 1924, the trajectory of the course of events in his life began to change.

Adriano was invited to the town of Piana dei Greci by its Mayor, a friend of his, Don Francesco Cuccia, to meet and hear a speech by the new, young Prime Minister of Italy and head of the fascist party, Benito Mussolini.

Mussolini arrived in Piana dei Greci escorted by his own police in large numbers. He was met in front of the Cathedral by Don Cuccia. Adriano, as the Mayor's invited guest, stood close by.

As *Il Duce* exited his car, his policemen lined the path. Mussolini first walked over to the Mayor's wife, whom he ogled longingly with his eyes, and whispered into her ear. When Mussolini finally stood in front of Don Cuccia, the Don pointed to Mussolini's police and said to *Il Duce*, "Here in Sicily, you are under my protection. You don't need your police here. You can send them on. I will protect you."

Adriano listened to what Don Cuccia had said, and took a step back when he saw Mussolini's face turn red in anger. *Il Duce* quickly rejected Cuccia's offer of protection, and said, "I will see you in the piazza in one hour for my speech." He turned and got back in his car and pulled off, with his police escort.

Don Cucccia was angry that his offer of protection was rejected by Mussolini, and against Adriano's counsel, he instructed the residents of Piana dei Greci to not attend Mussolini's speech. An hour later, Mussolini gave his speech to an almost empty piazza. *Il Duce* was outraged and before leaving, sent a warning to Don Cuccia, "Sicily will pay for this disrespect." He told those close to him his belief that fascism and the Mafia could not coexist on the island. Adriano believed that Don Cuccia had acted foolishly, as *Il Duce* was gaining great power throughout Italy.

Suffice it to say, Adriano's concerns were correct. Mussolini returned to Italy and retained Cesare Mori, a former policeman who had worked in Sicily as a young man and who later in life was highly successful in fighting anti-fascists in Northern Italy. Mussolini had one job for Mori, to eradicate the Mafia from Sicily.

Just a year later, Mori was named prefect of Palermo. Mussolini instructed him to bring total war against the Mafia. He had full powers to do as he pleased. He arrived in Sicily with two brigades of black shirts.

He became known as *Prefetto di Ferro* (Iron Prefect.) He knew the soul of the Sicilians from when he had worked there years ago. He knew that in order to succeed, he had to show the peasants that the fascist government could bring the island justice and protection, even more than what the Mafia could provide. He also knew he had to convince the peasants that the police were not their enemies, but instead their true enemy was the Mafia. To accomplish all of this, he knew he would have to outmuscle the Mafia. He said, "If Sicilians are afraid of the Mafia, I will show them that I am the strongest *mafioso* of all."

Mori, and his black shirt army, went from town to town, rounding up any and all suspect members of the Mafia. Confessions were extracted through beatings and torture. There were no trials. No jury. Justice was delineated by Mori. As more and more Mafia bosses were arrested, many left for America or went into hiding.

Adriano withstood *Il Duce's* war against the Mafia as long

as he could. Finally, the writing was on the wall. If he wanted the men of his *cosca* to survive, he knew he would have to leave Castelvetrano. He debated with his wife whether they should flee to America or go into hiding. They ultimately chose to go into hiding. He was too connected to the island. "Santa, my soul is part of this place," he told her during the debate.

In late December, 1925, he left his villa in Castelvetrano with Santa, his son, Giacomo and a few of his men, including Ernesto and Luca. They moved to the village of Gangi, a Mafia stronghold in the Madonie Mountains near Palermo. The great Mafia Don of Castelvetrano was now living in a small, humble home on a crowded street, just off the main square of the village.

With many members of other *coscas* living nearby, Adriano thought Gangi offered his family the best chance for safety from Mussolini's war. Just a week later, he would find out how wrong he was.

ON THE 1ST of January 1926, the Iron Prefect came to Gangi. He entered the empty main piazza and gave a grim warning to the town's residents, who listened from behind closed doors. Turn themselves in, or face dire consequences was the mandate.

Some of the men fled into the hills, leaving their wives and children behind. Later that day, Adriano sat Santa down at their small dinner table.

After a lengthy discussion between the two, Santa told him, "I want you to go. I want you to escape to the hills like the others. Mori will be back. He will arrest the men left behind."

"Santa, you are correct. He will be back, with all of his black shirts. But, unlike the others, I will not leave you and Giacomo here. I know the mind of Mori. He knows that to get to these men, he will bring suffering to their wives and children whom they left behind. That will draw these men out, and bring them back to face the consequences."

Santa asked, "And if the men don't come back? What will happen to the families?"

"Their families will pay a dear price. I will not leave you here alone."

"Where will we go?"

"We will go to the hills near Castelvetrano. I know that area like the back of my hand. There are caves near the area of Selinunte where we can live until the initial threat blows over. Eventually, we may be able to move into a farmhouse of some friends. We need to leave tonight."

"You really want me to go with you."

"*Si, Santa. T'amo.* Like your father said the day I first saw you, 'Women inspire the melody of the soul.' You are my melody. I will not leave you."

They kissed.

Later that evening, Adriano fled to the hills with his family. He told his *cosca* associates, who had come with him to Gangi, to flee and to emigrate to America if they could. The only member who stayed in Gangi was Ernesto, who said he was too old to live like a bandit. Luca Sperenza was the only member of his *cosca* who went with Adriano and his family.

Mori returned the next day with his two brigades of black shirts to carry out his threat. He ordered house-to-house searches, and began arresting everyone there. As Adriano had predicted, for those who had gone into hiding, Mori took their wives and children hostage. Violence throughout the next few days was widespread in the village, as well as reported rapes of the women and the teenage girls. Soon word reached the men that Mori had arrested their families, and rumors of what was happening to their wives and daughters. Most of the men came back to the village to turn themselves in.

As for the Umbretto family, they arrived at the hills in the area near Selinunte, about ten miles from Castelvetrano, and near the archeological site of the majestic, ancient Greek temples located there. It was in those hills that they settled in a deep cave. Some of the families whom the Don had once protected in and around Castelvetrano provided the Umbretto family with food and supplies. After a few weeks, they finally moved into a small, abandoned farmhouse, closer to Selinunte. Adriano's small farm had enough land to provide a meal a day to his family and Luca. Adriano purchased a few cows, and grew an herb and vegetable garden for the family. They would live there in the hills for many years, constantly at war with thieves, robbers, and those who supported the fascists. Even while living in exile, Adriano still looked out for his neighbors and helped them to protect their property against the roving brigands, who were at war with poverty and hardships themselves.

As luck would have it, if you would call such a thing luck, about two miles from Adriano's farm, another family who fled into exile eventually moved into a farm in the hills above Selinunte, and that family was the Genovese family. For now, the Umbretto family and the Genovese family lived in proximity to each other in peace. Yet, when Vincente Genovese learned who was living close to him, he thought back to the killing of his men and of his nephew by Adriano Umbretto. When the time was right, he would have his revenge.

While living in the farmhouse in the hills, Santa gave birth to their second child, their daughter Francesca. The wife of a nearby vineyard owner came to assist with the birth. The growing Umbretto family continued to live in the farmhouse, and scratched out a living as best they could. Don Adriano Umbretto had now become a farmer, and continued to fight for the survival of his family against those who desired to take his life and possessions away.

Eventually victory was announced by Mussolini, and Mori was called back to Rome. Umberto Albani replaced Mori, and he was nowhere near as ruthless as his predecessor. With the war against the Mafia settling down, some of the exiled Mafia Dons began to move from their secluded locations closer to the towns and villages around Sicily, still in hiding and still biding their time for the day they could try to regain control.

By the time Adriano finally left the hills in 1938 and settled in a secluded house with a small vineyard attached that was located in the hills directly above Castelvetrano, he had tragically lost both his wife, Santa, and son to the business. Don Vincente Genovese had finally exacted his revenge against Adriano, by bringing death to his family, just as Adriano had done in the killing of Vincente's nephew.

Adriano settled into his new humble home with his young daughter, Francesca, and his only remaining associate, Luca

Speranza. The once powerful Don Adriano Umbretto had returned to the area of Castelvetrano as a broken man.

ADRIANO'S EYES were damp from his tears as he remembered his life with Santa. He got up and walked over to the small bar in his study, and poured a glass of wine. He wiped his eyes and then took a drink of his wine. He fought his way back to power after exile and the war, and he would do whatever he had to do to protect his daughter. That was his entire life purpose. After-all, that was all that was left.

THE SOCIETÀ DI BELLAFORTUNA

Giuseppe Sanguinetti's last stop during his business trip that week was a visit to Carlo Viti, an old friend, and a wine seller in the capital city of Sicily, Palermo. It was midday that Thursday and Giuseppe unloaded the last of his wine cases.

"My boys will load your cart with the usual items," Carlo told him. "Is that good?"

"*Perfecto.*"

Carlo shook his head. "Do your fellow villagers know that you are trading most of your wine so you can obtain highly sought-after black-market items for them?"

"They need them. Let's leave it at that."

"Well, let my boys load your cart, and they will watch it for you. If you left it parked without watching it, there would be nothing left. Some of the residents of Palermo would love to get their hands on the foods and medicines you have in there. The black market is highly lucrative. While they watch your cart, I want to show you something."

Carlo took Giuseppe for a walk through the old town of Palermo. It was here that the Allied bombing during the war had done the most damage. Up and down every street, one could still see destroyed or heavily damaged buildings, houses, churches, and administrative buildings.

At one point, Carlo stopped at the *Santa Maria della Catena*. The damage to the Gothic church was substantial. Carlo pointed to the building. "Sicily paid a dear price for getting in bed with Hitler."

"Every time I come here, I'm amazed at the destruction of the city. It is unbelievable," Giuseppe replied.

"Some 40% of our houses were destroyed. Palermo now has a housing shortage."

"With each trip here, I see more and more building activity outside the center."

Carlo sighed. "As you can see, the Allied bombing did great damage to much of the city. However, it is the politicians and the Mafia who will do true damage to our cultural heritage. Their horrendous plan will change the landscape forever."

"How? What is the plan?"

"The decision was made to not restore the old city to what it once was, but instead, make a new Palermo."

"So, they will not rebuild the old town?"

"The corrupt politicians have been bought out and have turned over all the rebuilding to contractors with ties to the Mafia to do with this area what will make them the most money. These thugs have swept in and received the permits to construct apartment blocks. Come, let me show you the first one they built."

Carlo and Giuseppe walked about two blocks. A large, grayish concrete building stood before them. The building lacked any character at all.

"There was a beautiful little park in this area," Carlo pointed out. "A wonderful green spot to savor the Lord's blessings to us. They took the park away and built this monstrosity. They shortly will knock down the two buildings next to this one and build two more of these concrete eyesores."

"That's terrible," replied Giuseppe.

"That's just the start of the 'Sack of Palermo' as we call it. New construction will replace most of the majestic villas and palaces, some of which were untouched by the bombing. These buildings give Palermo its architectural grace. Now they will be torn down and replaced with these characterless, shoddily constructed, cement apartment blocks. More parks, like the one that was here, will be built on top of. There is even talk of building some of these buildings down in the *Conco D'Oro*. It is as if they are at war with anything green."

Giuseppe said, "The Dons of old that I knew would never be involved with this horrendous plan."

"Indeed not. With the opportunity brought by the war, these bastards will not let a chance to make money go by, and to hell with the cultural heritage of our City. This new breed of *mafioso* is fully aware of the money flowing into Sicily from the North, and how lucrative these contracts are and will be. They will do whatever they can to solidify their control and influence."

Carlo and Giuseppe spoke the entire way back to his

shop. When they turned down his street, a group of men stood by the corner, having an animated conversation. One of the men saw Carlo and ran over to him.

"They killed him, *Signor Viti*. They killed him."

"Who?" asked Carlo.

"The mayor of Monreale, Don Calogero Biscotti. He was murdered today outside his office."

Giuseppe's shoulders slumped, as his face lost all of its color.

"My God. Don Biscotti is dead," Carlo said out loud.

"Has this news been confirmed?" Giuseppe asked.

The man nodded his head in agreement.

Giuseppe exhaled deeply while feeling weakness in his knees. What that death would mean to Bellafortuna was unknown, but it had the potential to change the life of every resident of the village.

"I just saw him," Giuseppe said in a quavering voice. "Just the other day."

They walked quickly back to Carlo's shop. Many residents on the street were now outside discussing the disturbing news.

They entered Carlo's shop. "The news we have learned today is not good," Carlo told Giuseppe. "Not good for us. Not good for you."

"No, it is not. I'm sure all of Palermo will be talking about it just like the people of your neighborhood."

"Safe travels home, Giuseppe."

"*Grazie*," he said before he went to retrieve his cart and horse. The news of the death of Don Calogero Biscotti shook Giuseppe to his core. Word of the murder was quickly spreading across all of Palermo and soon all of Sicily.

It WAS late that Thursday afternoon when Giuseppe Sanguinetti returned to Bellafortuna. His horse-drawn cart traveled along the *Corsa Calatafimi*, the main road that ran between Palermo and Monreale. His wagon was packed with the black-market items he had obtained in Palermo.

About midway between the two cities, there was a small offshoot, a winding dirt road, the *Via Valle*, that eked its way through the valley to the secluded hilltop village of Bellafortuna. As Giuseppe turned onto the valley road, he loosened the tight grip of the reins. His horse knew this route very well and needed little direction.

Normally, when traveling in this part of the valley, Giuseppe would get lost in the views the valley afforded; the mulberry trees, with their gnarled branches, and the sea of olive trees and vineyards that stretched as far as the eye could see. But all of his thoughts this day centered on the news about the murder of the mayor of Monreale, Calogero Biscotti.

Giuseppe reached a clump of trees, and as he made the turn away from the trees, the village of Bellafortuna, high upon the hill-top, first came into view. He always loved this view, but today, the view did not bring him joy. He stopped the cart momentarily and looked up toward his beloved village. The news about Don Biscotti stirred in his heart. Gazing upward at his village made the tears begin to flow.

Giuseppe clicked his tongue, and his horse began moving once again. Just a tad farther, Giuseppe reached a fork in the road where the *Via Valle* splits off. One road, the *Via Boccale*, headed toward the Boccale Winery, where the best wine in

Sicily was produced, *Vino di Bellafortuna.* The other road led in the other direction toward Bellafortuna. Giuseppe thought about the winery and how devastating it would be to have the Mafia have any element of control over the facility.

Giuseppe's thoughts turned to the person or persons who murdered Don Biscotti. Whoever it was would soon come out of the shadows and make a move to take control of Monreale. Giuseppe suddenly remembered the car parked by the Boccale winery a few days ago, and his stomach turned. If Monreale would fall, so too would Bellafortuna. Giuseppe recognized that Bellafortuna would need the *Società* now more than ever to lead and protect the villagers. But he knew the embers of courage required to lead the *Società* were no longer glowing inside him. It had been extinguished with the death of his son.

After he pulled into the *Piazza Santa Croce* and began unloading his cart at his wine store, Giuseppe ran into Father Gianuzzi. He informed the priest of the death of Don Biscotti. Father Gianuzzi's face dropped as he said, *"Gesu, Maria.* Will the violence ever end?"

"Father, come join us tonight at the meeting of the *Società di Bellafortuna.* I need to let everyone know."

"I'll be there."

Giuseppe carried his last item from his cart into *Il Paradiso* and went upstairs to the living quarters where he would let his wife know of the death of Don Biscotti.

***

THE MEETING of the *Società di Bellafortuna* that night was held as usual in the dining room of the *Albergo di Bellafortuna,* the only hotel in the village. The large two-story building was located in the *Piazza Santa Croce*. Buildings surrounded the entire piazza. On the left side of the piazza from the hotel was the *Chiesa della Madonna,* with its bell tower and rectory. *Il Paradiso,* Giuseppe's wine store, was situated on the right side of the piazza from the hotel.

The *Albergo di Bellafortuna* had once been the home of the powerful Vasaio family, who had controlled the village for many years. A few years after the death of Santo's father, Vitellio, who was the last Vasaio to control the village, Santo sold the *Palazzo Vasaio* to the village, and he moved to the valley where he lived and ran the *Boccale Winery* and olive presses. Eventually, the *Palazzo Vasaio* was converted into a hotel capable of housing visitors from other parts of Sicily and Italy attending the annual summer opera festival held at the *Anfiteatro di Bellafortuna,* an old Greek amphitheater down in the valley that had been redesigned to hold concerts and opera.

A large solid mahogany table sat in the middle of the dining room, with a fireplace against the far wall. Portraits of the village leaders from the past graced the walls of the room, namely, Enzo Boccale, the founder of the village, Antonio Sanguinetti, and Vittelio Vasaio, Santo's father. Just a few years ago, after the war, another portrait was added to the wall, that of Father Biaggio Antonio Sanguinetti, Giuseppe's son.

Before the meeting started, Giuseppe introduced everyone to Father Gianuzzi. He spoke briefly with each member as everyone waited for the meeting to start. They were much impressed with the young priest from Cefalù.

The meeting was then called to order by the head of the

Società, Giorgio Monachino, as he banged his fist on the table, signaling that the meeting was beginning. Giorgio, the owner of a small trattoria, *Del Monaco's*, located next door to *Il Paradiso* on the piazza, had a fiery temperament, just like his father, Turridu, had before him.

Everyone took a seat. Giorgio began by thanking Father Gianuzzi for coming to the meeting. The priest informed everyone that Monsignor Mancini had gone to Cinisi for the rest of the week and offered his apologies for not being at the meeting. Giorgio proceeded to give the priest a brief breakdown of the importance of the *Società*, its role in the village, and a brief history.

When he finished, he said, "Before we turn to our food supply shortages, we will hear about a very important update from Giuseppe regarding some news he has just learned."

Giuseppe rose and quickly informed the *Società* of the death of Mayor Biscotti. Shock quickly turned to fear. The members asked their questions over each other. Giuseppe ended his report by saying, "I know I don't need to tell you how devastating this news is for us. During my recent trip, I went to see Don Biscotti, to inform him of some men Santo had seen down by the winery. We believe these men were members of a *cosca* from a powerful family. Now I'm beginning to think they may be from the family who murdered Don Biscotti. Don Biscotti had pledged his unwavering support to our village. But now he is dead."

"Do they know who killed him?" asked Santo Vasaio.

"Have they caught the killer?" asked Elizabetta Hofmann, the only female member of the *Società*, and the wife of Giuseppe's sole employee, Kurt Hofmann.

"Who will become the new mayor?" asked Giacomo Mascopuno, a farmer.

Giuseppe lifted his hands and said, "I know everyone is anxious. But I don't have answers to any of those questions."

There were murmurs as the members all spoke vigorously with each other. Giuseppe took his seat and remained quiet as Giorgio lifted his voice and said, "It is fair to say that whoever takes over as mayor of Monreale will be of great importance to our community. We should plan what we will do if the outcome is not good for us."

The members of the *Società* debated what that plan should be, with no real answer agreed upon. As the anxiety in the room reached a high level, Father Gianuzzi stood and asked, "I know I'm not a member of this fine group, but may I ask a question?"

"Certainly, Father," replied Giorgio.

"Can Biscotti's associates win the ensuing battle and keep Monreale for themselves? And in so doing, continue to protect your beloved village, as before."

Giorgio turned to Giuseppe. "What do you believe, Giuseppe?"

"I don't think so. Even though we don't know who killed him, I know for certain it was a man of power. Biscotti was supported by the Allies, so whoever took him down, is powerful in his own right. I don't think Biscotti's men can withstand the coming war."

Giorgio banged his hand on the table loudly, and looked into the eyes of each member of the *Società*. "Giuseppe is correct. War is coming. Take my word for it. We need to be ready to fight. Once Monreale is claimed by this murderer, his eye may turn to Bellafortuna and all of its blessings." He then turned to Santo Vasaio. "I'm sure they would love to take control of the Boccale winery."

Santo Vasaio stood and said with defiance, "Not without a fight."

Elizabetta asked, "Fight? But how? We are a village of farmers, vintners, and craftsmen."

The debate went back and forth. Giuseppe had taken his seat once again and remained quiet. Finally, as the debate reached a fever pitch, Giuseppe rose, and all the members' attention turned to him. In a hushed tone, Giuseppe said, "I do agree with Giorgio. War is coming. We must be ready."

Elizabetta asked again, "But how can we take on these powerful men, if and when they come?"

Giuseppe looked directly at her. "That's a question for which I have no answer, and I am sure that none of us do. But it is a question that together we'd better be able to answer soon." Giuseppe briefly remembered his walk with Carlo around Palermo and added, "For if we don't come up with an answer, our life here in Bellafortuna will forever be changed."

"But how?" she asked again.

At those words, Giuseppe hung his head.

Father Gianuzzi stood up and extended his hand upward, making everyone turn their attention toward him. In a dramatic fashion, he made the sign of the cross as he said to the members of the *Società*, "With God's help, that is the answer. The answer will come in time. *In nomine patris et filli et spirtu sancto*."

With an "Amen" voiced by all, the meeting continued late into the evening as the *Società* worked through their lengthy agenda, including all of the upcoming Holy Week celebrations, yet with an ever-present fear and dread over the news of the death of Don Calogero Biscotti.

When the meeting finally wrapped up, Giuseppe walked out of the building with Father Gianuzzi and into the piazza. The young priest said, "I hope that you did not mind me interjecting that God would provide the answer in response to *Signora Hofmann's* repeated question?"

"Not at all. As you could tell, I certainly had no answer for her."

Father Gianuzzi sighed. "Giuseppe, the truth of the matter is, Elizabetta, as is the case with most women, cut right to the heart of the matter. She wanted the answer as to how the villagers would fight in this coming war. I do believe deep down she knows the answer, as do you. I have seen first-hand the ruthlessness that the Mafia can bring into a situation and the carnage they can leave behind. Your village will not be able to win this war."

Giuseppe stopped walking. Father Gianuzzi stopped as well. Giuseppe glanced up toward the Boccale statue before saying, "I know you are correct, *Padre*. And that is what scares me."

"*Buona notte*, Giuseppe."

"*Buona notte*. Don't forget to come to the concert on Saturday."

"I'll be there."

They split up and went their way to retire for the night.

THE MAYORS

*A*t the exact moment that the meeting of the *Società* was wrapping up in Bellafortuna, Adriano was seated at his desk inside his mayor's office in the town center of Castelvetrano. He had just finished a meeting with Lorenzo Pitari, an olive farmer from Castelvetrano, who was in a dispute with the olive producer to whom he sold his olives. Lorenzo was convinced he was being cheated by the producer and wanted to seek Adriano's support in his dealings. Lorenzo smiled when Adriano had told him, *"E fatto."* (It's done.) When you came to Adriano with a problem, that response by him was all the assurance you would need that your request would be answered.

After Lorenzo had kissed Adriano's hand in gratitude, he left the office. Adriano sat quietly at his desk. He was a man with immense power. Yet, not knowing who sent the intruder into his home still perturbed him, and he found it hard to think of anything else.

He thought back to his first day he came into the office. He also remembered the first order he had issued from this very desk. He had ordered the death of Don Vincente Genovese. The death took place only two days after Don Vincente was named Mayor of Campobello di Mazara. Adriano was not interested in taking control of that city. That was not in his makeup. His was revenge against Vincente Genovese, not his family, nor the citizens of Campobello di Mazara. Adriano began to contemplate that perhaps he was wrong for not wiping out the entire Genovese clan when he had the chance.

Just then, there was a knock on the door.

"*Accedere*," yelled Adriano.

Into the office walked Giancarlo. He stood on the opposite side of the desk. His face looked tense and fearful.

"You look like you have seen a ghost."

"I have news," Giancarlo solemnly replied.

"What is it?"

"Calogero Biscotti has been murdered."

"Murdered? Adriano blurted out. "Calogero. No! No!" He leaned forward and rested both hands on his desk in silence as his head hung low. In almost a whisper, he finally asked, "Who has committed this outrage? Please tell me we know something."

"We don't know. Our contacts are still trying to piece it all together. But I would think his murder and the attempt on your life are not coincidences. Two mayors attacked. Someone is trying to take control over much of Sicily."

Adriano lifted his hands off the desk and turned his chair as he looked out the window. He closed his eyes as a single tear tracked down his face as he fought his desire to cry for the loss of a close friend. "Calogero was a man of honor. A man of integrity. What a sad time for all of Sicily. Does Luca know? He knew him so well."

"Yes, he knows. I told him as we discussed security measures. That's why he is not here now. He wanted to come tell you in person, but I made him stay at the villa. We are going to increase security even more, here at City Hall, as well as at the villa. He's putting a plan in place."

Adriano turned away from the window and bore his stare into Giancarlo's eyes. "I'm concerned for my daughter."

"She should continue to stay inside the villa until we get a handle on what is going on, and the threat is defeated. I will get my contacts in and around Palermo and Monreale to see if they can shed light on who killed Mayor Biscotti. I do believe that if we find out who killed Biscotti, we find out who ordered the attack on you, and who turned Mario against you."

"This news confuses me, and goes against what I truly believed to be true. I thought Don Sergio Genovese had made a move on me. But, if indeed the attack on Biscotti and me are connected, then Sergio would not be involved with that. He's not ready to take on all the Dons who will come to defend Biscotti."

"I agree. Sergio Genovese is not involved."

"We must make every effort to find who is behind it."

"I will."

He left Adriano alone in his office.

Adriano sat down at his desk. In the silence of his office, he thought back to his friendship with Calogero Biscotti.

ADRIANO FIRST BECAME aware of Calogero Biscotti when the younger man became the Don of Monreale for the brief period after Onofrio Fausto had fled to America. This was right at the time when Mori was exercising his brutal force against the Mafia. For the short time that Calogero was in his position of control, he was beloved by the inhabitants of Monreale, as his demeanor and nature stood in such stark contrast to that of his predecessor, Onofrio Fausto.

Calogero had been born in Noto, Sicily. As a teenager, his family moved to Palermo. That was where he got his start in the business, which ultimately led him to take control of Monreale. He had an expressive face, a kind countenance, and was very short in stature. He always said he was 5′5. No one would dare challenge him on that statement, although it was a stretch.

As Mori tightened his grip, Calogero eventually fled from Monreale and moved from village to village in the Sicilian hills. He eventually settled in the hills above Castelvetrano. In 1941, he got a job as a day laborer at a small vineyard, the vineyard owned and run by none other than Adriano Umbretto, who by that time was a widower, living with his daughter, Francesca, and his only remaining associate, Luca Speranza. That was how the two exiled Dons became more than just acquaintances, but friends.

Adriano, Luca, and Calogero worked hard around the vineyard during the day and would retire at night to Adriano's small home, where they would spend their evenings drinking wine while listening to the gentle singing voice of Francesca, serenading them with opera arias and Sicilian folksongs, as she stood by the fireplace. Francesca had developed a beautiful soprano voice, and when she was able, she studied singing with a lady from Castelvetrano who had sung in the opera as a younger woman. Calogero insisted that Francesca should pursue singing as a career. He joked that he could not wait to hear her sing one day at the summer opera festival held in the small village of Bellafortuna, which he had been to many times. He even was friendly with the head of the opera there, Giuseppe Sanguinetti, whom Adriano knew from the wine business.

While living in exile, Adriano and Calogero would take long walks in the evening, taking in the beautiful views the Sicilian landscape provided, as they discussed how they would once again run their business if and when they were ever able to be back in positions of power.

For the two exiled Mafia Dons, life suddenly had become routine. Yet the friendship that blossomed between them helped Adriano regain his confidence and his drive. It also gave him a momentary respite from the grief in losing his family.

As the years passed, and war engulfed all of Europe, Adriano began to long for the day when he would be back in control once fascism was defeated. He placed his hope and his life in the one thing that he believed could defeat fascism and Nazism, and that was the Allies. As the calendar turned to 1943, Sicilians had little idea what was about to happen on their island.

In January 1943, the tide of war was changing for the Allies. They had held off the German offensive in Africa while the Germans on the Eastern Front were being decimated by the Russians. The Allied leaders met in Casablanca to discuss plans for the war. They knew the only acceptable victory would be the unconditional surrender of Germany.

Some of the Allied leaders, led by the American President, Franklin Delano Roosevelt, favored a cross-channel invasion of Europe. Yet other Allied leaders thought the time was not yet ripe. Instead, England's Prime Minister, Winston Churchill, argued that a third front needed to be opened to draw German troops away from the likely invasion point, and Italy should be that front. The belief was that, in doing so, a cross-channel invasion into France months later would hopefully find the Germans weakened from the prolonged battle on the Eastern front and the raging battles in Italy. It was believed that this plan would provide a better chance of success for the invasion of Europe, or D-day as it was called.

Churchill believed that the invasion of Italy should start in Sicily. The operation became known as "Husky." The Allies moved quickly to prepare to invade Sicily.

The planners of the invasion drafted a report titled Special Military Plan for Psychological Warfare in Sicily that unbelievably recommended the "Establishment of contact and communications with the leaders of separatist nuclei, disaffected workers, and clandestine radical groups, e.g., the Mafia, and providing them every possible aid."

In other words, those members of Sicilian society who were disenfranchised by the fascists would now join the Allies in their fight against both fascism and Nazism. The report was approved by the Joint Chiefs of Staff in Washington on April 15, 1943.

Meanwhile, mob boss Lucky Luciano would become instrumental in the Allied plan. Lucky was born as Salvatore Lucania in Lercara Friddi, Sicily. As a young boy, he emigrated to America with his family. By the early 1930s, he was the undisputed *capo di tutti i capi* (boss of all the bosses.) By 1940, Luciano was being held in a New York jail, having finally been prosecuted for his criminal activities. He offered his services to the American War effort in an attempt to win his freedom. He first assisted with issues in and around the harbors of New York and the fear the American Navy had of sabotage of their boats by Germans and Italians living in New York. The harbors were run by the mob, and the Americans knew Luciano's mob connections could assist them with protecting the American Navy's interests. The Navy, the State of New York, and Luciano reached a deal: in exchange for a commutation of his sentence, Luciano promised complete assistance of his organization in providing intelligence to the Navy. Once he gained the trust of the Navy with his harbor work, the Americans reached out to Lucky to see what assistance he could give with the coming invasion of Sicily. He offered the names of Mafia Dons who were living in exile in Sicily and whom he believed would aid the cause. Two of the names that showed up on that list were Adriano Umbretto and Calogero Biscotti.

Soon, contact was made through intermediaries, and Adriano and Calogero offered their assistance. Their initial job was to provide pictures of certain ports in and around Sicily, as well as the drawing of maps showing the different terrains, so the Allies knew the best places to move their tanks and artillery. Adriano and Calogero, with the assistance of Luca, enthusiastically jumped into their "espionage" work and relished that their actions could help the Allies take down the fascists and, in return, perhaps give both men their own lives back. The Allies' faith in Adriano and Calogero provided a great benefit, as their work product provided great intel in the planning of the invasion. As the time of the invasion neared, the Allies expanded the exiled Mafia men's role and called on them to begin preparations to assist with the invasion. These one-time leaders began calling upon the old members of their *coscas* to assist them. They were provided with arms and directed by the Allies as to what was expected.

Adriano was able to find a few members of his *cosca*, but, being the natural leader that he was, he also began to get a small following of men who joined his little army based in the hills around Castelvetrano. Those new members included Giancarlo Fanucci, Giorgio Anselmo, and the man who would later betray him, Mario Zuchello.

On Saturday, July 10, 1943, the Allied Forces, under General George Patton for the Americans and Field Marshal Bernard Montgomery for the British, invaded Sicily. The invasion combined air and sea landings, involving 150,000 troops, 3,000 ships, and 4,000 aircraft, all directed at the southern shores of the island. They were met by German and Italian divisions. But truth be told, many Italian soldiers threw their weapons down and fled, refusing to shoot at American soldiers, who in many cases were Italian-American boys coming to free Italy.

As a foothold was established by the Allies on the island, Adriano, Calogero, and the men under them sprang into action. As General Patton's Third Division moved across Sicily, Adriano and Calogero, like other Mafia Dons in exile, protected the roads from snipers and arranged for enthusiastic greetings by the Sicilian villagers liberated by the advancing troops. At one point, Adriano and Calogero both climbed aboard an Allied tank and acted as a guide through the confusing mountain terrain.

As the Allied forces pushed farther and farther into Sicily during the summer of 1943, any remaining public support for the war and Mussolini quickly disappeared. The invasion of Sicily quickly led to events that would affect all of Italy.

On July 22, 1943, Palermo fell to the Allies.

On July 24, 1943, Victor Emmanuel II, the King of Italy, deposed Benito Mussolini. A new government was set up under Marshal Pietro Badoglio, who had opposed Italy's alliance with Nazi Germany from the start.

General Badoglio kept up the appearance of loyalty to the Axis. Yet, at the same time, he dissolved the Fascist Party two days after taking over and immediately began secret discussions with the Allies about an armistice. Finally, on September 8, 1943, Badoglio approved the surrender of Italy to the Allies. This action allowed the Allies to land in southern Italy and begin beating the Germans back up the peninsula.

With the retreat of the Germans from Sicily, the war in Sicily was over. But for the inhabitants of the island, the end of the war brought even more strife. Crime soared in the upheaval and chaos. Some members of the Mafia who had fled to the hills began banditry, and the black market thrived all across the island. The Allies occupied all of Sicily, but almost every institution had been destroyed. There was no order even though the American occupiers controlled most of the island. It fell to them to create a whole new society. Their first step was to depose the fascist mayors and appoint many of the former Mafia Dons in their place. These former Mafia

Dons resurrected their *coscas* and brought in some new blood from the marauding bandits.

Just a few months after the occupation of Sicily, Adriano Umbretto was appointed as the Mayor of Castelvetrano. In November 1943, Adriano, along with Francesca, Luca, and Giancarlo, and the other men who had joined his *cosca*, moved into his old villa outside of Castelvetrano. He had bided his time, and he was now back in control. His good friend, Calogero Biscotti, likewise was named the Mayor of Monreale. The Allies provided to both men the right to confiscate the abandoned trucks of the Italian army now strewn across Sicily. The two friends formed a trucking business, which brought them quick wealth, and when they sold it a year later to a businessman in Palermo, their fortunes were solidified, and their power was thought to be absolute.

ADRIANO'S THOUGHTS were completely consumed with his good friend, Calogero Biscotti. He was dead. Murdered. And by the same person who had ordered the attack on Adriano. He would avenge his friend's death. He would bring war upon the person who ordered the death of Calogero.

Probably due to both the stress he was under and the news he was just told, Adriano found himself uncontrollably crying alone in his office. He had lost too many people close to him over the course of his life, both family and friends. Too many. His tears streamed down his face.

A SPECIAL TREAT

By the time Friday arrived, Francesca believed it was one of the longest weeks of her life. To top it all off, her father had come to her room early that morning to inform her of the death of Calogero Biscotti. They reminisced about their days in exile with him and, in particular, the evenings when the men would listen to her singing.

As she lay in bed that morning, she thought about how she missed her singing lessons with *Signora Lucia*. A passion for music had stirred in Francesca's soul when she was very young. It took her to a place far away from the death of her mother and her brother, and she was able to get lost in the music. Opera soon became her favorite music to study and sing.

However, it was through *Signora Lucia* that her voice really began to come into her own. She knew over the past year that she had greatly improved, and perhaps a career as a singer could be a possibility. She was happy that at least her father agreed that *Signora Lucia* could start coming to the villa.

Her thoughts were interrupted by a knock on the door.

"Who is it?"

"It's Marco, *Signorina Francesca*."

She pulled the sheets up to her neck. "You can come in."

He entered the room.

"What is it?" she asked.

"*Signora Fulmicina* made you a special breakfast this morning. She asked me to bring you down to the dining hall."

"What did she make?"

"She would not tell me."

"Let me get dressed. It will be just a moment."

A short time later, Marco heard the door unlock and out into the hallway stepped Francesca. She was wearing a simple blue dress that fit her figure perfectly.

With his *lupara* slung across his shoulder, Marco smiled at her. "*Buon giorno, Francesca. Come va?*"

"*Va, bene.* I'm starving, so I'm glad you came to get me when you did."

"*Signora Fulmicina* came to tell me to get you. I saw your father this morning. He was quite upset about the death of Don Biscotti."

"Terrible news. They were very close."

"Most likely killed by the same people who ordered the attack on your father. That cannot be a coincidence."

"I would think not."

"You are safe here, *Signorina Francesca*. I stood guard outside your door all night. I will let nothing happen to you."

She extended her hand and patted his arm. "You must be exhausted?"

"I'll sleep later. *Andiamo*."

They walked together down the long hallway to the stairs. The dining hall was located to the right of the stairwell on the first floor. As they entered, the smell of baked dough wafting in from the nearby kitchen permeated the entire room.

Francesca smiled broadly. "She did not?"

"Not what?" asked Marco."

"I think she made her famous *sfincis*."

Just then, *Signora Elvira Fulmicina* walked into the dining hall carrying a platter of *sfincis* - morsels of sweet, fried ricotta donuts covered in juicy sultanas. But what made *Signora Fulmicina's sfincis* stand out was the addition of cinnamon. She always said that being from Palermo had allowed her to perfect this Sicilian delight.

Francesca said to her, "What's the occasion? You made my morning."

"I know you have been through a lot this week. I wanted to give you a surprise for the end of the week. Your father already had his before he left this morning."

She placed the platter down in the middle of the table. Francesca told Marco, "Bend over the table. Do it now."

"Now take a deep breath," Francesca advised.

Marco followed the order. The smell was incredible. The baked dough, the ricotta, and the hint of cinnamon were a complete pleasure to the senses.

Francesca turned to *Signora Fulmicina*. "My father is blessed to have you."

"For all that your father did for me, cooking for him and

his men is the least I can do," *Signora Fulmicina* responded. "Now, *mangia, mangia.*"

Marco pulled a chair out and, with his hand against Francesca's lower back, gently directed her to sit."

Signora Fulmicina said to Marco, "There is more than enough for you as well. *Mangia, mangia.*"

Marco walked to the other side of the table, laid his *lupara* against the wall, and sat across from Francesca as *Signora Fulmicina* left the room. Francesca and Marco both took a *sfinchi* from the platter and placed it on the plate before them.

Marco picked it up and lifted it toward Francesca. "*Mangia, mangia,*" he said, imitating *Signora Fulmicina's* voice perfectly.

They both laughed before biting into the *sfinci.*

"*Delicioso,*" stated Marco emphatically.

"I agree. She is a fabulous cook."

While eating, Francesca asked Marco, "You have stood guard outside my door the entire week. And yet, I know so little about you. So, how is it that you came to work for my father?"

"Well, it's the same story as I am sure it is for *Signora Fulmicina* and for most of your father's associates. Let's just say your father helped me at a time I needed help the most, so my working for him was the least I could do."

Francesca smiled at him. "It's all rather strange. People like you and *Signora Fulmicina* want to be a part of the family, while I want out."

"What do you mean?"

"I want to be a singer. That's all I ever wanted to be as a young child."

"Your voice is mesmerizing. You will make a great singer."

"Do you really think that I, the daughter of the head of a Sicilian *cosca,* has a chance of making such a career?"

"Certainly, I do. Your father's contacts alone will provide you with opportunities."

"His business could also hurt my chances in the pursuit of my career."

"Your father is a great man. A great man. A man of honor. Don't ever be ashamed of what he has made of his life. My father was a drunkard, a womanizer, and abusive to my mother. Let's just say the last time he gave my mother a bloody nose and a bruise below her right eye, your father made sure he would never touch her again."

"He had him killed?"

"No. But let's just say my father can no longer make a fist with either hand. Let's have another *sfinchi.*"

They both reached into the platter and pulled out another before taking a bite into it.

14

THE MUSIC OF BELLAFORTUNA

Saturday welcomed a spectacular day in Bellafortuna. The sky was a deep blue, with just a few clouds dotting the skyline. Father Gianuzzi was seated behind his desk in the rectory, preparing for his first Sunday sermon set for tomorrow. The words did not flow easily that morning. He turned his head away from the pages and peered out the window, which offered a glorious view of the valley below. His thoughts turned to the meeting with the *Società* two nights before and the concerns of the residents of Bellafortuna regarding the rise of the Mafia. He feared for the villagers.

He tried to leave his thoughts behind as he looked down and reread the Gospel for tomorrow, hoping for inspiration. It was one of the most famous parables told by Jesus to his disciples, the Pharisees, and others. It was the parable of the Prodigal Son.

In the story, a father has two sons. The younger son asks

his father for his inheritance. This son leaves the home, squanders his fortune, and eventually becomes destitute. He returns home and intends to beg his father to accept him back as a servant. To his surprise, he is not scorned by his father but is welcomed back with a celebration and a welcoming party. Meanwhile, the older son is jealous and angry that his father lavishes such celebrations on the prodigal son. He refuses to participate in the festivities. The father tells the older son: "You are ever with me, and all that I have is yours, but your younger brother was lost, and now he is found." Ultimately, it's a story of God's boundless mercy and love.

When Father Gianuzzi finished reading the passage again, the theme for his sermon finally leaped into his mind. Usually, when he heard teachers or priests discuss this passage, the father's actions were what took center stage. But Father Gianuzzi was more interested in the motivations of the prodigal son. What made him break from his father and his family? What was family life like once he came back? That's what the focus of his sermon would be. It would be on the lost son.

He worked the rest of the morning on his sermon. When the church bell of the *Chiesa della Madonna* tolled the noon hour, he put the final touches on it. He then gave it one last final read-through. He placed the pages of his homily inside his desk, just in time to go out to the *Piazza Santa Croce* for the Saturday afternoon concert given by the *Opera Orchestra di Bellafortuna.*

IN THE AGRICULTURAL world of Bellafortuna, the villagers worked tirelessly day in and day out among the vineyards and olive trees in the valley. Dating back many years, Siesta occurred every day in the village from 12:00 p.m. to 2:00 p.m., with all work ceasing in the village, the valley, the groves, and the vineyards. It was a time for the people to renew their energy for the rest of the day.

Unlike other villages where the residents went home during Siesta, in Bellafortuna, the villagers gathered in the *Piazza Santa Croce*, where under the shadow of the Enzo Boccale statue, they ate light lunches and discussed different aspects of life and, in particular, over the past few months, the post-war problems facing everyone.

Although Siesta occurred every day, it was on Saturdays that something unique and special to Bellafortuna occurred. The *Opera Orchestra di Bellafortuna* performed in the piazza every Saturday during the last hour of Siesta, a tradition begun many years before by Antonio Sanguinetti. The music they played ranged from classical, opera and Neapolitan love songs.

The *Opera Orchestra di Bellafortuna* had been in continuous existence in the village since the late 1700s. The orchestra consisted of fifteen full-time members. This was the same orchestra that played during the summer opera festival held in the valley on the site of an ancient Greek amphitheater when the orchestra would be supplemented by other musicians from the surrounding towns of Sicily.

On that Saturday afternoon during the last hour of Siesta, the villagers gathered around the Enzo Boccale statue, with most sitting on the ground while a few occupied chairs that were brought out from the nearby shops. Some of the children played with a ball off to one side. The orchestra had finished setting their chairs up in front of the *Chiesa della Madonna,* and they took their positions just as Father Gianuzzi walked out of the rectory and over to Giuseppe and Maria Sanguinetti, who were both seated near the Boccale statue. They had an empty chair next to them for him.

"Ahh, Father Gianuzzi, welcome to your first concert," Giuseppe responded as the young priest approached and took his seat in the empty chair.

"I can't wait to get lost in the music today. As you know, Monsignor Mancini went to Cinisi for the week. I'm giving my first sermon tomorrow and have been working on it all morning."

"We look forward to hearing you preach, Father," Maria said. "But for now, relax and enjoy the music on this beautiful day."

He smiled. "I will."

Santo and Mirella soon joined them. Mirella sat next to Father Gianuzzi. "I'm so glad you came to our concert," she told him.

"I'm thrilled to be here."

Suddenly, a thunderous eruption of applause rattled the sun-splattered piazza. The conductor of the *Opera Orchestra di Bellafortuna,* Vincenzo Occipinti, took his position in front of the orchestra, and the Saturday afternoon concert began with the *Intermezzo* from Pietro Mascagni's *Cavalleria Rusticana.*

After that, the next selections that afternoon were arias from some of the most famous operas ever written. The entire crowd sat quietly throughout all of the selections, save when they were singing along. The locals loved to sing along with the orchestra.

For the second half of the hour concert, the orchestra played Neapolitan love songs, which the villagers loved immensely. Father Gianuzzi sat in awe as he looked around the piazza, taking it all in as the melodic music filled his brain. He stared at the faces of the people, which reflected their deep love of music. He knew their feeling well. He grew up with music, and he too had a deep love for it. It was obvious to him that music for the villagers of Bellafortuna was more than just entertainment, it was a part of their very being, a part of their makeup, a part of their world.

As the concert came to a close, Mirella leaned toward Father Gianuzzi. "Now comes our tradition. This tradition is seared into the soul of every village member. The music you are about to hear is the anthem of our village and brought us our freedom many, many years go."

Maria added, "And may it always keep us free."

Father Gianuzzi nodded his head and waited anxiously to hear this anthem.

Kurt Hofmann, who was seated in the orchestra, put his instrument down and made his way to the front by Vincenzo Occipinti, who lifted his baton swiftly. The initial notes of Verdi's "Va, pensiero" from his opera *Nabucco* echoed throughout the piazza. The crowd - old, young, male and female – rose as one and stood. Even the orchestra stood.

Father Gianuzzi stood and looked around the piazza at all of the villagers. There was a soul to this place that was hard to describe but one that could easily be felt.

Verdi's chorus from his opera *Nabucco* is sung by Jewish slaves who are being held captive in Babylon. They sing of their homeland and the hope of ridding themselves of oppression. The opera's theme of freedom borne of oppression resonated with Verdi, just as it did with the villagers of Bellafortuna many years ago. One by one, the villagers in the crowd grabbed hands and began to sing.

This song had only grown in importance to the villagers of Bellafortuna during the time they had shielded Jewish refugees in their village during the war. That is why Kurt Hofmann now always stood in the front, as a remembrance of those people they had grown close to and had protected.

In one voice, the villagers all joined in and sang the song.

> *Va, pensiero, sull'ali dorate;*
> *va, ti posa sui clivi, sui colli,*
> *ove olezzano tepide e molli*
> *l'aure dolci del suolo natal!*
> *Del Giordano le rive salute,*
> *di Sionne le torri atterrate.*

> *Go my thoughts on wings of gold;*
> *go and settle upon the mountains and hills,*
> *where you feel and smell the*
> *sweet breezes of our native soil!*
> *Greet the banks of the river Jordan*
> *and the destroyed towers of Zion.*

Right at this point, the villagers sang the next line with great emotion.

> *Oh, mia patria,*
> *sì bella e perduta!*
> *Oh, membranza, sì cara e fatal!*

Oh, my country,
so beautiful and lost!
Oh, memory, so dear and so fatal!

As the last notes faded away, the entire piazza erupted in applause. Giuseppe asked, "Well, Father. What do you think?"

"Amazing. Wonderful. I have never seen or heard anything like it, actually. This place is truly blessed."

"Good people, Father. That's the true blessing of Bellafortuna."

The villagers began to file out of the piazza.

Father Gianuzzi thanked the Sanguinettis, told the Vasaios good day, and then returned to the rectory. Before he walked inside, he turned one last time and looked across the piazza. He was blessed to have come to this little village. Never in his wildest dreams could he have imagined the path that he had walked in his life. He thought back to the sermon he was working on earlier that morning. The life choices we make are up to us and are a consequence of our free will, which is a part of our makeup as humans. But what the Prodigal Son parable teaches us is that no matter what choices we make, God will never abandon us. After attending the concert today, Father Gianuzzi was convinced that God's providence had brought him to this small Sicilian village. God allows us to make choices, both good and bad, but He will always come to our aid, no matter what choice we make or paths we decide to tread upon, as long as we realize when it is time to come home and seek redemption for our actions.

Father Gianuzzi watched as the last orchestra members left their impromptu stage. He thought back to the meeting

Thursday night and he reflected on what the rise of the Mafia from the ashes would mean to Bellafortuna and all of Sicily. He knew one thing for certain. If the Mafia was fighting for control of the black market, then that would undoubtedly lead to violence and death.

A new battle would soon erupt, a war for power and control that would leave a legacy of violence and blood across the island. The death of Calogero Biscotti was just the opening shot in a soon-to-be all out war. The inhabitants of Sicily would be the insignificant pawns caught in the middle. And as for the villagers of tiny Bellafortuna, their quiet existence, while trying to recover in the post-war environment of Sicily, was about to be put to the test.

Father Gianuzzi mumbled under his breath, "So much violence," as he made his way into the rectory.

PART II

ALLIES

15

THE MEETING OF THE FAMILIES

Adriano was seated in his office in the Castelvetrano City Hall early that Monday morning. Within the past week, he had been betrayed, attacked, and his friend murdered. But what was on the forefront of his mind was that he still had no idea who was responsible for it all.

Luca and Giancarlo were seated across the desk. Adriano said to them, "We need to do what needs to be done to find out who has brought war upon us. I think the time has come to have a meeting with the families whom we know can be trusted. We need their assistance to bring war upon this unknown enemy. With Calogero's death, they will all agree. I'm sure they are thinking they will be next."

Giancarlo replied, "And if I can venture a guess, you mean the Campagnos from Trapani, the Mazzas from Catania and the Tumminellos from Corleone."

"Correct. Those are the three. I trust those men with my life. Let's set a meeting to take place in Selinunte. We can meet in the second-floor room at *Mosca's Trattoria* near there. If a war is coming, then I need to line up my allies. They will join me in avenging the death of Calogero."

"I'm concerned about your safety traveling to Selinunte," Luca said. "I know the meeting would be in secret, and you trust these men, but I'm still leery."

"Giancarlo will have a travel plan in place, right?"

"*Si*," Giancarlo responded.

"Then that's that. I leave it to the two of you to make contact and set it up. The sooner, the better. And Luca, don't forget to pick up *Signora Lucia* this afternoon for Francesca's voice lesson."

"Yes sir."

"Let me know when the meeting with the families has been arranged."

When Luca and Giancarlo left Adriano's office, they walked down the hallway together.

"Don Adriano is very concerned," Giancarlo said. "You can see it on his face."

"Wouldn't you be?"

Giancarlo nodded in agreement. "We will both go with him to meet the families. We will protect him."

"And the villa?" asked Luca.

"If your concern is another betrayer, I believe Mario acted alone. Our men will protect the villa and Francesca."

"If anything ever happened to her ..." he stopped mid-sentence.

"I know, Luca. I know."

TWO DAYS LATER, Adriano was walking amidst the majestic and beautiful ancient Greek ruins of Selinunte. He had been quiet and deep in thought during the entire drive from Castelvetrano with Luca and Giancarlo. Since his meeting Monday morning with them, he had developed a plan, and today he would lay out that plan to the other heads of the three families.

Selinunte was located on the coast in the southwestern part of Sicily and within the commune of Castelvetrano. In ancient times, it was one of the most important Greek colonies established in Sicily and now was known for having the largest archeological park in all of Europe.

In just two hours, Adriano would be attending the meeting at *Mosca's Trattoria*. But for now, he relaxed walking among the Greek ruins located upon an acropolis. Giancarlo and Luca stood guard nearby.

As he walked inside the shell of the former Temple of Hera, his mind flashed back to when he came here to assist the Allies in their quest to wrestle control of the island from the Nazi war machine. Looking around the temple, Adriano remembered the American GIs sitting inside, some using their helmets as water basins as they shaved. It was here where Adriano first met Colonel John Tessitore, the Allied tank commander, and with whom Adriano and Calogero would assist in navigating the Allies through the hilly terrain of Sicily on the Allied march toward Palermo during the Husky campaign.

Adriano left the temple and then made his way up a mountain trail to an old abandoned farmhouse. This was the farmhouse where he had lived in exile with his family after leaving the confines of the small cave above Selinunte when he had fled Gangi with his wife and son.

While Giancarlo and Luca waited outside, Adriano stepped inside. As he peered around the entrance room, he was suddenly overcome with emotion. He walked through the kitchen and remembered the smells as Santa would cook her delicious meals for the family. He then walked down a small hallway and entered his old bedroom.

He sat on the floor and remembered his life here with Santa, and his two children. He looked to the left corner of the room where his bed once sat, and he thought of his nights of lovemaking with Santa. His mind became intoxicated with the memory of her smell. He missed her deeply.

He looked up and noticed the beam which ran across the length of the room. His eyes focused intently on that beam as his mind flashed to the image of Santa swinging back and forth from the end of the rope. He still could hear the painful screams of his children when they saw their mother after returning to the home with Adriano from the afternoon out in the fields. He knew the moment that he saw his wife swinging from the end of the rope that Don Vincente Genovese had finally exacted his revenge.

His thoughts were interrupted when Luca entered the bedroom. "Don Adriano, it's time."

Adriano stood up and left the farmhouse with Luca.

***

MOSCA'S WAS a small *trattoria* located near the archeological park of Selinunte. The only light inside the restaurant's dining room was produced by the single candles sticking out of the wax-dripped wine bottles that sat on each of the tables. The restaurant was dark - dark for dark business - was how the locals described it.

Adriano, Luca, and Giancarlo walked in and were immediately shown to the upstairs room by the owner of the *trattoria*, Alberto Mosca. There was a long table with a single, long electric cord with a naked lightbulb hanging over the table. The other heads of the families were already seated at the table, with their respective associates all standing behind them. The heads of the families rose when Don Adriano Umbretto walked in. They all made their way to him and kissed his right hand. Although all of the Dons in attendance were powerful in their own right, they knew that the most powerful among them had just entered.

They all took their seats around the table. Adriano sat as they all waited for him to begin. He looked around the table before he said, "Thanks to all of you for coming." He then looked at each Don and said their name, all the while staring at each of them in a very personal way. "Don Paolo Campagno, Don Giuseppe Mazza and, finally, Don Vincenzo Tumminello. I called this meeting to discuss a very pressing matter. I know you have all heard of the death of Calogero."

"It's terrible," replied Don Campagno.

"It's horrific," replied Don Mazzo.

"It must be avenged," replied Don Tumminello.

"I agree with all of your assessments, and there is something I must tell you, but it must be kept secret."

"Of course," they all replied.

"Last Monday, an intruder came into my villa and attempted to kill me. He failed as I was able to plunge his own knife into his chest."

The Dons were visibly upset.

"Before you ask, we have been unable to determine whom this man worked for. We have no information on the killer of Calogero either. However, we don't think the attempt on my life is unrelated to what happened in Monreale."

Don Tumminello replied, "Don Umbretto, this is very disturbing news. Particularly in light of some news I have heard on my way here. Calogero's *consigliere* has been killed as well."

Don Mazzo added, "Shot yesterday at point blank range is what I heard."

Adriano shook his head. "This is indeed disturbing news."

"We have tried to ascertain the killer of Calogero, but we too have been unable to find out any information,"Don Tumminello added.

Don Mazza added, "But now with the news that your life was threatened, and the killing of Calogero's trusted associate, it makes finding out who is behind it all the most pressing of issues before us."

"I guess the move for control of Monreale has begun," Adriano replied. "I know the remnants of Calogero's *cosca* are still in place, but they will not be able to survive the war that is to come. And now with the news you bring of the death of Calogero's *consigliere,* I know my belief is true."

Don Campagno asked, "I wonder why they came after you?"

"Once we find the culprit, perhaps we will find out that answer," replied Adriano.

"I know why," Don Tumminello said. "Because if you are seeking control of Monreale, you better take out the powerful

Don Adriano Umbretto, whose family once ran that same city."

"We don't know who did this," replied Don Mazza. "I think our only option is to wait until we know."

Adriano stood up from the table and said in a defiant voice, "We cannot wait any longer." He pointed his finger at each of the Dons. "They may come for you, and you, and you, as well. Whoever our enemy is, they know the closeness I have to the three of you. We need to flush them out and destroy them."

"But how?" asked Don Mazza.

Adriano's eyes burned with intensity. "Our families will combine, and, together, we will make a move for control of Monreale. The combined strength of our families will crush the killer and his minions. He will have to come out to assert his control over Monreale. It will be a bloody war, but it's a war we have to bring, and it's a war we have to win. We need to bring the war to our enemy, before it overtakes all of us."

Don Mazza said, "I understand your reasoning, but I'm not sure we are strong enough to take on an enemy we know nothing about."

"I agree with Don Umbretto," Don Tumminello said. "We may not know whom we are up against, but we know what the outcome will be if we do not act."

Don Campagno asked, "So, how do we bring war upon an unknown enemy?"

Adriano sat back down. He said, "My *cosca* will remain in Castelvetrano and protect my endeavors there. In the meantime, I will move to secure my position of control in Monreale, with the assistance of some of your men and Calogero's remaining *cosca*. Each of you will have to give me some of your men to assist me. Together we will crush the head of the serpent once he pokes his head out. Once we attain victory, Monreale will be ours."

Don Mazza said sarcastically, "The Umbrettos will once again rule Monreale."

"No, Don Mazza. The Umbrettos will rule Monreale with all of you. This is my promise to all of you. Victory will be attained by all of us, and the reward will be divided equally among us."

"When do you propose we make our move?" Don Tumminello asked.

"Three days. In three days, I will go to Monreale and meet your men. Pick the best men you have."

Don Mazza asked, "And if you fail in gaining control of Monreale?"

Adriano was silent for a moment before responding. "Let me put it this way. Failure is not an option. We will flush him out and kill him. *Capice.*"

The three Dons nodded their heads.

Adriano pointed to Luca and asked him to get Alberto Mosca to come upstairs and take their food and drink orders now that their dark business was complete.

LATER THAT NIGHT, on their drive back to Castelvetrano, Luca, seated in the vehicle's passenger seat, turned to the back seat and asked Adriano. "Don Adriano, do you think your plan will work?"

"As a young man, Don Spatuzza taught me one thing. He always said, 'It's important to have a plan, but even with your plan in place, it's even more important to make sure that your gun is loaded.' Honestly, I don't know if it will work, but I will promise that if I go down, it will be in a fight, and not stabbed to death in my own bedroom."

"I want to go with you to Monreale," Luca replied. "Please, Don Adriano. You need at least one person you can trust. Giancarlo and the rest of the men will protect the villa and Francesca."

"You have been a loyal friend, Luca. A dear friend. I would be honored to have you with me."

"Francesca seems so happy, studying voice again with *Signora Lucia*. Her teacher told me the other day when I picked her up that your daughter possesses one of the best voices she has ever heard."

Adriano said, "She indeed has a glorious voice. But we need to crush my enemy, or all of us will suffer the consequences. For if we don't, Francesca's voice will be forever silenced."

They continued driving down the road late that night to Castelvetrano.

THE DEATH OF MUSIC

The next morning, Adriano was in his study at the villa, speaking with Luca and Giancarlo. They were discussing the best way to implement Adriano's plan.

After many ideas had been bantered about, Adriano said, "The key to our success on this mission is to make sure we have the unwavering support of the other three families. Without them, I do not see a path to victory."

"I concur," Giancarlo added. "I will protect your assets here, while you and Luca go to Monreale in a few days to meet up with the men the other families send to join you. There, along with Biscotti's men, you will bring war upon those who have brought it upon you."

"And Francesca?" Adriano asked. "You will assure her safety, Giancarlo?"

"Of course."

"*Bene,*" replied Adriano. "Now, there is one other item we must discuss."

"What is that?" asked Luca.

"Succession."

"Succession?" both men responded almost in unison.

"*Si*. What happens if I don't come back?"

Giancarlo said, "Don Adriano, you will come back."

"We are fighting an unknown enemy at this point. I have to prepare just in case." He turned toward Luca and bore his gaze deep into the younger man's eyes. "You have been with me since before my exile. You and I, along with Calogero, spent many a night drinking and talking about our lives in front of the fireplace or seated outside, drinking wine overlooking the vast landscape of Sicily set before us. You were with me when we came out of the hills, and returned to Castelvetrano, and I took power once again. Not only are you my *capobastone*, but I consider you my friend. If something happens to me, I want you to take over my *cosca*."

Luca gulped hard. "It would be an honor to do so."

Adriano then turned to Giancarlo. "And you, Giancarlo, although you have been with me for only a few years, since the time I was named Mayor, you have always been committed to me, and have carried out every one of my orders to perfection. You proved yourself well, and moved up to head of security quickly. If both Luca and myself do not return, then this *cosca* is yours."

Giancarlo nodded. "It will be done, Don Adriano," he replied.

"It goes without saying that whoever takes over from me will watch over and defend Francesca, and that everything I own will be hers."

"*Si*, Don Adriano," they both replied.

"Bene," Adriano replied again as the meeting came to an end.

As the two closest confidants of Adriano turned to leave, he said to them, "I thank the both of you for your dedication and loyalty to me. I will never forget it."

Luca replied, "No, Adriano. Thank you for your dedication and loyalty to us. We will never forget it."

"Thanks for meeting with me. And Luca, are you going to pick up Francesca's voice teacher in a bit?"

"Yes, a little later today."

"Great. On your way, stop at Cincilla's and buy us three dozen *Cuccidati* to take with us to Monreale to eat in the car."

"I shall. And I will make plans for one of the other men to pick up *Signora Lucia* when you and I are in Monreale."

"I'll see the two of you later then," said Adriano.

"*Addio*, Don Adriano," the men replied, and they left the study.

THREE HOURS LATER, Tommaso Giordano, a farmer under the protection of Don Adriano, showed up at the gates of the villa. His clothes were stained with blood. His eyes were red with tears. He demanded to see Don Adriano.

The forceful requests by Ferruccio at the gate to provide the reason for the farmer's visit, as well as for the blood on his clothes, went unanswered, as he only kept making his repetitive request to speak personally with Don Adriano.

Giancarlo was finally called to the courtyard, and he came and met the man at the gate. Giancarlo knew Tommaso, as the farmer and Luca had been friendly with each other over the years.

"*Signor Giancarlo*, something has happened. I must speak to Don Adriano."

"What has happened?"

"*Per favore, Signor.*"

Giancarlo said to Flavio, another of Adriano's soldiers standing by the gate, "*Aperto.*"

The gate was opened, and Giancarlo brought the farmer to Adriano's study.

Giancarlo knocked on the door of the study, and Adriano's voice called out from behind the door. "*Pronto.*"

Giancarlo opened the door and walked into the study.

"Don Adriano, Tommaso Giordano wants to speak with you."

The two men stepped fully into the study.

Adriano rose from behind his desk. "What can I do for you, *Signor Tommaso*?"

The farmer burst into tears. "I'm sorry, Don Adriano."

Adriano looked over at Giancarlo before asking, "Sorry for what?"

"It's *Signor Luca. Lui è morto*. He is dead," he repeated.

"Dead? Luca? What do you mean?"

"I found him dead in a car with a woman. The car is in a ditch right near my farm. Only about a mile away. The entire car is filled with bullets holes." Tears flowed again as he said, "They are both dead, Don Adriano. It's an awful scene."

Adriano banged his fist on his desk before he sprinted past the two men and out the room. Giancarlo and Tommaso turned and ran behind him.

Adriano arrived in the courtyard first, where four of his

soldiers, Flavio, Alessandro, Ferruccio, and Marcello, stood guard. Adriano demanded a car.

"Luca, Giovanni, and Roberto have three of the cars," Flavio responded. "The other one is being repaired. Luca should be ..."

Adriano cut him off. "Open the damn gate," he thundered.

As Alessandro went to do so, Adriano said again, but with more desperation, "Open the God damn gate."

By this time, Giancarlo and the farmer had entered the courtyard, along with other soldiers of Don Adriano who had heard the commotion. As the gate opened, Adriano sprinted out. Giancarlo was yelling for him to wait.

"What happened?" Ferruccio asked Giancarlo.

"It's Luca. There has been a shooting up the road. Bring me a car."

Flavio responded, "There are no cars available."

"*Fanculo*," Giancarlo responded angrily. He pointed to the Don's men, standing guard by the gate. "The three of you come with me." He then yelled toward the men who had just come out of the villa. "All of you stay here and protect the villa."

He took off running after Adriano, followed closely behind by Marcello, Ferruccio, and Flavio. Tommaso ran next to Giancarlo toward his farm.

MARCELLO, Ferruccio, and Flavio ran at a full sprint, along with Giancarlo and Tomasso, but they could not catch up to

Adriano. As they got near the site, Tommaso pointed the car out to Giancarlo, just a bit ahead of them.

The car had left the road and was stopped in the ditch that ran along the road. Smoke bellowed from the hood. But the smoke was not what caught Giancarlo's attention. It was the figure of a man, sitting in the middle of the road with a body lying across his lap.

As Adriano's men arrived, they all stopped and took in the scene before them. The powerful Don Adriano Umbretto, holding tightly to the bloodied body of Luca Sperenza strewn across his lap, was crying uncontrollably. This was a shock to his men, as they had never seen their boss cry.

Adriano picked his head up and looked directly at Giancarlo. "They killed him, Giancarlo. They killed him."

Giancarlo walked over and knelt down next to Adriano. He looked at the bloody face of Luca, and his own tears began to track down his face. He grabbed Adriano's right shoulder.

"I pulled him out of the car," Adriano said. "Look how many times he was hit. He never stood a chance."

Giancarlo looked over toward the car and saw *Signora Lucia* slumped over in the passenger seat, her head and chest covered in bright red blood. "Let me go take a look."

Giancarlo got up and walked over to the car, calling Flavio, Ferruccio, and Marcello over to him. *Signora Lucia* was slumped over toward the driver's seat. All around the front seat were the *Cuccidati* that Luca had purchased. The bag that carried them had been ripped apart by bullets entering the vehicle.

Giancarlo said to the men, "Get her out of the car and lay her on the side of the road."

Ferruccio, his face somber, said, "Giancarlo, we will take care of this. You take care of the Don."

As Giancarlo turned toward Adriano, he called Tommaso over. "Can you go to your farm and get us your truck so we can take the bodies?"

Before Tommaso could respond, Adriano stood up and began walking down the middle of the road carrying Luca's body in his outstretched arms. The men removing *Signora Lucia* from the car stopped and watched the events unfolding before them in silence and with great emotion.

Giancarlo ran up to Adriano. "Tommaso is getting his truck. Let's lay Luca down and wait."

Adriano stopped walking. He turned toward Giancarlo. "I promised his mother. I promised her. I killed her husband. That man deserved to die. But she was ill. I promised her that I would take her son in and protect him. I promised her that nothing would happen to her boy. I failed her. He never knew I was the killer of his own father. Now he is dead. Leave me be. I am taking him home."

With that, he continued walking down the road carrying the body of Luca Sperenza, his *capobastone*, and his friend, back home to his villa.

17

A GLIMPSE INTO THE SHADOWS

A large farmhouse stood in the valley of the stunningly beautiful *Conca d'oro*, just a few miles from the city of Monreale. Behind the house were rows and rows of lemon trees and a smaller building, which once housed the tenant farmers who worked for the Donati family who owned this land. The Donati family had stopped housing the tenant workers years ago, and now the little building had been abandoned; that was until a few weeks ago when they welcomed an old friend.

That friend, his son, and a patchwork of associates now were living in the little building. Some would say the place was their hideaway. Those occupying the little place would say this was their headquarters as they set forth the plan that had been developed over the last year.

The leader and mastermind of this odd assortment of men sat in a chair in the main room of the building, smoking a long pipe by the fireplace. He rubbed his knees as they ached from the coolness of that Sicilian afternoon. Those knees had walked this earth for 78 years and had taken this man to the pinnacle of power and wealth, both in Sicily and America. But he had returned, and his sights were now set on his return to power in Sicily.

The man took a deep, long draw on his pipe, held the smoke inside his mouth, and then exhaled, enjoying the smell of the tobacco wafting in the air. He viewed smoking his pipe on that afternoon as a celebratory smoke. He was bringing war to Sicily. And so far, he was winning. The news he had just received brought him great joy. Luca Sperenza, the *capobastone* of Don Adriano Umbretto, had been murdered a short time ago upon his orders. His thoughts were interrupted when his son walked into the room and sat in the chair opposite him.

"Smoke?" asked his father.

The son raised a glass in his hands. "*Negroni* instead. *Salute.*"

"*Salute, mio figlio.* You just got back from your deed. I already heard the news. Tell me how it went down?"

"*Bellissimo.* We knew he would take that road back to the villa. So, we took our positions on the road near a farm. We could have just shot him while he drove by, but instead we blocked the road and pointed our guns at him."

His father smiled.

The son laughed. "The look of fear on the woman's face with him was quite a sight."

"Guessing that was the daughter's voice teacher?"

"Yes. Our contacts provided perfect information. Don Umbretto, we believe, thinks that he rid his *cosca* of all his traitors. He is wrong."

"So, what did Adriano's *capobastone* do when he saw our men in the road pointing their guns at his car?"

"He swerved the vehicle. But his tires slipped off the road and he lost control. His car went down a little embankment and smashed into the bottom of a ditch. Smoke began pouring from the hood. We could see him frantically trying to get the car going again. The woman with him was crying uncontrollably."

The old man laughed.

"We slowly walked to the front of the car. The man stopped trying to get the car moving again as his eyes locked onto mine through the window. He knew his fate was sealed. We opened fire."

"Excellent, my son. Excellent."

"On the way back, I took the men who were with me to a brothel on the outskirts of Monreale. I wanted to treat them for their great work today."

"I heard. I also heard you left one of the girls bloodied."

The younger man smiled. "Unlike the wives of the men under our protection in New Orleans, this girl would not do what I asked." He raised his fist toward his father and said, "Let's just say by the end I could put it where I wanted."

"Don't hit women, Castranzio."

"She was a whore."

The old man took an even longer draw on his pipe before exhaling again. "We will make our move soon. Until then, we must avoid doing stupid things that can lead us into having a run in with the local authorities. Taking out Don Biscotti and Don Adriano's *capobastone* were just the beginning of our path of terror. Don Umbretto escaped death. He won't escape next time I move against him."

"When will we make our move against the others on your list?"

"*Notte oscura.*"

The younger man laughed and repeated, "The black night."

The old man laughed even harder than his son. He said, "That's the night when all of Sicily will know we are back in power."

"But when?"

"The Saturday before *Domenica delle Palme*. On that night before Palm Sunday, our members and those associates under our wing across Sicily, will take out the remaining forces against us."

"Who?"

"Giangiacomo Zancanaro, Monreale's police chief, as well as its chief Judge, Alfredo Saltafamaggio, as well as a few others of importance to help us gain complete control. We will also wipe out the remaining *cosca* members of Don Biscotti. And finally, we will take down once and for all, Don Adriano Umbretto."

"Don Umbretto? Why are you so set on taking him down, father?"

"Monreale will be our base of operations. By controlling this area, we can control the fertile area of the *Conca d'oro*. Our control of Monreale will also allow us to take over the farmlands and wine production in Bellafortuna. Don Biscotti was beloved all over Sicily. His death has sent shockwaves around Monreale, as the citizens of Monreale, and Bellafortuna for that matter, know what the death of their protector will mean. There is one thing I know more than anything else in this world, the mind of a Sicilian. These people in their despair and fear will fondly remember Don Calcedonio Umbretto. In their lost state, they will seek out the assistance of his grandson, the powerful Don of Castelvetrano, Adriano Umbretto. Today, I took out Don Adriano's most trusted associate. That will bring him much pain. He will make a stupid move, and when he does, we will take him out before the citizens of Monreale turn to him for assistance. My son, once we are in power, all of this will soon be yours."

His son took a sip of his *Negroni* and said, "Sicily will remember your 'black night' for years to come."

"Indeed. Like it was when I ordered the killing of Calcedonio Umbretto's wife and his *cosca* members after I shot him. My only regret is that young Adriano had fled Monreale the morning it all happened. I would have loved to have stabbed him that day."

"Soon, Papa. Soon. And then all of Monreale will bow down to Don Onofrio Fausto and his son, Castranzio, who have both returned from America, where they controlled the ports of New Orleans. Soon, we will control Monreale, and the entire wine production facility and vineyards of Bellafortuna."

The old man took another long draw on his pipe before he said, "*Uccidere mi dà ancora un'erezione.* (Killing still gives me a hard on.) Even at my old age."

His son laughed as he raised his glass of *Negroni* in a toast to his father.

18

ANOTHER BETRAYAL

*L*ater that evening, Adriano sat in his study inside his villa. Across the desk from him was his *consigliere,* Salvatore Battaglia. Adriano's face was red with anger. His stomach churned. His clothes were still stained with the blood of Luca.

Just over two hours ago, he had finished turning the bodies of Luca and Lucia over to the *impresario di pompe funebri.* (Funeral Director.) He thereafter had called Lucia's husband, to whom he wished his deepest condolences. Adriano promised her husband that he would personally avenge her death on his behalf.

Since placing that phone call, Adriano's mind became fixated on a comment that Lucia's husband had made. The man probably thought nothing of it, but for Adriano, that comment stung his heart and made everything make sense.

He advised Salvatore of that conversation and what he now believed to be the truth. And because of it, his main concern was now the safety of his daughter. The two men spoke at length as to what they each believed was the way to proceed. Salvatore was both persistent and persuasive in pushing a plan he believed was the best approach. After much debate, Adriano assured Salvatore that he would consider his plan.

Their conversation was halted when Adriano placed a phone call to Giancarlo and asked him to send Marcello to the study at once. After hanging up the phone, he said to Salvatore, "And now we wait."

"You have been very wise in using my nephew to protect your daughter. Your belief that there are still traitors among us rings true. I know you have deep concern for her. I hope I did not speak out of turn in advising you where she should go to be better protected."

"No, I appreciated your advice, as always, and I do believe that it might be the best option."

"I will go with you to make the arrangements."

"I hate sending her away."

"I think my plan is your only option. Don't you agree?".

Before Adriano answered, there was a knock on the door. Adriano stood and said to Salvatore, "The traitor is here." Adriano then shouted toward the door, "Enter."

Salvatore stood and walked around the desk and stood next to the Don.

Giancarlo entered first. His eyes were still red with tears from the loss of Luca. He was followed by Marcello Tedesco, one of Adriano's *cosca* members.

Upon entering, Marcello shot a puzzled look when he saw Salvatore standing next to the Don. He quickly turned to Adriano. "Giancarlo said you wanted to speak with me."

Adriano took a deep breath, trying to calm himself down. "I do. Thanks for coming."

"You are welcome. I'm so sorry about Luca."

Adriano stroked his chin with his right hand. "I called *Signora Lucia's* husband to offer my condolences. In the course of that conversation, he mentioned that he had received a phone call earlier today confirming the pick-up time for his wife. The person who called him was you."

Marcello stood quietly, sweat forming on his top lip.

Adriano continued, "I know why you made that phone call."

Marcello spoke quickly. "Luca had asked me ..."

"*Basta*," thundered Adriano as his attempt to remain calm disappeared, and he punched the top of his desk with his fist. "I thought Mario was the only betrayer among us. I should have known there was another. I was stupid and lazy."

Marcello said, "I was calling to make sure..."

"*Taci*," Adriano bellowed, demanding Marcello to be quiet. Adriano turned toward Salvatore and nodded.

Salvatore walked toward Marcello and stood behind him.

"*Perdoni me*, Don Umbretto," Marcello pleaded. "I beg you. They contacted me, just as they did Mario. They threatened our families. What were we to do?"

"And you never came to me. Instead, you betrayed me. You sold me out. You turned Luca over to these butchers. Who contacted you?"

"Four men. They worked for a powerful Don, but they never said who."

"Who?" thundered Adriano again. The veins in his neck bulged, and his face reddened with anger.

"I swear, I do not know."

Adriano walked from behind the desk. Marcello fell to his knees.

Adriano stood over the man kneeling before him. "You came into my study a moment ago and offered your condolences to me for the loss of Luca, a loss that you arranged to happen. You followed me to the scene earlier and saw his bloodied body for yourself. I'm glad you are on your knees. Because while you are down there, you can pray for your soul."

Marcello turned to look at Salvatore, who was standing behind him. "*Aiuto*. Help me."

But Salvatore remained silent.

Adriano lifted his eyes up from Marcello and looked at Salvatore. Adriano again gave a simple nod of his head. Salvatore grabbed Marcello by the back of the neck and stood him up.

Marcello seemed resolved to his fate as Salvatore led him out of the study.

Giancarlo closed the door and walked back to the desk. Adriano slumped into his chair.

"Don Adriano, I will personally interview every one of our soldiers to make sure there are no more betrayers."

"It's a concern, as we have enemies both outside and within. "Have you increased our security around the villa?"

"I have, Don Adriano."

"I'm deeply concerned for Francesca's safety staying here. It's the most pressing of issues on my mind."

"I know. I will have Giorgio stand guard outside her bedroom with Marco at all times."

"I do fear the forces we are up against. A war is upon us, and we will need all the allies we can get."

Just then, there was a knock on the door. Giancarlo walked to the door and spoke to Flavio. Giancarlo closed the door and said to Adriano, "Don Giuseppe Mazza is on the phone for you. Flavio thought you would want to speak with him."

"Yes, I will take it right here. And Giancarlo, stay and listen in on the other phone."

Giancarlo walked over to a small table on which sat a phone. He waited as Adriano sat at the desk and then picked up the phone on his desk.

"*Pronto,*" Adriano said.

Giancarlo picked up the phone across the room and listened in.

"*Buona sera,* Don Umbretto," Don Mazza said. "The news we have heard earlier today is awful. Just awful. I offer you my condolences for the loss of your *capobastone*"

"*Grazie.*"

Don Mazza took a deep breath. "Don Umbretto, with that news, our circumstances have changed."

Adriano's mouth curled, as he shot a glance toward Giancarlo, before he asked, "What do you mean, Don Mazza?"

"I've had the opportunity to speak with both Don Campagno and Don Tumminello. We are all in agreement that we should not take sides in this war. Let this faceless enemy take control of Monreale. They have killed Biscotti, they killed his *consigliere* as well as your *capobastone*, and they tried to kill you. We don't want this."

"What are you saying?" asked Adriano.

"To put it simply, we will not be sending any of our men to Monreale to assist you in defending it."

Adriano was quiet until he asked Don Mazza, "Are you seeking a response from me?"

"Yes. I want to make sure you understand where we are coming from."

Adriano stood up from the desk. "I do understand what you are saying. And here is my response. *Fanculo a tutti voi.* (Fuck all of you.) You fucking coward," he snarled. "This enemy is not coming just for Monreale. Like a weed, if you allow it into the garden, it will soon take over the entire area. We must pull out the weed by the root, and do so now. That's what I will do, I will crush this weed, and will do so on my own if I need to. So, please do me a favor and tell Don Campagno and Don Tumminello when they ask what I said, be sure to tell them verbatim, '*Fanculo a tutti voi.*' They will all come to regret this."

"Don Umbretto, please understand, we …"

Adriano slammed the phone down, as he slumped back into his chair.

Giancarlo hung up the phone he was listening in on. The look of exhaustion and sadness on Adriano's face caught Giancarlo by surprise.

"*Santo cielo,*" (My God) Adriano said.

Giancarlo walked over to a small table on the opposite side of the room on which sat a bottle of limoncello and a few glasses. He poured one glass, walked over to the desk, and handed it to Adriano.

Adriano lifted the glass in a toast. "To our allies," he said with irony."

They are scared," replied Giancarlo.

"They will be even more afraid when they are staring at the wrong end of a *lupara*."

"So now what?"

"I'll have to take some of my own men with me to Monreale. In two days, we will join forces with Biscotti's men. That is where the war will take place. But that will leave this villa exposed."

Knowing what was on the Don's mind, Giancarlo said, "I will protect her, Don Adriano."

"I know you would, or die trying. But after the events of the last few days, I don't know who I can trust. I have been debating and debating with myself what to do about Francesca. Although I know it goes against what my heart is telling me to do, I think I will have to go with my brain and put Salvatore's plan into action. I know of no other solution."

"What is it?"

"Go get Marco and Francesca and bring them both here. I will then let all of you know the plan."

"Yes, sir."

Giancarlo turned to leave but then quickly turned back toward Don Adriano. "Don Adriano, I don't mean to speak out of turn, but I have always had much respect for Don Mazza. Don't hold his decision against him. He's scared. You could hear it in his voice."

"One thing comes to mind about Don Mazza. *Avere le braccine corte.*"

"Giancarlo asked, "What do you mean he has short arms?"

"He's stingy, both with his money and with his willingness to put his neck out. I'll say this. I hope they all soon change their minds and join the fight."

"I'm sorry for not realizing Marcello had joined forces with Mario. I will speak with the men I trust the most and see if they have any information on any others. I do believe that you have rid your *cosca* of the rats."

"Before I went into exile, I never had to worry about disloyalty. This new breed knows little about loyalty. All they care about is themselves. No question. I leave it to you to check out the men. My main concern at this point is the safety of Francesca. Marco and Giorgio, like you, I trust completely. They are the only ones I trust to guard Francesca."

"Yes sir. I'm anxious to hear your plan. I'll go get Francesca and Marco and bring them to you."

Giancarlo turned and left the study. Adriano brought his hands up as his head fell into them.

19

A REUNION

The next morning, Adriano was in the back of his car, which was being driven by Giancarlo. Salvatore was seated in the passenger seat. They had left early that morning to implement the plan that Salvatore had devised. The plan had been discussed with Giancarlo, Francesca, and Marco late the night before. Adriano's hope was that the plan would provide Francesca with safety away from the threat against his family. Salvatore had convinced him that the plan about to be put into motion was the only option available. In truth, Adriano had only related part of that plan. He did not tell them everything. He needed to keep a part of it secret. That part was known only to him and Salvatore. It had to be that way. He was convinced that his plan gave Francesca the best chance to remain safe, far away from the villa.

They passed the outskirts of Monreale, as Giancarlo purposefully avoided driving through the city. They soon reached the *Corsa Calatafimi*, the road that runs between Monreale and Palermo. About halfway between the two cities, there was a small dirt road that traveled south. Giancarlo turned onto the dirt road, the *Via Valle.*

They followed the winding path amidst the spectacular valley vineyards until they passed a clump of trees when they first got their glimpse of the village of Bellafortuna that sat high up on the hill. The buildings of the village glistened in a golden hue under the brilliant Sicilian sun as the car began climbing the hill.

As Giancarlo pulled the car into the village, he made his way to the *Piazza Santa Croce.* He parked very near *Il Paradiso.* A few of the residents who were out in the piazza gawked at the long black car. While it was true that motor vehicles often came to the village, they were not the mode of transportation of most of the villagers of Bellafortuna.

Adriano got out of the car with Salvatore. He told Giancarlo to stay there. Then he and Salvatore walked over to *Il Paradiso* and went inside.

Giuseppe Sanguinetti was bending down over a box of wines, cutting it open with a knife. Kurt Hofmann was on another aisle placing wine bottles on a shelf. When Giuseppe heard the door open, he turned and glanced toward what he thought was a customer. He quickly realized who it was, and he stood up.

"Don Adriano Umbretto, what brings you to our little village today? Wine?"

"*Ciao, Signor Sanguinetti.* It's nice to see you again. It's been quite a long time. No wine for me today. You have not been over to Castelvetrano as of late."

"Yes, it's been a long time. How are the olives over in Castelvetrano?"

"About as tough a sale as your wine?"

Giuseppe laughed. "Don Umbretto, this is my employee, Kurt Hofmann."

Kurt waved over the top of the shelf in front of him.

"Nice to meet you," replied Adriano. "This is my associate, Salvatore."

Giuseppe nodded to the big man standing next to Don Adriano before replying, "I offer to you my condolences on the death of Don Biscotti. I know the two of you were close."

"He was a dear friend of mine. He will be missed. I'm sure I don't have to tell you the turmoil that his death brings to the region."

"No, you do not. It has been on the forefront of my mind and on the minds of all of the villagers of Bellafortuna since we heard the news. Do you know who killed him?"

"Not yet. But that death is what brings me here. I have come to meet with you and the priest."

"Monsignor Mancini?"

"No, the young priest who just arrived here."

Surprised, Giuseppe asked, "Father Giulio Gianuzzi?"

"*Si*, him."

"You know him?"

"I do."

"He should be over at the rectory."

"*Bene*. I have an urgent matter that I need to discuss with him, and with you."

"Me, Don Umbretto?'

"Yes, you. Let's go now."

Giuseppe turned toward Kurt. "I will be right back. Tell Maria I went over to the church if she is looking for me."

Giuseppe, Adriano, and Salvatore departed the wine store. Giancarlo was standing outside by the car.

"We are going to the church. Stay by the car, Giancarlo. We won't be too long," Adriano said.

"Yes, sir," he replied.

They crossed the piazza to the church. Adriano asked Giuseppe about the summer opera festival and how he would love to come to the opera again as he did many years ago and bring his daughter. He told Giuseppe about the beauty of her voice. They reached the rectory and knocked on the door.

The door was opened by Monsignor Mancini.

Giuseppe said, "Monsignor, you remember Don Adriano Umbretto?"

"Of course. Nice to see you again, Don Umbretto."

"Pleasure to see you as well," replied Adriano. "This is my associate, Salvatore."

"Pleasure. How can I be of assistance, Don Umbretto?" Monsignor Mancini asked.

"I need to speak to Father Gianuzzi."

Surprised, Monsignor Mancini asked, "Father Gianuzzi?"

"Yes. You may join us in my meeting with him. I have the most urgent of matters to discuss with all of you."

"He should be in his office. Come, follow me."

Monsignor Mancini led them down a small hallway to an office at the end of the hall. Monsignor Mancini knocked on the door, and a voice inside said to enter.

Monsignor Mancini entered first. Father Gianuzzi was seated behind his desk. As Giuseppe walked into the office, the young priest looked up and nodded toward him. When Adriano and Salvatore entered the room last, Father Gianuzzi's eyes suddenly widened, and he quickly stood up from behind the desk.

Monsignor Mancini said, "Father Giulio, may I introduce …"

Adriano cut off the Monsignor in mid-sentence and said, "*Buona sera*, Giacomo."

The young priest gulped hard and responded to Adriano, "*Buona sera*," before pausing momentarily and finishing his greeting by saying, "Papa."

A BREAK FROM THE FAMILY

With those words uttered by Father Gianuzzi, Giuseppe and Monsignor Mancini looked at each other in dumbfounded shock. Adriano turned to Monsignor Mancini and said, "Please close the door. This meeting between my son and me, does involve all of you. But what is spoken here is for our ears alone, just the five of us."

As Monsignor Mancini went to close the door, the young priest, visibly shaken, took a seat behind his desk. His mind suddenly was filled with images of his past and the decisions he had made many years ago.

In 1937, Giacomo Umbretto was just 17 years old. At that time, he was living in exile with his parents and his sister, Francesca, who was only 8 years old then. Luca Sperenza, who was Don Adriano's only remaining associate since being forced to flee, also resided with the family. At that time, they were all living in the small farmhouse in the hills close to Selinunte.

The home sat on the top of one of the many rolling hills in the area. Adriano, with the assistance of Giacomo and Luca, worked the nearby fields, which provided the family with all of their needs.

One September afternoon, Adriano was out checking some of his crops, where he was joined by Giacomo and Francesca. Santa was home cooking dinner while Luca was working in fields further away from the farmhouse. When Adriano completed his work for the day, he and his children made their way back to the home. They played hide and seek among the crops on the way back.

At one point, Adriano, trying to find his children, walked out of the crops and onto the dirt road that led toward the farmhouse. Just as he did so, a car came barreling down the road away from the area of his farmhouse. Adriano was surprised to see a car on the road, as he was not expecting anyone today. As the car passed, Adriano's heart raced as he got a quick glimpse of the man in the back seat of the car. It was none other than Don Vincente Genovese. The car sped on down the road. Adriano's mind flashed to his farmhouse and to Santa who was home alone.

Adriano stepped back inside the crops, quickly calling for his children to stop playing and to come out of their hiding spots at once. They ignored their father at first, thinking he was still playing with them. But when he yelled out again in a more commanding tone, they knew he was no longer playing. They came out of their hiding spots and followed their father home. He said not a word on the way back, walking at a brisk pace that made it hard for his children to keep up.

Adriano had a feeling of dread. He hoped he was worried for nothing. But something kept telling him he had every reason to worry.

When they reached the farmhouse, Adriano noticed the front door was wide open, He told his children to wait outside, until he called for them. His children complained, but stood outside as Adriano entered the home.

He entered the kitchen, calling for Santa. His calling went unanswered. He looked around the kitchen and noticed a bowl of salad that was spilled upon the floor.

He yelled again for his wife, but again received no answer in return. He quickly made his way to his bedroom. The moment he walked into the room, he fell to his knees. Above him, Santa was swinging naked from the end of a rope from the main beam in the ceiling. Just then from behind him, Adriano heard the bloodcurdling screams of his children who had disobeyed him and had entered the farmhouse and came to the bedroom.

Both of his children had collapsed on the floor. Adriano ran over to Francesca and picked her up in his arms. The image of Vincente Genovese in the car resonated in his mind. Adriano held Francesca tightly, holding her face away from the sight of her mother gently swinging back and forth at the end of the rope. Giacomo was sobbing loudly on the floor.

"Come, Giacomo. Come to the kitchen," ordered Adriano.

"She is dead, Papa. She is dead."

"I know, Giacomo. Come to the kitchen."

Giacomo stood up, but before leaving the bedroom, he glanced one more time at his beloved mother's body.

As they left the bedroom and headed to the kitchen, Luca entered the farmhouse. The children's tears made him quickly realize something was wrong.

Adriano said, "Luca. It's Santa. In the bedroom. Cut her down for me and lay her on the bed. I'll keep the children here."

Luca, in disbelief, responded, "Cut her down. What happened?"

Adriano replied, "Vincente Genovese finally took his revenge."

Giacomo was crying with his head down on the dining table in the kitchen. He lifted his head and stared at his father. His emotions went quickly from pain to anger.

Luca left the kitchen and went to perform his morbid task.

A little while later, Luca was inside the kitchen with Francesca. Adriano was outside with Giacomo in a heated discussion.

Giacomo said, "Vincente Genovese. You keep saying Vincente Genovese did this."

"That's right. I know he did it."

"No, Papa. You did this. Your choice of life did this. You killed Mama. You did it."

Adriano stammered, "How dare you say such things to me."

"What would you expect. You dragged her from her home. You made her move to Gangi. Then you made her go into exile with you. Yet, you never could escape your past. And today it caught up with you. Vincente Genovese took his revenge. This life you lead, this life of revenge, of vendettas, and of violence, you put Mama in harm's way. Your hands have her blood on them."

Unable to control his anger, Adriano replied, "Go away from me. I don't want to see you."

"Great. I don't want to see you either." Giacomo turned and began to walk into the farmhouse. However, he stopped, and turning to his father once again, he said, "As a matter of fact, I don't want to see you ever again." Giacomo turned and ran inside the home.

Adriano stayed outside, trying to calm himself down from the argument with Giacomo.

Meanwhile, Luca, who had heard the fight, left Francesca in the kitchen momentarily and went to the children's bedroom, where he found Giacomo stuffing his clothes inside a bag.

"What are you doing, Giacomo?"

"Leaving."

"Leaving? Where are you going?"

"Away from here. Away from him."

"Giacomo, he just lost the love of his life. The mother of his children. He's upset."

"As he should be. He killed her, Luca."

"He did no such thing."

"If he does not want to see me, I'll make it easy for him."

With that, Giacomo picked up his bag and walked out of his bedroom and into his parents' bedroom. Luca followed behind him.

Santa was laid out on the bed. She looked to be asleep, but Giacomo knew better. Luca had placed her hands as if in prayer on her chest. Giacomo bent down and kissed her. He looked up and glanced out the window of the bedroom. He could just climb out the window and run down the road. But he changed his mind.

Luca left the bedroom and went back to the kitchen, and sat on the floor with Francesca, where she was playing with a doll. He could see Adriano out the front window, crying.

Giacomo walked into the kitchen carrying his bag.

"Take care of her, Luca."

"Where are you going?"

"Away from him and his life. Protect her, Luca. Don't let her suffer the same fate as my mother."

Giacomo bent down and kissed Francesca on the top of her head. Tears began rolling down his face.

Luca pleaded, "Don't go, Giacomo."

"*Addio*, Luca."

Giacomo left the kitchen, glancing one last time at Francesca.

"Where do you think you are going?" asked Adriano when Giacomo walked outside the farmhouse.

"Away. I wanted to jump out the window in your bedroom after I told Mama goodbye and just leave without seeing you. But I wanted to at least say goodbye."

"If you think I'm going to apologize for the life I have led, you are gravely mistaken. I lived my life the way I had to. I confronted every curve in the road, and continued on the path that was set forth in front of me. You may disagree with my choices, but you did not walk the path that I had to walk. You question things that I did. You. You are but a boy. Nothing but a boy. A boy who has grown up under my protection."

"Protection? Like the protection you offered Mama. You killed her, and because of it, you are dead to me."

Adriano clenched his teeth and swung his right hand, slapping Giacomo's face.

Giacomo rubbed his cheek and then stood up straight, putting his chest forward. He said in a defiant tone, "Don't look for me. Don't ever look for me."

Adriano reached toward his son and tried to grab his shoulder, saying, "Giacomo, I did not mean to do that. You made me angry."

"Goodbye, Papa."

With that, Giacomo quickly ran down the path away from the farmhouse.

Adriano's urge was to chase after him but knew he could not catch him. He stood outside the farmhouse, watching his son leave.

ADRIANO THOUGHT once his son got over his grieving, he would surely return. But he had not returned later that evening. By the end of a week, he still had not returned. Adriano began to use his contacts all across Sicily to search high and low for the whereabouts of Giacomo. It was around that time that Adriano met Salvatore Battaglia. Adriano had been told by an acquaintance that if you needed to find someone, Salvatore was the best person to hire to find them. It was about a month and a half after Giacomo had left that Salvatore informed Adriano that he successfully had tracked his son's whereabouts. Through Salvatore's connections with the Archbishop of Palermo, it was discovered that Giacomo had entered the *Seminario Vescovile di Acireale* (Seminary of

Acireale.) It was the oldest Catholic seminary in Sicily, having been founded in 1881.

Adriano made the trek to the eastern coast of Sicily and to the city of Acireale. There he met with the rector of the seminary, who informed Adriano that his son was now known as Giulio Gianuzzi. Although Giacomo refused to see his father, the rector was adamant with his young seminarian that a meeting take place. In the small chapel inside the seminary, Adriano met with his son and pleaded for his return. His son remained quiet the entire time until he finally said simply, "I am with my true father now." He got up and left his father alone in the church, who began to weep loudly. That was the last time Adriano had seen his son.

When Adriano returned home, he told both Luca and Francesca that he had confirmation that Giacomo was dead. The both of them believed that to be the case over all of these years. Adriano continued using his contacts to keep track of his son. And once Salvatore came to work for Adriano, one of his jobs was always keeping tabs on Giacomo. It was Salvatore who informed Adriano that his son had been ordained to the priesthood and that his first assignment was to the small village of Bellafortuna.

ONLY ADRIANO and Giacomo seemed to be the participants at the meeting inside the rectory, as Giuseppe and Monsignor Mancini said not a word, still in shock as to the revelation about the true identity of the young priest.

Adriano laid out his plan to his son, who listened in

silence. At one point, Adriano said, "Giacomo, Luca has been murdered."

Tears welled up in Giacomo's eyes.

"These same people tried to kill me," Adriano continued. "They succeeded in taking down Biscotti. I fear for your sister's life."

Giacomo rose to his feet from behind his desk and looked directly at his father before saying, "I have not seen you for ten years. I have not seen Francesca since she was 8 years old. You said she believes that I am dead. But today, out of nowhere, you show up in my office and ask for my help."

Salvatore interjected, "If you have any love for your sister, you will do what your father asks of you."

Giacomo turned quizzically toward Salvatore and asked sarcastically, "And who are you?"

Adriano said, "Giacomo, Salvatore is one of my closest associates."

Giacomo replied, "Of course, I love my sister. And of course, I would do anything to protect her."

Adriano's face showed relief. He replied to his son. "Take her in. Here in the village. She will not know that you are her brother. It's probably better that way. But it will allow you to watch over her."

"Where will she live?" asked Giacomo. "She can't live in the rectory."

"I'm sending her to you with Marco, one of my most trusted men, and the nephew of Salvatore. Francesca and Marco will come here pretending to be husband and wife, married just a short time ago. By pretending to be married to Marco, he will be in a position to protect her at all times. They will say they are related to someone in the village and they moved here for a bit."

Salvatore added, "That's the reason they are here. To stay with relatives."

Monsignor Mancini interjected for the first time. "I don't mean to interrupt. But she can be related to me. That way both myself and Father Gianuzzi can keep an eye on her as well."

Giuseppe added, "I will speak to my wife, but I'm sure they can live with us. We will have our eyes on her as well."

Adriano nodded. "*Bene.* I will provide Marco with funds to provide to you, *Signor Sanguinetti,* for your willingness in taking her in under your roof. Salvatore will come by often to check in as well, and to report how everything is going here back to me and of any concerns I should be made aware of."

Giacomo looked at Monsignor Mancini and Giuseppe before saying, "I'm glad you are all willing to help. But it's my decision if I agree to this plan or not."

Adriano said, "I know you are disappointed in me. But you have never truly understood how I have had little control over the events of my own life. My parents and brother were killed when I was but a child. My grandfather and grandmother were killed thereafter, and I was left alone in the world. I was taken in by a man who loved me. He happened to be in the business and he raised me in that business. My first true love, I found her nude, raped, and with a bullet hole in her head. I never thought I would find love ever again, but I did, and then Mussolini forces me to live with my family in the hills like a bandit. And my wife is soon found ravaged and swinging from the end of a rope. A man of honor, Don Biscotti, who was like my brother is killed, along with a young man who was like a son to me. The only thing I have control over at this point is putting Francesca somewhere safe. You are the only option I have."

Giacomo rubbed his mouth with his hand while deep in thought. He finally said, "At any point, you could have chosen a different path. It may have been difficult. It may have led you through the woods or rocky terrain. But ultimately, you would have found a path, a better path. But you kept down that path that led to destruction. A path lined with corpses because of your choices. As I told you 10 years ago, your actions brought death to my mother. But, even with that said, I will do whatever is necessary to protect Francesca, my beloved little sister. Rest assured, I do so not for you, but for her and for her alone."

Adriano bit his lip as he wanted to correct his son but thought better of it. He simply replied, *"Grazie."* He then followed up with, "In two days she will come here with Marco, driven over here by Salvatore. I will be in Monreale."

"Why Monreale, Don Adriano?" asked Giuseppe.

"To defeat the enemy who is trying to take it over. I will join forces with Biscotti's men, and fight this war."

Giacomo added, "And I will protect Francesca with my life if I have to."

Giuseppe smiled, "I hope you are successful in that war, Don Umbretto."

With that, the meeting came to an end. Leaving Giacomo in his office, they all walked into the hallway. Adriano said, "I thank the both of you for your willingness to help." He then turned to Giuseppe and said, "I particularly thank you for taking my daughter into your home. I know my plan envisions Francesca and Marco coming to your village as husband and wife, as that will afford her the most protection. I leave her honor in your hands. Marco will be sleeping in the same room with her." He paused and said, "But you will make sure he sleeps on the floor."

Giuseppe said, "I will speak to my wife, and will arrange the bedroom to give them both privacy. We will watch them closely."

"*Bene,*" replied Adriano.

They left the rectory and entered the piazza. Adriano said, "I don't need to tell both of you that my children's true identity must always remain a secret. Otherwise, it would be dangerous for them both, as well as for the village."

Giuseppe said to Adriano, "War is coming to Monreale. I fear for Bellafortuna as well."

"As well you should. We don't know who the enemy is, but you have my word, I will fight this enemy in Monreale, and I will defend Bellafortuna with all of my heart and soul. After all, my children will be here."

They reached his car. Giancarlo opened the back door and let Adriano in.

"*Grazie,*" Adriano said to Giuseppe and Monsignor Mancini. "Thank you for your help. Now I go back to Castelvetrano. Francesca and Marco will be here in two days, and I will be in Monreale. Take care of them."

Giancarlo and Salvatore got in, and with a final wave from Adriano, the car pulled out of the piazza.

Once gone, Giuseppe turned to Monsignor Mancini and smirked. He said, "Well, for better or worse, we will soon have both the son and daughter of one of the most powerful Dons in Sicily living right here in Bellafortuna."

"And their father stationed right over in Monreale. He will protect them, and in so doing, will hopefully protect us."

"Amen to that, Pietro. Amen to that."

Monsignor Mancini asked, "And if he wins the war, what happens to Bellafortuna?"

Giuseppe shrugged. "I know what happens if he loses. That's for certain."

"I might as well bring it up. I know Don Adriano wants no one to know the identity of his children. But, do you think the *Società* should be told who will be moving into the village and the true identity of our young priest?"

Giuseppe took a deep breath. "Against what I know is right, I say no. Not at this time. Perhaps that is best for now."

"You're probably right."

Giuseppe said, "I know it's strange that we are involved in protecting the daughter of a Don, but it affords our little village the protection it will need in the upcoming war. It's as if an answer to our question as to how to protect ourselves fell into our lap. I think we welcome her here and protect her. Our action is selfish, no doubt. I also know our village cannot save Sicily from the scourge of the Mafia. But if we take certain actions that protect our little world here and our fellow citizens, then I say so be it."

"I agree. And the *Società* will understand if and when they find out."

"I guess that depends on the ultimate result. I know we are putting our trust in Don Umbretto. Yet, from what I know of him, he is a man of honor. A man of tradition, at least in the world of the Mafia that is."

"I think we have no other option."

"I wonder what truly happened between Adriano and his son."

"I wonder as well. Let me go back to the rectory to speak with Giacomo, or Father Gianuzzi, or whatever we are to call him. He must be upset from his visitor tonight."

"Strange times, Pietro."

"Indeed, strange. Strange and very dangerous."

"Take care. I'll see you later."

"*Addio*, Giuseppe."

READY FOR A FIGHT

Two days later, Francesca was in her bedroom inside the villa. She finished closing her two suitcases that had been lying open on the bed. She had finally come to grips with her father's plan. She actually looked forward to leaving. She no longer felt safe in the villa. There was a knock on the door. She opened the door, and Marco walked into the bedroom.

"Ready, *Signorina Francesca*?"

She placed her hands on her hips. "If you are going to be my husband from this point forward, then you better just call me Francesca."

He laughed. "I understand, *Signori...*" He stopped and corrected himself, "Francesca."

She chuckled. "Now you have it, Marco. Do you know where we are going?"

"I do not. I know your father did not tell us when he laid

out his plan. I guess he wants to make sure no one knows where you are going."

"Do you think my father is correct in sending me away?"

"If you were my daughter, I would do whatever I needed to do to protect you. Your father knows what he is doing. I owe everything to that man. He knows I will protect you."

"And you will do so because you are following his orders. I have lived my entire life with people caring for me, watching over me, speaking with me, not because of who I am, but merely because their boss ordered them. If and when the time comes to protect me, my hope is that you will do so not because of his orders, but because you want to. No one has ever done that for me." She paused and then said, "Never mind. I'm talking out of my head. Forget what I'm saying. I have finally come to accept my father's plan. But I want to tell you something."

"What? What do you want to tell me?"

"I have never had a boyfriend. And now suddenly I am supposed to act like I am a married woman. Let me know if I'm doing it wrong."

"You think I know. I've never had a girlfriend or been married either."

"I guess we will learn together. Let's go."

"Yes, *Signori*...." He caught himself again and then said, "Francesca. Salvatore is waiting for us."

"He scares me."

"He's fine. He's the person you want with you in a dark alley in Palermo."

She picked up her suitcases and walked into the hallway with Marco. His two bags were sitting outside the bedroom. His *lupara* was leaning up against one of them. He slung the *lupara* over his shoulder and picked up his bags, and then Marco and Francesca walked down the hallway together.

Meanwhile, Salvatore pulled a car into the courtyard of the villa. Adriano walked up to him as he exited the vehicle. Adriano spoke directly to him so no one else could hear.

"Drive them directly to Bellafortuna. Do not pass through Monreale."

"Yes, Don Adriano," replied Salvatore.

"After you drop them off, come meet me in Monreale."

"I shall."

Adriano inched closer and said, "Tell no one where you brought her. Do you understand?"

"I do, and I swear upon the grave of my mother, I will remain silent."

Just then, Francesca and Marco walked into the courtyard with Giancarlo. They carried their bags in their hands. Adriano had told the other members of his *cosca* that she was going to Monreale to be with him.

Francesca walked over to her father and kissed him.

"Take care of yourself and be safe," he told her.

She climbed into the car.

Meanwhile, Marco walked over to Adriano and said, "You have my word I will protect her."

Adriano leaned over and whispered into his ear. "I know you are supposedly married. If you touch her, I will come find you and personally cut your balls off, and then stuff them down your throat."

Marco gulped hard and said again, "I promise I will protect her."

Marco got in the car, and Salvatore drove out of the gate of the courtyard.

Don Adriano Umbretto stood silently by the open gate as he watched the car taking his daughter away. Giancarlo walked over to him. He said to his boss, "Salvatore was correct in his recommendation to you. You made the right choice."

"I hope so. Are we ready for the meeting with the men before I leave for Monreale? Just one last meeting to discuss the measures in place protecting the villa while I am gone."

"Yes, the men are ready to meet. I will protect the villa while you are gone."

"Round them up, Giancarlo."

"Yes, sir."

As Giancarlo left him, Adriano slowly began to walk toward the villa, but before entering, he stopped and looked out the gate down the road. He could no longer see the car. He went inside.

———

LATER THAT DAY, Adriano arrived in Monreale with his handpicked *cosca* members accompanying him. He arrived at Biscotti's villa, which had been, many years before, the home of Don Calcedonio Umbretto and the very home where Adriano had been raised by his grandfather. Biscotti's men welcomed Don Adriano outside the villa, along with the six *cosca* members Adriano had brought with him.

As his men unpacked the cars, Adriano introduced himself to each of Biscotti's men, who kneeled and kissed his right hand. They thanked him profusely for coming to assist them. He promised he would flush out the enemy and bring war upon them.

It was not lost on Adriano that the last time he had stood in this spot was when his grandmother had kissed him goodbye before he departed to live with Don Spatuzza.

He walked to the front door and into the villa. He had not been back to this place since he was twelve years old. The images and sounds of his childhood and of his grandparents came flooding back to him.

His thoughts were interrupted when some of the household staff came up and introduced themselves. After the introductions, Adriano called Ferruccio over, who had just entered the villa. The household staff began to take Don Adriano's luggage to his bedroom upstairs.

Ferruccio said, "This place is stunning."

"It was once the home of one of the most powerful and great Dons Sicily has ever seen, Don Calcedonio Umbretto. Ferruccio, there is a dining room down the hall. Arrange a meeting with our men and Biscotti's men in an hour."

"Yes sir."

"I'm going to unpack. See you in an hour."

As Adriano began to walk up the stairs, he stopped momentarily and thought about Francesca and Giacomo. A smile came to his face as he thought about how his children would be together.

He continued up the stairs to his bedroom. He was back home.

MOVING INTO BELLAFORTUNA

Francesca and Marco arrived early that Sunday afternoon in Bellafortuna, when most of the inhabitants of the small village were sitting out in the *Piazza Santa Croce*, enjoying the spectacular weather.

Salvatore had pulled the car into the piazza and dropped them off right in front of *Il Paradiso*. Giuseppe and Maria met the young couple as they exited the car.

"*Benvenuti*. Welcome to Bellafortuna and to our home," stated Giuseppe.

Marco extended his hand toward Giuseppe, and as they shook hands, he said, "Nice to meet you, *Signor Sanguinetti*. My name is Marco Moretti." He smiled and then said, "And this, as you know, is my wife, Francesca."

"It's very nice to meet the both of you as well. This is my wife, Maria."

Maria said, "Welcome to the both of you."

"I thank you both for your willingness to assist us," Francesca replied.

"Come, we will show you to your room," replied Giuseppe.

Marco and Francesco removed their luggage from the trunk.

Salvatore walked to the back of the vehicle and extended his hand to Marco. "Be safe, nephew," he said. "I'll be back now and then to check on you."

"*Grazie,*" replied Marco.

"*Signora Francesca,* take care of yourself," said Salvatore.

"I shall."

"*Addio* to the both of you."

Salvatore then walked over to where Giuseppe was standing. Under his breath he whispered to Giuseppe, "Keep her safe, *Signor Sanguinetti.*"

Giuseppe only nodded his head in return.

As Salvatore climbed into the car, Marco and Francesca followed Giuseppe and Maria inside *Il Paradiso* and up to the living quarters.

Maria walked them into her son's old bedroom. A single bed sat against the nearby wall. A small curtain sat on a cord that split the room in two; however, it was pulled off to one side. A bedroll was in the far corner of the room opposite the bed. Once the curtain was closed, the bed and the bed roll would be completely separated.

Giuseppe carried Francesca's bags into the room. When he placed them down, he turned to Marco, who was behind him carrying his own bags. His *lupara* was hanging on his shoulder. Giuseppe pointed to the curtain. "I promised her father. Please pull it closed at night. And act like you have separate rooms. Also, the bedroom door is to always remain open."

"I promise," replied Marco. He placed his bags down and stood the *lupara* in the corner near his bedroll.

Maria, meanwhile, was speaking with Francesca. "Make yourself at home. If you need anything, please let me know."

"I will. *Grazie*," replied Francesca.

Giuseppe said to both of them, "Unpack, and then come meet me down in the wine store. Your father, Francesca, mentioned how much you love music. I want to show you around our little village and someplace that is very special to me."

"I would like that very much. Marco and I will be down in a bit."

Giuseppe looked at both of them and said, "You will be safe here. I promise."

Francesca smiled and said in reply, "My father must have known what he was doing in sending me here to you. I trust you when you say that I will be safe."

"We will see you both downstairs," replied Giuseppe.

The Sanguinettis departed the bedroom.

Francesca turned to Marco and said, "Well, here we are. My father's plan has been put into action. Do you think *Signor Sanguinetti* is correct that I am safe here?"

He walked over to his *lupara* and picked it up. He placed it on his shoulder. "Yes. I think you are safe. And on top of everything, this place is beautiful. Let's go see it all with *Signor Sanguinetti*."

They began to leave the room, and as they did so, Francesca slipped her hand into his. "Isn't this what we are supposed to do."

Marco smiled as they departed the room and went downstairs to the wine store.

When they walked into the wine store, Giuseppe advised Marco the *lupara* would not be necessary. Marco took it off and placed it behind the store counter.

Giuseppe told the couple, "Let's go see Bellafortuna."

Giuseppe took the young couple around the main square first, introducing them to some of the villagers out in the piazza. Giuseppe made sure to say that Francesca was a relative of Monsignor Mancini's and that they would be staying with Giuseppe for an extended time in the village.

Shortly thereafter, Kurt Hofmann brought Giuseppe's horse and cart around from the Pandolfini stables.

"Francesca and Marco, this is Kurt. He works with me."

"Pleasure to meet the both of you," Kurt replied as he climbed down out of the cart.

"Where are we going, *Signor Sanguinetti*?" asked Francesca.

"Down to the valley. I want to show you something."

As Giuseppe and Francesca climbed into the cart, Marco quietly asked Giuseppe, "Are you sure I shouldn't take my *lupara*?"

"No, Marco. You don't need that here." He paused and said, "Not yet. And on top of that, you would stick out like a sore thumb in our little world here."

Marco hopped aboard, and the cart made the short trek down to the valley.

GIUSEPPE TOOK them first to the Boccale Winery, where they met with Santo, along with his wife and son. They also took a very brief tour of the wine facility. Giuseppe followed that visit with a trip to *Antica Campanèlla*, which was the original location of the village down in the valley before a devastating earthquake forced the move from the valley to its present hilltop location under the guidance of Enzo Boccale. With that move came the new name for the village, *Bellafortuna* (Beautiful fortune).

Antica Campanèlla still contained remnants of the old buildings which once stood there, now overgrown with weeds. Nearby was the abandoned chapel, the *Capella di Campanèlla*, which sat on the banks of the beautiful and tranquil *Stagno Azzurro*. Very near the ruins of the chapel were gates that led to the ancient Greek Amphitheater, the *Anfiteatro di Bellafortuna*. This had now become the place where the village of Bellafortuna held its summer opera festival. Before the War, Sicilians from all over the island would make the trek over to the amphitheater to enjoy the opera performances. Giuseppe was the head of the festival, and it was his brainchild many years ago that brought this place to fruition.

As they walked through the gates, Giuseppe said, "This is where I bring the most perfect art form in the world to my people. This is where we hold our summer opera performances. Some of the greatest singers have graced this stage."

Francesca took in the sight of the rows of stone benches leading down toward the amphitheater stage. She said to Giuseppe, "My father came here once with my late brother. But with the rise of the fascists and then the War, my father never came back. My voice teacher always would tell me about this place. She used to come here to see performances."

"Perhaps you can bring your voice teacher here again, *Signora Francesca.*"

Francesca looked down and said, "That's one of the reasons I am here, *Signor Sanguinetti.* She was murdered by the very same men who are out to get my father."

"I'm sorry to hear that. I truly am."

"*Signor Sanguinetti,* I want to be fair to you and to your villagers. Do you know what you are getting yourself into by allowing me here?"

Giuseppe was quiet for a moment and then replied, "I do. And we welcome you. This place, this village, these people, they are good, decent people who love life. They love each other. They love God. They love music. Yes, music. Music is in their soul. Music gives them a purpose beyond their everyday life. Music is the pulse of our community. Your father raves about your voice. Go on the stage and sing something for us."

"*Scusi.* Sing now?"

"Yes. Just for me and Marco. A solo concert of one song."

She shrugged her shoulders. "Any suggestions?"

"Puccini. Anything Puccini," replied Giuseppe.

She walked over to the stage and walked up the three steps that led to it. Marco and Giuseppe walked down the second row and took a seat on the stone bench directly in the middle.

Francesca stood near the front of the stage and announced, "*Si, mi chiamano Mimi* from *La Bohème.*"

Giuseppe clapped his hands and settled in. Francesca began the aria. Her phrasing was exquisite, and her singing of the famed aria was delicate in the beginning. However, when she reached the part of the aria about the warmth of spring, her voice opened, and she poured forth an emotion that made the hair on Giuseppe's arms stand up. As she sang about the pedals of a flower, her voice played with the words, punctuating each syllable. When she reached the end of the aria, both Giuseppe and Marco were on their feet, cheering.

Giuseppe quickly left his seat and ran up the stairs of the stage. He extended his hands to her.

"Bellisimo, Signora Francesca. Bellisimo."

"That means so much to me, knowing all the great singers you have heard from this stage."

"Your voice is outstanding. I will have to have you sing at our next Saturday concert in the piazza."

"I would love to."

"I'll introduce you to Vincenzo Occipinti, our conductor, and a great vocal coach at that. He will work with you this week to prepare you to sing Saturday."

"I can't wait. It will be great to start singing again."

Just then, Marco joined the duo on the stage. He said, "I'm a very proud husband."

They all laughed as Giuseppe said, "Well, I hope you enjoyed your tour down here in the valley. We only have one more stop."

Francesca replied, "Marco and I have both been blown away by the beauty of your village."

"Wonderful. Now, let's go to our last stop."

They walked out of the amphitheater and over to the cart and horse parked at the gates. They climbed aboard and began the ascent toward the village.

Giuseppe spoke to the couple the entire time as they made their way from the valley and back up to the village. He pulled the cart into the piazza and parked it by the rectory. Giuseppe told them, "Come, I want to introduce you to our two priests here in the village."

They all climbed out of the cart and made their way to the front door of the rectory. Their knock was answered by Monsignor Mancini.

Giuseppe said, "Monsignor Mancini, may I introduce you to your relatives, Francesca and her husband, Marco."

Monsignor Mancini extended his hand to her. "It's a pleasure to meet you. Pleasure to meet you both."

"Thanks for your willingness in assisting me, Monsignor," stated Francesca.

Footsteps behind Monsignor Mancini made him suddenly turn away toward the hallway as he noticed Father Gianuzzi coming to the door. Monsignor Mancini said, "Francesca and Marco, this is Father Giulio Gianuzzi. He knows why you are here."

The young priest stepped into the doorway as he intently bore his gaze at the beautiful young woman standing in front of him. He slowly extended his hand to her. His eyes never left hers. He clasped her hand and said, "It's is so good to meet you. I'm glad you are here."

She smiled back at him and replied, "We are glad to be here as well."

Giuseppe interjected, "They have had a long day of sightseeing. I'm sure Maria has a nice plate of food ready for them. I just wanted to come introduce them."

"*Ciao*," replied Father Gianuzzi. "We will see you both around."

"*Buona sera*, Father. *Buona sera*, Monsignor," said Francesca.

"*Buona sera*, my child," said Monsignor Mancini as the two priests disappeared into the rectory.

LATER THAT EVENING, after dinner, a perfectly prepared *Pasta Bolognese* by Maria, the couple sat at a table outside *Il Paradiso*. The *Piazza Santa Croce* was empty so late in the evening on a Sunday.

Francesca and Marco sat at the table with the Sanguinettis enjoying a glass of *Vino di Bellafortuna*. They were soon joined by Monsignor Mancini and Father Gianuzzi. They made small talk until Giuseppe related to the two visitors the history of his village, beginning from the time he was a child. They were fascinated with his story as the entire group drank more and more wine. Father Gianuzzi was quiet during the entire time he was seated at the table, but he could not take his eyes off of Francesca.

After Giuseppe finished his stories, everyone retired to bed while the young couple sat alone at the table.

Marco said, "There is a little more wine in the bottle. Want some more?"

"No. I've really never had more than a glass with a dinner. I had enough."

"Mind if I finish it, and then we will go to bed."

"Sure, I don't mind."

Marco drained the bottle into his glass. As he did so,

Francesca asked, "Mind if I ask you a question? I've always wanted to ask, but never had the chance before. However, now that you are my husband and everything, I feel it is okay to ask."

He laughed and said, "Of course. Ask me anything."

"I know you told me before about your mother and father and how you ended up working for my father in the business. What do you exactly do for him?"

"A fair question. My abusive father eventually left my mother and me. My mother was a seamstress. We were poor. Very poor. My mother's brother is Salvatore Battaglia."

"He scares me."

Marco laughed as he said, "I know. And yes, he scares me as well. So, when your father was named Mayor of Castelvetrano, Salvatore spoke to him on my mother's behalf. Your father took me in. If he had not, I don't know where I would be today. Before the attack on your father, I guess you could say my job was to simply serve your father in anyway that I could. That all changed. Now my job is to protect you. He entrusted your care to someone he knew he could trust. Who better than Salvatore's nephew."

Francesca leaned forward across the table and asked quietly, "Have you killed for him?"

Marco frowned and said, "Don't ask me that. Never ask me that."

"I'm sorry. I know all about my father's business. I guess because of my own mother's death, I know more than most children. I pay attention. I listen. And I watch. You're not like my father's other men. You're different somehow. He even treats you differently. I do apologize for my question."

Marco replied, "It's fine. I have so much respect for your

father. Sicily is a brutal land. Politicians kill. Neighbors kill neighbors. Thugs and thieves roam the land. The police are corrupt. What your father offers to the residents is protection, law and order."

Francesca turned and looked around the piazza. She then said, "And in stark contrast to the brutality, sits this beautiful village."

"Indeed." He took his last sip and said, "Ready for bed?"

"I am."

They stood up as Marco picked up the two wine glasses. They walked inside, and he placed the glasses on the counter. As they began to walk up the stairs, Francesca slipped her hand into his. He wrapped his fingers around her hand.

When they reached their bedroom, Marco walked across the room and up to the curtain. He grabbed hold of it. Before he pulled it closed, he turned and said, *"Buona notte, Francesca."*

She smiled and replied, *"Grazie. Buona notte, Marco."*

He pulled the curtain shut, separating the room.

THE CALM BEFORE THE STORM

*E*arly on that Monday morning, Adriano was seated at a table in Don Biscotti's study. Salvatore, who had arrived yesterday after dropping off his passengers in Bellafortuna, sat with him.

"I guess they are settled in?" Adriano asked his *consigliere*.

"Indeed. *Signor Sanguinetti* met them and took them inside his store. I'm sure she will be safe there."

"Later today, join me in my final meeting with Biscotti's men. Tomorrow we will begin the process of bringing the rat out of his hole. Tomorrow, with Biscotti's people, we will arrange a meeting with the largest *pizzo* providers. They will start paying me, as they were paying Biscotti. Word of this will reach the rat that I have moved in for control. That will flush him out into the open."

"And then what?" asked Salvatore.

"A fight to the death. He will come for me. We will move against him. The winner takes the prize."

"If you lose, Don Adriano, what happens to your holdings back in Castelvetrano?"

Don Adriano was silent for a moment before saying, "We cannot lose."

There was nothing left to be said. Salvatore got up and told Don Adriano he would see him in a bit at the meeting, leaving Don Adriano alone in the study.

OVER THE COURSE of the next week, Adriano worked tirelessly with his men and Biscotti's men to solidify his control over Monreale. And as promised, he had his meeting with the landowners and instructed them that all future *pizzo* payments would be made to him, and in return, they would have the full protection of Don Adriano Umbretto.

The landowners were surprised yet extremely thankful that, once again, a member of the Umbretto family was in charge. All Adriano could do was wait. He knew word would reach the ears of whomever it was seeking control. They would have to come out of the darkness, and that's when Adriano would attack.

FRANCESCA, meanwhile, was slowly settling into her new life in Bellafortuna. Giuseppe did introduce her to Vincenzo Occipinti, who immediately began meeting with her in his home to practice for the upcoming concert. Marco never left her side. He would sit quietly across from the piano that was in Vincenzo's front room. Marco was always amazed at the beauty of Francesca's voice, but now even more so this up close to her. He also was becoming more and more infatuated with her. But it was an awkward "marriage."

They walked hand in hand together all around Bellafortuna, but that was the only outward sign of affection. Francesca enjoyed her time with Marco and was glad she was getting to know him. She knew a relationship with the nephew of Salvatore Battaglia was impossible, so she just relished being with him.

Francesca most enjoyed vocalizing every evening with *Signor Occipinti* and was excited to be singing arias at his request. They chose three arias for her to sing at the concert and practiced those three every evening. He was an even better teacher than *Signora Lydia.*

And then, every night after practice, she and Marco would end their day at the table outside of *Il Paradiso*, drinking wine, often joined by Giuseppe and Maria, and the two priests, before retiring to bed.

THAT SATURDAY USHERED in a gorgeous day in Bellafortuna. The village was abuzz that morning with excitement. Palm Sunday was the very next day, and the preparations for the Easter celebrations were in full swing. Francesca and Marco woke up on the day of her performance and, after getting dressed, made their way to Maria's kitchen, where a hot espresso was awaiting them.

Later, they went down to the wine shop, where they found Giuseppe speaking to Mirella Vasaio. But it was the gentleman who was standing with them who gave Francesca pause. It was none other than Salvatore Battaglia.

"Francesca," said Giuseppe, "look who stopped by."

"Nice to see you, *Signor Battaglia*," she replied.

"Francesca." And then turning toward Marco, he said, "Nephew. How goes everything?"

Marco replied, "It's been wonderful here, and Giuseppe and his wife take great care of us."

Giuseppe smiled and said, "I was telling Salvatore about your performance today. I asked him to stay and he has agreed."

Francesca feigned excitement as she said, "I'm glad."

Giuseppe said, "You remember *Signora Vasaio*."

"Of course. She gave us such a wonderful tour of the winery," replied Francesca.

Signora Vasaio replied, "Nice to see the both of you. I've been speaking to *Signor Battaglia* about the winery and I am taking him to meet my husband so he can have a look at our winery."

"She is a great tour guide," Marco said.

Salvatore looked toward Francesca and Marco and said, "Before I go, can I speak to the two of you for a moment, outside?"

They walked outside of *Il Paradiso*. Once outside, Salvatore got in close to the both of them and said to Francesca, "Why would you put yourself in front of all of these people? You are here to be protected. To blend into the shadows." He put his finger into Marco's chest. "You are supposed to be protecting her. Her father did not send her here to sing."

Marco hung his head as Francesca replied, "I was sent here for protection, but I still need to live my life."

"Your father would be disappointed in the both of you. You will not sing today."

Francesca's nostrils flared as she replied, "I'm going to sing. You can tell my father you tried to stop me. But I was adamant."

"You are not going to sing one note. Not one."

"Then I will let every person living in this village know my true identity. That is exactly what I will do, if you try to stop me. I'm singing today."

Marco shot a glance toward Francesca, shocked at her strength and courage.

"So be it," replied Salvatore. "It probably does not matter."

They all went back inside *Il Paradiso*. Salvatore said, "Well, *Signora Vasaio*, let's go see the winery so I can be back in time for Francesca's performance." He looked toward Marco and said, "I'll speak with you when I get back."

Marco gulped hard as Salvatore left the wine shop with *Signora Vasaio*. Giuseppe asked Francesca, "What time are you meeting Vincenzo?"

She replied, "At 10:30 this morning to practice one more time. Marco and I are going for a walk until then."

"I can't wait till our villagers hear your voice. I'll see the both of you later."

As they walked out of the wine shop together, Francesca's face was radiant with excitement.

"I stood up to him, Marco. I stood up to him."

Marco shrugged his shoulders and told her, "For better or worse, you certainly did."

"I want to be a singer. Today I have an opportunity to sing to people. He was not going to stop me."

"You are an amazing woman." He paused before saying, "And that's why I made you my wife."

They both laughed. Francesca slipped her hand into his as they walked across the piazza.

By mid-day, the piazza began filling with the inhabitants of Bellafortuna coming up from the vineyards and olive groves. They all settled around the piazza for their afternoon break. With the news that week of Biscotti's death, the villagers' mood was somber and worried.

As the orchestra began to set up, Giuseppe and Maria, carrying two chairs, placed them down next to other chairs that were near the front and took their seats. They were soon joined by the Vasaios and Salvatore.

"How was the wine tour?" asked Giuseppe.

"Amazing. The place is very impressive, and the Vasaios are terrific tour guides."

"He was quite attentive to everything," replied *Signora Vasaio.*

"And he knows his wine," added Santo.

Just then, Father Gianuzzi and Monsignor Mancini walked up. "*Buon giorno,*" the priests said.

They all told the priests hello, and everyone took their seats, just as Vincenzo Occipinti made his way across the piazza, walking with Francesca and Marco.

When they reached the orchestra, Marco whispered into Francesca's ear and then made his way over to the empty chair next to Salvatore. Francesca, wearing a simple but stunning, blue dress, walked with Vincenzo, who took his place in front of the orchestra. Francesca sat in the chair right in front of the orchestra, facing the crowd out in the piazza.

Vincenzo bowed to the crowd and asked the orchestra to stand. The villagers clapped for their beloved orchestra. Vincenzo turned. The orchestra sat down, and the Saturday afternoon concert began.

The Overture from Verdi's *La Forza del Destino* was the first selection. As the orchestra played, Francesca gazed out across the crowd. Nerves were creeping in, but she couldn't wait to do the thing she loved more than anything else in the world.

As the first musical selection ended, the crowd cheered. Vincenzo turned to the crowd. He said, "Today, we have a real treat. Monsignor Mancini's relative will be living in our little part of the world with her husband over the next few weeks. We are blessed because of it. She has a beautiful soprano voice, as you will be able to confirm for yourself in a few seconds. May I present, *Signora Francesca Moretti*."

From the moment she stood up from her chair, Father Gianuzzi never took his eyes off her. He sat up on the edge of his seat and folded his hands.

Francesca gracefully stood and moved to the front. The men out in the piazza all noticed her beauty. As she faced the crowd, she bowed. Once out of her bow, she said, "I will sing "Semper Libera" from Verdi's *La Traviata*.

She turned and nodded her head toward Vincenzo. He raised his baton, and the music began.

Verdi's aria requires a master singer to bring out all of the qualities of the piece. The singer must convey the character's mental state, torn between the call to true love, illness, and the pursuit of pleasure. The aria is known for its virtuoso runs and stunning high notes.

As Francesca's voice soared out across the piazza, the crowd sat in mesmerized silence. The villagers' sour mood disappeared due to the power of music. Giuseppe, a man with a deep love of music, sat in awe at Francesca's voice and her perfect legato. But what he found most impressive was her work in the *passagio*, that tricky part of the voice for a singer where the voice travels from the singer's chest and transfers over (or passes through, thus the term *passagio*) into the head voice, which allows the singer to reach the astronomical high notes with power.

As the aria drew to a close, Francesca hit the final note perfectly, as the villagers leaped from their seats and awarded her with a thunderous ovation. Salvatore leaned over to Marco and said with a smile, "Your wife's voice is spectacular."

Marco smiled back and said, "She is a wonderful woman."

Father Gianuzzi stood, staring at his sister, as a single tear tracked down his cheek, overcome with emotion.

Francesca bowed to the audience as Vincenzo clapped his hands, standing next to her. Francesca then took a step forward and said, "*Grazie.* Next, I will sing "Vissi darte" from Puccini's *Tosca.*

The crowd cheered and waited anxiously to hear her sing again. As her voice soared out, the listeners were entranced once again. After her final selection, "La mamma morta" from Giordano's *Andrea Chenier,* the crowd erupted. She bowed to the audience and then walked to the side as the orchestra completed the afternoon concert with two musical pieces. The concert ended with Kurt Hofmann taking his usual position and everyone joining in with the signing of the chorus from Verdi's *Nabucco*, the village anthem.

When the afternoon performance ended, many of the villagers rushed to Francesca. They offered their congratulations, telling her they hoped she would sing at every concert while she remained in Bellafortuna.

Giuseppe walked over to Father Gianuzzi and said, "She is wonderful."

"She has a fabulous voice," he replied.

Salvatore, meanwhile, told Marco, "This is on you. She is the talk of the entire village now. You have allowed her to be in danger now."

As the villagers began to leave the piazza to return to their work for the rest of the day, Francesca walked over to the chairs where Marco had been seated. As she approached, Giuseppe was the first to meet her. "You have brought happiness today to many."

"*Grazie, Signor Sanguinetti.* I owe this all to you. I was so nervous."

"There was no sound of nerves in your voice, not one."

Marco came up and kissed her on both cheeks. "Glorious, Francesca."

She raised her hand and patted him on his chest.

Father Gianuzzi came up with Monsignor Mancini, and they both offered their congratulations. Father Gianuzzi offered her his hand, which she took as he replied, "Beautiful."

Their conversation was cut short by Salvatore, who walked over to where Francesca was standing. "I'm leaving and returning to Monreale. I will tell your father about your performance. Rest assured; I'll be back to check in again."

Francesca said nothing in return. As Salvatore passed Marco, the young man said, "*Addio, Zio.*"

Salvatore pointedly said to him, "Do your job, Marco."

Salvatore turned and walked away.

Maria said to all those standing around Francesca, "Please, all of you, come by *Il Paradiso* tonight, and we will have a toast to Francesca.

They all agreed to come.

THAT NIGHT, Francesca and Marco sat at the table outside *Il Paradiso*, with the entire contingent of people Maria had asked to come. The village's priests were there, the Vasaios, the Hofmanns, as well as Vincenzo Occipinti. Maria and Giuseppe Sanguinetti had sat up an extra table outside their wine store as they all sat under the moonlight celebrating the events of earlier that day. The wine was flowing, with most of the group tipsy. As they all drained another bottle of wine, Giuseppe said, "The villagers were stunned at the beauty of your voice."

"*Grazie, Signor Sanguinetti.*"

Santo Vasaio added, "You are the second-best singer whose voice has ever echoed among the buildings surrounding the piazza."

She laughed and said, "Second-best, huh. Who was the first?"

Giuseppe replied, "You wouldn't believe him if he told you."

"Try me."

Santo said, "Tell her Maria."

"Enrico Caruso," Maria said in return.

Francesca replied, "You are joking?"

Giuseppe gave a broad smile and said, "Nope. He sang right here in our little village when I was a child. As a matter of fact, the room you are staying in is the very same room he slept in the night before."

"What did he sound like?"

Monsignor Mancini said, "The most glorious sound you ever heard."

Giuseppe added, "He made the hair on your arm stand up. Give me a moment."

Giuseppe walked into *Il Paradiso* and placed a record on the victrola close to the door. Soon the majestic voice of Caruso thundered out of the horn as the great tenor sang *Vesti la Giubba* from Leoncavallo's opera, *Pagliacci*. Upon completion of the aria, they all cheered.

Giuseppe said, "That's just a fraction of what he sounded like in person. He loved singing here and loved our little concert." Giuseppe went on to relate to both of them the story of how Caruso had come to the village as well as the significance and importance of the weekly concert and the orchestra.

When Giuseppe finished relating that history, another bottle was produced, and the drinking continued. Finally, Maria said, "Well, I think it's time to retire to bed. The wine has taken its effect."

They all laughed.

Giuseppe said, "I will end the night by saying again, your voice touched so many people today."

"*Grazie*, and thanks to all of you for your kind words."

With that, the group wished her a goodnight. The last was Father Gianuzzi, who reiterated to her how much he enjoyed her singing. After everyone had left, Giuseppe and Maria said they were going to bed. Francesca and Marco told them they were going to sit outside a little longer.

When the Sanguinettis had left, Marco asked her, "Another glass?"

"I've already had too many tonight. But it's so good."

As he poured her one more glass, he said, "These people loved your voice."

"Do you really think so? I hope so. I love this place and the people."

"Of course, they loved you. I heard them talking about you. The passion in your voice when you sing. It's hard to explain . . ."

As Marco tried to explain what her voice meant to him, Francesca was not focused on his words but instead on his expressions. He spoke animatedly, using his hands to punctuate his point. His dimples appeared with each smile and then would retreat as he chatted more. She had never had feelings for someone like this before. She drew her attention to his eyes and was smitten. So much so that she did not realize he had stopped talking.

"Um, did you hear me?"

She quickly gathered herself and picked up her wine glass. "Too much, I told you. I had too much. I'm sorry, what did you ask me?"

He laughed and repeated his question. "How do you sing those high notes?"

"With practice. A lot of practice."

"You will bring much joy to people in your life."

They finished their wine and then went to their bedroom, hand in hand once again. Before crossing the room, Marco turned to her and said, "You did really well today." He leaned over and kissed her cheek. She blushed.

He said, "Your face is red. Have you never been kissed before?"

She paused and then replied, "Not until just now."

He smiled at her. He then leaned in and kissed her on her lips.

When he pulled away, her face was even redder.

"I better go to bed," she said.

She stumbled when she turned.

"All good?" he asked with a chuckle.

She shrugged her shoulders and replied, "Just too much. Way too much."

He walked over to the curtain, turned to her, and said, *Buona notte*, Francesca."

"*Buona notte*, Marco."

He pulled the curtain shut.

She walked over to the dresser and pulled out her nightgown. She could still feel the blush of her face. Exhausted and drunk, she quickly got dressed and slipped into bed. When she laid down, she noticed that the curtain had not fully been closed. The moonlight coming through the window illuminated the entire room.

She was lying on her side in the bed and could see Marco standing with his back to the window with his shirt off. His chest and stomach were muscular. He turned toward the window and removed his pants. The top of his buttocks could be seen over his underpants. He turned and walked over to his bedroll. Her gaze went downward, and while staring at him, she suddenly felt an urge, a sensation that she had never felt before. He did not use a sheet, so when he laid down on the bedroll, his entire body was exposed to her view.

She rolled onto her back while the room began to spin in her drunken state. She continued looking at him. Her breathing picked up in pace. Her hand reached down, and she slowly hiked up her nightgown. She placed her hand between her legs and felt her underwear moist from her excitement. She had never had these feelings before. She lifted her hand and slid it under her underwear. She spread her legs even further as she began to move in rhythm. She fought the desire to moan out loud.

Her eyes remained locked on him until pleasure overcame her, forcing her legs to close. She closed her eyes tight and got lost in her sensations.

She rolled back onto her side and drifted off to sleep.

MEANWHILE, the little farmhouse on the land of the Donati family was alight with excitement. Men gathered in the study, some carrying their *luparas* while others had pistols.

Onofrio Fausto sat in the big chair facing the fireplace. He said not a word. His men let out a yell when Castranzio Fausto walked into the study toward the chair where his father was seated.

He said to his father, "All the cars are gassed up. We have the list. Two men for each person on the list."

Onofrio smiled. "And our other associates across Sicily all

are aware that tonight is the night when their service will be needed?"

"Indeed, father."

Onofrio smiled again as he stood up from his chair. He turned to all of the men in the room, who all listened intently. "Tonight, all of Sicily will tremble before us. Tonight, all of Sicily will remember us. Tonight is *Notte Oscura.*"

All the men in the study yelled in unison, "*Notte Oscura.*"

Onofrio Fausto raised his hand and shouted, "Let it begin."

The men quickly filed out of the study. The last to leave was Castranzio, who kneeled down and kissed his father's hand. "I will make you proud, Papa."

"*Notte Oscura, mio figlio.* Make them tremble."

Castranzio Fausto stood up and grabbed a pistol from the table. He then darted from the study and out the farmhouse to meet his men who were getting into the cars. Onofrio Fausto followed and stood in the doorway as his men started the cars.

As the cars began heading out, the headlights lit the dirt road. Onofrio Fausto stood alone in the darkness, watching as the cars traveled down the road. It was good to be back in Sicily. And tonight, everyone would know that he had returned to the land of his birth. And they would remember *Notte Oscura* for the rest of their lives.

PART III

THE MAFIA WAR

NOTTE OSCURA

A strong west wind blew across the valley of Bellafortuna during the pre-dawn hours on that Palm Sunday. The sound of the wind was what awakened Mirella Vasaio. She turned and looked at Santo's side of the bed. He had told her when they returned from *Il Paradiso* earlier that night that he would be in the wine cave for only an hour. But at this late hour, she noticed that the sheets and cover on that side of the bed were undisturbed. Santo would always be in bed by this time of the night, save the few times he had fallen asleep in the wine cave after a long day's work. He was most likely drunk from drinking with the Sanguinettis and had passed out in the wine cave, she thought.

She got up and pulled a robe on top of her nightgown. She passed by her son's bedroom, whose door was closed, and headed out the front door.

As she walked the dirt path leading to the wine cave, the

trees swayed in the howling wind as Mirella's nightgown bristled with each gust. The sky was littered with stars in the darkness. The smell of jasmine, with its distinct smell, permeated the air.

She came to the double doors of the wine cave, opened them, and then descended the stairwell. The still-lit lanterns that illuminated the cave below confirmed her belief that her husband had fallen asleep.

When she got to the bottom of the stairs, she saw her husband slumped over a wine barrel. She giggled to herself and said, "Poor man." She then called out, "Santo."

But there was no response. She walked over to him and gently placed her hand on his back. She shook him, saying, "Santo, wake up."

Her act of shaking him shifted his body just enough that he rolled off the barrel, falling to the ground face-up.

It was the blood on top of the wine barrel that first caught her attention. As she began to bend down toward him, the gruesome scene became clearer. The wine thief, which had been transformed into an instrument of death, protruded out of his right eye. His face was covered with blood.

Mirella screamed and fell to her knees next to her husband. "*Aiuto! Aiuto!*" she bellowed.

But no help came.

She suddenly heard a noise. She looked to her right as a man appeared from the shadows from behind the wine barrels.

She brought her hands up to her mouth. "You. But why?"

The man said not a word. He calmly walked over to her, reached down, and pulled her up by her hair.

"Please, please don't hurt me. I have a son."

He smiled at her and patted her cheek with his other hand, all the while holding her hair tightly with the other. He then pulled her close and forced her face toward his. He rammed his tongue deep inside her mouth as his hand quickly fondled her breast. She tried to push him away, but he was too strong. His hand left her breast and slipped around her neck, which was soon joined by his other hand.

Tears began flowing down her face. She brought her hands up and wrapped them around the man's hands, trying to remove them, which were now tightening even more around her neck. She tried to yell, but nothing came out. She then felt him pushing her toward the ground before everything went dark.

When her hands went limp and plopped down on either side of her, the man, knowing his job was complete, finally released his hands from around her neck. He picked up her body and laid it next to that of her husband's. Before leaving the wine cellar, he took his finger and dipped it in the blood on Santo's face. He then walked over to a wine barrel and, on the top of it, scribbled a short message with his bloody finger for all to see.

It simply read: *Onofrio Fausto è tornato.* (Onofrio Fausto has returned.)

He bent down and wiped his finger on Santo's pants and then made his way to the stairwell, leaving the dead bodies of Santo and Mirella Vasaio lying next to each other in the wine cave of Bellafortuna.

It was 4:30 that morning when Flavio opened the front door of Biscotti's villa. Two of Adriano's men, along with two of Biscotti's men, were standing guard outside. Flavio asked, "All quiet."

"Yes, sir," replied Ferruccio Fonsato. "Is the Don still sleeping?"

"Yes. Do any of you need anything?"

They all replied negatively.

Flavio asked, "Have you checked with Dondo by the back door?"

"Yes, I just came back from seeing him," Ferruccio responded.

Flavio looked at the men. "Stefano and some others will relive you at 6. Keep guard until then. Keep walking the grounds."

"We shall," they all replied.

Flavio retired back inside.

He went to the dining room and sat down at the table. He positioned his chair so he could watch the staircase leading upstairs and to the bedroom of Don Umbretto. The hallway was dark in the wee hours of the morning.

About fifteen minutes later, and while Flavio was fighting off the temptation to fall asleep, he heard voices by the backdoor. Flavio stood up and headed toward the backdoor of the villa.

As he walked down the hallway and approached the door, he could hear the knob turning. He reached for the knob and opened the door expecting to see Dondo Gufinisti coming inside. Instead, two men in dark clothes stumbled inside when he opened the door. One of the men held the limp, bloodied body of Dondo.

The two intruders were just as startled by Flavio as he was by them. Before Flavio could utter a word, the taller of the two men lifted a knife that he held in his hand and plunged it into Flavio's neck. He crumbled to the ground, blood pouring from his wound. The man went to his knees and hovered over Flavio. He clamped one hand over Flavio's mouth, which made his screams of pain muffled. The man removed the knife from Flavio's neck, lifted it high above his head, and then plunged it deep into Flavio's chest, killing him instantly. The other man dumped the body of Dondo on top of Flavio. They then stepped over the bodies and headed to the stairwell.

Don Umbretto was sleeping soundly in his bed. So much so that he did not hear the floor creak as the two men crept into the bedroom.

The man who had stabbed Flavio lifted the bloody knife in his hand and pointed it toward the bed as he walked forward. The shorter of the two men slowly made his way to the other side of the bed. As they both reached the bed, the man with the knife nodded toward his associate. The shorter man lifted his hand and then quickly clamped it down over Adriano's mouth, pushing the back of his head into the pillow and holding him down.

Adriano's eyes flashed open. He began to kick his legs wildly as he brought his hands up and grabbed the man's hand, which was draped over his mouth. He tried to yell out, but the man's hand over his mouth only allowed for a muffled sound. The other man raised the knife over his head and said softly, "Onofrio Fausto has returned. And this is his gift."

As he began to bring his arm down, Adriano was able to

overpower the smaller man who was holding him down, which allowed him to shift his body just enough so that the knife came straight down into the Adriano's left arm and not his chest where the man had been aiming. Adriano let out a scream of pain, followed by a very forceful, *"Vaffanculo."* (Fuck you.) *Fanculo a entrambi."* (Fuck you both.) He pushed against both of the men, who were surprised by his brute strength. Breaking free, Adriano quickly climbed out of bed. Lights came on in the hallway outside his bedroom, and many footsteps could be heard throughout the villa.

Alessandro, who had been sleeping in a room nearby, had heard the commotion and was the first to enter the bedroom. He saw Adriano, blood streaming from the wound on his arm, standing by the window like a caged animal as the two men stood nearby.

The man with the knife turned toward the door, reached into his pocket, and pulled out a revolver. He lifted it and shot Alessandro point-blank in the face. Clutching his face, Adriano's associate hit the floor with a thud.

The man then turned toward Adriano and pointed the gun directly at him. He said forcefully, "No, Don Umbretto. Fuck you."

He fired, and the bullet ripped through Adriano's body. Adriano spun around and fell face first onto the floor.

It was at that very moment that Ferruccio arrived to the scene and stood in the doorway. The blast from his *lupara* shook the entire room. His shot struck the man with the revolver directly in the middle of his back. He fell forward. Ferruccio then lifted his *lupara* again as the other man quickly turned and sprinted across the room toward the window.

Ferrucio took his shot but missed, just as the man jumped out of the open window.

More of Biscotti and Adriano's men entered the room. Ferruccio leaped over the lifeless body of Alessandro and ran toward the window. As he peered down, he saw the man getting up from the ground and running with a limp out of the courtyard.

Ferruccio yelled to the others in the room, "After him. All of you after him."

The men ran out of the bedroom as Ferruccio looked around the room at all of the bodies. He took a few steps forward and saw the crumpled body of his boss lying on the floor. He went to his knees and buried his head in his hands as he sat over the body of Don Adriano Umbretto.

THE AFTERMATH

It was Monsignor Mancini banging on the door of *Il Paradiso* which stirred the Sanguinetti household early on that Palm Sunday morning. Maria heard the knocking and woke Giuseppe up. They both stumbled out of bed and hurriedly left their bedroom.

Marco and Francesca also heard the knocking. Marco, still shirtless, stood up from the bedroll and pulled a shirt on. He told Francesca to stay in the bedroom. Before leaving, he grabbed his *lupara*.

When he left the room, Francesca rubbed her temples as she felt the aftermath of a night of drinking. She removed the covers and got out of bed.

Marco went down the stairs and found Giuseppe and Maria speaking with Monsignor Mancini. Both of the Sanguinettis were holding tightly to each other. Maria was in tears.

"What happened?" Marco asked.

Monsignor Mancini announced, "Santo and Mirella Vasaio have been killed. Their son discovered the bodies this morning."

"*Gran Dio*," replied Marco.

Just then, Francesca came down into the wine store.

Marco turned and walked over to her. "I thought you were going to stay upstairs."

She looked at the faces of everyone in the store and knew something terrible had happened. Once she was told, she felt the air leave her lungs, and she found herself trying to catch her breath. When Giuseppe agreed to go with Monsignor Mancini to the winery, she finally caught her breath and asked to join them. She said it in such a way that it really was more of a statement than a question.

Giuseppe replied, "We will all come, Pietro." Giuseppe looked at Marco, pointed to his *lupara*, and said, "I think it's time that you carry that with you."

Marco nodded, and the group left the wine store and quickly made their way to the valley and to the Boccale Winery.

A SHORT WHILE LATER, they all stood over the bodies of the Vasaios down in the wine cave. Matteo Vasaio stood off to the right side, being held in the arms of Maria. Neither could look at the gruesome scene before them. Monsignor Mancini was kneeling down over the bodies, praying and blessing them. Francesca stood on the opposite side, holding tightly onto Marco's hand. She stared at the dead bodies.

Giuseppe Sanguinetti was standing off to the side near the

wine barrels. Looking upon the bodies of his dear friend and his wife made Giuseppe's entire being feel like he was standing on the precipice of a deep hole, staring into it with no end in sight and feeling the strong pull to jump into the nothingness. Monsignor Mancini's voice, as he recited the Latin prayers, echoed throughout the cave.

Suddenly, the church bells of *Chiesa della Madonna* could be heard down in the cave. Monsignor Mancini stopped praying and said to the group, "I asked Father Gianuzzi to ring the bells." That custom had been in existence in Bellafortuna for a very long time to announce to the villagers the death of one of them.

Monsignor Mancini finished his last prayer, stood up, and said, "Let's take Matteo back to his house so he can get dressed. I'll go get some men to help with the bodies. I'll see all of you later this morning at our Palm Sunday mass.

The group approached the stairwell, save Giuseppe, who stood quietly near the bodies. Giuseppe turned toward the wine barrel that Monsignor Mancini had pointed out to him on which the perpetrator had written in blood the name "Onofrio Fausto." Giuseppe knew what the killing meant and that his fears of the Mafia making a move to take over the winery were now a reality. And he now knew who was behind it all. Onofrio Fausto, the most hated Don of them all, had returned.

Giuseppe felt the pains of emptiness in his heart that he had felt a few times in his life. He hated knowing the black space of despair he would be entering over the next weeks. Merged with his feelings of despair was the realization that his village was about to face one of its toughest tests with the reemergence of Onofrio Fausto. And for the first time in his life, Giuseppe believed there was nothing that the villagers of Bellafortuna could do to defeat the impending evil about to descend upon the village.

As he began to walk toward the stairwell, he stopped. He turned toward the bodies and said, "I'm so sorry, Santo. I'm so sorry."

Giuseppe looked one last time at the bodies of his friend and his wife and then turned and went up the stairs.

MONREALE CHANGES HANDS

Giancarlo had awoken early that Palm Sunday morning at Don Umbretto's villa on the outskirts of Castelvetrano. It was a relatively uneventful morning until a car came to the gate and was immediately let inside by the associates guarding it. One of the men stationed by the gate ran inside and found Giancarlo seated in the Don's study behind the desk.

"*Signor Fanucci,* it's Salvatore Battaglia. He has returned and says he must speak with you at once. It is extremely urgent."

Giancarlo left the study and hurried out toward the gardens. However, before he reached the door, the towering figure of Salvatore Battaglia entered the foyer.

"The Don has been murdered," he said gravely.

"What? How?"

"He has been killed by Onofrio Fausto."

Giancarlo looked dumbfounded at Salvatore before finally responding, "He has returned."

"Yes, and with his son. I was at Biscotti's villa when they attacked. I had returned from Bellafortuna earlier that night and was sleeping. The murder happened very early this morning."

"What about our men and Biscotti's men?"

"We have lost Monreale."

"What about the Don? Where is his body?"

"I don't know. I left to come here at once to let you know what happened and to prepare."

Giancarlo sighed heavily. "What about Francesca?"

"She is safe, for now. The Don knew what he was doing when he agreed to send her away."

"She will be devastated when she hears this news," Giancarlo replied.

"Don Adriano's remaining *cosca* members still here in the villa must show strength to survive. The succession of the next Don must occur."

"The Don appointed me as his successor, after Luca," Giancarlo interjected. "So with Luca gone, I am to assume the role of Don."

Salvatore was silent for a moment and eyed Giancarlo up and down, almost as if sizing him up as boxers do in the middle of the ring prior to a fight. He then said, "And who heard this conversation, besides you, Luca and the Don?"

"Just us."

"So you are now the only person alive who was a participant at that meeting?"

Giancarlo cocked his head to one side and then, looking up

to the much taller man, replied forcefully, "If this conversation is going where I think it is going, you can stop now. All of these men at the villa are loyal to me. This conversation ends now."

Salvatore said in reply, "I'm just preparing you for the possible attacks against your succession." Salvatore then went to a knee and reached for Giancarlo's hand. He kissed it, saying, "I pledge my life to you, Don Fanucci."

"Come Salvatore, we need to let everyone know what has occurred."

GIUSEPPE AND MARIA were seated with Francesca and Marco by a table inside *Il Paradiso*, which sat by the window overlooking the piazza. The curtains were closed. They had returned from the Boccale Winery, where they had sat with Matteo until other relatives of his had arrived. One of the relatives had voiced her concern over and over again to Giuseppe about Matteo's future now with the death of his parents. Giuseppe had assured the relative, "You have my word. I will take care of it. I will be with him every step of the way as he takes over the winery."

By the time they had returned to the village, they were too late for Mass that morning, so they went straight to the wine shop. A great sadness enveloped the room.

Grief works in many strange ways, and people respond to their feelings of grief in all sorts of ways. Giuseppe had not spoken much since the unfolding of the events of that morning. However, inside the wine store, he turned to stories to help cope with his feelings. He related to Francesca and Marco how he and Santo had first met, how Santo had confronted him on his way to school one morning, how ultimately a deep love and respect came to fruition, and how together they had assisted with the removal of the Vasaios from power in Bellafortuna. As he finished his stories, he said, "Santo became like a son to my father. And that is how he came to run the winery."

Maria held tightly to her husband's hand the entire time.

Francesca said, "I'm so sorry for your loss, *Signor Sanguinetti*. I'm so sorry." She broke into tears. "This is my fault. This is all my fault. Santo and Mirella would still be alive if I were not here."

Marco put his arm around her to comfort her.

Giuseppe reached across the table and grabbed her hand. "They were coming for the winery with or without you here. These are grim times. Men like your father and Don Biscotti were men of a different age. This new breed will bring a type of brutality that this island has not seen."

While they were talking at the table inside the store, a long black car pulled into the piazza and stopped by the Boccale statue. The driver quickly got out of the front seat. He scanned the piazza until his eyes rested on the sign above the wine store. He sprinted across the piazza toward the wine store.

Francesca was about to respond back to Giuseppe during their discussion when the door to the wine store flew open, and the man quickly came inside.

Marco turned in his seat and gasped. "Ferruccio."

Ferruccio blurted out, "*Aiuto*! Don Umbretto has been shot. He's passed out in the back seat."

They all sprinted out of the wine store to the car.

AFTER THEY HAD LAID Don Umbretto on Francesca's bed upstairs, Marco walked into the hallway to speak with Giuseppe and Ferruccio.

Ferruccio said, "Don Umbretto has only gained consciousness twice since he was shot. The first time he had the strength to ask me to take him to Bellafortuna and to your wine store. He said this is where his daughter would be. The other time he came around, he only said the name 'Fausto.' He repeated that name three times before he passed out."

"He must know Onofrio Fausto has returned. He is behind this attack," Giuseppe said.

Ferruccio continued, "He has not awoken since then. Will he recover?"

Marco looked over Ferruccio's shoulder and could see Francesca sitting beside the bed, tightly holding her father's hand. Marco said, "I have no idea. *Signor Sanguinetti*, what do you think?"

Before Giuseppe could respond, Maria came up the stairs with Lorenzo Baldini, the *farmicista*. Lorenzo walked into the bedroom and examined Don Umbretto while the others stayed in the hallway. Francesca, still seated next to her father, said to Lorenzo through her tears, "*Salvalo, per favore.*"

Lorenzo smiled at her in return and patted her arm. He then left the room and told those out in the hallway, "I bandaged his arm. I also checked the bullet wound. It seems the bullet went clean through. But he has lost a lot of blood. A lot of blood. I believe the next few hours will determine the outcome. His injuries are far beyond what I can do to help him."

Giuseppe turned toward the others. "Ferruccio, can you and Marco take your car and go to Palermo? I'll give you directions to Dr. Frances Incaprera. Ask him to come quickly."

Marco said in reply, "I'm not leaving Francesca's side. Especially not now."

"I understand, Marco. I'll get Kurt to go with Ferruccio."

"*Grazie,*" replied Marco.

Giuseppe replied, "Come, Ferruccio. I'll walk out with you and get Kurt. Then I will go over to the church to let the priests know what has happened. I will ask them to come pray over him. *Andiamo.* Thanks Lorenzo. Will you stay with the Don until Dr. Incaprera comes."

"*Certo,*" Lorenzo replied.

Meanwhile, inside the bedroom, Francesca sat next to her father, holding his hand. Marco came back into the bedroom and took a knee next to her. As he looked upon the body of his Don, tears began to stream down his face.

Francesca looked at him and said, "You truly love him."

"I do, Francesca. With all of my being, I do."

She smiled back at him.

GIUSEPPE MET the priests outside of the church just as the Palm Sunday Mass had ended. The villagers filed out of Church, all of them holding palm branches in remembrance of Jesus' triumphant entrance into Jerusalem just before His Passion. As they came up to complement Monsignor Mancini on his homily, Giuseppe walked over to the priests. He grabbed Father Gianuzzi by the arm and said, "Father, I need you to come to *Il Paradiso* at once. There has been an incident."

"What sort of incident?"

"It's very serious. Someone is very sick."

"Let me grab some oil. I'll be right back."

He ran toward the church as Giuseppe moved over to where Monsignor Mancini was standing. "*Scusi mi, Pietro.*"

"Giuseppe, what do you need?"

He led Monsignor Mancini a few steps away so their conversation could not be heard by the villagers nearby.

"It's Don Umbretto. One of his men rushed him here to us. He's been shot and may be dying. He's in bed in my house."

"Have you told Father Gianuzzi?"

"I did not tell him who was gravely wounded. He went to grab some oil."

"When he comes back, I'll join you. Let's tell him on the way."

FRANCESCA WAS STILL SEATED near the bed, holding the hand of her father. Marco was standing next to her. Lorenzo Baldini was sitting close by. Monsignor Mancini was standing over Don Umbretto, saying prayers and blessing him. Father Gianuzzi had turned that job over to Monsignor Mancini when they arrived in the bedroom. He stood behind Francesca, holding onto her shoulder. His face was stoic and showed very little emotion. Giuseppe stood in the doorway.

While Monsignor Mancini was still praying, Francesca

stood up and walked over to Giuseppe. She whispered to him, "Is the doctor coming?"

"Yes. They left to go to Palermo to get him. It will be a little while, but he is coming."

"Help my father. Please don't let him die."

"I will take care of him. I promise you."

She smiled and returned to the bed. She got back on her knees and clasped her hands together into prayer.

When Monsignor Mancini finished his prayers, he came over to Giuseppe and asked him to step in the hallway, leaving Lorenzo, Marco, Francesca, and Father Gianuzzi alone in the room.

Monsignor Mancini looked kindly at Giuseppe and asked, "How are you doing, Giuseppe?"

"I'm fine."

"I'm concerned for you with the loss of Santo. And now this."

"I'm fine, Pietro."

"With Don Umbretto being attacked, don't you think the *Società* should meet?"

Giuseppe shrugged his shoulders and replied, "I guess so."

Monsignor offered a quizzical look and then said, "You told me that a few villagers out in the piazza witnessed you carrying Don Umbretto into your home. Keeping it a secret is impossible at this point. I'm sure once word reaches everyone about the attack on Don Umbretto, a meeting will be called for immediately. We must come up with a reason why the Don's man brought him here." He turned and glanced toward Francesca before continuing, "Her identity must still be kept secret, especially after the events of today."

"Probably so," Giuseppe replied before turning and walking back into the bedroom.

Monsignor Mancini walked down the hallway toward the kitchen, where he found Maria making espresso. As he entered, he said to her, "Sad times, Maria."

"Indeed, Monsignor."

"Maria, I'm concerned for your husband. He seems distant."

"He's trying to be strong, Monsignor Mancini. But I know his sadness is great."

"I think his emotions are overwhelming him. It's hard to explain, but he seems disconnected. Continue to be there for him, Maria. This village will need him, probably now more than ever. Not only are these sad times, but they are dangerous times."

"I'm scared for us, Monsignor. I'm scared for our entire village."

"Me too, Maria. Me too."

Monsignor Mancini walked back toward the bedroom, where he found Giuseppe, who was standing by the Don's children and Marco. Lorenzo was seated nearby. The room was silent with nothing being said as they all watched the Don's chest slowly move up and down with his shallow breathing.

WORD SPREAD QUICKLY around Bellafortuna about the attack on Don Umbretto and of his presence in the village. The shock of the news of the death of Santo Vasaio and his wife and the attack on Don Umbretto resonated among all the villagers.

As Monsignor Mancini predicted, a meeting was quickly called for by the *Società* to meet that afternoon. Monsignor Mancini and Father Gianuzzi were both asked to attend. However, Father Gianuzzi declined and stayed with Francesca awaiting the arrival of Dr. Incaprera from Palermo.

At 2 pm that afternoon, the room at the *Alberga* was filled with every member of the *Società*, save two – Lorenzo Baldini and Giuseppe Sanguinetti were not there. Monsignor Mancini pointed out to the group that Lorenzo was with Don Umbretto. When one member asked if they should wait for Giuseppe, another villager pointed out that he was seen walking out of the village and down toward the valley. Monsignor Mancini guessed where Giuseppe was headed but said nothing. He would go find him after the meeting.

During the meeting, the members all voiced their fears that were now running very high with the latest news. There was no doubt that the winery and Bellafortuna itself were in the crosshairs of Onofrio Fausto. As the discussion moved to what options were available to them to protect the village, members over and over again would add, "Well, if Giuseppe was here..." and "What would Giuseppe think ...".

As the meeting came to an end and with no solution, the fears of every member had only increased exponentially. The question as to why Don Umbretto was brought to the village of Bellafortuna went unanswered by Monsignor Mancini.

When the meeting ended, everyone left to comfort their families, while Monsignor Mancini walked out of the piazza and down the street that led to the valley.

DOWN IN THE VALLEY, there was a knoll located on the opposite shore of the *Stagno Azzurro*, directly across from the amphitheater in *Antica Campanèlla*. On the little hill, three simple crosses stood under a single tree. Here were the final resting places for Antonio Sanguinetti, Father Biaggio Sanguinetti and Biaggio Spatalanata. Seated between the burial locations of his grandfather and son sat Giuseppe Sanguinetti.

Giuseppe looked up as Monsignor Mancini approached. The priest nodded his head and sat down next to his good friend. Not a word was spoken at first as the two dear friends stared over the blue waters of the *Stagno Azzurro*.

Monsignor Mancini finally broke the silence, turned his head toward Giuseppe, and said, "You were missed at the meeting."

Giuseppe, still staring across the water, said in reply, "I had nothing to offer."

"They are in fear, Giuseppe. All of them."

"They should be."

"You are probably right. But they need you, Giuseppe. You are their leader, like it or not. You always have been. You have always been the light in the darkness for our little world here."

Giuseppe finally turned to his friend. "That light is extinguished, Pietro." He pointed to the grave of his son. "It was buried years ago. I just did not have to face it until now."

"Santo's death has affected you greatly. You need to grieve. It's understandable. God will provide you with the strength to get through this. Just as he did when your son died."

Giuseppe exhaled deeply. "I'm mad at God, Pietro."

"God loves you, Giuseppe."

For the first time since Santo's death, tears began to flow down Giuseppe's cheeks. "You don't understand, Pietro. Everything is silence."

"What do you mean? What or who is silent?"

"God, Pietro. God is silent. When my son died, I thought God would let him speak to me through prayers or signs, to keep his soul alive within me. I've prayed daily to my son, both to him and for him. But all there is in return is silence."

"Giuseppe, God does not act according to the laws of human life. You may not hear his voice or those of his angels, such as your son, but rest assured your son is communicating in God's way with you, daily. As is the same with God Himself."

"I'd rather hear his voice speaking to me."

Monsignor Mancini smiled. "There are many Saints throughout Church history who credit their pursuit of a saintly life to hearing the voice of God. But I say, blessed are those who pursued a saintly life just on faith. It's easy to believe if you actually hear God's voice speak to you. In contrast, it takes your whole being to stay the course when all you have is faith, as you must constantly fight the temptations of the devil whose one desire is to turn your faith away. Again, it's easier to defeat those temptations if I have actually heard God speak to me, as otherwise, you must only rely on faith to defeat Satan's test. Your faith is strengthened by the graces sent to you by God, by your father, by your son, by your dear friend, Biaggio Spatalanata, and soon, by Santo.

Those graces are the voices coming down from heaven. That is God's voice speaking to you through his angels. That is how your faith grows and you grow in closeness to God and you are strengthened which gives you assistance in your war with the devil. Once you understand this, then your heart is opened to the graces touching your soul daily, and it opens your connection to God and his angels through prayer even more. You come to understand that indeed God is speaking directly to you."

Giuseppe buried his head into his hands as he sobbed loudly. "It's too much to bear, Pietro. Too much."

"Life moves on, Giuseppe. And so must you, which you will. You need to grieve Santo's death, outwardly, which you are doing now through those tears. That will begin the healing process. Your feelings were locked up. You have opened them, which in turn, will lead you to a much better place. God will provide, and in so doing, will give you the assistance you will need to give aid to your fellow villagers in the coming days and weeks. There is no getting around the fact, my friend, that they will rely on you for a solution. Whether that solution works or not is not of concern at this moment, only your readiness to be called upon to offer it."

Giuseppe lifted his head up and looked directly at Monsignor Mancini. "Don Adriano Umbretto lies dying in my home, his son and daughter are living in secret in our village, the head of our winery and his wife have been murdered, and Onofrio Fausto has returned to our shores to take control. There is no solution."

Monsignor Mancini pointed over at the grave of Giuseppe's father. "You are the son of Antonio Sanguinetti. You took on the powerful before, against great odds, and brought freedom to your village." He then pointed to the grave of Giuseppe's son. "You accepted your son's request to hide Jews here in the village against pure evil itself, and they survived. There is no one else I would put my trust in to protect this village and its people. God's finger has touched this place. We owe it to Him to fight for it. We owe it to Him to give our entire being and effort to protect this place and its people. That is how we show our true thanks for His blessings."

With tears streaming down from his eyes, Giuseppe turned toward him. "You have always been a dear friend, Pietro. I promise I will do what I can. I agree we owe it to Him." He then looked over the graves around him. "And I owe it to each one of them as well."

Monsignor Mancini smiled. "*Bene.* Let's go back to *Il Paradiso.* Kurt and Ferruccio should be coming back with Dr. Incaprera at any time."

They stood up and returned to the village.

SALVATORE WALKED down the hallway of the Umbretto villa in Castelvetrano. The mood inside the villa was grim as the men who worked for Don Umbretto tried to come to grips with the news of his death.

Salvatore looked over his shoulder and saw that no one was behind him. He opened a door in the hallway that led to a small parlor with a table next to a chair. On the table was a phone.

He closed the door and walked over to the phone. He sat in the chair and picked up the phone. But then he paused. He hung the phone back up as his mind turned to the events of last night.

The killing of the wine man and his wife was not what he was thinking about. They were an afterthought. It was the children of Adriano Umbretto who were in the forefront of his mind. He had told Don Onofrio Fausto that Francesca was living in Bellafortuna. With that information in hand, Don Fausto gave him the order to kill the wine man. The wine man's wife was a bonus, as she had just happened upon the scene, as luck would have it. He had no regrets in letting Don Fausto know that Adriano's daughter was hiding in the village. But Salvatore had never informed Don Fausto of the fact that there was a young priest in the village who was actually the long thought dead son of Adriano. Something held him back from revealing that to Don Fausto.

Sitting in the chair, he wondered if now was the time to come clean and tell Don Fausto. What did it matter, especially now with Don Umbretto dead. He made that statement to himself again. Don Umbretto is dead. He still had feelings for a man he considered a friend, but in this business, friendship meant nothing. He had tried to convince Don Umbretto that the Mafia was changing after the war. The way of the Dons of old was over. Don Umbretto would have to change to compete. But he had refused. Don Umbretto still viewed himself as a man whose purpose as Don was to actually protect those under his care, where the new breed was in it all for themselves and those who worked for them. Salvatore had tried many times to convince his boss, but he would not change. He never would. Then, Salvatore began hearing rumors that Don Fausto and his son had returned to Sicily from America. A chance encounter with an old friend of his who had recently joined the newly formed *cosca* of Don Fausto soon led to a meeting between Salvatore and Don Fausto.

At that first meeting, the words Don Fausto used and how he spoke about the power and money that were available throughout Sicily after the war matched Salvatore's own beliefs. Don Fausto, from his time in America, had learned what the new Mafia was all about. He was the epitome of what Salvatore thought Don Adriano should become.

After that initial meeting, Don Fausto had to put Salvatore to the test first, to see if he was trustworthy. Salvatore's first job was to find conspirators within Don Umbretto's own *cosca* who would help by lessening security at the villa so that Don Fausto's assassin could take out his rival. Salvatore knew this was the most dangerous part of his mission. Finding two associates of the Don who would not immediately run to the Don and tell him of Salvatore's betrayal would be difficult. Of course, his nephew, Marco, worked for Don Umbretto, but he was infatuated with the Don and would never agree to it. There was one person, though. He had been with the Don a long time, and Salvatore had heard some of his mumblings about Don Umbretto. That person was Mario Zuchello.

He approached Mario one evening and had a conversation with him. The lengthy talk started cautiously, but soon, Salvatore knew the man could be turned. Mario agreed to assist him and would work secretly for Don Fausto. Mario advised Salvatore that Marcello would join him, without a shadow of a doubt, as they had both become disillusioned with Don Umbretto's old ways. They were missing out on all the new money flowing into Sicily.

The trio devised a plan that would allow Don Fausto's

assassin to gain access at an unwatched part of the fence surrounding the villa. Neither they nor Don Fausto had contemplated that Adriano would end up stabbing the intruder to death. Later that night, after the attack, Mario met Castranzio Fausto in nearby Corso Borgatti, where he made his report of the events that had occurred.

Although the plan had failed, Don Fausto was convinced of the loyalty of Salvatore and his two co-conspirators. Later, his assistance in providing key information to Don Fausto regarding Luca Sperenza, which ultimately led to his killing with the voice teacher, brought Salvatore even closer to the trusted inner circle of Don Fausto.

When Adriano discovered the betrayal of Mario and Marcello, Salvatore had no other choice but to silence them. It did not matter to him. They were only needed to prove his loyalty to Don Fausto.

However, it was his revelation to Don Fausto that Francesca Umbretto had moved to Bellafortuna that truly brought Salvatore into the fold, and Don Fausto put complete trust in him.

But what had kept him from telling Don Fausto right from the start of the existence of Don Umbretto's son? What?

Sitting in the chair, Salvatore pondered that question. Deep down, he thought he knew the answer as to why he said nothing. His years of working for Don Umbretto had taught him one thing. It was the one thing that Don Umbretto demanded. Adriano was not a violent man. He actually hated violence. But there were times when certain actions needed to be taken, where a strong response was required, sometimes even death. Yet, Adriano only took actions against the person to whom he was seeking revenge.

Other family members or associates would be left alone by Don Umbretto.

Francesca was fair game for Salvatore to advise Don Fausto of her living in Bellafortuna. It provided an opportunity and opened the door for Don Fausto to establish a foothold in the small village and its winery. So, of course, he told him about her. But the priest had nothing to do with it. He was a nobody. He served no purpose. In Don Umbretto's world, he was to be left out of the equation. All those years working for his friend, Salvatore still had some of Don Umbretto's sense of justice buried deep within. And that's why he never told Don Fausto about Giacomo Umbretto. Something was instilled deep within him. It would not change today either. He decided then and there that Don Umbretto's son would remain a secret.

He picked up the phone and placed his call. He told the person who answered the phone that he needed to speak to Castranzio Fausto.

A few seconds later, a voice came across the phone line, *"Pronto."*

"Signor Fausto, questo e Salvatore."

"Si."

"E fatta. L'uomo del vino e sua moglie." (It is done. The wine man and his wife.)

Castranzio asked for clarification. *"Anche moglie?"*

"Si. Anche la moglie." (Yes. The wife also.)

Castranzio laughed. *"Eccellente. Faro sapere subito a mio padre."* (Excellent. I will let my father know at once.) Castranzio paused, and added, *"Sara motto contento. Saremo in contatto al piu presto."* (He will be very pleased. We will be in touch soon.)

The line went dead. Salvatore sat back in the chair. If Don Fausto ever discovered the identity of Giacomo Umbretto and that Salvatore knew he was living in the village, it would mean certain death for him. Over time he would have to come to grips with Don Umbretto's influence inside him and destroy it. But that would take time. That's the only downfall to friendship in this business. The influence it can bring.

So the Don's son would continue living in obscurity. What would ultimately happen to Francesca and what Don Fausto had in mind for her now with Don Umbretto being dead was of no concern to Salvatore. He hoped his nephew, Marco, would be left untouched, but if he got caught up in it all, so be it. Marco and his mother were weak. His sister could never stand up for herself. Marco was of the same breed. Don Umbretto was right about his nephew. He was too kind for this business. He regretted allowing him to work for Don Umbretto. But that was all in the past. Salvatore's path now lay clearly before him. Soon, when the time was right, he would make his move and kill Giancarlo Fanucci. Then he, Salvatore Battaglia, would be the Don of Castelvetrano. He would give Marco one chance, one chance to join him. If he refused, he would send him back to his mother, and he would never speak of him again. He was ready to take control, but he knew he needed to bide his time for now and wait.

He stood up from the chair and left the parlor.

By that evening, the events of *Notte Oscura* came to light across all of Sicily and revealed to all the staggering body count. News spread of the murder of the much loved and respected Roberto Dimaggio of Monreale, who was a leading banker in the city, as well as Giangiacomo Zancanaro, Monreale's police chief, and its chief Judge, Alfredo Saltafamaggio. Three policemen were also killed, and a businessman who was a vocal critic of the Mafia. Sicilians also came to learn of an attack on Don Biscotti's villa and the rumor of the murder of Don Adriano Umbretto. Word also spread of an attack in the quiet, secluded village of Bellafortuna.

For even the most hardened of Sicilians, the unprecedented bloodshed from one night of violence was surprising and revealed a sophisticated killing machine that they feared would soon become the new normal across the island.

And on the tongues of every Sicilian was the name of Onofrio Fausto, who had returned to Sicily with his son, using such vicious savagery to solidify their control. By nightfall, the surviving *cosca* members of Don Biscotti and Don Umbretto had all fled from the villa in Monreale, which was now once again under the control of Don Onofrio Fausto. Many questioned if their was anyone who could stand up against death itself, take on the Faustos, and rid Sicily of the brutality.

Meanwhile, in the village of Bellafortuna, Dr. Incaprera cared for his patient throughout the long night. Although gravely wounded, Don Adriano Umbretto exhibited a strength and a strong heart that provided optimism to those inside the bedroom where he rested that he might recover from his wounds.

THE DON LIVES

*M*onday of Easter week began with gloomy weather over much of the island of Sicily. It perfectly matched most of the inhabitants' feelings, particularly those in Monreale and Bellafortuna. In Castelvetrano, a wet fog welcomed the morning hours.

It was early that morning when a car left the villa in Castelvetrano. Giancarlo was alone in the car on his way to Bellafortuna to meet with Francesca and to let her know about the death of her father if word had not reached her yet.

Before leaving, Giancarlo had told Salvatore, "I'm gravely concerned Onofrio Fausto will move against the Don's holdings here. You will stay behind and assist with the protection of the Don's holdings until I return."

"Your holdings now, Don Fanucci," Salvatore had said with an ironic smile.

Giancarlo thought about the Don and Luca the entire time he drove. If there was one thing he could do for the man he loved, it would be to protect his daughter at all costs. The car continued in the fog, headed toward Bellafortuna.

GIANCARLO ARRIVED in Bellafortuna just before noon. The fog had lifted, although the day remained dreary with a grey, deep cloud cover. He parked in the piazza and made his way toward *Il Paradiso*. Kurt Hofmann was alone inside when he entered.

"I'm here to see Giuseppe Sanguinetti."

"He is upstairs," Kurt replied. "I will go get him. Stay here please."

Kurt left Giancarlo in the wine store and went up the stairs to the living quarters. Moments later, Kurt returned with Giuseppe.

Giuseppe said, "Can I help you?"

"*Signor Sanguinetti*, I am Giancarlo Fanucci. I came to your village a few weeks back with Don Umbretto."

Giuseppe extended his hand. "I don't think we actually met when you were here last time."

"I am here on the most urgent of business. I must speak with Francesca at once. Her father, Don Umbretto, has been murdered."

Giuseppe rubbed his chin with his hand. "You have been told the Don is dead?"

"Killed in Monreale."

"Please, come upstairs with me at once."

He followed Giuseppe up the stairs.

GIANCARLO STOOD in shock over the bed where his Don was lying. Francesca and Marco were much surprised at his arrival. Ferruccio was also in the room, along with Dr. Incaprera.

Giancarlo asked, "The Don's alive? How did he get here?"

Ferruccio spoke up. "He asked me to bring him here to be with his daughter."

"Francesca and Marco have not left his side," Giuseppe added. "They are exhausted and must get some rest today."

Francesca shrugged her shoulders in response.

Giancarlo asked, "Doctor, will he live?"

"Last night was the hurdle, and he overcame it well. I was able to do a straight donor to patient transfusion all last night. The Don can thank Francesca for that, as she provided her blood to him. I also probed the wound. Don Umbretto was struck just above the liver. Somehow, nothing vital was struck. I packed the wound, which seems to have stopped the bleeding. I think he will recover and hopefully will awake soon."

Giancarlo went to his knees, overcome with emotion, and exclaimed, "My God, the Don lives."

Francesca stood up and offered her hands to help Giancarlo up. "It means so much for me and my father that you came. He always loved you."

"I know, Francesca. You don't know what stirred in my heart when I heard the news of his death. But now, to walk up these stairs and see your father lying in this bed; I can't describe my emotions. Now, if you excuse me one moment, let me speak with Marco and Ferruccio."

The two men followed Giancarlo out into the hallway.

Giancarlo said, "Onofrio Fausto did this."

"We know who did it," Marco replied. "He had his men kill the owner of the winery here in Bellafortuna, Santo Vasaio, along with his wife."

Giancarlo replied, "Oh no."

"Yes, he and his wife," repeated Marco.

Ferruccio added, "The Don knows who attacked him. He said the name Fausto to me before he passed out."

"Discovering that Don Umbretto lives, now throws my plans into the wind, which I greatly welcome," Giancarlo said. "I'm not sure where we go from here but I know one thing for certain. My guess is Don Fausto believes that Don Umbretto is dead. We must let him continue to believe that."

"I agree," replied Ferruccio. "I'm not even sure our own men in Monreale know exactly what occurred. It was utter chaos inside Don Biscotti's villa. When Don Umbretto asked me to take him here, I left immediately without seeing any of our men."

Giancarlo said, "Ferruccio, you saved the Don. I will stay in Bellafortuna with you. We must protect him and his daughter. If Don Fausto finds out he is alive, he will move in for the kill. I'm not sure what you have heard, but Don Fausto ordered the killing of many people last night. His attack on the winery means he is making a move not only for control of Monreale, but for the wine production of Bellafortuna. This is a dangerous place for the Don, but we can't move him just yet."

"And what about our men and the villa in Castelvetrano?" Ferruccio asked.

Giancarlo answered. "No doubt, they are in danger. Salvatore came back to Castelvetrano yesterday and informed me of what had happened to our Don. He believed he had died. He said he was at the villa in Monreale when it happened, but was asleep. He has remained in Castelvetrano to assist with its protection."

Ferruccio slumped his shoulders and was about to respond but instead kept quiet.

Marco asked, "So you are staying?"

"With the news I just discovered, I will stay until I can speak with the Don and find out what he wants me to do."

Ferruccio added, "If he wakes up."

Marco said, "Giancarlo, there is a hotel in the piazza."

"I'll go get a room and shall be back shortly."

"I'll take a walk with you," Ferruccio said.

The two men made their way down to the wine store. When they entered the wine store, they ran into Giuseppe and Maria, who were speaking to Father Gianuzzi.

Giuseppe turned to Giancarlo. "This is Father Gianuzzi."

Giancarlo extended his hand to the priest. "Nice to meet you. I'm Giancarlo Fanucci."

Father Gianuzzi took the man's hand. "I just came to check to see how Giuseppe's guest is doing. Giuseppe gave me the positive news."

Giancarlo replied, "Yes, I hope he wakes up soon. Father, may I ask a favor?"

"What is it?"

"I'm sure you know who it is that lies upstairs?"

Father Gianuzzi's face twitched as he was uncertain as to where the conversation was going and if Giancarlo knew who he actually was. He finally responded, "I do."

"A man of his stature, we must try our best to keep it secret that he survived the attack. I'm sure you know what would happen if the perpetrator found out he was alive. It would not only be bad for him, but for those rendering aid to him."

"I understand. I will do my best to quell any and all discussions that I may hear among the villagers. I will do my best, as I'm sure Giuseppe will do the same."

"Thank you, Father."

"Nice meeting you. I'm going back to the rectory."

The priest left the wine store. Giuseppe then introduced Giancarlo to his wife.

Maria asked, "Will you be staying in Bellafortuna?"

"Yes."

Giuseppe said, "Great. You can find a room at the *albergo* across the piazza."

"*Grazie.*"

Giuseppe added, "I am in great fear for our little village with the attack on our winery."

"My Don is under your roof and alive in your village. We will do what we can to protect this village. I thank you for everything you have done for the Don."

"You are most welcome."

He said to Giuseppe, "I'll go across the piazza and see about a room."He then looked at Maria and bowed his head slightly. "*Signora Sanguinetti.*"

"Pleasure meeting you."

Giancarlo and Ferruccio walked outside and into the piazza.

Ferruccio turned to Giancarlo. "So Salvatore is at the villa in Castelvetrano?"

"Yes," replied Giancarlo.

"I need to tell you something. I am greatly disturbed with something you said."

"What is it, Ferruccio?"

"Salvatore told you he was sleeping at the villa when the attack occurred?"

"Yes. He said he had returned from Bellafortuna and went to bed."

Ferruccio folded his arms. "I did not want to say anything upstairs to you in front of his nephew. Granted, after the shooting, it was utter chaos inside the villa. Who of our men I saw is a blur. People coming and going and running all over the place. However, I am certain of one thing, and of that I have no doubt."

"Get to the point, Ferruccio."

"I stood guard outside the villa all night. Salvatore never came back to the villa. He was not sleeping there the night of the attack as he told you."

AWAKE

*L*ater that afternoon, Monsignor Mancini knocked on the door of Father Gianuzzi's small office door. When he entered, he found the young priest seated behind his desk reading his breviary.

Father Gianuzzi lifted his eyes from his prayer book and said, *"Buona sera,* Monsignor."

"Buona sera. I thought you and I could talk plainly."

"Of course. But first, I've been so caught up with the goings on at *Il Paradiso,* I wanted to ask how poor Matteo is doing."

"Giuseppe is with him now. He and Maria are helping the family with the funeral arrangements. I would love to have you concelebrate with me."

"It would be an honor. I did not know Santo as well, but Mirella was a very kind soul, who loved both her husband and her son. I got to know her well the short time I have been here."

"Matteo is in good hands. Giuseppe knows the wine industry so well, and he ran the winery for many years. He will show him the ropes, when Matteo is ready."

"The whole episode only proves once again what I know for certain. The Mafia only brings sorrow and death, while they hide behind their pledge of *omertá*. Where our Lord calls for windows to be open, light to be let in, where the fresh breeze cleans all, the Mafia demands just the opposite. Shadows, darkness, and whispers is where it thrives."

"And what of your father?"

The monsignor's question caught Father Gianuzzi off guard momentarily. He finally asked in return, "And what of my father?"

"What are you feeling toward him, lying under Giuseppe's roof?"

He stood up from the desk and folded his arms. "Why does it matter?"

"It matters because I care about you, and am concerned about what you must be going through."

"I appreciate your kindness. I really do. I'm just not sure how to answer your question, as I'm not sure of my own feelings. I'm angry. I feel guilty for what happened to the Vasaios. Yet, if you want to know, I was happy to hear that my father will live."

Monsignor Mancini smiled. "And that is what I was hoping to hear."

"I disagreed with my father's choices. I never believed his excuses that he did what he had to do. While I no longer could live under his roof, I never wished him ill. And that is still the case."

Monsignor Mancini smiled again. "You are well on your way on becoming an outstanding priest. You will have many people in your flock who wish ill upon those whom they turned away from. We must show them what God demands of us. You're well on your way with your feelings toward your father."

"Would you mind praying with me for the Vasaios?"

"I would love to."

They both kneeled as Monsignor Mancini began by quoting from Psalm 23, *"Though I walk though the valley of evil, I have no fear for you are at my side."*

MARIA MADE Francesca and Marco leave the Don that evening to come have dinner in her kitchen. As she plated her chicken cacciatore, she turned from her stove and said to the two of them, "You both must get some sleep tonight."

Francesca replied, "I know."

Maria carried the two plates to the small table in the kitchen. "Why don't you get a room at the *Albergo*. Giuseppe and I will pay for it. The both of you would be comfortable there."

Francesca said in return, "I'm fine sleeping on the floor with my father. I promise I will sleep."

Marco laughed and said, "My sleeping arrangements have not changed. I will stay with her as well on the floor. And yes, *Signora Sanguinetti*, I will sleep as well."

They both took a bite of the food.

Marco looked toward Maria. "This is excellent."

"It was my grandmother's recipe. She was a great cook,

and was well known for her cooking in Monreale where she lived."

"Is that where you are from?" asked Francesca.

"Yes. My love for Giuseppe brought me here to Bellafortuna."

"My father was from Monreale as well," replied Francesca.

"I knew all about your family, Francesca. My parents knew your great-grandfather, Calcedonio and his wife."

"I wish I had the opportunity to know them," Francesca stated.

"By the time I came along, your father was already in Castelvetrano."

"Does Giuseppe know my father from his wine dealings?"

"Yes. He always liked your father and Don Biscotti."

"I really have enjoyed my time speaking with your husband. He's such a kind person and so full of stories. What does he think of my father's life; his life in the Mafia?"

The question caught Maria off guard. She pretended to be stirring the remaining contents of the pot sitting on the stove in front of her. She wanted to respond to the question by relating how her own parents suffered in having to provide *pizzo* payments to all of the Dons of Monreale. But instead, she simply replied, "Giuseppe has much respect for your father."

Francesca said, "Your food is absolutely delicious."

"*Grazie*, I'm glad you both agreed to come eat."

They finished their meal and then went back to the bedroom.

Castranzio Fausto stood over two of his father's men who were busy wiping blood stains from the floorboards in the bedroom inside Don Biscotti's villa in Monreale. He smiled as the men's rags went back and forth against the floor, sopping up the blood of Don Adriano Umbretto.

He left the men to their work and went downstairs to the dining room where his father was seated alone. He said to his father, "They are almost done cleaning. However, we should have just burned this place to the ground instead of following your desire to move in. The citizens of Monreale would feel the pain as they watched the flames lick the sky as this place burned."

"My son, just as I think you will make a great Don one day, then you open your mouth, and I have to reevaluate my thoughts. This villa has been the seat of power for so many years, it is only appropriate that we move in. That is how we will show everyone that the Faustos are back in control. And with the death of Don Umbretto, we begin our march to total control of this area."

"You are correct, as always. With Salvatore's report yesterday he provided to us about killing the wine man and his wife, Bellafortuna must be in disarray."

Don Fausto replied, "They must be in disarray indeed. Salvatore has been an invaluable asset to us. His brilliant move in recommending that Adriano move his daughter to Bellafortuna gave him the perfect opportunity to go where the Don's daughter was in hiding and to exact the turmoil that he did there. This will help us in solidifying our control in Bellafortuna. Now my son, do you trust Salvatore?"

"I do. I remember when he came to us and explained why he threw his support behind you. He knows your leadership style is what Sicily needs after the War. I remember him saying Don Umbretto's way was done. That Don Umbretto refused to change. He would not listen to him."

"So, I ask you again, do you trust him?"

"Yes. Yes, I do."

"And yet again, it shows my faith in you might be misplaced. You have much to learn. Trust is a strange thing, my son. We gave Salvatore the task to kill the wine man, which he did with perfection, and even did the wife. But, he has shown his soul to me. He was close to Don Umbretto. Very close. And yet, he betrayed him. I asked you if you trust him. You said you do. That's because you are not wise yet. Heed my words. Before this is all over, I will have Salvatore killed, so that one day he will never have the chance to turn against me. That is the nature of trust. Trust is a fickle friend."

"When will we go to Bellafortuna?"

"Soon, my son. Soon. But first, let's celebrate the death of Don Umbretto with a smoke.

FRANCESCA SAT in a chair next to the bed of her father. She was sleeping with her upper body bent over by the waist with her head lying on the bed near her father's hip. Marco was the only other person in the room. He was seated on the floor, leaning up against a wall, asleep as well. Maria's food had filled their bellies, and their lack of sleep had finally caught up with them. It was around nine in the evening.

Adriano was asleep in the bed on his back. Suddenly, his eyes began to flutter. Then with a jerk of his head, his eyes flashed open. He brought his right hand up to his eyes and rubbed them. His hands brushed against his face, which revealed a two-day stubble. He looked down toward his hip and saw the clump of blonde hair. He smiled and reached for the hair with his right hand. He ran his fingers through it, saying, "My Santa."

Francesca moved slightly, and then when her father ran his fingers through her hair one more time, she woke up, just as he said again, "My Santa."

She sat up and said, "Papa. Papa. It's me Francesca."

"Francesca." He tried to focus his eyes on her. His face then broadened into a bright smile. "Francesca," he repeated.

"You are ok, Papa. You are ok."

Marco woke up, stood up from the floor, and walked over to the bed. He picked up Adriano's hand and kissed it, saying, "Praise the Lord, Don Umbretto."

"Marco, thanks for protecting her."

"She has never left your side."

"Neither did he, Papa."

"What happened to me? I guess I am in Bellafortuna."

She replied, "Yes, you are in Giuseppe Sanguinetti's house. Giancarlo and Ferruccio are here. Before I tell you what happened, let Marco go get them. Go, Marco. Go get them, as well as Dr. Incaprera and Giuseppe."

Adriano stared into his daughter's eyes and was about to ask about his son, but then he remembered she had no idea that he was in the village. Instead, he merely said, "And the priests. Ask them to come as well."

She turned toward Marco. "Go round everyone up. Tell them he is awake and he will live."

Marco left the room, leaving father and daughter alone.

Once he was gone, Adriano grabbed his daughter's hand

tighter. He slowly brought her hand to his mouth and kissed it gently. He then said to her softly, *"Mio figlia."*

They held hands until they were soon joined by everyone coming in to see the Don now that he was awake. The last to arrive was Father Gianuzzi. His father's eyes locked onto his.

His son bent down and kissed his father's forehead, saying, "May the Lord bless you, Don Umbretto."

His words brought a smile to the Don's lips as Father Gianuzzi made the sign of the cross over him.

The Don's bed was surrounded by everyone Marco had called. Giuseppe and Maria stood near the doorway while the Don's men spoke excitedly with him. The incident of a few days ago was not discussed. That would be for tomorrow. For now, everyone just relished in his being awake. The night finally came to an end when Dr. Incaprera ushered everyone out of the room so his patient could get some rest. Dr. Incaprera did allow Marco and Francesca to remain along with Father Gianuzzi, who had requested to stay to pray.

His prayers only lasted a short time, as Adriano, Francesca, and Marco all fell asleep. Father Gianuzzi left the room with one final sign of the cross over Adriano. Francesca and Marco slept in the chairs next to the bed all night.

A FUNERAL

It was six o'clock in the morning the next day when Giuseppe and Maria lay in bed awake discussing the day in front of them. Giuseppe had not slept much all night. He dreaded the first event of the day. The funeral of Santo and Mirella Vasaio. Matteo had asked Giuseppe to say a few words, which he had struggled writing much of the day before. He had finished but was not pleased with what he wrote. Perhaps it was too upsetting. Later that afternoon, he would be attending the final meeting of the *Società* before the Easter week celebrations. There was talk among several villagers that perhaps those celebrations should be canceled. Giuseppe knew it would be a contentious meeting. But with the death of Santo, the *Società* and the return of Don Fausto were far from Giuseppe's mind.

As he lay in bed next to his wife that morning, he held her hand as they spoke with each other. At one point, she said to him, "You do have a lot on your plate today. I know it will be hard. But I'm proud of you, Giuseppe. Pietro is worried about you."

"He spoke to me a few days ago. I know he is worried about me. I'm fine, Maria. I just can't believe Santo is gone. Why would they kill him and Mirella? Who would do such a thing? I will miss him so much. You, of all people, know how close we were. I'm just tired. Tired of it all."

She rolled onto her side and placed her hand on his chest. "I will be here with you always, my love."

"I know. I know. Our village is in such a precarious position now, but I've decided to just take one event at a time. Complete that task, and move on to the next. It's too overwhelming otherwise. So, first the funeral, and then the *Società*, which I'm sure we will discuss Don Umbretto living in our village."

"Will you tell them about his daughter?"

"I don't think. Not yet."

"Francesca seemed so relieved last night. She is such a sweet girl, one would never know her roots."

"One does not choose one's roots, Maria. I like her a lot. And her voice is amazing. I guess we should start our day."

Maria smiled at her husband. "I added one more item to our agenda."

"What is that?"

Maria hiked up her nightgown and climbed on top of Giuseppe. He whispered, "They will hear us."

"I'll be as quiet as a church mouse." She then bent down over him and whispered into his ear, *"Sei la mia anima gemella."* (You are my soulmate).

He enveloped her in an embrace, and then whispered

back, *"Sei la ragione per cui vivo, per cui omni giorno sorrido."* (You are my reason for living, why I smile every day.)

"T'amo, Giuseppe."

Giuseppe smiled, removed his pants, and then they kissed deeply.

ALMOST EVERY VILLAGER attended the funeral of Santo and Mirella Vasaio. Black was by far the predominant color of the villagers' outfits in attendance.

Matteo sat in the front pew of the *Chiesa della Madonna* with some of his family members. Giuseppe and Maria sat directly behind him. Francesca, with Marco at her side, sat with them.

Giancarlo and Dr. Incaprera had stayed behind with Don Umbretto as his recovery marched forward. Monsignor Mancini and Father Gianuzzi stood at the altar facing the two caskets that were before them in the middle of the aisle.

Maria held tightly onto Giuseppe's hand. Seeing the caskets in the church stirred horrible memories for both of them. Giuseppe could not look at the casket of his good friend. Tears flowed down the faces of many of the villagers as they thought of their own friendships with the Vasaios over the years.

After reading the Gospel of the raising of Lazarus, Monsignor Mancini said a few brief words and then invited Giuseppe up to the altar. Maria squeezed his hand as he stood up in the pew and then approached the altar. He went up the small stairwell and into the pulpit.

He took a deep breath and pulled out the two sheets of

paper he had worked on. He stared at the first line and then picked his head up and looked at all of his fellow villagers seated in front of him. His eulogy centered on Santo and Mirella's life. But looking out across the church filled with his friends and fellow villagers, something deep inside Giuseppe stirred, a feeling of complete and utter love for his people and his village. He loved his villagers, and they loved him in return. And more than anything, he loved Bellafortuna. When he and his father began the journey to remove the Vasaios from power, the villagers stood with them. When his own son recommended to the people closest to Pope Pius XII that Jewish musicians be hidden in the village, the villagers rose up, and they hid and protected those musicians even at great peril to themselves.

He looked down at his paper one more time. His crafted speech was too tame to truly grasp the grief he held in his heart for the death of his friend, Santo Vasaio. His death could not be in vain. Something good needed to come out of it. Giuseppe folded the papers up. He would speak from his heart. He took a deep breath and began.

"Many years ago now, when our village was at a turning point, Santo Vasaio stood up on the side of righteousness, confronted his father, and aided us in throwing away the shackles of oppression that had overtaken our community. He stayed here in the village, and fell in love with the daughter of Giacomo and Nannetta Terranova, two people whom I know we all loved. Santo and Mirella married and had a child together. As Santo's life became more and more entrenched in our village, he came to love this place and its people. But now violence and evil has come to our village, and Santo and Mirella have paid the ultimate price. The church is filled this morning in an overflowing show of love and support for their memory and for Matteo, who will need all of us to assist him. Our grief is great. Our sadness is deep. Our commitment to keeping the Vasaios in our hearts is constant. Our love for Matteo is immeasurable. And in our very soul we feel the drumbeat sending forth its musical notes of our absolute resolution that evil will not triumph in our village. We will overcome the machinations of the devil that reared its head in our community. The Vasaios shall not have died in vain. This village, this little village, touched by God's hand many years ago, shall continue to thrive. Evil has no place here. Our community will become stronger because of the deaths of the Vasaios. A strong, loving community is what is needed to crush and repel evil. A strong and loving community is what evil despises. A strong and loving community is what defines Bellafortuna. We will overcome evil. I will miss this man and his wife beyond measure. I ask all of you to pray daily for Matteo, and to give him the strength to find the courage to continue everyday. And take it from one who knows, that is exactly what is needed, courage. Grief and sadness do lessen, over time. But memories last forever. In the days ahead, we will need to call upon the memories of these two wonderful souls as we face one of the toughest tests our village has seen. We will pray that through our prayers, they will be able to send God's grace down to our village and protect it. But that's all for another time. Right now, we celebrate the life and love of Santo and Mirella Vasaio."

There was hardly a dry eye in the church as Giuseppe finished. He made his way back to his seat and sat back down. Maria turned to him and gently whispered,

"*Bellissimo.*"

He nodded to her in return and then slipped his hand into hers. Out of the corner of his eye, he saw Francesca in tears.

The mass continued, and when it reached the conclusion, both priests came off of the altar and stood before the caskets. In Father Gianuzzi's hands was the *aspersorium*, which held the holy water, while Monsignor Mancini had the *aspergillum*.

Monsignor Mancini dipped the *aspergillum* into the holy water, and then as he began sprinkling the holy water, he said a blessing over the casket of Santo.

He then turned the *aspergillum* over to Father Gianuzzi. The young priest stood over the casket of Mirella. In his mind, he remembered his tour of the winery with her and their lengthy conversation. His eyes welled up as he began to sprinkle her casket. He composed himself and gave a blessing. He said, "I bless this gracious woman, this beautiful angel, this wife and mother…" he paused before he added, "this woman who is the true melody of Sicily."

Francesca never heard another word Father Gianuzzi said of his blessing. The words spoken by Father Gianuzzi had gone directly to her soul, and they opened her eyes. She kept staring at the priest, trying to compare that face to the face of the person she knew so long ago. No one would call a woman the true melody of Sicily except for the son of Adriano Umbretto. But how? How could this be her brother? Yet, now it started to make sense. Perhaps, that was why her father sent her here in the first place.

After the blessing, the caskets were processed from the church and out into the piazza, where they were loaded on carts pulled by two horses each. Then the villagers followed behind the carts as they made their way to the village cemetery down in the valley, where Santa and Mirella Vasaio were laid to rest, next to the resting place of Santo's father, Vitellio Vasaio.

After the funeral, the villagers went up to the priests and said how beautiful the ceremony was, while others thanked Giuseppe for his stirring words. Before leaving, everyone paid their respects to Matteo.

Francesca walked over to where Father Gianuzzi was standing. The young priest smiled at her as he said, "Francesca, I'm so happy to hear your father is doing well."

"Thank you, Father. The ceremony was lovely. Very touching."

"It was beautiful for two beautiful people."

As Francesca went to hug him, she stared into his eyes. And it was in those eyes that she confirmed her belief. After their embrace, she simply said, "Have a good rest of your day."

She walked over to Marco, grabbed his hand, and began walking back to the village.

Everyone soon began returning to the village. The caskets had been interred, and mud now covered the graves. A lone figure remained standing over the graves. Giuseppe Sanguinetti stood in silence and would remain there for quite some time before finally making his way back to the village.

THE DEBATE OF THE SOCIETÀ

As the graveside service was concluding down in the valley, Adriano sat up against his pillows in the bed inside the Sanguinetti home. He was in a deep conversation with Giancarlo and Ferruccio. They had related to him everything that had happened in Monreale. Well, in truth, almost everything. Giancarlo had withheld one item. He finally brought it up last.

"Don Adriano, there is one last thing to tell you. It concerns Salvatore."

"Is he ok?"

"Yes, Don Adriano. He is at the villa in Castelvetrano. He, like the Faustos, believe that you are dead. I told him to stay there to help protect the villa. But there is something very odd."

"What is it?"

"The day of your attack in Monreale, Salvatore was in Bellafortuna."

"That's correct. I knew he was coming here to check in on Francesca."

"He left Bellafortuna at some point, and claimed to me that he was at the villa in Monreale and asleep when the attack happened. Ferruccio has confirmed Salvatore was not there."

"Yes, Don Adriano," Ferruccio added. "Salvatore was not at the villa."

Adriano stirred in the bed and sat more upright than before. He looked directly at Giancarlo and said, "I trust that man with my life. What exactly are you saying? What is it you are trying to tell me? Tell me your thoughts now. Hold nothing back, Giancarlo."

"I'm not sure what to think. Why did he lie? I don't know."

Adriano rubbed his temples before saying, "I feel like you have not told me all of your feelings on this subject. Am I correct?"

"There is something that I keep trying to wrap my head around. It's pure speculation. But it's there."

"What? Say it."

"At first, I wondered if he was merely using your believed death at the hands of the Faustos to take control of your *cosca*. But now I am wondering if it is more sinister? What if he was involved in the plot against you with the Faustos? What if Salvatore is the real betrayer in your *cosca*? What if he was the man who brought Mario and Marcello into his little group of conspirators to take you down for the Faustos?"

Ferruccio interjected, "But Salvatore killed both Mario and Marcello for their betrayal."

Giancarlo shook his head and said, "He told the Don he

killed them. Did he? Or if he did, did he do it to keep their silence? Their price for being caught."

Adriano sat quietly for a moment and then said, "If he is working with them, then he would have most likely informed Onofrio Fausto that my daughter is here."

"Most likely that is correct," Giancarlo replied. "We know Salvatore was here the day the Vasaios were killed. Was he the perpetrator? Was that the order Don Fausto gave him?"

Adriano sighed. "These are all questions that we have no answer. Yet, I cannot believe that he would have betrayed me. My mind is cloudy. My thoughts are all over the place. I don't know what to think. Lying in this bed, it is hard for me to fathom that he would betray me. Yet, if he has, then it means we are in a horrible predicament. Our betrayer is at our villa, while the Faustos solidify their control in Monreale. You said early on that you believe the Faustos and Salvatore all believe me dead. We must keep it that way for now. I need to get my strength back."

"I know, Don Adriano," Giancarlo said. "Let's continue this conversation later. Try to get some rest."

Adriano smiled at Giancarlo and said, "Thanks for your honesty with regard to your feelings. My faith in you has been well placed. Today you spoke to me as Luca used to. A Don needs honesty when dealing with tough situations."

"*Grazie*, Don Adriano. And I would be wrong for not mentioning to you the absolute loyalty that Ferruccio has shown during these past few days."

Adriano turned to Ferruccio and said, "I would expect nothing else from one of my most loyal soldiers."

Ferruccio went to a knee, grabbed Adriano's hand, and kissed it.

"Get some rest, Don Adriano," Giancarlo said. "We will continue this conversation again later."

The two men left Adriano alone in the bedroom, although they stood guard just outside in the hallway.

Adriano laid back down and tried to sleep, but his mind was racing with his thoughts of Salvatore.

FRANCESCA AND MARCO walked back to the village from the gravesite holding each other's hands. His *lupara* was slung across his back. Francesca said not a word as she was deep in thought. Finally, Marco asked her, "You're so quiet. Is everything alright?"

"Over these past weeks, I have grown to trust you, more than anyone else my entire life. I feel like I can tell you anything."

"Indeed, as I feel the same about you."

She stopped walking, let go of his hand, and then turned to him. "The young priest."

"Father Gianuzzi?"

"Yes. That's not his real name."

"Not his name. What is it? Do you know him?"

"His name is Giacomo Umbretto. He is my brother. I have no doubt."

"Your brother? I thought he was dead. How do you know?"

"He called Mirella Vasaio the true melody of Sicily. Only someone close to my father would use that phrase. I stared into his eyes. I recognized his soul. It's him. He's not dead. He's here. Perhaps my father knows, and that's why I am here. If my brother knows who I am, that's a question I don't have an answer to yet."

"Are you certain it is him?"

"Without a doubt."

"Will you speak to him about it?"

"Not yet. Let's keep it between us for now."

"As you wish. *Mamma mia.* Don Adriano Umbretto's son lives."

THAT AFTERNOON, the meeting of the *Società* happened in the dining room of the *Albergo.* Every member had arrived early except for Giuseppe.

Elizabetta went up to Monsignor Mancini and asked, "Is he coming?"

"I think so," replied the Monsignor.

She walked over to Giorgio and said, "Monsignor Mancini thinks Giuseppe is coming."

"We will wait a few minutes."

Father Gianuzzi was standing next to Monsignor Mancini. He heard Elizabetta's question and said to Monsignor Mancini, "Giuseppe certainly means a lot to these people."

"Bellafortuna is him. His love for this place and these people is unending and unmeasurable."

Just then, Giuseppe came into the dining room. All of the other members turned and looked at him as he walked in. Many of them came up and offered their hands to him. Giorgio asked everyone to take a seat so that the meeting could begin.

Monsignor Mancini began the meeting with a prayer,

asking the Lord to protect the village and for a special blessing for the Vasaios. When he finished, Giorgio began the meeting.

Giorgio said, "Dark clouds hover over our beloved village. Two of our fellow villagers have been murdered. And now we know that our greatest fear is a reality. The Mafia has set their sights on our village. Onofrio Fausto has returned to Sicily, and he has brought his evil ways to our little world here. How we proceed from here is what we must debate today. I know we also need to discuss the Easter celebrations. But I believe this issue is the most pressing, so we will cover it first. I call upon Giuseppe who wanted to say a few words first."

Giuseppe stood up from the table as all eyes turned toward him. He said, "For those of you who are unaware, the very same night that the Vasaios were killed, there were numerous attacks on people in Monreale. Onofrio Fausto has brought his evil not just to our little world, but he is solidifying his control in this part of Sicily. It is my understanding that Don Adriano Umbretto had taken some of his men and joined Don Biscotti's men at the villa in Monreale, to defend the city from the takeover by Don Fausto. The villa was attacked that night, and Don Umbretto was gravely wounded. One of his men drove him here, to our secluded village. Why here? Close proximity. His man was unaware of what had happened here. Be that as it may, the Don is recuperating at my home. Dr. Incaprera came in from Palermo and believes the Don will recover completely. The belief of the Don's men who are here is that Onofrio Fausto thinks Don Umbretto is dead. They advise that it is best if Don Fausto continues to believe that. That's why I waited to tell you as a group." Giuseppe sat back down.

Elizabetta said, "So we are right in the thick of it."

Giuseppe smiled at her. "We were in the thick of it the moment the Vasaios were killed."

Giorgio stood up. He said, "Giuseppe, I listened to your moving words at the funeral of Santo and Mirella. Your words spoke about overcoming evil. Don Fausto is the epitome of evil. He is the devil himself. The only way to defeat evil is to kill it. We must avenge the deaths of the Vasaios and protect the village with the killing of Don Fausto."

A few members voiced their support for the words of Giorgio. Some groaned while others sat quietly with worried looks on their faces. Soon a vigorous debate erupted between those in support of Giorgio's suggestion and those who opposed it.

Giuseppe rose once again, and the debate quickly drew to a close. Giuseppe said, "If you took my words as a call for violence at the funeral, then you misunderstood them. We are farmers, craftsmen, shop owners, and vintners. We cannot win a war against the Mafia. And if we fail, what would be the outcome. The death toll would be staggering."

Giorgio, still standing, said, "So in your mind there is no solution. We just let the Faustos take over our lives. No, Giuseppe, I say we fight."

The debate raged once again until it was finally disrupted by a bang on the table by Monsignor Mancini. "Listen to yourselves. Let me remind you of a key fact. An eye for eye will only result in two people losing their eyes. It's not a solution. What happens if you kill Onofrio? Who takes over? His son? You kill him too? And then whoever takes over after him, you kill him too? It's a never ending cycle."

There was no response to the words from Monsignor Mancini from anyone seated around the table. Finally, Giuseppe rose and said, "Many, many years ago, this group entrusted me the task of going to meet with the leading family to attempt to set us free from the oppression they had placed on us. I ask you once again to trust me. I will go see Don Fausto. At the end of the day, he is a businessman, ruthless and evil, but a businessman nonetheless. On Easter Monday, I will go to Monreale and seek a meeting with him. I will make him an offer he cannot refuse. An offer to take Bellafortuna off the table."

Father Gianuzzi asked, "And what type of offer would that be to make him turn his eye away from this place?"

"It will not affect any villager in Bellafortuna."

Elizabetta said, "I agree with Giuseppe. Let him speak with Don Fausto."

Those opposed to Giorgio's position all shook their heads in agreement with the statement made by Elizabetta.

Giorgio pointed to Giuseppe and said, "You still haven't said what your offer would be. So what is it?"

"That's between Don Fausto and myself. It will not affect you in any way."

Lorenzo Baldini quickly stated, "I agree that we should let Giuseppe go speak to him. Monsignor Mancini has shown the foolishness of the other position."

The debate roared again until Giorgio raised his hand and asked for quiet. He then said, "We will let Giuseppe do his thing. If it fails, then we know what action we will need to take. Now, we have discussed this enough. Let's talk about the Easter celebrations."

There was an entirely new debate on whether or not the Easter celebrations should happen, but ultimately all of the villagers came to the agreement that they should, as that was exactly what the Vasaios would have wanted to happen.

As the meeting came to a close and the members started to file out, Elizabetta came up to Giuseppe and asked, "At the Good Friday event, do you think Francesca would sing the *Regina Coeli* for us."

"I will ask. That would be beautiful."

Everyone left the room except for Giuseppe, Monsignor Mancini, and Father Gianuzzi. Monsignor Mancini smiled at his old friend. He said to Giuseppe, "You have no idea what your offer will be, do you?"

"Not a clue. But I had to answer the hotheads. After all, hotheads can create a mob. A mob that would be wiped out by Onofrio Fausto."

Father Gianuzzi added, "Understandable that you have no clue. They don't negotiate. They take. That's the way of the Mafia."

Monsignor Mancini said, "Well, that might be true, but let me know if I can be of any assistance to you. Your words at the funeral today were beautiful."

"The Vasaios deserved them."

"Indeed they did. Take care of yourself, Giuseppe."

"Both of you take care," replied Giuseppe.

Giuseppe walked out of the dining room.

As the meeting was wrapping up, Francesca and Marco sat next to the bed of Don Umbretto. Adriano said, "I'm getting my strength back. You look tired, Francesca."

"I'm fine. Worried about you, but fine."

"You need to rest. Tonight, you will sleep at the hotel. Marco, you will sit outside her bedroom door and guard her. You can sleep lying up against her door, if need be. But just be there to protect her."

"I will do as you ask, Don Umbretto."

"Papa, these people think he is my husband. What will they think if someone sees him sitting outside my door?"

"They will believe you had a spat. And that's that. *Capice.*"

Marco chuckled at Adriano's comment as Francesca responded, "Yes, sir. Can I ask what the plan is going forward?"

"Giancarlo wants me to return to Castelvetrano soon. Most likely after Easter. We will have much to do. I will need you more than ever. I have no idea what the status of my *cosca* is currently."

Francesca asked, "What are we going to do about Onofrio Fausto?"

"Revenge can come in many forms. But his actions against Luca, Don Biscotti, your grandfather and grandmother, and me can only be satisfied with one result, his death."

Marco stood up from the chair and said, "Just say the word. Say the word and let me do the deed."

Adriano smiled at his loyal soldier and said, "I promised your mother when you came to work for me that you would never take a life. You would join my *cosca*, but your hands would be clean from that part of the business."

Francesca lifted her hand to her chin. She remembered back when she had asked Marco if he had killed for her father. He did not give an answer back then. But now she knew.

Marco sat back down and said, "I would do it for you, Don Umbretto."

"I know, my son. I know."

<hr>

LATER THAT EVENING, Francesca and Marco left Adriano in the bedroom with Giancarlo and Ferruccio as they carried their bags downstairs, heading over to the Albergo. As they walked out the front door, Giuseppe and Maria were outside, seated at the table drinking wine.

"I made all the arrangements," Maria said. "You have a room over at the albergo. Marco, are you sure I can't get you a room as well."

"No, *Signora.*" He then patted his *lupara* slung on his back and replied, "Here is my pillow for my sleeping spot outside her door."

Maria said in response, "Well, before you leave, join us for a glass of wine."

They put their bags down and sat at the table. As Maria went inside to grab two glasses, Marco laid his *lupara* on top his bag and sat down. Maria soon joined them back at the table. As Giuseppe poured the wine, he said, "I spoke with Dr. Incaprera before he left to go back to Palermo this afternoon. He was much impressed with your father's strength. He said your father is well on his way to recovery."

"Yes, *Signor Sanguinetti.* And it is all thanks to you and

Maria. We will never forget what the both of you did for him." She paused before asking, "How's Matteo?"

"I'm meeting with him tomorrow to help him with the winery. He's still in shock."

"And how are you, *Signor Sanguinetti*?"

Giuseppe smiled back at her. He said not a word, picked up his glass, and took a big sip.

Marco added, "If you need any help at the winery, let us know, as we would love to lend a hand."

"*Grazie*. That's very kind of the both of you. Francesca, I almost forgot to ask you. On Good Friday, we have a procession in the village that ends here in the piazza. The committee in charge of the event would love to have you sing when the procession reaches the church. You will sing the *Regina Coeli*, if you agree to it."

"I would be honored."

"*Mille grazie*. How's the wine?"

"Delicious."

Giuseppe asked, "Would anyone mind if I do one thing?"

"Not at all, whatever it is," replied Francesca.

Maria laughed and said, "Oh, I know what it is."

Giuseppe stood and walked inside *Il Paradiso*. He put a record on the phonograph and then began to play it. The voice of Caruso blasted out of the open door of the wine store. He joined them back at the table.

As the moonlight covered the piazza in a mystical, bright white light, the booming voice of Enrico Caruso singing *Recondita armonia from* Puccini's *Tosca* bounced off the buildings. The little group sat quietly at the table, drinking their wine, listening to the magical voice, and forgetting their grief and worries momentarily. Francesca thought back to her first days sitting at the table with Marco, drinking late into the night. With her other hand, she slipped it under the table and grabbed his hand. He gently stroked her hand with his finger.

Upstairs, Don Adriano Umbretto told Giancarlo and Ferruccio to leave him as he was tired. Before they did, he asked that they open his window. After they left him alone, he lay in bed as the voice of Caruso wafted in through his open window. He thought of Don Biscotti and his nights of listening to music with him during his time of exile. He thought of his own son and the time they came to Bellafortuna together to see an opera. And he thought of Francesca and her wonderful voice. A smile came to his face as he relished listening to the voice of the opera great.

FRANCESCA AND MARCO made their way over to the *albergo*. One aria had turned into two, which had turned into three, and then more. Of course, each aria brought forth another pour of wine. They were both pretty tipsy by the time they made their way over to the hotel.

Francesca's room was on the second floor. Marco opened the door to the room and let Francesca in. She turned to him and said, "You can put your bag inside if you want."

As he did so, she said to him, "My father is alive, and now I have discovered that my brother lives. My emotions are all over the place."

"I'm so happy for you, Francesca."

He picked up his *lupara* and stepped out into the hallway.

"*Buona notte*, Francesca. I know you will enjoy your night's sleep in a bed once again."

"*Buona notte*, Marco. Thanks for everything."

"You are most welcome."

"Do you think when my father returns to Castelvetrano, we will have to go back with him?"

"I have not heard, but I would think with the Vasaios murder and the Faustos being in control of Monreale, I guess he will most likely want you back with him."

She sighed, then looked directly into his eyes. "It's sad. As I have come to love this place." She smiled at him.

He said in return, "I've fallen in love myself ...," he paused and added, "with this place."

"*Buona notte*," she repeated as he closed the door.

He took a seat in the hallway next to the door. Inside the room, she changed her clothes and put on a nightgown. As she removed the bedspread on the bed, she paused. She never wanted anything in her life as much as she wanted him. She walked to the door, turned the knob, and opened it. She said not a word as she went to the bed and climbed in.

Marco heard the door open and was expecting to see her. But she never came out into the hallway. He said out loud, "Francesca, what is it?"

There was no response.

He stood up, went to the door, and stood in the doorway. "Francesca, what is it?" he asked again.

She was in bed, her back up against the pillows, with the bedsheets at the bottom of the bed. She simply responded, "*Chiudi la porta.*" (Close the door.)

He came into the bedroom and then turned and closed the

door. As he turned around, she sat up and pulled her nightgown over her head. He stared at her nakedness.

She said, "Before I return to my old life, I want one memory to hold onto; and that memory is you."

He walked over to the bed. He looked at her breasts and then down to her intimate area as he quickly began to undress. He climbed on top of her as she welcomed him, and they embraced. He whispered to her, "Your father wanted me to wait outside."

"Tell him we made up," she whispered back.

He kissed her lips. Their kiss became more passionate. He then began kissing her breasts as her nipples became erect with each stroke of his tongue. He looked up at her, smiled, and then shifted his body down further. She spread her legs wider as he began to kiss her womanhood. As he entered her with his tongue, she rubbed his hair with both of her hands as his head went back and forth. Her hips began to match his moments. She began to moan as waves of pleasure tingled her body. Just as she was about to climax, he stopped and got on his knees. She looked at his excitement and wanted him more than ever. She sat up and pulled him on top of her. He entered her, and she moaned even louder than before. Their motions soon matched each other as the pace quickened. She came quickly, soon joined by him. As he kissed her and laid his head on her shoulder, she said, *"T'amo, Marco."*

"You are so beautiful, Francesca. *T'amo."*

They lay in each other's arms for a few moments. When he got out of bed, he noticed the blood on the sheets.

She laughed and said, "Don't worry about it. I'll tell them my monthly visitor came and I was unprepared."

As he began to dress, he said, "I really would kill Onofrio Fausto for your father."

"I know, Marco. But I also know why he would not want you to. He knows the feeling that killing brings, even when it is justified. I think in you, he sees the goodness which I see in you myself. He wants your soul untouched by the blackness that surrounds his at times. He would not want to be the reason for that blackness."

He finished latching his belt. He was about to turn to the door, but instead, he looked directly at her and said, "*La tua memoria e la mia memoria. Uno che non dimentchero mai.* (Your memory is my memory. One that I will never forget.)

She jumped from the bed and ran into his arms. They kissed deeply before he left to stand guard outside her bedroom door.

THE POLITICS OF SICILY

The next morning, Giuseppe attended his morning Mass as usual. He prayed to his son, asking for assistance with his plan in dealing with Don Fausto.

After Mass, and with his mind filled with the events of the past few days, he decided to take a stroll around Bellafortuna. He took a side street that ran west out of the piazza. The narrow, twisting cobbled street was lined with two-story buildings on either side. Small balconies protruded from the second floor, most of which were decorated with geraniums. From the railings of some of the balconies, the inhabitants of the home had hung their laundry to dry, which included their unmentionables.

He turned down one small alley. Midway down the alley was a single niche wall fountain with the face of a lion from which a stream of water purred gently and produced the most distinct pleasing sound as the water collected in the basin below. At the end of the alley was a *carretto da gara*, a

Sicilian cart used for festivals. In just a few days it would be used for the Easter celebrations. The cart was painted a bright red and yellow, representing the colors of Sicily. On either side were scenes of life in Bellafortuna. One panel had the vineyards, one panel had the church, one had the *Stagno Azzurro*, and one had the Boccale winery.

Seeing the winery made him think of Santo. He continued out of the alley and turned right where the street peered down over the expanse of the valley below. He stopped and stared across the valley. He always had loved Bellafortuna. It was in his soul. He would try to protect it as best he could. But what could he offer Don Fausto to keep him away?

Then it dawned on him. It was too simple. It made perfect sense. If you are going to make a deal with a Don, why not ask another Don what offer would be attractive. Adriano Umbretto could assist him in coming up with an offer. He would speak to him. He would help Giuseppe. He owed it to him for protecting his daughter.

He began walking at a quick pace, making his way back to the wine store.

ADRIANO WAS LYING IN BED. Giancarlo was standing next to him. When Giuseppe walked in, he asked Adriano, "How are you feeling?"

"Better each day, *Signor Sanguinetti*."

"I was wondering if I could speak to you about a pressing matter?"

"*Certo.* Giancarlo, go to Ferruccio and discuss with him our conversation. Come see me in an hour."

"Yes, sir."

He left the room as Adriano asked Giuseppe, "What do you need?"

Giuseppe stepped further into the room. "I come to you for advice. I don't need to tell you what the death of the Vasaios at the hands of Onofrio Fausto has stirred within my people. Some of course are calling for revenge."

Adriano smiled. He cut Giuseppe off and said, "I am sure that you told them the foolishness of such action. They would be crushed by Don Fausto."

"I did."

"There is much more going on than just Onofrio Fausto, Giuseppe. Sicilian politics does not play much of a role in your little secluded part of the world, I would bet. There are many forces pushing and pulling at each other on this island. Some who want complete Sicilian independence from Italy. Others who want the status quo. Others fighting for the rights of the landowners. Others trying to maintain power, while others seek more power and control. In politics, the Communist Party is gaining strength, supported by the peasants and workers of Sicily. They are demanding change, in particular, land reform. The powerful Christian Democrats are losing popularity, and fear that at the upcoming election, they will lose control. The Mafia hitched itself to the Democrats, and they will do whatever needs to be done to stay in power. For example, Nunzio Sansone and Leonardo Savia, communists in the forefront arguing for land reform, were recently silenced by the Mafia. What my little history lesson shows you, Giuseppe, is that your advice to your fellow villagers to be careful with a call for revenge was correct."

"Don Umbretto, politics does have a limited role here. Music, love of God, love of each other, hard work, and community is what matters here the most. Don Fausto can take all of that away from us. And that's what I wanted to come speak to you about. Before Don Biscotti died, he pledged his support and protection to Bellafortuna, as he had always done. Now we find ourselves exposed. I want to meet with Don Fausto and make him an offer to take Bellafortuna off the table. Would making him an offer work?"

"Don Fausto's soul is pure evil. He also wants what the new breed wants, power. Sure they love the money, but it is power they are after. They do not care one bit about the people under their protection. Your offer, if it's large enough, would most likely be agreed to. But, very soon thereafter, he would be back again to take more from Bellafortuna. More land, more payments, and more blood."

"Is there any hope for us?"

"My *cosca* is wounded. When I am back in Castelvetrano, I will need to rebuild it. Once we have regained strength, I will pull together Dons from Palermo and we will bring war upon Don Fausto."

"But how long will that take?"

"Time. The other Dons would need to feel that my power is back before they would join me in such an undertaking. In the meantime, you will have to deal with life under Don Fausto. Heed my words, Giuseppe, you do not want to cross him. Patience is the key. Wait, bide your time, and then when the time is right, actions will occur that will give you the result you desire. I pledge to you that I will do whatever I can that whomever ultimately takes over from Don Fausto will leave Bellafortuna alone, just as Don

Biscotti and my grandfather, Don Calcedonio, did. This I swear."

"*Grazie*, Don Umbretto."

"The kindness you have offered me and my daughter will never be forgotten."

"Well, Don Umbretto, if you were nothing more than a simple peasant, we would have treated you the same here in Bellafortuna. We act out of compassion and righteousness. Never expecting to get anything back in return."

Adriano laughed and said, "You do know that's not the way of the world."

Giuseppe shrugged and said, "It's the way of Bellafortuna."

Adriano looked right at Giuseppe and said, "I've always liked you. You have qualities that are hard to find in people; loyalty, trust, leadership, goodness, kindness and intelligence. There have been only a few people in my life who had those same elements. One of those was my *capobastone*. Don Fausto had him killed. Just imagine if you took over that position. We could do great things."

Giuseppe laughed. "I'm flattered. Although you would hate all of my advice."

Adriano burst out laughing and said, "I forgot to add one more quality, a wicked sense of humor. Giuseppe, it means a lot to me that you would come seeking my advice. Put your trust in me, and in time, you will see the reward. But it will take time."

After thanking Adriano, Giuseppe walked back down to the wine store. He had walked into that meeting with Don Umbretto optimistic with his plan. He left with his thoughts in disarray. The feeling he had when all of this started was in the forefront of his mind. There really was nothing Bellafortuna could do.

AN HOUR LATER, Adriano held a brief meeting with Giancarlo and Ferruccio in the bedroom. The last topic concerned Salvatore.

Adriano said, "Giancarlo, I understand your belief that Salvatore is and has been the betrayer amongst us. I still have a hard time believing it to be true. But I must say, if it is true, it stings more than you know. His betrayal assisted with the death of Luca. We will leave for Castelvetrano on Monday. Salvatore will be shocked to see me. I will look into his eyes, directly into his soul, and I will find the truth."

Giancarlo said to his Don, "I'm so sorry for everything that has happened."

Ferruccio asked, "Do you think Salvatore killed the wine man and and his wife?"

Adriano said in reply, "I know I'm getting better as my mind is becoming clearer. If he betrayed me, then the killing of the Vasaios makes sense. He recommends Francesca to come here. I agree to send Marco with her. Salvatore comes to the village to check on them for me. In so doing, Don Fausto now has his agent in place to do his dirty work. If all true, Salvatore will pay dearly for his betrayal. But I still have a hard time believing it to be true."

Giancarlo asked, "What about the Faustos?"

"I just had this conversation with Giuseppe. He's very concerned about his village as he should be. But, the time for revenge is not ripe. I need to regain complete power. I need to rid myself of the rats within my organization. And then I can make my move against the Faustos. It will take time."

Ferruccio asked, "Do you have any concerns about Marco?"

"No. While it's true he is related to Salvatore, I think he is loyal. I take that back. I know he is."

Giancarlo added, "For now, you will get more and more of your strength back so we can go back on Monday."

"My trust in you, Giancarlo, has always been well placed."

"*Grazie*, Don Umbretto."

A WITNESS TO A BETRAYAL

*H*oly Thursday morning brought forth a stunning blue sky across the valley of Bellafortuna. Inside *Il Paradiso*, Kurt Hofmann and Giuseppe were doing a quick inventory. Kurt placed the last bottle he had pulled from a box on the floor onto the shelf.

He said to Giuseppe, "That's the last of them."

"Ok. We need to take a few bottles of *Vino di Bellafortuna* over to the rectory. Monsignor Mancini always has a big lunch at the rectory for Easter Sunday."

Kurt walked over to the shelf that housed *Vino di Bellafortuna*. Giuseppe, meanwhile, grabbed an empty box and walked over to Kurt, who began to hand the bottles to him.

"Here you go," said Kurt.

"*Grazie.*" Giuseppe grabbed the first bottle and stared at the label. "Poor Santo and Mirella."

"Elizabetta told me the meeting yesterday was contentious."

"It was indeed."

"She said you were great in toning down the flames calling for revenge."

"Monsignor Mancini's words made those calling for revenge see the foolishness of their proposed action."

Just then, the door to *Il Paradiso* opened. Into the wine store came Enzo Adarato, a farmer down in the valley.

Giuseppe welcomed him to the store. *"Signor Adarato, come va?*

"Molte bene, Signor Sanguinetti."

"What can I help you with this morning?"

"I don't need anything. I wanted to come talk to you about something." He turned to Kurt and said, *"Signor Hofmann, come va?"*

"Bene."

Enzo turned back to Giuseppe and said, "You know my farm is one of the furthest from the village. It's location along the *Via Valle* gives me the perfect opportunity to see who comes and goes from the village. I was the first to see the American tanks heading toward our village to liberate us from the Germans."

Giuseppe glanced at Kurt, who smiled, as any conversation with Enzo Adarato, no matter who he was speaking to, would always include that tidbit of Bellafortuna history.

Enzo continued, "It broke my heart to hear about Santo and his wife. They were such good people. He treated me fairly with my vineyards over all these years."

Giuseppe said, "If you are fearful that things will change with Matteo now in charge, have no fear. He will match and perhaps even surpass his father's fairness."

"Oh no, that's not why I am here. I have been so depressed these past few days with his death, that something I noticed slipped from my mind. I guess it just did not make me think it could be related, but now I am thinking it does."

"What did you notice?"

"The night Santo died, I couldn't sleep. I went outside and was seated on my porch, having a smoke. It must have been 3am. Suddenly, from out the darkness, I saw the lights from a car coming from the direction of the village on the *Via Valle*. The car sped right past my home and where I was seated."

"What type of car?"

"A long, black car. Unsure of the type."

"Did you see the driver?"

"Well, you know, my beautiful little farmhouse sits so close to the road. I think of all the farms in the valley mine is the closest to the road. It allows me a perfect opportunity to see a lot."

"I know," replied Giuseppe, with a glance over to Kurt.

Enzo continued, "The car was driven by the man you were speaking to at the concert. He was that big man with the bushy mustache."

"You are certain that is who you saw?"

"Yes. It was definitely that man you were speaking to."

"*Grazie*. Thanks for letting me know."

"Like I said, I just did not think anything about it, and it slipped my mind. But this morning, looking across my vineyards and thinking about Santo, I remembered that car and the driver. It was so late at night. No one drives down that road late at night."

Giuseppe grabbed a bottle of Spanish wine from one of the racks. He handed the bottle to Enzo, saying, "This is for you. A token of thanks for what you have told me today."

Enzo looked at the wine label and said, *"Della Spagna.* I once met a lady from Spain in Palermo. She was beautiful. Her kisses tasted like wine. I can't wait to taste this."

"Thanks again. Thanks for coming."

The farmer left the wine store as Kurt walked close to where Giuseppe was standing. Kurt said, "You are thinking what I am thinking?"

"I am."

"Do you remember his name?"

"Salvatore, I think. He worked for Don Umbretto."

"Do you think Don Umbretto was involved? Have we been misled this whole time?"

"I don't think so. I think Salvatore's allegiance, for whatever reason, was to Don Fausto. I think he was working under his orders."

"What will you do with this information?"

Giuseppe glanced to the ceiling above him and then told Kurt, "I think someone upstairs would like to know. I'll be back." He turned and made his way to the stairwell.

ADRIANO WAS SITTING up in bed, eating scrambled eggs that Maria had made for him. As most Sicilian women did, she stood nearby as Adriano took his first bites, waiting to see if the food met his expectations. Francesca and Marco were standing close by.

Adriano, after his initial bite, assured the cook that the eggs were delicious, just as Giuseppe walked in. Adriano asked, "How do you stay so thin with a woman who can cook like this?"

Giuseppe laughed and, patting his belly, said, "It's a struggle. A daily struggle." He looked at everyone in the room and then said to Adriano, "I have some news, but I can come back later."

"Whatever you have to say, you can say in front of everyone in this room."

Giuseppe nodded and then proceeded to tell Adriano about the conversation with Enzo Adarato. Adriano never lifted his fork from his plate again as it sat on his lap in the bed. When Giuseppe finished, the first to speak was Francesca, "I always said that man scared me."

Marco, with tears in his eyes, said to Adriano, "Do you really think he would betray you?"

"Although it is hard for me to even consider such a thing, if he was seen leaving early that morning, it raises many questions. One thing I do know. If he killed the Vasaios, he did so under the orders of one person and one person alone."

"Don Onofrio Fausto," replied Giuseppe.

Maria said, "Why did he have to kill Santo and his wife?"

Adriano replied, "Because that was the order. The wife probably because she happened to be there. I can't give the Vasaios back to you. All I can do is promise you that they will have justice. Salvatore will pay for his crime. Giuseppe, thanks for telling me this. Would you and your wife leave me a few minutes to speak with Marco and Francesca alone?"

"Not at all."

As Maria and Giuseppe began to leave the room, Adriano said, "Thank you both. And Maria, thank you for my breakfast."

WHEN THE SANGUINETTIS HAD LEFT, Adriano told his daughter and Marco about Giancarlo and Ferruccio's belief of Salvatore's betrayal and how he had lied about being at the villa in Monreale on the night of the attack. He ended his brief summation by saying, "Giuseppe's conversation with the farmer confirms my fears. Salvatore Battaglia has betrayed me."

Marco said, "Don Umbretto, please believe me when I tell you I had no idea. I pledge my loyalty to you."

"I know, Marco. I have not one worry about you. Salvatore has been the poison within my *cosca,* and I missed it. He had conspirators working with him, and I failed to see that he was the leader of them."

Francesca said, "How could he betray you? He was so close to you."

"There will come a point in the next few days when down on his knees he will tell me why he did so as he pleads for his life. Now, go get Giancarlo and Ferruccio at once. This changes our plans."

Marco went to a knee, grabbed Adriano's hand, and kissed it, saying, "My Don."

With that, they left the room. Adriano placed his plate of food on the floor. He was no longer hungry. Giancarlo's intuition about Salvatore was right, but Adriano did not want to believe it. But it was all true. Salvatore Battaglia betrayed him. He would use today and tomorrow to develop a plan for their next steps. They would now go back Saturday to Castelvetrano and take care of business. He looked out the window of the bedroom and could see the top of the church and the vineyards spreading for miles in the valley behind it. Don Fausto was in control of Monreale, and soon he would be coming to take control of the economic life of this village, and there was nothing to stop him for now. However, one thing was certain in Adriano's mind though: Salvatore would pay dearly for his betrayal.

AFTER LEAVING ADRIANO'S BEDROOM, Giuseppe made his way to the kitchen, where Maria made him a strong espresso. Their conversation soon turned to Don Fausto and the precarious position of Bellafortuna.

Giuseppe said, "I've decided to try to reason with Don Fausto. I want to make him an offer that will keep him from harassing our villagers."

"What type of offer?"

"I'm still working on it. As you know my grandfather and father left us with an enormous amount of wealth. I'm thinking a large payoff to keep Don Fausto out. I will tell you I spoke to Don Umbretto about it, and he thinks it will not work."

"You know I trust everything you do, and support every decision you make, but on this I would have to agree with

Don Umbretto. I remember when my own parents had to deal with the Mafia in their simple candle shop. Don Fausto was in charge of Monreale back then. He would come to the shop every Tuesday and collect his blood money from my father. I remember when my friend's father did not make his payment for his cobbler shop. Her father was hanged from a lantern pole with shoe strings from some of his shoes in his shop. His body was left on that pole for four days. I had to pass it everyday. That's the type of person you are dealing with, Giuseppe, in Don Onofrio Fausto."

"But I have to do something. My entire being is driving me to one result and that is to save the village in anyway that I can. This is the only way available to me. This is it."

"I know, Giuseppe. But you are dealing with a man who has accumulated bad money. You are throwing good money at bad. Good money thrown at bad money will result in only one thing, more bad money. Just think about it, that's all I ask before you take action."

"I will. I promise. At least we now know who killed the Vasaios, Salvatore Battaglia."

"I was surprised he was related to Marco. I like that boy."

"He seemed very upset when he figured out his relative betrayed Don Umbretto. I guess Don Umbretto trusts that he is loyal to him."

Maria laughed and said, "He is loyal to Francesca. He loves her, Giuseppe. They slept with each other recently."

Giuseppe threw his hands up and asked, "How would you know that?"

"A woman knows, Giuseppe. Before you came into the bedroom, I could tell the way she looked at him and touched him while they were talking. There is a closeness that was not there before. They flirted before when we would sit out drinking wine at night. I knew there was an interest between the two. But today I noticed a closeness that only occurs once you have been intimate. A closeness that shines like a beacon in the night. A closeness that makes new love sparkle. Don Umbretto has no worry about Marco betraying him."

"I hope Don Umbrettto does not have a woman's intuition or Marco will be thrown down the hill of our village, or worse." Giuseppe then grabbed Maria and pulled her into an embrace.

She asked, "What are you doing?"

"Showing the world that we are close. That we have been intimate. Sending forth a beacon."

Maria laughed and said, "After so many years of marriage the beacon fades, the sparkle is gone, as is the case with us. Now it's replaced with a deep love and respect for each other."

"We can rekindle the spark of new love, or at least try."

She tilted her head up and kissed him. She said to him, "I love you with every fiber of my being."

"I know. And I love you too."

"Be careful in all of your dealings with Don Fausto. He brought so much misery to my parents and to all of Monreale. The fact that he is back in charge of Monreale and soon taking over control of Bellafortuna makes me extremely scared and sad all at the same time."

"Me too, Maria. Me too. After I finish my espresso, I'm going over to the winery to meet with Matteo. I will be back for dinner and then we can go to the Holy Thursday Mass tonight."

"You're getting your feet washed by Monsignor as usual?"

"No, I gave up my spot for Matteo."

"That's a nice gesture. And what about Good Friday? The procession is all set?"

"It is. And Francesca will sing when we reach the piazza. Should be a glorious time for all."

"Our village needs the distraction after the death of the Vasaios."

"It does."

She handed him his espresso, which was now ready. He took a sip and then said to her, "No sparkle, hmmm."

She laughed and said in reply, "Get over it, old man."

He laughed before leaning in and kissing her.

———

DON FAUSTO SAT in the oversized chair behind the desk which once belonged to Don Biscotti. His son stood off to the side.

A business owner from Monreale was on his knees in front of the Don. Sweat beaded on the man's lip. A result of his overworked nerves. The Don extended his hand to the diminutive man before him. The business owner promptly kissed it, saying, "I pledge my loyalty to you, Don Fausto. I promise to make timely payments to you for your protection."

"Do so, and you will have peace. *Va.*"

The business owner left the room, leaving Don Fausto and his son alone. Castranzio closed the door and walked back toward the desk. He told his father, "That's the last of them. That's every major business owner and farmer in Monreale, all who pledged their loyalty to you. They all feared you. You could see it in their eyes."

"It's good to be back here, my son. We need to repeat this scene in Bellafortuna. It won't take as long as there are just a few we need to meet as the rest will fall in line soon enough. None of it matters, as it's the winery we want anyway. Let me tell you my plan and how we will deal with the daughter of Adriano Umbretto."

THE FAMILY

*L*ate that afternoon, Francesca finished her rehearsal with Vincenzo Occipinti for the small concert tomorrow that would take place at the end of the Good Friday procession.

As she walked down the street leading back toward the piazza with Marco, she said to him, "I've decided to confront my brother. I want him to know that I am aware of his identity. I will let my father know as well. I think the time is right."

"Are you sure?"

"Yes. I'm going to the rectory now, and will tell him to come with me to Giuseppe's home."

"If you are wrong, that would make for quite an awkward conversation."

She laughed and said, "It would. But I'm not wrong. He's my brother."

They walked into the piazza. Marco went to sit by the Boccale statue while Francesca continued to the rectory.

———

WHEN FRANCESCA ARRIVED in the bedroom with Father Gianuzzi, they found Adriano walking on the arm of Giancarlo.

Giancarlo said, "We just got back from strolling around the wine store and going up and down the stairs twice. Your father, Francesca, is making remarkable progress."

"I'm so glad to see you up and about, Papa."

Adriano laid back in bed. He said, "Progress is exhausting."

Father Gianuzzi said, "The more you do it though, the less exhausted you will be."

"One can only hope," Adriano said as he made himself more comfortable. He said, "Father Gianuzzi, what brings you to me this afternoon?"

"Francesca asked me to come."

Giancarlo said, "Don Umbretto, I will go over to the hotel but will be back shortly with Ferruccio."

"*Grazie*, Giancarlo," replied the Don.

When he left the room, Francesca walked over and closed the door behind him. She then turned and walked back to the bed.

Adriano said, "I'm sure Father Gianuzzi has much to prepare for Holy Thursday mass tonight. Why did you want him to come?"

Francesca looked over toward the priest and then down at her father. She said, "I will get right to the point. At the

Vasaio funeral, Father Gianuzzi referred to Mirella Vasaio as a woman who was the true melody of Sicily. There are only two men in all of this God-forsaken country who use that term. Mamma's father and you." She turned to the priest and said, "Your words opened my eyes and my heart, Giacomo."

The shock on his face was telling, such that Adriano knew there was no use denying it. He said, "He is your brother."

She turned to her father and said, "Why did you keep this from me all these years?" Then turning back to Giacomo, she said, "Why would you abandon me after Mamma's death?"

Giacomo raised his hand toward his father and said, "Papa, this is for me to explain, not you. After Mamma's death, I was angry. I was angry at him for the life he led. That life led to revenge against Mamma and her death. We argued. I left. I wanted nothing more to do with that life. I had no idea what to do when I left. I had no money. I had nowhere to live. I was trying to get to Palermo. I found myself in Monreale where I found lodging at the Benedictine Monastery. They allowed me to stay there for a few weeks. It was in their small chapel, at dawn during morning prayer, that I heard the gentle call to the priesthood. Until then, trust me, I expected I would return to the family. But as I was filled with God's grace more and more, I knew my past life was over. I left the monastery and eventually went to Cefalù where I went to the seminary."

Francesca asked, "Papa, did you know he was alive all along?"

Adriano sighed before saying, "I did. I went to the seminary to confront him and convince him to come home. He refused. And that was that."

"So you told Luca and I that he was dead?"

"*È così,*" Adriano replied. He then looked at his son and said, "He wanted it that way. He cut all ties with us. Yet, I still followed his career. And when he became priest, I knew he was installed here. That's why I moved you here."

"Giacomo, so you knew I was your sister all along?"

"The only reason I agreed to anything that father asked was because it was for you."

Francesca asked them both, "Is my being here the reason death has come upon this place?"

Giacomo said, "I, more than anyone else, would love to believe that you being here brought the Mafia and everything that goes with it to this place. But I agree with Giuseppe Sanguinetti that Don Onofrio Fausto was coming to this place no matter what. Your being here did not matter."

She looked at his father and said, "Does Don Fausto know I am here? Does he know your son is here?"

"I don't know. Salvatore knew. And he has betrayed me so I have no idea if he told Don Fausto. I have come to believe Salvatore is working with the Faustos and is the killer of the Vasaios. I have become certain of this, as all the facts point to that as the truth. We are leaving Saturday to go back to Castelvetrano."

"All of us," she asked.

"Yes, all of us."

She turned to her brother and asked, "And what about you, Giacomo, what will you do?"

"I am fine. I have nothing to do with it. The antiquated traditions of loyalty, honor, *omertà* and vendettas are all rooted in evil. They should have no place in this world. How one can sit idly by and witness a killing, and then because of some old tradition of silence not say anything is beyond me. It goes against who I am."

Adriano quickly retorted, "My son, that's because you have never understood life in Sicily. I'm not fighting with you. I'm too old and too tired. But I will say this. In Sicily, corruption runs deep. Let me ask you this. You have fallen in love with Bellafortuna, right?"

"I have. With all my heart. I love this place and the people."

Adriano smiled and said, "I think back often to when you were young and we came to the opera here together."

"I remember it well."

"This place that you love was touched by death. A murder of two of their most beloved villagers. Has the village called upon the Sicilian authorities to come in and investigate? Have they contacted anyone to come in and arrest Salvatore Battaglia for the murder? No, of course not. Why? Because they know how corrupt it all is. Now if Bellafortuna was under my protection, I would be both the enforcer and the judge. That's the way of Sicily. That has been my life, despise it or respect it, I don't care, as this was what was forced upon me by my life's journey."

Giacomo smiled and said, "I've changed over all these years. In the past, I would not hold back my words. But now, I will just smile. As our Lord says, sometimes it's better to shake the sand from your sandals and move on from that place if you know your words will not lead to conversion."

Francesca cut off any response from her father by asking Giacomo, "Do you think you would have eventually told me who you were?"

"Well, you figured it out, so I guess we don't need to worry about that."

Francesca walked to where he was standing and hugged him.

While staring at his two children in their embrace, Adriano's mind flashed to an image of Santa as he took a deep breath. At least for now, the family was back together again.

PART IV

THE CONFRONTATION

GOOD FRIDAY

*S*ettimana *Santa* (Holy Week) is a celebration throughout all of Sicily showcasing the deep faith of the inhabitants across the island, a celebration of life overcoming death in the form of the Lord's Passion and Resurrection. These celebrations, from festivals, to processions, and re-enactments of Christ's passion, have deep roots in the history and traditions of each and every community. The one constant among them all is the role of music. Each village or town selects which day of Holy Week is the one they celebrate more expansively. Across the entire island, from the larger cities down to the smallest of villages, events take place in celebration. For Bellafortuna, it was *Vernerdi Santo* (Good Friday), the most solemn of days, which was the culmination of the entire week.

For the Sanguinettis and the rest of the villagers of Bellafortuna, *Vernerdi Santo* began at 6 am at the *Chiesa della Madonna*. The event that morning began with a brief prayer by Monsignor Mancini. Then Father Gianuzzi read from the Book of Isaiah of the Old Testament. The passage was the same every year. It concerned the suffering servant of God, which Christians have long considered a prophecy of the coming of the Messiah. When Father Gianuzzi reached the following lines of the passage, everyone in attendance stood up to remember what the entirety of the day before them was all about: *"But he was pierced for our transgressions, he was bruised for our iniquities: upon him was the chastisement that brought us peace, and with his wounds we are healed."*

Finally came the Gospel read by Monsignor Mancini; of Jesus's trial before Pontius Pilate. Upon its conclusion, there was no homily. Instead, everyone kneeled and prayed in silence.

The service ended with the "Our Father." Then a group of twenty-four men, known as the *Maestranze* (skilled workers), walked up on the altar to perform the *scinnuta*, which means the taking down. Giuseppe Sanguinetti was a member of the *Maestranze*, along with Santo Vasaio, whose position was now taken over by his son, Matteo. Eight members surrounded the statue of Mary, while eight surrounded the statue of St. Joseph. The other eight members, which included Giuseppe, surrounded the statue of the crucified Christ. Each statue had a wooden base, called a *vara*. This base would allow the statue to be easily carried and would also tend to make the statue dramatically sway during the procession, which added to the entire spectacle. The men slid a long pole along the base of the statue on either side and then, with four men on each side, removed the statues from their pedestals. The statues themselves dated back to the time when the village of Bellafortuna was located down in the valley, back when it was called *Campanella,* and before the earthquake that made the village leaders at that time move from the valley once and for all, so many years ago now. The *Maestranze* cared for the wooden statues throughout the year, repairing them and getting them ready for today's celebration.

Each group of men laid the poles upon their shoulders, and then they carried their statue down the aisle and out of the Church, followed behind by the congregation. When they came out into the piazza, a small marching band greeted them, playing solemn music. The priests took the lead in front of the procession and led the band, followed by the *Maestranze* and then the villagers. They processed out of the piazza. When they reached the spot where the road leads down the hill toward the valley, the priests, band, and villagers stopped as the *Maestranze* continued carrying the statues down to the valley to prepare them for the much larger procession later that day.

The *Maestranze* made their way to the Silveri barn down in the valley. This barn had a special connection to the village of Bellafortuna. The barn was originally owned by Renato Silveri. He had allowed the first secret meetings of the *Società* to happen inside when the Vasaio family was in charge. Even after his death, the barn remained in the Silveri family. Within the barn, three tables had been set up, upon which each of the three statues were placed. Soon, the barn would be a whirlwind of activity as the *Maestranze* would paint each statue if need be and then decorate each of the statues for the coming procession just a few hours away. It was somewhat of a competition among the *Maestranze* as to whose statue looked the best. Their work began immediately as months of planning, drawings, and designing would all quickly come together before their work was put on full display in front of the whole community. During the war, the processions had ceased. But once Sicily was liberated, that first Easter, the beloved procession began again.

Maria Sanguinetti had watched with pride as her husband carried the statute of Christ out of the village. Being a member of the *Maestranze* was a high honor in the village, one for which both Giuseppe's father and grandfather had been chosen. When she could no longer see the group of men carrying the statutes, Maria returned to the village. As she walked toward *Il Paradiso*, she found Francesca and Marco walking with Adriano.

Maria said, "Don Umbretto, it's good to see you outside this morning."

"Yes, it's good to be outside."

Francesca added, "He made it around the entire piazza."

Adriano chuckled and said, "Which means I won't be out of the bed for the rest of the day."

"You look better, Don Umbretto," Maria said. "Your strength is returning."

"One can hope," Adriano replied.

Francesca said, "He wanted to come hear me sing later today, but I told him its too hot for him to be seated out in the piazza. He can leave the window open and sit in a chair next to the window to take it all in."

Maria said, "She will bring our celebration today to a fitting close."

"I know she will. Now, it's back to bed for me."

They all went inside the wine store and waited for the celebration to begin later that day.

AT NOON, the marching band processed to the Silveri barn. They waited outside the doors as the frantic work of the *Maestranze* continued inside. In the piazza, the orchestra was setting up the stage where they would perform to end the celebration when the procession reached the church. And inside the kitchen of almost every home, the women began preparing the meal that would be eaten after the festivities.

By 12:30 pm, some of the villagers began to show up outside the barn, waiting for the first glimpse of the statues as the procession would start. Villagers who remained up in Bellafortuna began to line up along the road leading to the piazza, waiting for the procession.

At 1:25 pm, the double doors to the barn were thrown open. The villagers outside the doors were giddy with excitement. The first statue to come forth was that of St. Joseph. The eight *Maestranze* carrying the statue wore black robes. The statue did not depict how the father of Jesus is normally portrayed as a worker. Instead, St. Joseph was holding Jesus as a child. The men in charge of this statue did not do much to the statue itself but instead spent their time exquisitely decorating its base. A wreath of yellow plumeria encircled the feet of St. Joseph. The flowers seemed to suspend the Saint as though he were floating on a cloud of delicate blossoms. The villagers standing nearby clapped and voiced their approval.

Next came the stunning statue of Mary. She was on her knees, depicting the moment the Angel Gabriele informed her of God's plan and her acceptance to do God's will. The *Maestranze* for the Madonna had repainted her robes, which were a beautiful light blue, almost matching the blue sky above. The base of the statue was decorated with gardenias that were strewn at her feet. The thick, sweet scent preceded her arrival, a herald of her strength and virtue. This year, the *Maestranze* wanted to do something with the arms of the statue, the same arms that had held not only Christ at his birth but at his death. They placed a large, beautiful bouquet of Easter Lillies in her arms, which she cradled as she did the infant Jesus. The men carrying her were dressed in light blue robes. The crowd cheered even louder upon seeing the craftsmanship of the decorations for this statue.

Last came the statue of the crucified Christ. The statue depicted the very moment of Jesus's death. His body, with arms outstretched, feet nailed together, and a crown of thorns on his head, showing the horrendous death that crucifixion brought and of the unselfish love the Lord had for the World. The men carrying the statue were adorned in robes of bright red, symbolizing the blood of Christ. Deep red roses surrounded the base. And an arch of roses encircled the entire statue, making one's eyes focus on the face of the Lord. At the insistence of Giuseppe, a gold paint had been added to the body of Christ, except where the wounds of Christ were located. Those areas were repainted with red paint but were also draped with swags of red roses, as though his dripping blood had bloomed with hope for the people of the village.

There was an audible gasp from the crowd as the sunlight hit the golden paint, making it shine bright and contrasting with the blood-red paint of Christ's body and the deep red roses all around. The gasp soon turned into cheers and yells from the villagers. Giuseppe smiled at the other members of his group, much satisfied by the crowd's reaction.

The men carrying the statue of Jesus turned to their left, where the Mary statue had been stationed. They walked toward that statue, and as the two groups met, the men carrying Jesus's statue bowed, making it look like Jesus was bowing to his mother.

The band took their position in the front, and then the *Maestranze* got into order, the same order they had come out of the barn. The band began to play a funeral march, and the procession began making its way toward the village. The *Maestranze*, carrying the poles on their shoulders, walked slowly and swayed side to side, in step with the music.

The procession soon reached the hill leading up to the village. By this point, the road leading from the crest of the hill all the way to the piazza was lined with villagers on either side.

The procession climbed up the hill along the road between vineyards and olive trees. When it reached the summit, the crowd pushed in closer to get a glance as the *Maestranze* came into view. As the procession reached the village, the music of the band echoed off the buildings, making the sound reverberate throughout the entire village. Not all of the villagers were on the street. Some were standing on their balconies, and as the statues passed, they threw flowers from where they were standing, making for a beautiful sight. Although the villagers thought the statues of Mary and St. Joseph were beautifully decorated this year, it was the crucified Christ which was truly awe-inspiring, glistening under the Sicilian sun. Everyone knew who would take home the prize this year.

The procession slowly made its way to the piazza.

Monsignor Mancini checked his watch. Right on time, as usual. After all these years, he had perfected it.

They entered the piazza right at 3 pm, the hour of the Lord's death. The piazza was packed with the rest of the villagers who were waiting for the procession and the concert. The procession continued into the piazza, where it circled two times around, giving time for the other villagers to arrive at the piazza, as the bell from *Chiesa della Madonna* tolled.

Inside the Sanguinetti home, Adriano sat by the window, with Giancarlo and Ferruccio standing nearby. Adriano took in the procession around the piazza and thought of the celebrations he had seen throughout his life.

Maria, Francesca, and Marco were seated in chairs outside *Il Paradiso*. Francesca wore a simple but elegant black dress that Elizabetta gave her, assuring her they were the same size, which they were, thankfully.

Francesca, at one point, turned to Maria and said, "I really could stay here forever. I love this place and the people."

"When Giuseppe asked me to marry him, I knew I would be leaving Monreale for this small, secluded village. It's the best decision I ever made in my life. I too love this place and its people."

Marco was taking in the procession, mesmerized by the entire spectacle. As the statue of Christ came by *Il Paradiso*, he noticed Matteo Vasaio at the end struggling as he walked with the weight of the statue, yet with a look of pride upon his face. Marco knew the thoughts of his father had to be on his mind.

As the procession ended, the band members scrambled to take their place with the orchestra as the *Maestranze* made their way into the church to place the statues back onto their pedestals. Over the next few days, the flowers and other decorations would be removed, and the statues would once again just become part of the décor of the church and would not garner much interest until they were taken out into public once again next year. That was the beauty of the celebration; each year, new plans were laid, and new designs were tried, and it was through that work these pieces of art came to life.

Monsignor Mancini stepped in front of the orchestra and asked for a moment of silence. He then led everyone in the "Anima Christi" prayer.

When he finished, Vito Occipinti came forward with his baton. Monsignor Mancini walked to his seat in the front, next to Father Gianuzzi. Vito bowed to the crowd, turned to the orchestra, and they began to play the first selection, *Ave Maria* by Gounod.

The crowd cheered as the orchestra played the final note. Vito asked the orchestra to stand and accept the applause. He then asked them to sit as he prepared the next selection, a symphonic version of Antonio Vivaldi's *Stabat Mater*, depicting Mary standing in sorrow at the foot of the cross. He raised his baton, and the orchestra began the solemn piece. The orchestra played it exquisitely. Again, a thunderous eruption of applause greeted the orchestra at the end. Vito Occipinti made the orchestra stand once again. As they did so, Francesca made her way forward. Vito said to the crowd, "Now we will hear a different version of *Regina Coeli*. Francesca Moretti will sing for you the Easter Hymn from Pietro Mascagni's opera, *Cavalleria Rusticana*.

A small group of villagers walked up and took positions off to the right of the orchestra. These men and women were members of the summer opera festival chorus who would be lending their support today. Francesca took her place in front of the orchestra and curtsied to all. A nod of Francesca's head assured Vito she was ready, and the music began.

Pietro Mascagni wrote the opera in just two short months in order to enter it in a competition. He won first prize. The opera was based on a short story by Giovanni Verga and concerned dark passions lurking within the lives of people living in a small Sicilian village.

The Easter Hymn begins with a brief religious-sounding introduction before the chorus sings the famous words of the *Regina Coeli*.

As the chorus sang, a car come up the valley road and stopped just short of the square, unnoticed. Seeing the large crowd, the driver parked on the side of the road. A man with a limp got out of the passenger side with a *lupara* slung on his back. The driver also got out, grabbing his gun as well. They opened the back doors on either side. From the back seat emerged Don Onofrio Fausto and his son. They had decided that they would celebrate Easter not only in control of Monreale but of the Boccale Winery in Bellafortuna.

They stayed in the front of the car, taking in the music sung by the chorus. Then, suddenly as if out of nowhere, Francesca began to sing.

Inneggiamo, il Signor non è morto.
Ei fulgente ha dischiuso l'avel,
inneggiamo al Signore risorto
oggi asceso alla gloria del Ciel!

Let us rejoice that Our Lord is not dead,

And in glory, has opened the tomb!
Let us rejoice that Our Lord is risen again
And today is gone up into the glory of Heaven!

The crowd sat in stunned silence as Francesca's voice echoed across the entire piazza. Father Gianuzzi sat in his chair with a wide smile on his face. Giuseppe Sanguinetti was seated with Maria and Marco. He, too, was smiling, relishing her voice. Looking out from the bedroom window, her father had tears streaming down his face.

Castranzio, leaning up against the hood, turned to his father and simply said, "What a voice. It has to be her. Salvatore said she had a gorgeous voice, but he never said how beautiful she is."

Don Fausto replied, "You are right on all accounts."

As the piece reached its climax, the chorus repeated the word *"Signore,"* and soon Francesca joined them as her voice soared over both the orchestra and the chorus. At its conclusion, the villagers stood as one, offering a thunderous applause to both the orchestra and singers. But it was when Vito Occipinti bowed to Francesca that the crowd gave the largest ovation of the day.

As she turned and walked away from the front of the orchestra, the first person who met her was her brother. He hugged her, saying, "That was stunning. Absolutely stunning."

"Grazie."

She returned to *Il Paradiso*, where she was met with congratulations by Marco, Giuseppe, and Maria. After she hugged them all, she looked up and saw her father peering down. He placed one hand over his heart and, with his other hand, blew her a kiss.

Some villagers came over to *Il Paradiso* to congratulate Francesca on her voice. Her father, meanwhile, closed the window and got back in bed with the help of Giancarlo.

Don Fausto, meanwhile, said to the men with him, "Let's go."

They walked into the piazza. They saw two priests speaking with villagers close to the church. They started heading toward them. The villagers who passed them on their way back to their homes scurried out of their way. They did not know who they were, but their demeanor showed they were not here for the Easter celebration.

Monsignor Mancini was speaking to a villager, and as their conversation ended, he turned to Father Gianuzzi and asked, "Ready to go back."

"Yes. What a glorious day."

It was at that point Monsignor Mancini saw the men making their way over. He said out loud, "My God."

"What is it, Monsignor?" Father Gianuzzi asked before turning and seeing the men walking toward them.

Monsignor Mancini said, "If I had to guess, here comes the Faustos. And so it begins."

Father Gianuzzi replied, *"Il cielo ci aiuti."* (Heaven help us.) He then made the sign of the cross as the men approached them.

TAKING BLAME

The two men with Don Fausto stopped a few feet before the two priests as Don Fausto and his son continued toward them. They both walked right up to the two priests.

"I am Don Onofrio Fausto. This is my son, Castranzio."

"I am Monsignor Pietro Mancini. And this is Father Giulio Gianuzzi." Monsignor Mancini thought carefully of his next words before saying, "We have been expecting your visit. What can we do for you?"

Don Fausto chuckled and said in reply, "Yes, Monsignor. Your expecting me does not come as a surprise. You can help arrange a meeting for me."

"With whom?"

"Matteo Vasaio, Giuseppe Sanguinetti, and the daughter of Don Adriano Umbretto."

Father Gianuzzi bristled at the mention of his sister's name. Monsignor Mancini placed his hand upon his arm and then responded to Don Fausto. "The daughter of Don Umbretto?"

"Monsignor, do not play games with me. Please don't start off on a bad foot. It will not be good, both for you or this place. Her father is dead. I suggest you do what I ask. Arrange this meeting in the next fifteen minutes. We will meet in your rectory. The young priest here will take us over there, while you go get everyone. My two men will stand guard outside the doors of the rectory, just in case anyone in your village wants to be stupid. Father Gianuzzi, let's go."

They began walking to the rectory with the group as Monsignor Mancini quickly headed over to *Il Paradiso*.

GIUSEPPE AND MARIA were inside the wine store. Francesca and Marco had already gone upstairs to see her father. Giuseppe was opening a wine box on the counter with a knife. He had just received this new wine produced by a winery located on the slopes of Mt. Etna and was looking forward to trying it tonight. When Monsignor Mancini walked in, Giuseppe laid the knife on the counter. He could tell something was wrong the moment he saw Monsignor Mancini's face.

Maria was the first to respond after Monsignor Mancini told them who was in the village. "Oh my God. What do they want?" she asked.

"A meeting. A meeting with your husband as well as with Matteo and Francesca. They know who she is."

"Oh my God," she repeated again.

Giuseppe said, "I knew they would come for the winery

one day. But the fact that he knows about Francesca. That's not good news." He turned to his wife and said, "Say nothing to Don Umbretto or his men or even Francesca about them being here in the village. Monsignor Mancini, I will go alone and negotiate. Don Fausto must not find out who lies upstairs. For if he does, I fear our village will pay dearly for it."

Maria asked, "How can you handle this?"

Giuseppe leaned over and kissed his wife, saying, "I'll think about it on my walk over. Let's go, Pietro."

Giuseppe and Monsignor Mancini walked out of *Il Paradiso* toward the rectory as Maria picked up another box off the floor and opened it using the knife from the counter, trying to keep herself busy while all of her thoughts were focused on who had come to the village.

WHEN MONSIGNOR MANCINI introduced Giuseppe and said that he wanted to speak with Don Fausto without the other requested people in attendance, Don Fausto responded, "I'm a patient man, Monsignor. Very patient. Yet, when I ask for something, I expect and demand that my request is met with no deviation."

Giuseppe said, "I asked for a meeting with you."

Don Fausto said, "Giuseppe Sanguinetti. I knew your grandfather and father. I did not have many dealings with them as back then my relatives, the Vasaios, ruled this place."

"Your relatives," replied Giuseppe. "If you care for them, leave Matteo Vasaio alone." Pointedly he then said, "You have already done enough."

Don Fausto laughed and said, "Santo's father, Vitellio, was weak. He gave this all up. I will not make the same mistake."

"What is it that you want, Don Fausto?"

"I want exactly what I asked for. I want a meeting with you, Matteo Vasaio and the daughter of Don Umbretto, who I know is here."

"Let's you and I talk first."

"I'll tell you what. I know Francesca Umbretto has been staying in your home. The young priest here, he and my son will go over to your home and together will bring her here. Monsignor Mancini, in the meantime, will go get Matteo Vasaio. As they are bringing everyone to our little meeting, I will meet with you to discuss whatever it is you want to say to me. You have as long as it takes for the others to get here."

Giuseppe quickly said, "I have no idea where Francesca is."

"Well, we can start at your house. Castranzio, take the priest with you and go find her. Monsignor, go fetch Matteo."

Giuseppe took a hard, long stare at Monsignor Mancini.

Castranzio Fausto and Father Gianuzzi headed out of the room, as Monsignor Mancini followed close behind.

When they left, Don Fausto said to Giuseppe, "So what is it that you want to say to me."

FATHER GIANUZZI SAID NOT a word to Castranzio as they walked across the piazza. He knew he needed to find a way to leave Castranzio downstairs so he could go and tell his father who had arrived in the village. They reached *Il Paradiso* and went inside. Maria Sanguinetti had finished unpacking boxes and was standing by the counter.

Upon entering, Father Gianuzzi saw Maria and quickly knew how he would get upstairs. He said, "Maria, this is Castranzio Fausto."

She nodded to the young man, who responded by saying, "You must be Giuseppe Sanguinetti's wife. My father never told me how beautiful Giuseppe's wife would be."

Ignoring his comment, she asked, "Can I help you with something?"

Father Gianuzzi said, "His father would like to meet with Francesca. She must be upstairs. *Signor Fausto*, stay here with Maria and I will go get her upstairs."

Father Gianuzzi walked toward the stairwell as Castranzio came over by Maria, who was standing in front of the counter. He said to her, "I'm going to like seeing you when I come pick up the *pizzo* every month."

"I know all about your family, *Signor Fausto*. I am from Monreale. My family was under your father's so-called protection, if you want to play that game and call it that. You can have your blood money. Because that's what it is."

"Do you have any idea who you are speaking to? My father will be the head of the most powerful *cosca* in all of Sicily."

"I know exactly who I am talking to."

"You better be careful how you speak to others, particularly those who are more powerful than you."

"Power? Power comes and goes. Decency, humility and goodness last forever. Things that you and your father know nothing about."

"Let me tell you something, *Signora Sanguinetti*. I have

done nothing to you to warrant such biting words coming from your mouth. I will reiterate to you once again to be very careful. Very careful. I can make life a whole lot easier for you and your family. Perhaps we can come to some type of arrangement to lower the amount your husband will have to pay."

"What type of arrangement?"

He reached down and grabbed his crotch, saying, "I think you and I could work something out. It would make it so much easier."

Maria laughed and said, "Does your father know you make such offers to the wives of those under his protection?" She then took a few steps toward him and said in a sarcastic tone, "It's probably the only way you can be with a woman anyway."

His face turned red. He laid one arm across her chest and pushed her back against the counter. His body weight pressed against hers. He said to her with an authoritative tone, "I told you to be careful. If you piss me off too much I will be collecting the *pizzo* from your husband's widow."

As his body pressed harder against her, she said to him, "Get off of me."

He pressed his body even harder against hers as he leaned over and kissed her cheek.

"Get the hell off of me," she said angrily.

"You have my proposition. I won't need an answer until I come next time to collect. I hope you understand how important it will be for you to answer correctly."

She could feel him as he thrust his pelvis against her. She closed her eyes momentarily as she spread her hands on the counter to support herself. As she did so, her eyes flashed open when her hand hit an object.

He said to her, "Trust me, answer correctly, and I will make things go very smoothly for you. You will need it for what's in store for your village."

"Trust you? Your family killed Santo and Mirella Vasaio."

"They had to die. You, on the other hand, have the power to save your husband." His hand grabbed her right breast, and he fondled her.

She tried to push him off but could not.

He said again, "Answer me correctly, and all will be well." He pushed against her even harder. His hand then left her breast and went down by her thigh. He grabbed the folds of her dress and began hiking it up. He then grabbed her crotch and pressed his two fingers into her through her undergarment.

"Stop it," she begged, but it only made him press his fingers harder into her. As he did so, Maria's right hand wrapped around the handle of the object sitting on the counter, the knife she had used earlier to open the boxes.

"You can wait till I come back, or you can answer now. Your choice?"

"Here is my answer," she said to him as she raised the knife high behind him and then plunged it deep into his back.

He crumbled to his knees at her feet, reaching around toward his back with one hand for the spot where he had been stabbed. He tried to stand but stumbled forward. Maria stood over him, the bloody knife in her hand.

He yelled out, "*Aiuto! Papa, aiuto!*"

Footsteps could be heard hurrying down the stairwell from upstairs. Father Gianuzzi and Giancarlo were the first to enter the wine store, just as Maria leaned over Castranzio Fausto and shouted, "May God save your soul." Then with an underneath swing of her arm from her right hip, she plunged the knife into his chest.

Her momentum made her fall on top of him as he fell backward onto the floor. Father Gianuzzi and Giancarlo ran over to her and helped get her up, just as Francesca and Marco came into the wine store.

Maria stood up and stared at her hands. She then looked at Father Gianuzzi and said, "I killed him, Father. I killed him."

Father Gianuzzi looked toward Giancarlo, who was kneeling next to the body of Castranzio Fausto. Giancarlo felt for a pulse, looked up toward Father Gianuzzi, and shook his head. Francesca, meanwhile, ran over to Maria and held her tight.

Just then, Ferruccio and Adriano Umbretto walked into the wine store.

Ferruccio asked, "What happened?"

Maria, who was in tears, said, "I killed him. Oh my God, I killed him."

Adriano walked over to Maria. Francesca looked at her father as she released Maria from her embrace. Adriano pulled Maria into his arms. He removed the knife from her hands and put it in his pocket. He looked down at the body lying by his feet.

Maria said, "He would not get off of me. He was propositioning me and letting me know things would be bad for me and Giuseppe if I said no."

Adriano shrugged his shoulders and said, "*È così!* You did what had to happen." Adriano then turned his head and looked at everyone around the room. He said, "Now listen to me – all of you. What happened in this place today will never be known to anyone. I killed Castranzio Fausto." He then looked at Maria and said to her, "Not you, my dear. You did not do this. Does everyone understand?"

They all nodded their head, except for Father Gianuzzi, who was now kneeling over the body of Castranzio Fausto, saying the final prayers for his soul.

Adriano hugged Maria tighter in his embrace. Maria, still with tears tracking down her face, said to him, "Why will you take the blame?"

He looked kindly at her and then told her, "You acted boldly, and were merely defending yourself and your husband. But our society does not approve of strong willed women, at least not yet. But it is women like you who are the true melody of Sicily. You, who have been through so much, you don't deserve any of this. Your kindness and goodness emanates from your very soul. For these reasons, I will take the blame."

Before Maria could respond, Marco, looking out the window, blurted out, "Don Umbretto, I see Giuseppe Sanguinetti walking across the piazza with three men. The older one must be Don Fausto." Adriano quickly walked over to the window and looked out.

Watching Don Fausto walking across the piazza made Adriano think of his grandparents before the image of Luca came to the forefront of his mind. This man walking toward the wine store was the man who had brought so much pain to him.

Adriano said, "Ladies, go upstairs. Gentlemen, *luparas* at

the ready. Both of you take care of his associates. Leave Don Fausto to me."

Marco, Ferruccio, and Giancarlo readied their guns as the ladies went to the door that led to the stairwell but stopped by the counter. Father Gianuzzi stood up and faced the door of *Il Paradiso*.

Marco and Ferruccio moved into position on either side of the door as silence inside the room took hold.

Adriano moved back and stood over the body of Castranzio Fausto. He broke the silence by saying, "And now I put an end to it."

Giancarlo, who was standing to the left of the window, said quietly, "Here they come. Gentlemen you will have one chance to disable his men."

Maria and Francesca held on to each other to see what would happen.

Don Fausto walked next to Giuseppe while his associates were just a few steps ahead. They approached *Il Paradiso*. Inside, Marco and Ferruccio waited on either side of the door.

A DEATH AVENGED

As the group reached the door, Don Fausto said, "What was taking my son so long to bring *Signorina Umbretto* to us will now be answered."

Dennario, holding his *lupara* with both hands, said, "Don Fausto, let me and Vincenzo go in first. Just to make sure."

Dennario reached for the doorknob and entered the door. As he came through the door, he felt the muzzle of Marco's gun against his temple. Marco, with his other hand, grabbed the man by his shirt and pulled him toward the floor of the store, sending the man's gun sliding across the floor. Giancarlo reached for the man's *lupara* and picked it up. The commotion at the door confused Vincenzo, Don Fausto's other associate, who had been unable to see exactly what was happening. His eyes darted to the right to see where Dennario had gone. It gave Ferruccio just enough time to grab Vincenzo's *lupara*. The two men struggled until Ferruccio wrestled it free.

Giancarlo, standing a few feet away and holding his own gun as well as the one he had picked up off the floor, shouted to both men, "On your knees. Get on your fucking knees."

Don Fausto and Giuseppe Sanguinetti were by the doorway. Don Fausto saw his men go to their knees, but it was the man lying on the floor that caught his attention. He ran into the room and over to the body. He went to his knees and held his son without realizing who it was standing over him. He yelled, "Who did this? Who did this?"

Adriano stood upright and replied, "I, Don Adriano Umbretto."

Holding onto his son, Don Fausto said, "You. But I thought you were dead."

Adriano laughed and said, "Your men failed."

"You killed my son, you bastard."

"You have killed many people close to me. Now you shall know the feeling of grief. But don't worry, your torment will be short-lived."

"Short-lived, what do you mean?"

From his pocket, Adriano withdrew the knife that he had taken from Maria.

"No, Don Umbretto. Please," begged Don Fausto.

Giuseppe was standing in the doorway when suddenly, from behind him, came Monsignor Mancini and Matteo Vasaio. They peered into the room, trying to make sense of it all.

Don Fausto said again, "I beg you, Don Umbretto."

"Admit to me that you came to Bellafortuna to kill my daughter. Admit it."

"No, Don Umbretto."

"Admit it to me!" he yelled.

Angrily, Don Fausto responded. "I won't admit anything to you. You want to kill me, then just do it." He grabbed his son's body tightly, saying, "You took the only thing that mattered to me."

Father Gianuzzi stepped closer to Adriano. He told his father, "Don't do this." Then with even more emphasis, he said, "Don't do it, Papa."

Francesca, standing with Maria, glanced at her father's men, who all wore a look of shock on their faces after the priest had referred to Don Umbretto as his father.

Meanwhile, Don Fausto let go of his son and stood up on his knees. He raised his fist toward Adriano and with a look of defiance on his face, screamed, "*A fanabla!*" (Go to hell.)

Adriano laughed and said, "You can let me know how it is down there, since you will get their first."

Father Gianuzzi said again, "Papa, no. Don't."

Adriano glanced at his son and then turned back toward Don Fausto. He said, "Make peace with God, Don Fausto."

"*Vaffanculo,*" Don Fausto sneered back at him.

With all the force he could muster, Adriano plunged the knife deep into the chest of Don Fausto. Don Fausto raised both hands to his chest as he gave out a death yell. His body then fell forward on top of the dead body of his son.

Adriano stepped back. He dropped the knife to the ground and exclaimed, "Both my daughter and Bellafortuna are safe, and the death of my grandparents and my *capobastone* are avenged."

"Papa, you killed him," his son said loudly.

Adriano looked at his son and then looked at the dead bodies. He said, "*È così!* I had no other choice. If I had let him go, it would mean a constant threat of revenge on me and my men, and it would certainly mean difficulties and perhaps even death for many of these villagers if he remained in control of this place and Monreale. The very same villagers who you have come to love."

Father Gianuzzi said not a word in response.

Monsignor Mancini said to Giuseppe, "What the hell happened?"

"I don't exactly know, Pietro."

Adriano walked over to Don Fausto's two men. He was closest to Dennario. He said, "I remember you from the villa, you bastard. You should have killed me in the bed."

"Please, Don Umbretto. Let us go."

Adriano smiled and said, "You are both lucky. You deserve to die. But I will let you both live for one purpose. Go back to Monreale. Tell your remaining men that Don Adriano Umbretto lives. Tell them to leave the villa by nightfall. As once again, an Umbretto will rule Monreale. Did you drive here?"

"Yes."

"Yes, Don Umbretto," Adriano corrected him.

"Sorry, Don Umbretto. Yes, we drove, Don Umbretto."

Adriano said, "Marco and Ferruccio. Walk this man to his car. Have him drive it to the store. Then he and his friend can load the car with this filth lying on the floor. That way, all of the remaining associates will know what will happen if they cross Don Adriano Umbretto."

Marco pulled Dennario up and said, "Let's go."

Adriano turned and noticed Francesca and Maria in the back of the store. His eyes locked onto Maria's. He slowly nodded his head to her. She did the same back to him.

He then turned to his son. Before he could say a word, his son walked to the door and left the wine store.

Ferruccio stood the other man on his feet. Giuseppe, meanwhile, made his way over to his wife. They all waited for the car to come around.

After Don Fausto's men had left, everyone stayed in the wine store. Giuseppe had just finished relating how he had tried to make an offer to Don Fausto but there was no interest. "It was obvious, he wanted one thing and one thing only. He was coming for the winery and all of its production." Giuseppe turned toward Francesca and said, "I also think the day would have ended with your demise, young lady. It was something he said about tying up all of the loose ends of the Umbretto family. Don Umbretto, your actions today, in killing both Castranzio and Don Fausto, saved your daughter's life."

Adriano looked toward Maria and then said, "I did not kill Catsranzio Fausto, Giuseppe. That young lady over there, your wife, is one courageous woman. She rejected his proposition with a knife."

Giuseppe brought his hand over his mouth as he grabbed his wife. He said to her, "I had no idea. Are you ok?"

"I'm fine, Giuseppe."

Adriano said, "When my wife was killed many years ago, I swore upon her grave that I would protect my daughter, at all costs. Sometimes, we have to do what we have to. *È così*! My daughter is safe. Just as your wife is safe. That is what matters most. The killing of Castranzio Fausto will fall on me, not your wife."

Giuseppe asked, "And what does the death of the Faustos mean to Bellafortuna? Who will come after Don Fausto to rule Monreale?"

Adriano said in reply, "I will rule Monreale. I pledge my life to you, that this place and its people will live in peace."

Ferruccio and Marco, both confused by Adriano's words, looked to Giancarlo, who shrugged his shoulders.

"And for that, we will be eternally grateful," responded Giuseppe.

Adriano said, "We leave tomorrow. I have some business I must attend to in Castelvetrano." He looked toward Maria and then back to Giuseppe. "I thank the both of you for all that you have done. Now I must go upstairs. Perhaps, later we can have one last meal together."

Adriano went upstairs with Ferruccio and Giancarlo as Giuseppe hugged his wife.

———

ONCE IN THE BEDROOM, Adriano climbed into bed, exhausted from the events downstairs. He said to his two associates, "We have much work to do."

Giancarlo asked, "What did you mean that you will rule Monreale?"

"We have other items to discuss first. After the death of Luca, I never thought I could find a replacement for a *capobastone*. I know that I have now. Ferruccio, your loyalty to me has been steadfast and proven. I would be honored if you would agree to taking the position of *capobastone* within my *cosca*."

Giancarlo's mouth dropped open as he stood next to Ferruccio in silence.

Ferruccio replied, "I would be honored and accept your offer." Ferruccio went to a knee and kissed Adriano's hand.

Adriano turned and asked Giancarlo, "Do you think Don Fausto's men will flee from Monreale?"

Putting his hurt feelings aside for being passed over, he responded, "I do. Once they know the great and powerful Don Umbretto is alive and well, they will flee."

Adriano said, "Which leaves Monreale easy for the taking."

"Yes it does. Don Umbretto, may I ask you a question?"

"Certainly."

"Did I do something that made you not trust me?"

"Why would you ask such a thing?"

"I'm just asking."

Adriano laughed and said, "You're mad that I named Ferruccio as my *capobastone*? You can speak freely."

"I just thought after Luca's death, I would have been next in line."

Adriano smiled and said, "I trust you with my life, Giancarlo. I do have a job for you. One that is more important than my *capobastone*. You will become the Don of Castelvetrano. I will take over Monreale, and that's why I said an Umbretto will rule once again in Monreale. For now, we will split our men. We will have to act quickly to muster more men, but with men whom we can trust. Ferruccio, you will come with me to Monreale."

With surprise in his voice, Giancarlo asked, "I am to be Don?"

"It will be tough. You will have many forces against you. But I know you have it in you."

"Congratulations," Ferruccio told him.

"*Grazie*, Ferruccio." Giancarlo then turned back to Adriano and said, "I will not let you down."

"I as well, Don Umbretto," said Ferruccio.

"I know, gentlemen. That's why I chose you. So, we leave tomorrow for Castelvetrano, where I need to deal with Salvatore."

"Thank you so much for putting your trust in me," replied Giancarlo.

"I'll see the both of you later at supper."

Giancarlo went to his knee and was about to reach for Don Umbretto's hand. Adriano stopped him, saying, "From this day forward, you bow to no one, Don Fanucci."

Giancarlo stood up and thanked Adriano once again and then left the room with Ferruccio.

When he was alone, Adriano thought about Salvatore and how to deal with him.

GIACOMO UMBRETTO

Monsignor Mancini returned to the rectory. He went to his office and sat down behind his desk. His mind was a whirlwind from the events that day. He needed a moment to collect his thoughts before he would return later that evening for dinner at the Sanguinettis' home.

Father Gianuzzi, meanwhile, was in his office. His mind to was running back and forth over the events of earlier in the day. Everything he hated about the Mafia was now smack in his face. He knew who had killed Castranzio Fausto, but now it would be expected that it never be spoken. The truth never to be told. That was the way of the Mafia and of *Omertà*, its code of silence.

On top of that, his father killed a man even when he had begged his father not to do so. And yet, deep down, he was glad his father did it. He knew his father was correct. Don Fausto was going to bring pain, regret, and death to this place. On top of that, his sister would probably be dead, killed at the hands of Onofrio Fausto. And without question, the future for this village that he had come to love was bleak. But his father's actions, and that of Maria's as well, had put an end to all of it, and as a result, Bellafortuna would be safe. For that, he was thankful as he had come to love this place since coming here.

He should be outraged that his father did not listen and spare Don Fausto's life. But there was no outrage inside of him. And that is what distressed him the most. How could he remain a priest with such feelings?

As he sat at his desk, he lifted his hand to his neck and removed his Roman Collar. He held it in his hands, staring at it. He then laid it on his desk. He took a sheet of paper and began to write.

He wrote a few paragraphs, and when he finished, he signed it at the end with "Father Giulio Gianuzzi." He thought for a moment and wrote next to his signature the word – "formerly." Then underneath, he simply signed it, "Giacomo." He folded the pages and wrote "For Papa" on the outside.

He retired to his bedroom to pack his things.

Once packed, he laid the letter on his bed and then headed down the hallway to speak with Monsignor Mancini.

IT WAS early evening when everyone gathered back at the Sanguinetti home. Two long tables had been set out in the piazza. Two lanterns on each of the tables served as centerpieces.

As everyone began to sit around the table, Monsignor Mancini asked Don Umbretto to step into *Il Paradiso*.

Once inside, Monsignor Mancini said, "Your son took off his Roman Collar and left this afternoon. He asked me not to tell you till this evening, which I swore I would do. I had one of the villagers give him a ride to Palermo."

"So he is gone."

"Yes. He left this note for you which I think explains everything."

Adriano took the note. "I will read this later. I'm sure it's all about what a terrible person I am."

Monsignor Mancini said in return, "Just read it, Don Umbretto. I think your son has come to understand you better. Now let's go eat."

ADRIANO RETURNED to the table where he sat between Giuseppe and Maria. As he sat down, Giuseppe asked, "All is well, Don Umbretto."

"My son has left Bellafortuna. He has left the priesthood, I believe. I will discuss more of this later with you."

"I'm sorry, Don Umbretto."

He turned to Maria, "And now we relish in the food cooked by the magical hands of this woman of Sicily."

Maria smiled, as she said, "I hope you like it, Don Umbretto. Care for some wine, a little *Vino di Bellafortuna*."

"I would love a glass."

Giuseppe poured him a glass, just as the others around both of the tables did the same. When all the glasses were filled, Adriano stood up from the table and the people seated around the table became quiet.

Adriano raised his glass toward Maria and said, "As we await the arrival of the food, I want to give a toast, a toast to the Sanguinettis for their hospitality."

Everyone raised their glasses and shouted *"Salute"* before drinking.

Giuseppe stood, and said in reply, "It was our pleasure, Don Adriano. And I'm glad you are feeling better. And I would like to make my own toast." He raised his glass, as everyone followed suit. Giuseppe said,"First, to a lady whose voice earlier today echoed against the buildings of this piazza, the same buildings that enjoyed hearing the voice of Enrico Caruso. You, my dear Francesca, have a wonderful voice."

Everyone seated at the table cheered loudly. Then Giuseppe turned toward Maria. He said, "And lastly, to my wife, Maria. I'm blessed to call her both my wife and my friend. We salute your food even before we eat it, as we know what we are about to experience will be *perfecto. Salute.*"

"Salute," everyone replied.

"Grazie," replied Maria. Now, if some of you ladies can come upstairs with me, we can start bringing the food down."

As she started to walk away from the table, Adriano grabbed her by the hand. He said nothing to her, but simply smiled and nodded his head.

EVERYONE ENJOYED MARIA'S MEAL, but most importantly, they enjoyed being together after a very long, trying day. After the meal, Adriano had pulled Francesca and Marco aside and told them about Giacomo. He promised that he would tell her more later.

Monsignor Mancini also told Giuseppe the news about Giacomo, but Giuseppe advised that Adriano had already mentioned it to him. Giuseppe told Monsignor Mancini how much he hated hearing the news as he liked the young man and thought he would make a fine priest.

Maria was busy picking up plates. Giuseppe got up and helped her. They each carried a stack to the kitchen upstairs.

After placing the plates down, Giuseppe said, "We have not been able to speak since the events of earlier. How are you doing?"

"Staying busy, so I don't have to think about it."

"I'm so sorry, but I am thrilled you are fine."

Tears began to flow down her face. "I hope I was right in my decision. I took his life, Giuseppe."

"What does your heart tell you?"

"I felt at that moment I had no other option."

"I love you with all of my being, Maria."

"I love you too, Giuseppe."

They hugged, as Maria said, "Take that box of cannolis downstairs for me."

"Cannolis? I love your cannolis."

"I'll see you downstairs."

AFTER DESSERT WAS EATEN by all, with some partaking of a cappuccino, Adriano wished everyone a good night. He went upstairs alone, exhausted from the events of earlier, and he retired to the bedroom.

However, he did not immediately get ready for bed. He had been waiting to read the letter from his son since the moment Monsignor Mancini had given him the letter.

He pulled his son's note from his pocket. He unfolded the pages and began to read them.

PAPA:

After the events of today, I am leaving; I am leaving both Bellafortuna and the priesthood. But I wanted to explain myself to you. I watched you standing over Don Fausto today. I tried to stop you from killing him. I begged you not to. And yet, you did it anyway. I thought I would be filled with outrage at what you did. But deep down, I was relieved. Relieved that you saved the people of this village from suffering.

As a priest, I knew such feelings were wrong. As a man, I was glad you did it. As such, I knew I could not continue as a priest with such different positions. So I am leaving the priesthood. I will find work, and I will make you proud of me.

I have come to realize Sicily is confronted with the same opposing forces that I have been confronted with today. The absolute beauty of this island is contrasted with its brutality.

As I have gotten older, I reflect many times back to when I left the family after Mamma's death and my words to you and yours to me in return. I remember like yesterday you telling me that I never understood the path that life had forced you down. I do understand now. The harsh, corrupt underbelly of this island requires strength to combat it. And that is what you have provided to many, strength. Strength to those to whom you offered your protection. Please, do not take from my words absolution. I still think there were different ways. But, I have come to appreciate why you made some of the choices that you did.

With all of that said, I will leave this place, this place that I have fallen in love with. Bellafortuna stands as the beacon of decency in a world where decency has no place. Please do not look for me. I shall send word to you once I know what I'm going to do.

As for Francesca, I hate leaving her again. Tell her I love her and that she truly has a voice sent by God.

Take care, Papa.

Formerly Father Giulio Gianuzzi

Giacomo

ADRIANO HAD tears rolling down his cheeks as he folded the pages back to how they were and then placed them on his nightstand.

GIUSEPPE, Maria, Francesca, and Marco sat out at the table in the piazza long after everyone had retired, drinking one last bottle of wine. They knew this would be the last time they would enjoy each other's company outside of *Il Paradiso*.

Giuseppe said, "It seems like ages ago, but your voice today was perfect."

"Thank you. It has been a long day. I never got the chance to tell you how impressed I was with the concert and all of the festivities earlier today. The procession was beautiful."

"It is a wonderful time."

Marco added, "And congrats on your victory, as I heard your statue was voted the best."

"Yes, it was. I will get to relish my group's victory for an entire year." He laughed and then asked Francesca, "So, what happens when you leave with your father?

"What do you mean?"

"Will you still pursue your singing."

"I want to. I hope to."

"Please do. I know some wonderful voice teachers in Monreale, including Maria's brother. Perhaps I could put a good word in for you."

"I would love that."

Maria interjected, "We will miss the both of you."

We will miss you as well," Francesca replied.

Giuseppe and Maria finished their wine and retired to bed, leaving Francesca and Marco alone. He poured the last little bit of wine into her glass.

He then said to her, "Well, we return to Castelvetrano tomorrow for a short time. Giancarlo informed me that I'm coming to Monreale with you."

Francesca smiled at him. She took a sip of her wine. She looked up at the moon and then around the piazza. She said to him, "I love this place, and I love you."

"*T'amo*, Francesca. What will become of us?"

"I don't want to think about it. Not tonight, at least." She took her last sip of wine. "Let's go to the hotel. I'm getting tired."

He stood up, offered her his hand, and helped her stand up from the table.

They walked across the piazza under the moonlight. She asked, "You will be standing guard outside the door again?"

"Of course."

She smiled at him and then whispered under her breath, "I'll leave the door open."

"Walk faster," he said with a laugh.

They reached the hotel and went inside.

THE NEXT MORNING, a cloudless sky welcomed the villagers of Bellafortuna. Word spread quickly about the events of yesterday, culminating in the death of the Faustos at the hands of Don Adriano Umbretto.

Adriano met with Giuseppe to discuss a few matters. At one point, Adriano said, "The actions of your wife forced me to take steps quicker than I originally planned. Monreale is now ripe for my taking. Can you fulfill the requests that we just spoke of?

"I promise. I will do so."

Just a little before 9 am, a car driven by Giancarlo pulled in front of *Il Paradiso*. Adriano made his way to the car with Francesca, Marco, and Ferruccio. With tears in her eyes, Francesca gave both Giuseppe and Maria a hug.

Francesca told Maria, "Thank you for your kindness to me."

Maria whispered into her ear, "Fight for Marco. Love is all that matters."

Francesca smiled as she turned to Giuseppe. "I'm going to miss this place, and I am especially going to miss you."

"Keep singing, Francesca. Promise me."

"I promise."

Marco hugged the Sangunettis as well, just as Adriano walked over. He extended his hand to Giuseppe, who shook it. Adriano said, "You have my word, I will keep Bellafortuna safe. Just as my grandfather did in the past. Everyone will know it is off limits." He then turned to Maria and said, "I am thankful to you for everything. I thank the both of you for the kindness you have shown my children and me. It will not be forgotten."

With that, he got in the car. Giancarlo started the engine, and they drove away, out of the piazza, headed toward Castelvetrano.

SALVATORE BATTAGLIA

Salvatore Battaglia was in the study at the villa in Castelvetrano that Saturday afternoon. Not one of the men standing guard that afternoon ran in to tell him of the arrival of a car and the return of Don Adriano Umbretto. The Don's men in the courtyard were thrilled to see him alive, having thought he was dead this entire time.

Adriano got out of the car and quickly went to his old study. Giancarlo and Ferruccio followed behind. Adriano did not knock but opened the door. He stepped inside while the other two men waited in the hallway.

"Don Umbretto. I can't believe my eyes," Salvatore said as he stood up and began to step around the desk.

"Stay where you are, Salvatore. And keep your hands away from the desk drawers. I have some news for you. Don Fausto and his son are dead. I killed them myself."

Salvatore rubbed his temples with his hand. He then said, "What great news."

Adriano shook his head. "Don't. Don't even try, Salvatore. I know you betrayed me."

Salvatore began to say, "No, Don Umbretto —"

Adriano cut him off forcefully, saying, "*Taci*. Quiet. Don't lie to me. Not now. I know what you did."

Salvatore went to his knees. "I'm sorry Don Umbretto. I thought they were the future."

"You chose wrongly."

"Please forgive me."

Adriano walked over to where he was kneeling. He said to him, "Now listen to me. If your betrayal had only resulted on attacks on me, so be it. Perhaps I could forgive you. But your betrayal led to the death of Luca. Because of that, make your confession to God. Do so now."

"Please, Don Umbretto."

"You were going to allow them to kill Francesca."

"Please, Don Umbretto, I beg you."

"Yet, Don Fausto never knew my son was living in Bellafortuna. You never told him. For that, I am grateful. For that, your life will be spared. Provided you do exactly what I say."

"Anything."

"Giancarlo and Ferruccio are going to drive you to Palermo. They will buy you a ticket to New York for a ship that leaves in the morning. Be on that ship, and never come back here. Never come back to Sicily. If you do not obey me, I will hunt you down, and kill you. Now, get out of my sight."

Salvatore began to speak but was quickly cut off by Adriano. "Don't say a word, not a fucking word. Just leave and never come back.

Salvatore quickly stood up and went to the door.

Giancarlo and Ferruccio were outside the door. They walked him out to the car.

BY EASTER MORNING, all of Sicily was abuzz with the news of Don Umbretto and the demise of Don Fausto. Word even reached Castelvetrano that all of Don Fausto's men had fled from Monreale. Tomorrow, Adriano would pick his men, and then he and Ferruccio would go to Monreale, along with Francesca and Marco, where he would take up residence at the Umbretto villa. Once again, an Umbretto would rule Monreale.

In Bellafortuna, the villagers celebrated Easter with Mass. They then all returned to their homes and ate lunch as a family. The feeling of dread over the village was gone and was now replaced with the hope that Bellafortuna would be safe again.

THE END OF IT

Two weeks later, early one morning, Giuseppe was in the valley assisting Matteo in learning the barrel roasting process. Matteo paid close attention as the workers discussed in great detail how the craft was done. Giuseppe had explained to Matteo that he would have to understand every part of the process to run the winery successfully, just as Santo had worked hard to achieve.

Giuseppe finished his work with Matteo well before lunch. When he departed, he did not go back to the village but instead headed over to the knoll of the hill overlooking the *Stagno Azzurro*. In his hands, he held the small box that he always kept under the counter in the wine store. He made his way over to the grave of his son. Maria had placed a beautiful bouquet of tulips on top of the grave earlier in the morning to remember her son's birth 36 years ago this very day.

Giuseppe sat on the ground next to the grave and opened the box. He pulled out a small sheet of paper; a letter addressed to Giuseppe and Maria Sanguinetti. He unfolded it. He said aloud, "Biaggio, this first one is from Ary Boehm." He began to read:

Caro Signore e Signora Sanguinetti:

I hope this letter finds you well. I just wanted to drop you a note to let you know that Miri and I are expecting our first child. I can't tell you how excited we are. I've accepted a position with the Israeli Philharmonic Orchestra and cannot put into words what it means to be playing music again. Without question, it's because of what your son, you, your wife, and the villagers of Bellafortuna did for us that I have these blessings. You protected us and gave us life. What everyone did for us will never be forgotten.

Yours truly,

Ary

Giuseppe neatly folded the letter and placed it back in the box. He pulled out another letter and said, "Biaggio, this next one is from Heinrich Bergman."

He read that letter as well, as he did with the rest of the letters in the box, as was his custom since his son's death on the anniversary of his birth. All throughout the year, he would keep the letters he had received from the Jewish musicians and their families who had been hidden in Bellafortuna during WWII. Every one of them who had stayed would write to keep the Sanguinettis up on what was happening in their life and would always end with a word of thanks.

After reading the last letter, he wiped the tears from his

eyes. He then placed the letter back in the box. Just as he stood up, Monsignor Mancini walked up the hill.

"Maria said I could find you here."

"It's his birthday."

"I know. I prayed for him this morning when I was reading my Breviary."

"Thank you for that. But you did not come to find me to tell me that. I can tell by the look on your face."

"You are correct, Giuseppe. I wanted somewhere private where the two of us could talk. I received some news, some very distressing news."

"What happened now?"

"A few days ago, on May 1st, hundreds of Sicilians, mostly poor peasants, went to Portella della Ginestra for the International Labor Day parade. They also went to raise their voices in protest to the dire predicament they are in, in large part due to the Mafia. During a speech, gunfire broke out. It seems machine guns had been fired from the surrounding hills, and by men on horseback."

"Oh no," replied Giuseppe. "How many were killed?"

"Eleven killed and twenty-seven wounded," replied Monsignor Mancini.

"Sicily bleeds once again. Who perpetrated this attack?" asked Giuseppe.

"The bandit Salvatore Giuliano has taken responsibility. But many believe it was orchestrated by factions of the Mafia."

Giuseppe shook his head and replied, "The anti-Mafia forces did better in the election than people thought. Don Umbretto told me one day that the Mafia would fight back, show its strength, and convince everyone that it still rules

Sicily. I think even he would be shocked at this news of opening fire on peaceful peasants of Sicily. It only confirms what I believe. This new version of the Mafia is brutal and wicked. This news shows what the future will be like on this island. The likes of Don Umbretto are quickly becoming a thing of the past. But luckily for us, he has established his foothold in Monreale. He has pledged his protection to us. I agreed to some things that will assure that commitment. Pietro, some would say our reliance on him is a deal with the devil."

Monsignor Mancini said in return, "Our life in the village has been unmolested by the Mafia. And the only reason for that is because of two strong willed individuals who kept them out all these years by playing nice with the families close by in Monreale. You and your father, Giuseppe, the both of you have been our protectors. You have been the equivalent of a Don for us, a protector for us. The both of you used your wine business connections to keep these men at bay, to keep them away from us, yet at the same time, have them provide to us an aura of protection for our little world here. And now it seems, with Don Umbretto pledging his protection to us, we are shielded once again. I believe we are between periods, as one gives way to another. This next phase will be a battle, a battle for control of Sicily. Hopefully, at the end of it all, Sicily will rise united against the forces of the Mafia. But for now, the most important thing we can do is protect our village. And that is what your family has assured for us. The Sanguinettis, from Antonio, to Biaggio, to Maria, and to you, all of you have shown an undying love for this place and its people. And for that we are eternally grateful."

"I do love this place, Pietro. I know I'm a changed man.

Because of that, I did not think we had any way out of the mess that confronted us. Somehow, it worked out."

"How's Maria doing?"

"She still gets upset about it all. But she is doing well. I keep telling her to come speak to you. Just to clear her head."

"She has been through so much in her life."

"She has. We all have. By the way, Pietro, have you heard from Father … I mean Giacomo Umbretto."

"No. Not since he left. I don't know what happened. Where he has gone is a mystery."

Giuseppe said, "It's a shame. I think he was a very good priest, with his heart in the right place."

"I agree. But I guess with his father and sister here, it got too much for him. He was so close to Mirella Vasaio. I know her death affected him greatly."

"Poor Santo and his wife. I miss them so much. Matteo is slowly learning everything. It will take time, but he will get it, with help."

"I'm sure he will, and I know you will be there to lead him every step of the way. Thank you for all that you do for this place, Giuseppe. The world needs more places like Bellafortuna. A place of decency, hope, love, and mercy. People should get to know our story."

"Would the world of today even want to know or believe our story?"

Monsignor Mancini smiled and said, "It's not a question of wanting to know. Sometimes it just needs to be told."

Giuseppe stood up, picked up his box with his letters, and then extended his hand to Monsignor Mancini. "Thanks for being my friend."

They began walking back to the village.

A LITTLE WHILE LATER, Giuseppe was seated at a table inside the wine store. In front of him were a few pages of paper. The first page had a paragraph he had just written.

Kurt Hofmann came up to the table. "I'm going to go home and have lunch with Elizabetta, if that is ok with you."

"Of course."

"Giuseppe, she is expecting."

"That is wonderful news. You lived through it all, and now you bring a new life into the world."

"*Grazie*. I will see you later."

"Take your time. Please tell Elizabetta congratulations from us."

"Giuseppe, if we are blessed with a son, his name will be Biaggio."

Giuseppe stood up and extended his hand to Kurt. "I would be honored by it."

As Kurt left, Maria came down to the wine store to find her husband. She said, "I made you a late lunch upstairs."

"Elizabetta is expecting."

"What great news. I'm so excited for them. What are you doing down here?"

Giuseppe placed his hands over his writing and said, "Just working on something."

"What are you working on?"

"Something."

"Giuseppe," she said in a tone that meant she expected a response.

"It was something that Monsignor Mancini said that made me began to think. The world should know about this place.

The world should know about the people of Bellafortuna. I want to tell their story."

"That's wonderful. So that's what you are doing. Telling the story of this place."

"I am."

"But where do you begin?"

"With my father, when I was only nine years old, and a trip down to the valley, a very long time ago, while the Vasaios were in power here."

"That is when it all truly began. What have you written so far?"

"Well, I have outlined the history of our village. As for writing the story, this is all I have written." Giuseppe removed his hands from the pages. "I've only written one paragraph."

He lifted the top page off of the stack and handed it to his wife. She grabbed it and began to read:

There is an ironic paradox in that courage requires fear. Fear provides the opportunity for courage. However, one must be willing to face the hard demands of courage, confront that fear, and ultimately triumph over it.

Tears tracked down her face as she handed the pages back to Giuseppe. "It's so beautiful. I can't wait to read the whole thing when you are done. Your words about courage are wonderful."

"The history of Bellafortuna is a study of courage."

Maria shook her head in agreement and said, "Yes. Both courage that is acted upon intentionally and other times when one is forced to call upon it to act."

"Exactly," replied Giuseppe. "You are courageous, Maria. By your actions, you forced Don Umbretto to act earlier than he thought was possible in securing Monreale, and in so doing, protecting us."

"Giuseppe, I did not act with courage, I acted because of fear."

He pointed to the paper in her hand and said, "And that is why I wrote what I wrote. Courage requires fear. That's the paradox. That's the thread of life that runs through the history of our village. You are now part of that history."

"Well, come upstairs and make your sandwich history. Then you can get back to your story."

Giuseppe stood up from the table and walked over to the Victrola. He looked at the drawing of Caruso and the Star of David on the wall. His village's story really was a story of courage. The world needed to know about this place and its people, which would include the story of his own son, Father Biaggio Sanguinetti. Meanwhile, Maria walked over to him and stood next to him.

"I miss him so much, Giuseppe. So much, it hurts."

"I know, Maria. I know. Kurt said if they have a boy, he wants to name him Biaggio."

"That would be a wonderful tribute to our son and to our village. I have been reflecting on everything these past few days, and I've come to the absolute realization that I love this place, and I would do anything to protect it. What will your story say about me."

He looked deep into her eyes. He then pulled her close and said, "In the words of a friend, you are the true melody of Sicily. You are a beautiful, courageous woman, who loved her God, her community, and her family. And who is a fabulous cook to top it all off."

"*T'amo, Giuseppe.*"

T'amo, Maria," he said in response. "*Tutto la mia vita.*"

She smiled at him in return and said, "You are my whole life as well."

He wrapped his hands around her waist. He then pulled her close and kissed her. They then grabbed hands and walked together to the stairwell that led to the living quarters.

THAT AFTERNOON, Adriano stood in the hallway of the villa in Monreale. He was waiting for the last of the four largest landowners in Monreale to come visit. The three others had already been there to pledge their loyalty to Adriano and, in return, receive his protection. His *cosca* was small, but he knew it would expand quickly. Ferruccio, his *capobastone*, stood close to him as they discussed the horrific news from Portella della Ginestra, and the murder of the peasants.

As their discussion ended, Ferruccio walked away just as Francesca came down the long hallway with Marco. Adriano stared at his daughter, who was talking animatedly with Marco, all the while giggling and touching him then and again.

The duo quickly separated when they saw Adriano standing in the hallway. Adriano motioned them over to him. It was true that he was a Don, but he was also a father. He could see there was more than just a friendship between the two. He noticed it first back in Bellafortuna.

Francesca approached her father, while Marco was a step behind.

Adriano looked at them both and then said, "Before we left Bellafortuna, Giuseppe Sanguinetti gave me the name of the top voice teacher here in Monreale. It is his wife's brother, Rodolfo. He himself had a long singing career, but has retired and returned home to Monreale where he now teaches. I have already called him. You start tomorrow."

Tears began to run down Francesca's face. She said, "Thank you so much, Papa."

"Giuseppe told me yours is one of the best young voices he has heard. He will have you sing at the Bellafortuna opera festival in a year or two. I agree with his assessment of your voice."

She smiled, however her smile quickly disappeared when Adriano turned to Marco and said, "You shall be leaving us."

Francesca stared at Marco, her face showing anguish.

Marco asked, "Leaving? What do you mean, Don Umbretto?"

"This life is not for you. You are a good person, Marco. A very kind soul. My daughter has seen…" he stopped and looked at her and then back toward him and finished his sentence… "the type of person you are and has fallen in love."

Francesca went to correct her father, but he cut her off. "I'm very intuitive, Francesca. If you marry him one day, he cannot be a member of my *cosca*. Marco, I am sending you to Bellafortuna. You will work in the winery with Matteo Vasaio. Before I left, I discussed this with Giuseppe. He agreed. You will get a job, and leave this life behind you. In time, if you apply yourself, and prove to me you can be successful, you may come talk to me about my daughter."

Francesca leaned her body into Marco's as they both smiled at each other.

"Marco, you leave tomorrow."

"Don Umbretto, I cannot thank you enough for all that you have done for me."

"I promised your mother that I would protect you. With this move, I have fulfilled that promise. At least that's one promise to a mother I will be able to keep."

"I will not let you down," he replied.

Francesca and Marco turned and walked down the hallway together. Adriano's mind turned to his wife. He had also lived up to his promise to her. Francesca was safe.

Just as he was about to retreat to his office, there was a knock on the villa's door. The last of the landowners must have arrived. Adriano turned and walked a few feet to the door and opened it.

The man at the door wore black pants and a white shirt and carried a small suitcase. Adriano stared in disbelief.

The man at the door simply said, "I'm back, Papa."

Adriano smiled broadly at Giacomo. He opened the door wider and let his son inside the villa.

FINITO

AUTHOR'S NOTE

Pietro Mascagni's one-act opera, *Cavalleria Rusticana,* gave the world an inside glance into Sicilian life and, although never mentioned by name, the Mafia. *Cavalleria* is "akin to the official ideology of the Sicilian Mafia," John Dickie wrote in his splendid book, *Cosa Nostra.*

The opera was based on a short story published in 1880 by the Sicilian writer, Giovanni Verga. Verga wanted to create a realistic story of what life was truly like on the island. He thought instead of setting the love story in the usual urban middle-class milieu of most literature of the day, he would set it "in the mud of Sicily."

Just a few years later, Mascagni, a struggling, young opera composer, was looking for a story to turn into an opera to enter into the Sonzogno Competition. The winner of the competition was guaranteed to have their opera performed in Rome. Mascagni chose Verga's story for his opera. Mascagni went to work, but after completing the opera, he lost hope in the work. In a twist of fate, on the very last day to enter the competition, and unbeknownst to Mascagni, his wife sent the work in. The opera won first prize.

Cavalleria Rusticana premiered on May 17, 1890 at the Teatro Costanzi in Rome, where it was met with great enthusiasm. The opera was most likely the first, in what came to be known as the *Verismo* (real, true life) movement, which reached its pinnacle with Mascagni's Milan Conservatory roommate and friend, Giacomo Puccini.

The title of the book and opera, translated as *Rustic Chivalry*, demonstrates what the author and composer created with their works: a romantic version of the violence of Sicily. As Roberto Dainotto wrote in his *The Mafia: A Cultural History*, Verga's own Sicilian pride had been wounded by depictions of Sicily as irredeemably violent. "To rehabilitate Sicilian honor, the Mafia had to be either denied as the defaming invention of northerners, or – better yet – reframed as a more romantic and beautiful thing: a rustic chivalry of sorts."

That has been the battle since that time. There is the true, vulgar, violent world of the Mafia, in comparison with the romantic version as shown in opera, literature and film.

Then, in 1969, along came a book that would forever alter the view of the Mafia and would make the Mafia a household name. Of course, that book was Mario Puzo's, *The Godfather*.

When Puzo began writing his novel, he was broke. He decided to turn his skills toward writing a blockbuster. Unlike many authors who set out with that goal, he delivered - big time. His novel would provide a detailed glimpse into the world of Vito Corleone and his rise in the criminal underworld. He initially called the book *Mafia*. Before the book was even published, Paramount optioned the book for a film. Once published, and with the name changed to *The Godfather*, the book spent 67 weeks on the *New York Times* best-seller list and sold over 10 million copies. The movie was released in 1972, and became the highest grossing film of all time (at that time.)

Some critics complained that Puzo's work romanticized the world of the criminals. Author and journalist Nicholas Pileggi answered the critics best when he wrote, *"The Godfather* emphasized their peculiar code of honor rather than their seedy, greedy little maneuverings. It dealt with their strong sense of family and their passionate loyalties. It romanticized and exaggerated their political power, wealth and influence in legitimate business. But most important, it humanized rather than condemned them."

The Sicilian Mafia was once all-powerful and all-encompassing. It evolved over time. What began as a rural, protection force, soon moved into a grab for power and control. For the inhabitants of the island who stayed and did not immigrate to America, the Mafia was a part of their reality on a daily basis. They knew the Mafia families, spoke with the Dons, and dealt with them in business and other endeavors. They also witnessed the violence and savagery. But just as Puzo did in his novel by humanizing them, for the Sicilians, these *mafioso* were living, breathing people.

As an author, I am fully aware of my obligation to not romanticize what the Mafia stood for, nor attempt to hide the darkness and sadness they brought. Yet, at the same time, they are a part of the history of Sicily. They loved, they cried, they performed good works, and they also did bad acts. Through the life of Adriano Umbretto, I attempted to show

how one man's path could lead to a way of life he would have never imagined. In contrast with the story of Adriano Umbretto, is the beauty of the village of Bellafortuna, and the goodness of the Sanguinetti family and their fellow villagers who are faced with the forces of darkness.

That is why I decided to bring to life the story of *Sicilian Melody*. Part of me knew the story of Bellafortuna would need a final book to complete the tale. I wrote in the epilogue of Book 2, *Saving the Music,* that "the winery flourished until the arrival of the Mafia, but that is another story." Even back then, something was telling me the story of Bellafortuna was not over.

Saving the Music was published in March 2020. Little did I know what the future held for our nation. Within the month, New Orleans was shutdown, as our society dealt with the ramifications of Covid. I started writing *Sicilian Melody* just as my kids were sent home from school and worked online. My wife and I were home, working as well. One would think, with the world at a standstill, it would be very easy to write. For me, in those early months, I found my writing hampered by the feeling of utter hopelessness in living under Covid.

However, I persevered As conditions improved, I increased the pace of my writing, and soon I reached the final chapters. I struggled with the ending of the story. I think the real reason was because I knew this would be the end of the series and I wanted to get it right, or maybe, deep down, I hated to see it end.

In May, 2022, my wife, Wendy, asked me what I would like to do for my birthday. I wanted to go to the beach for a few days and finish the novel. I thought writing on a balcony with the sound of the crashing waves was the inspiration I needed. My family went to Pensacola, where for three days, every morning, I worked on the novel, before relaxing in the Gulf of Mexico for the rest of the day with my family. Thanks to that trip, the book was finished.

Just a month later, I found myself in Key West to celebrate my son's twenty-first birthday. I took the first draft of the novel with me, where under the inspiration of visiting Hemingway's home and partaking of a few drinks at his old watering holes, I did my first read through.

For me, I always knew ending the series would not be easy. Bellafortuna, its people, and its history were part of me. They were always on my mind, as I would think of where the story would go.

This series encompassed my life for many years. When it started, my son, Matthew, was 4 and my daughter, Gabrielle (Ellie), was 2. They are both now in college, LSU and Auburn, respectively. Loved ones have passed away. Life has moved on. However, I was always able to escape all the trials of this life, as I could always return to Bellafortuna to tell its story.

I have received numerous emails over the years from readers asking me where Bellafortuna is, as they can't find it on a map, and they would love to go see it on their trip to Sicily. I'm sure they are dejected when they find out its fictional. Yet, as I tell them, it survives in their heart. It has been a pleasure to bring these stories to my readers about a place of decency and hope. The joy it has brought me has been immense.

I first would like to thank the readers of all of my previous books who encouraged me and pushed me forward to write this final book of the series. An author never tires hearing from readers and the impact the stories have on them.

Next, I have to thank Kathy Schott. She is that one person that every author needs. The person who reads the manuscript as it is being written, discusses the entire story, advises what works and what does not, and shares insights as to where the story should go. Kathy has been with me throughout the writing of this entire series, and for that I am eternally grateful.

Next, Ana Gregorio-Voicu of Stuggart, Germany, who has designed every book cover in this series. Her talent is incredible. Her work is masterful. Of course, the proof are the accolades I have received from readers for the book covers, as well as having the cover of *Saving the Music* selected as a finalist in the International Book Award for best cover.

My aunt, Janet LoCoco, an author herself, is another of my initial readers of my books, who always is spot on regarding changes that need to be made. It has been a wonderful collaboration with her over the years.

To a fellow New Orleans writer, Elisa Speranza (Author of *The Italian Prisoner*) who read the manuscript, provided some useful notes, and most importantly, assured me that she loved the story, I thank you for all of your support.

I must also use the opportunity to thank Bob Neufeld. Bob, with his distinctive, lyrical voice, has been the narrator on all of the Audiobooks in this series. He grew up in Wichita, Kansas where he studied voice, opera, and theater. His career with audiobooks began when his niece asked him to record the same fairy tales for her kids that he had recorded for her when she was little. It has been a joy working with him and bringing my written words to listeners all across the world.

To my sisters, Pam LoCoco Montz (Greg) and Beth

LoCoco Doody (Michael), and all of my in-laws (the Hemels), I thank all of you for your continued support of me in my writing endeavors.

To my mom, Lynda Goodier LoCoco. This book is dedicated to you. From an early age, you taught me two things, which have influenced my writing journey. First, you taught me the love of reading. As far back as I can remember, you always read in bed before going to sleep. A habit you still have today. It taught me the joy that reading can bring to someone. Secondly, you also taught me a love of storytelling. Be it novels, film, musicals or plays, you, and dad for that matter, surrounded all of us with stories. This has had the most impact on my being a writer, for at the end of the day, I consider myself a storyteller. And for that, I thank you and dedicate this book to you.

To my children, Matthew and Ellie, no matter where life takes you, find time for music and stories.

Lastly, my wife, Wendy Hemel LoCoco. The women in my novels are very strong, intelligent, motivated people. I find it very easy to describe these women, as they are the epitome of my wife. As I write this, we are celebrating our 25th wedding anniversary this week. In the words of Errol Flynn from the movie, *They Died with their Boots on*, "Walking through life with you, ma'am, has been a most gracious thing." She has encouraged my writing from day one. She has inspired me to keep writing.

To all my readers, it has been my joy to bring this series to you. Although this series comes to an end, it is my hope and desire that there is another story in me waiting to be told.

Chip LoCoco, New Orleans, January 2023

THE MUSIC OF SICILIAN MELODY

We have put together a Spotify Playlist with music from the
novel along with some traditional songs from Sicily to give
the reader a flavor of this magical region in the world. Be sure
to follow it to get updates.

The Spotify Playlist can be found as:

THE MUSIC OF SICILIAN MELODY

ABOUT THE AUTHOR

Chip LoCoco's love of music, stories and of his Sicilian-American heritage shines in all of his novels. His novels have won awards and have been ranked on Amazon as Bestsellers and Top Rated novels.

His first novel was *Tempesta's Dream - A Story of Love, Friendship and Opera*. Tempesta's Dream was awarded the Pinnacle Award in Historical Fiction.

Chip's next novel, *A Song for Bellafortuna*, forms Book 1 of his much beloved Bellafortuna Series. That novel won the B.R.A.G Medallion Award in Historical Fiction and was named a short-list finalist in the prestigious William Faulkner Writing Competition.

Book 2 of the Bellafortuna series is *Saving the Music*. It too has been listed as a Top Rated novel on Amazon and as a Bestseller in Italian Historical Fiction. It was selected as the Winner of the 2022 American Fiction Award in Historical

Fiction. It was also named as a Finalist in the 2022 International Book Awards in the Historical Fiction Category and Best Fiction Cover Design.

Sicilian Melody is Book 3 of the Bellafortuna Series.

Chip is an estate planning attorney in New Orleans, where he lives with his wife and two children. He is a member of the Italian American Writers Association. Chip has given extensive talks to book clubs, organizations, and has appeared on WWL Radio in New Orleans and The Catholic Channel on Sirius Radio.

For more information, visit his website at www.vincentlococo.com.

facebook.com/Authorchiplococo

twitter.com/VincentBLoCoco

amazon.com/author/vincentlococo

MORE INFORMATION

THE STORY OF BELLAFORTUNA CONTINUES

Be sure to check out the earlier books in the
Bellafortuna Series

A SONG FOR BELLAFORTUNA
SAVING THE MUSIC

If you would like to let others know about this novel, please
consider leaving a review on Amazon.
http://www.amazon.com/review/create-review/?asin=
B0856Z5CBL

If your group or book club is interested in inviting Mr.
LoCoco to discuss his novels or the writing process in person
or by Skype, please use the contact form on his website at
www.vincentlococo.com.

www.ingramcontent.com/pod-product-compliance
Lightning Source LLC
Chambersburg PA
CBHW021410310726
48971CB00005B/1281